EPICERIE

THE MATCHMAKER OF PÉRIGORD

THE MATCHMAKER
OF PÉRIGORD

Julia Stuart

Doubleday

LONDON · TORONTO · SYDNEY · AUCKLAND · JOHANNESBURG

TRANSWORLD PUBLISHERS
61–63 Uxbridge Road, London W5 5SA
a division of The Random House Group Ltd
www.booksattransworld.co.uk

First published in Great Britain
in 2007 by Doubleday
a division of Transworld Publishers

A CIP catalogue record for this book
is available from the British Library.

ISBN 9780385612029 (cased)
ISBN 9780385612807 (tpb)

T　　　　　　　　　　　　　　　　　ot,
　　　　　　　　　　　　　　　　　t,
i　　　　　　　　　　　　　　　　at
　　　　　　　　　　　　　　　　　ɔn,

Addre：　　　　　　　　　　　　　: the UK

The l　　　　　　　　　　　　　re that
the 　　　　　　　　　　　　　: been
legal　　　　　　　　　　　　　ɔrests.
Our paper procurement policy can be found at:
www.randomhouse.co.uk/paper.htm

Typeset in 11.25/14.25pt Golden Cockerel by
Falcon Oast Graphic Art Ltd.

Printed and bound in Great Britain by
Clays Ltd, Bungay, Suffolk

2 4 6 8 10 9 7 5 3 1

To my mother, who read to me, and my
father, who inspired my love for France

1

GUILLAUME LADOUCETTE WIPED HIS DELICATE FINGERS ON HIS trouser leg before squeezing them into the glass jar. As he wiggled them around the cold, slippery fat he recognized what he felt was an ankle and his tongue moistened. He tugged it out and dropped the preserved duck leg into the cassoulet made by his mother thirty-one years ago and which had been on the go ever since. The ghostly white limb lay for several seconds suspended on haricot bean and sausage flotsam before disappearing from sight following a swift prod with a wooden spoon.

Custodian of the cassoulet now that his mother had gone cuckoo, the barber gave the dish a respectfully slow stir and watched as a goose bone appeared through the oregano and thyme vapours. The flesh had long since dropped off, his mother having first added it to the pot nineteen years ago in celebration of his opening a barber shop in the village. Initially, Madame Ladoucette had strictly forbidden the bone's removal out of maternal pride. Years later, her mind warped by grief following the death of her husband, she convinced herself that her son's good fortune at starting his own business – the only happy memory to surface during that difficult time – was proof of the Almighty's existence. It was a conviction that led to her irritating habit of suddenly standing up at the table and dashing over to whichever unsuspecting dinner guest had mistakenly been served the grey bone. With a pincer-like motion, she would swiftly remove it from their plate with the words 'not so fast', in the fear that they would make off with what she had come to consider a holy relic.

From amongst the beans emerged an onion dating from March 1999, several carrots added only the previous week, a new thumb of garlic which Guillaume Ladoucette failed to recognize and a small green button still waiting to be reclaimed by its owner. With the care of an archaeologist, he drew the spoon around the bottom and sides of the iron pot to loosen some of the blackened crust, which, along with an original piece of now calcified Toulouse sausage, were, the barber insisted, the secret of the dish's unsurpassable taste. There were those, however, who blamed the antique sausage for turning the pharmacist Patrice Baudin, who had never previously shown any sign of lunacy, into a vegetarian, a scandal from which the village had never recovered.

Keeping the cassoulet going was more than just the duty of an only son, but something upon which the family's name rested. For the cassoulet war had been long and ugly and there was still no sign of a truce. All those fortunate enough to have witnessed the historic spectacle agreed that the first cannon was launched by Madame Ladoucette when she spotted Madame Moreau buying some tomatoes in the place du Marché and casually asked what she was making. When the woman replied, Madame Ladoucette recoiled two paces in horror, a move not appreciated by the stallholder on whose foot she landed.

'But tomatoes have no place in a cassoulet!' Madame Ladoucette cried.

'Yes, they do. I've always used tomatoes,' Madame Moreau replied.

'The next thing you'll be telling me is that you put lamb in it as well.'

'Don't be so ridiculous, I would never commit such a perversion!' Madame Moreau retorted.

'Ridiculous? Madame, it is not I who puts tomatoes in a cassoulet, it is you. What does your husband have to say about this?'

'He wouldn't want it any other way,' came the terse reply.

Moments later, several onlookers witnessed Madame Ladoucette striding up to Madame Moreau's husband, who was sitting on the bench by the fountain said to cure gout watching an ant struggling with a leaf five times its size. Monsieur Moreau looked up to see a pair of crane's legs, whose owner was carrying a straw basket which his nose immediately told him was full of fresh fish.

'Monsieur Moreau,' she began. 'Forgive me, but it is a matter of utmost importance and a true Frenchman such as yourself will know the definitive answer. Should a cassoulet have tomatoes in it or not?'

Monsieur Moreau was so startled by her sudden appearance and line of questioning that he could think of nothing but the truth: 'The correct method of making a cassoulet is always a source of contention. Personally, I prefer it without tomatoes, as my mother made it, but for God's sake don't tell the wife.'

According to Henri Rousseau, who happened to be standing next to Madame Moreau as she was paying for her tomatoes, Madame Ladoucette walked straight back up to her and repeated the entire conversation, adding that it was her civic duty to cook a cassoulet correctly. Precisely what Madame Moreau called her in return Henri Rousseau failed to catch, a crime his wife never forgave and which led to her insisting that he wear a hearing aid despite the fact that he was not in the least bit deaf. There was no doubt, however, about what happened next. Madame Ladoucette reached into her basket, pulled out what was unmistakably an eel and slapped Madame Moreau across the nose with it, before leaving its head wedged firmly down her cleavage and stalking off. She had made it halfway down the rue du Château, when, much to the delight of the villagers who couldn't have wished for better entertainment on a Tuesday morning, Madame Moreau put her hand into the brown paper bag she was holding and hurled a tomato at Madame Ladoucette. It landed with such force her victim momentarily staggered.

While the pair never spoke again, the salvoes continued. From that day, Madame Moreau insisted on keeping a large bowl of over-ripe tomatoes near her kitchen window, which she used as ammunition from behind her white lace panels whenever her enemy passed. Madame Ladoucette retaliated by always doing her eel impression whenever she caught her adversary's eye in the street. And while Madame Moreau's throwing arm was not what it used to be, and Madame Ladoucette's eel impression, which was never that good to begin with, had for several years been hampered by a pair of ill-fitting dentures, the two kept up their insults well into their senility, when they became almost a form of greeting.

Leaving the duck leg to heat up, the barber decided to fetch a lettuce from his potager. By the time he reached the back door the soles of his bare feet had collected a small sharp black stone, a ginger-coloured feather, two dried lentils and a little sticky label from an apple bearing the words 'Pomme du Limousin.' Resting his right foot on his left knee, he first removed the stone, lentils and label. Then, with a muttered blasphemy, he picked off the feather which he immediately carried to the bin.

Crawling his hairy toes into a pair of brown sandals by a

sack of walnuts from the tree in the garden, Guillaume Ladoucette opened the back door just wide enough to poke his head round. After scanning the top of the walls, still warm in the evening sun, and the lawn he would cut in two days' time when the moon was waning and passing in front of Pisces, he bent down to look underneath the lacy pink hydrangea. Satisfied that the coast was clear, he ventured out, quickly locking the door behind him. Filled with the pleasant anticipation of supper, he headed past the tiny well with its stone roof and the old rabbit hutches which he used to store flowerpots. The only sound was the thwack of cheap supermarket leather against dry heels and the cuckoos' incessant two-pitched mating call, which revealed a spectacular lack of imagination.

Legs wide apart over his oak-leaf lettuces, he picked enough of the burgundy-blushed leaves for a good serving. As he collected a couple of tomatoes, he congratulated himself on their aroma and glanced at his tiny potato plants hoping that they wouldn't come under attack from Colorado beetle again that year.

Silently unlocking the kitchen door, he peered inside. After casting his eyes along the tops of the cupboards, he bent down to check underneath the table. Relieved that he was still alone, he rinsed the salad and tomatoes thoroughly so as not to fall victim to the horror of worms. Arranging them in a bowl, he placed it on a tray along with a fork, a small blue jug of dressing and a white napkin with his initials embroidered in red in the corner. He then added a glass of disappointing Bergerac, which he had vowed never to buy again, but which he'd decided he might as well finish. Next to it he placed a packet of his favourite Cabécou goat's cheese, despite the fact that he had already reached his self-imposed weekly ration. After a final stir, he spooned out a bowlful of cassoulet, making sure that it included the duck leg. For several seconds he looked at the portion.

Remembering the sight of his stomach in the bath the night before, which, considering it was May, he could no longer dismiss as his winter plumage, he returned three spoonfuls to the pot and headed towards the back door with the tray. Just before opening the door, his eyes slid back to the disturbed pile of beans he had just returned. Dashing back to the pot, he scooped it back up again into his bowl. Before guilt could get its grip, he quickly strode out of the back door and kicked it shut behind him.

Guillaume Ladoucette settled himself at the warped wooden table and chair speckled with lichen underneath the walnut tree, where he often ate, cooling his feet on the grass, while admiring the veritable splendour of his potager. Picking up the fork, the barber selected a piece of plump sausage for his first mouthful. But, as he went to spear it, he suddenly stopped and stared blankly for several minutes. Then, very slowly, he put down the empty fork. As he sat back, a warm fat tear slid down his crow's-feet, shot over a tiny scar, rattled over his stubble and came to an abrupt halt at the bottom of his chin where it hung quivering.

It was not the realization that he had tweaked his moustache while cooking and that his world would forever smell of duck fat that had upset him. Nor was it the view of Lisette Robert's underwear pegged out on the washing line in the distance, a sight said to have broken at least seventeen bachelors' hearts. Nor was it the tiny pair of black eyes he'd just spotted bearing down on him from his neighbour's roof. The reason for his sudden despair was the memory of Gilbert Dubuisson's head when he walked into the barber shop that afternoon for his regular eight-week appointment and sat down in the chair with the words 'same as usual, please'. For, when the postman took off his cap, Guillaume Ladoucette looked down and saw to his utter horror that the man was almost completely bald.

2

HAIRLESS CUSTOMERS WERE NOT A PROBLEM GUILLAUME
Ladoucette had foreseen when, at the age of fifteen, he left
school and entered the Périgord Academy of Master Barbers.
Initially, his father had had other ideas for his only child, who
had taken so long to be conceived that his wife had resorted
to travelling to Brantôme to rub the church's lock in
accordance with the ancient fertility ritual. But while
Monsieur Ladoucette's joy at its success was unparalleled, it
led to his wife embracing all manner of peasant poppycock,
which became a source of utmost irritation for the rest of his
life. A worker in the disused stone quarry that had been
turned over to the cultivation of button mushrooms, he had
spent many an afternoon bent over the piles of horse
manure, his back in as much distress as his nostrils, imagining the baby his wife was carrying grown up and sitting
comfortably on a plump chair in a bank. But when the child
was born, there was no doubt as to his future employment,
for the boy's fluttering fingers were the most sublime things

he had ever seen. Whenever Madame Ladoucette showed off their newborn, proudly opening the nappy so that all could admire his considerable japonicas, her husband could talk of nothing but his fingers. Even before he was able to sit up, the child pulled himself over to his mother's sewing basket, extracted a pair of scissors and snipped his blanket into what was undeniably her profile. As soon as he was able to crawl, she was obliged to hide all the scissors in the house after returning from the garden one day to find the sitting-room curtains refashioned into the shape of a walnut tree.

The obsession followed him into school. When asked for a thousand-word essay on the Revolution, the boy handed in a cut-out working model of the Bastille, complete with miniature guillotine. He discovered the joy of cutting hair, and its life-changing effects, when his schoolmate Émilie Fraisse offered him the summer truffles she had just picked in exchange for shortening her butter-coloured tresses, which she found a source of great vexation when climbing trees. Guillaume Ladoucette, who would have agreed even without the fungal bribe, insisted on using his favourite pair of scissors, which he kept hidden under a large stone in the garden. He never regretted accepting the request, even when forced to stay in his room for the remainder of the holidays after Madame Fraisse appeared on his doorstep demanding an explanation for her only daughter's sudden resemblance to her cockerel.

Guillaume Ladoucette, who had never previously applied himself to learning, was the most studious of his year's intake at the Périgord Academy of Master Barbers. With ferocious concentration he watched as his teacher performed the cornerstone of gentlemen's hairdressing: the short back and sides. He stared, hearing nothing but his tutor's voice, as the man combed a section of hair with his right hand, slipped it between the fingers of his left and cut it off with a pair of scissors which suddenly, as if by magic, had replaced the comb in his right. It was a move that for Guillaume Ladoucette had all the appeal of a conjuring trick. He looked in wonder at how the two sides of the model's head were perfectly symmetrical, how the line on the back of the neck was as straight as his schoolteacher had always wanted his margins, and how a dab of gentleman's pomade, applied with a movement so fast it resembled sleight of hand, sealed the work of art.

But his excitement at mastering cutting hair, trimming beards, waxing moustaches and wet shaving was nothing compared to that felt when, at the beginning of a class, his teacher struck a match, lit a thin wax taper and approached the model (who had only a hint of terror in his eyes). Grasping a section of hair between his index and middle fingers, the instructor then drew the flame across the ends, quickly drawing his fingers up the shaft to extinguish the smoking orange glow. He proceeded in the same fashion around the head, describing the technique as the ultimate cure for a gentleman's split ends, while the room filled with the monstrous smell of singed hair. For Guillaume Ladoucette, the spectacle was more wondrous than anything he had seen at the circus.

He studied the Périgord Academy of Master Barbers' *Revised Guide to the Art of Barbering*, Second Edition, with such intensity that his mother feared he would go blind. So nervous was he before the final exam that for four days he refused to eat and Madame Ladoucette had to resist the urge to sit him between her legs and force-feed him like a goose. By the time he entered the examination room, he had checked that his pen was still in his pocket thirteen times out of fear that it might vanish into thin air, and had turned the colour of an oyster. When he read the first question – How Should a Barber Comport Himself? – his appetite instantly returned. Triumphantly he wrote: *A barber must combine nobility and honour with trustworthiness and cleanliness. It is most necessary to*

15

avoid stagnant breath and obnoxious body odours. The partaking of daily bathing is vital. In order to retain his customers' patronage, the successful barber must avoid at all costs quarrels, loss of temper, boisterous attire, blasphemy or the spreading of gossip.

By the time the boy read the second question – How Should a Facial Hairpiece Be Applied? – he felt vomitous with hunger as he answered verbatim: *In the case of a moustache, apply spirit gum to the upper lip, wait until tacky, position moustache and gently press down with a suitable cloth. If the moustache happens to find itself in an unfavourable position, first give warning to the customer and then remove in one strike with utmost speed and determination. Reposition and then trim in the desired style. For a beard, repeat, but apply spirit gum to the chin area.*

By the third – What Should You Remember When Tapering? – he started to nibble his question paper as he recalled: *That it is better to taper with caution and clarity of mind. One must remember that after the hair is cut it cannot be replaced.*

Unlike one of his fellow students whose model was taken to Périgueux Hospital with second-degree burns during the practical examination, Guillaume Ladoucette left the Périgord Academy of Master Barbers with a distinction. The following day, his mother put the certificate into a frame. It was the first qualification a member of her family had achieved, and not all of them could read it. The frame caused the boy considerable embarrassment as he carried it from village to village, and from town to town, searching for a position. But his shame soon came to an end when Pierre Rouzeau agreed to take him on at his shop in the town of Nontron. For the first week the hour-and-forty-three-minute cycle ride made him walk as if he had a *pain de campagne* wedged between his thighs.

Initially, the apprentice was charged with sweeping up the trimmings and putting them into bags which were sold to a mattress-manufacturer, a profitable sideline which a number of customers blamed when they left with less hair than they had bargained for. It also explained Pierre Rouzeau's enormous turn-ups, which he emptied before locking up every evening. After several months, the boy was given his first client, chosen by his boss for the man's habit of never leaving the house without a hat. But his caution was unnecessary, for Guillaume Ladoucette, whose fingers were by now fluttering with such a desire to get started that he could barely control his bicycle, did such a wondrous job that the customer foreswore his malodorous beret.

As the boy lived too far away to return home for lunch, the seasoned barber insisted that Guillaume Ladoucette ate with him and his wife. But while Francine Rouzeau was a formidable cook, and Guillaume Ladoucette could see her considerable cleavage whenever she served him, he was never entirely comfortable at the couple's table. For while barbering was also the boy's passion, he had no desire to talk about it *all* the time, and his boss never strayed far from the subject over the courses. Inevitably, the conversation would come round to his entry for the World Barbering Championships in Illinois, which he always pointed out to the youngster was in the United States of America. But despite his plans – the precise angle of tapering down the neck, the brand of pomade he would use that wasn't even available in Paris, and his savings for a return flight to Illinois which he kept in a tin up the chimney – Pierre Rouzeau never once submitted his application form. Guillaume Ladoucette, who soon knew every detail of the competition entry, nodded between mouthfuls, his mind on the pretty summer dresses he would have bought for Francine Rouzeau with the money which was smoked each night during winter.

Despite Pierre Rouzeau's propensity for repetition at mealtimes and (to Guillaume Ladoucette, even more infuriating) habit of finishing off the Cabécou, the boy developed a deep affection for his boss, even more than that he felt for the man's wife. The barber shop was a happy place to work and he even had enough money left over from his wages each week to start saving for a moped. Two years later, when he counted all the coins he had dropped into the ancient chamber pot under his bed that had served four generations of Ladoucettes, he finally had enough. On his next day off, he got a lift into Périgueux, the nearest city. He rode back home half terrified, half thrilled by his new machine. When he arrived, he immediately cleaned it, despite the fact that it was still spotless. The first person he took out on it was Émilie Fraisse. The pair swayed hesitantly down the rue du Château, both pairs of feet reaching for the comfort of the ground. They picked up speed as they passed the memorial erected to the *Three Victims of the Barbarous Germans, Shot on 19 June 1944.* Then, tucking in their legs, they flew out of the village, the breeze drying their teeth as they grinned with fear.

Guillaume Ladoucette's only disappointment as they shot past the maize fields was not being able to concentrate fully on the fact that Émilie Fraisse's thighs were finally around him. The hair her mother had forced her to grow back streamed behind them like a butter-coloured magic carpet. But when she turned to look at the retreating village behind them and batted her tresses away in order to see the view, the sudden movement upset the moped's balance and Guillaume Ladoucette lost control. They mounted a small bank, both emitting the sort of wail that follows the sudden realization that something painful is about to happen. In the end, Émilie Fraisse only suffered toothache, having landed on top of her friend with her mouth still open. Guillaume Ladoucette's biggest injury was to his pride. Not only did he have to explain the limp, but also that the nearest thing he got to a kiss was the bite mark on his cheekbone.

No one had expected the death of Madame Ladoucette's father. Some, however, had hoped that the day would come sooner rather than later as the old man had started to forget to put on his trousers before leaving the house, a sight which frightened even the men in the village, particularly when it was windy. Guillaume Ladoucette had been at his grandfather's house the day before he died, wondering why, at the age of twenty-four, he still wasn't allowed to go anywhere near his fig tree. Madame Ladoucette explained that it was because her father still hadn't forgiven his grandson for the time when, at the age of five, he had discovered a pair of hidden scissors, climbed up a stepladder and snipped off all the tree's branches, which took seven years to bear fruit again.

The house was left to Madame Ladoucette, who, despite adoring her son even more than her precious husband, immediately suggested that he moved there. For the young man's snores would float down from his gaping mouth on to the floor, tumble across his bedroom, roll underneath the door, pass through the draught-excluder stuffed with wild-boar hair, skate across the hall, bump down a steep flight of wooden stairs, turn two corners and penetrate the thick stone wall of her bedroom with its painting of the Virgin Mary. Monsieur Ladoucette insisted that his son's ability to sleep peacefully while manufacturing such a monstrous sound was a result of his mother having continually disturbed him when slumbering as a baby to check that he was still alive. However, her perturbation was far from over after he sailed through infancy without a single illness. For, at the age of six years and three months, she suddenly noticed to her horror that he had developed a habit of sleeping on his back with his arms straight down the sides of his body. 'He looks as though he's already dead in his coffin,' she would wail to her husband, who would have to get up from his seat beside the fire to prevent her from rearranging the boy's limbs.

Guillaume Ladoucette happily moved into his grandfather's house, taking with him the family chamber pot containing his savings, as well as his framed certificate from the Périgord Academy of Master Barbers. Suddenly discovering a freedom he hadn't even known existed, he left the dishes until the next day, ate entire packets of Cabécou in one sitting and walked around in the nude getting as much air to his japonicas as he pleased. When Pierre Rouzeau noticed that he was unusually quiet, he assumed he was still grieving for his grandfather. But Guillaume Ladoucette hadn't even wept because he couldn't believe that the old man wasn't going to walk into the family home at any moment in just his shirtsleeves and be chased upstairs with a broom to put on a pair of trousers. What was actually weighing on Guillaume Ladoucette's mind was the fact that he had decided to spend his small inheritance on setting up his own barber shop and was wondering how to break the news to his beloved boss.

In the end, it was Francine Rouzeau who came to his rescue. When, one lunchtime, she asked why he hadn't finished his rabbit with prunes, he replied that he had come into some money and was still deciding what to do with it. Her response was immediate: 'You must open your own barber's, of course. Mustn't he, Pierre?'

After helping himself to the rest of the Cabécou, Pierre Rouzeau replied: 'It's what every barber aspires to. That and never to have a customer in his chair with more hair on the tops of his ears than on his head.'

The sum Guillaume Ladoucette's grandfather had left him was in no way sufficient to buy premises in the village, equip it with a chair and washbasin and pay him a salary while it was getting on its feet. But he soon came up with a solution that kept him awake until three o'clock in the morning, his heart as tight as a green walnut with excitement. As he lay on his back, rubbing the palms of his hands on the bottom sheet while his feet waved in and out, his mind scattered over everything that was needed to convert his grandfather's kitchen into a barber shop.

With the help of his best friend Stéphane Jollis, the baker, who was used to humping around large sacks of flour, it didn't take long. First they built another small kitchen at the back of the house and then pulled out the existing one. Guillaume Ladoucette ordered just one sink for the shop to begin with, as expansion was something to consider in the future, and a black leather chair, the same make as those used by Pierre Rouzeau. Didier Lapierre, the carpenter, put in a bench along the wall facing the mirror for which Madame Ladoucette made cushions. But her son ended up hiding them because he didn't want to horrify his customers with frills.

A set of shelves was built and mounted next to the window to hold the products the barber hoped to sell to boost his profits. He took over an hour arranging the combs, pots of pomade, shampoos, boxes of razors, false sideburns, lather brushes, hair tonics and pencils to colour greying moustaches. Once he had finished he stood back, cocked his head to one side, and started again.

If Émilie Fraisse was Guillaume Ladoucette's first love, the shop came a very close second. Business picked up within weeks of opening, and, after two months, there was an average of three people waiting at any one time on the bench on a Saturday. Not all, admittedly, were customers. Some villagers came simply to warm up and even, on occasion, had the impudence to nip out to the grocer's for a packet of Petit Beurre Lu biscuits to make themselves feel more at home. The barber put up with the volleys of crumbs – which, much to his irritation, eventually found their way into his supermarket leather sandals – simply because so many bodies gave the impression that his services were in demand, which was good for business. They continued the habit of sitting around the place well into spring, claiming that the showers drove them in. In the summer, they would complain about the heat, shouting at everyone to close the door behind them to keep out the hot air that hung around the streets like an unwanted guest. When the shop was particularly busy, the barber would shoo them off the bench and they would scatter like a herd of wild goats. Much to his annoyance, he would then sometimes find one in the living room with his feet up watching the television or sitting on his lavatory reading his Lucky Luke books.

Guillaume Ladoucette never forgot his training, in particular the words of the Périgord Academy of Master Barbers' *Revised Guide to the Art of Barbering*, Second Edition. Every morning, before coming downstairs, he made absolutely certain that he was a Living Example. After emptying his bladder, he wouldn't leave the bathroom until his hair and moustache were of sufficient splendour to arouse his customers' interest in similar services. He took particular pride in his finger wave. Twice a week, after washing his hair and applying styling lotion, he would carefully position a finger on the front section of his hair, form a ridge with the help of a comb and then continue the procedure around the rest of the head. He named his three variations the Troubadour, the Pompadour and the Ambassador. And while there was not much call for any of them – most men objected to having to wear a hairnet whilst their hair was being dried – Guillaume Ladoucette took great satisfaction from simply knowing that the service was available should anyone request it.

After the initial wave of interest, business remained healthy for almost two decades, with customers returning every four weeks, seduced by the barber's mantra that 'a gentleman never needs a haircut'. As the years passed, he gradually built up a small, yet curious collection of old barbering utensils, which he found in the numerous antique fairs held in the streets of neighbouring towns and villages. Amongst the tat and over-priced treasures, he discovered several shaving bowls with a semi-circle cut out of one side to enable them to hug the neck. He also purchased a number of wooden balls which would be placed inside the cheek to facilitate shaving. Then there were the little brass moustache tongs which, after being heated, created the most magnificent of curls, and the numerous cut-throat razors, his favourite of which had a mother-of-pearl handle. He displayed the collection on a table in the front corner of the shop as a tribute to his profession, whose members were once of such high social standing that up until 1637 they were charged with the most prestigious task of bloodletting.

On the wall above the wooden bench was mounted another of his finds: an original advert for Dr L. Parker's electricity cure for baldness, bearing a picture of a faithful customer with a treatment cap strapped to his head. It claimed that the method not only had cured five thousand people in one year alone, but was recognized by the International Congress of Electrology at the Milan exhibition on 7 September 1906, two facts that aroused genuine enquiries from a number of Guillaume Ladoucette's customers.

Despite his passion for his profession, the barber eventually grew tired of living in the same place as his work, to say nothing of finding customers on his own lavatory, complaining that there was no more paper. When, three years ago, his widowed mother could no longer cope alone in the family house and moved to a one-bedroom place in the centre of the village, Guillaume Ladoucette returned to his childhood home with its splendid walnut tree in the garden and immediately took over custody of the family cassoulet, a duty which he performed with utmost devotion.

The barber had never heard of Jean-Baptiste Rigaudie until he saw his neighbour Yves Lévèque up a ladder attending to the curved salmon tiles on his roof. The barber, who had just started on a pigeon braised in half a bottle of Pécharmant while sitting at the wooden table speckled with lichen, immediately stood up. Slipping his hairy toes back into his sandals, he thwacked his way across the garden as fast as supermarket leather would allow. Once at the wall he called: 'Hey, Yves! Are you all right? What's happened?'

Yves Lévèque glanced down to see his neighbour looking up at him, a piece of onion caught in his moustache. 'Some of the tiles are loose and they're keeping me awake at night,' he explained.

'Not that,' called the barber. 'I mean you. Are you all right? You look as if you've been in the wars.'

'What do you mean?' he asked.

'Your hair.'

Yves Lévèque slowly climbed down to the last but one rung, looked at his neighbour and then at the ground.

'I'm sorry, Guillaume, it's just that I haven't been with a woman for such a long time. It's hard on a man. You know what torture it is. I've seen you night after night eating your supper alone out there. Surely it's not too much to ask to have the soft mounds of a woman's breasts against your back at night.'

'I'm not with you,' said Guillaume Ladoucette.

'A man has to do what he can to make the most of himself and I'm not getting any younger. As you know, I've tried the Troubadour. And the Pompadour and the Ambassador just aren't me. Someone told me about this new barber in Brantôme called Jean-Baptiste Rigaudie. They say he was trained in Paris. What do you think? It's called the pine cone.'

'It wouldn't be right for me to comment on another artisan's work. Good luck with the roof,' Guillaume Ladoucette replied, returning to his pigeon. But its tiny succulent breast had lost its appeal.

Four days later, the barber was walking home from his shop looking forward to a bath after the day's relentless heat, which had made him fear that he was producing obnoxious odours, when Didier Lapierre rounded the corner. From the sideburns up the carpenter looked as though he had been caught in a cataclysmic typhoon. Guillaume Ladoucette, who had been wondering why he hadn't seen him in his chair recently, knew precisely where the perfidious wretch had been. As soon as he saw him, the carpenter looked down and hurried off. The barber watched him disappear down the rue du Château, the first time he had ever seen him doing anything at speed. 'Turncoat!' he muttered.

The following week, as the barber was waiting to be served in the village's Bar Saint-Jus, his eyes travelled up to its owner's hair, which looked suspiciously like a pine cone.

'Ah, Guillaume! Hello,' said Fabrice Ribou, turning round. 'What can I get you?'

'A glass of red, please, Fabrice,' Guillaume Ladoucette replied evenly.

The bar owner poured out a glass and pushed it towards him across the wooden counter. Realizing that the barber was studying his hair, his eyes dropped, shot left, right and then returned to his customer.

'Oh, by the way, Guillaume, I was meaning to tell you. The reason why I've stopped coming to the shop is that my mother's started to cut my hair.'

The barber, who was just about to take a sip, halted his glass below his lips. He had heard Fabrice Ribou tell more convincing lies to his ex-wife.

'Is that so?' he asked.

'Absolutely! I was at her house the other day and she said she'd always wanted to take up hairdressing and was thinking of doing a little course and she asked whether she could practise on me to see whether she'd take to it.'

'Fabrice,' said Guillaume Ladoucette, resting an elbow on the bar. 'We both know that your mother is ninety-two and was registered blind last year.'

'That's the whole point, she's got a great sense of touch!' Fabrice Ribou replied.

Over the following few weeks, Guillaume Ladoucette

began to notice a sharp drop in the number of people waiting on the bench on Saturdays, despite the ferocious sun which had baked the lizards as hard as biscuits so that some villagers had started to use them as doorstops. If the barber was already troubled, it was nothing compared to how he felt when he spotted Henri Rousseau, whose hair he cut to help hide the hearing aid that his wife made him wear, coming out of the grocer's. As soon as he saw the barber, Henri Rousseau, who had never shown any interest in his appearance, immediately started running up the rue du Château as if he had just been caught in bed with another man's wife. Guillaume Ladoucette tore after his customer as fast as his shopping basket would allow. Henri Rousseau then charged down an altogether different rue du Château, and sprinted in the direction of the ancient wooden weighing platform where farmers were once charged a *franc* for each horned beast that stepped on. He hared past the Bar Saint-Jus, up yet another rue du Château and was in such a state of panic he didn't even turn to see whether Lisette Robert's underwear was on the line. Just as he had made it past the Romanesque church he found himself cornered by a tractor.

'Forgive me, Guillaume,' he called out as the barber approached, panting. 'Blame my wife. She said that everyone was trying out this new barber in Brantôme who knew all the latest styles. I was quite happy with the way you always cut it, but she said I had to go as it was she who had to look at me all the time.'

'What's it called?' asked the barber.

'The forelock,' replied the fifty-eight-year-old, looking at him with his right eye, his left covered by a long flop of hair stretching from as far back as his crown.

As Guillaume Ladoucette sat in front of his bowl of cassoulet, remembering the sight of Gilbert Dubuisson's freckled scalp earlier that day, he thought of all his other regulars who had deserted him on account of having gone bald due to their advancing years. Despite employing his best salesman's techniques, he had only managed to convince four of them to wear a hairpiece. Again he wondered whether he should move with the times and learn the pine cone and the forelock. But such monstrosities went against everything he had learnt. Anyone who had read the Périgord Academy of Master Barbers' *Revised Guide to the Art of Barbering*, Second Edition, would know only too well that each hairstyle should represent a work of art which emphasized the best features of the customer in order to make them look more attractive for their age, weight and height. He just couldn't do it. Wouldn't do it. The barber then counted up how many regulars he had left and thought of the letters from the bank asking him to come in for a talk that he had ignored. As Guillaume Ladoucette realized that his days as a barber were over, the tear on his chin dropped to the floor.

3

A BREEZE SNIFFED ROUND THE ADJUSTABLE SIGN AT THE ENTRANCE
to the village that read: 'Slow Down! There Are Only 33 of Us'.
A day never passed without a wind blowing. None of the
myopic meteorologists from Paris who made regular visits to
the tiny community in the north-western tip of the Périgord
Vert could agree on a cause for the curious microclimate.
Some in the surrounding hamlets pointed to the gusts as an
explanation for the reputation of the place, for wind was
widely accepted as a cause of madness.

There were numerous explanations as to how the village
came to be called Amour-sur-Belle, only one of which was
true. Belle, as everyone correctly pointed out, was the name
of the river that lolloped its way through. It wasn't much of a
river, no wider in places than Stéphane Jollis was tall, a fact
noted by those who happened to see the baker fall in while
picking wild mint one afternoon. He lay for several minutes
unable to move, his giant stomach sticking out of the clear
water like a half-moon. The sight was so arresting it took a

while for those on the bridge to stop staring and help the man get back up on to his ridiculously small feet.

Lisette Robert the midwife had insisted that the name referred to the love that permeated generations of her family, one of the oldest in the village, until it was pointed out that her great-great-grandmother had pushed her great-great-grandfather down a well after he had shown his donkey too much of the wrong sort of affection; that one of her uncles had never lived with the mother of their five children as she smelt too fiercely; and that Lisette Robert herself, who was a widow, hadn't even come close to finding love again, despite her unrivalled beauty.

Gilbert Dubuisson claimed that the village was named after St Amour. According to the postman, the fifteenth-century former heretic converted to Christianity on seeing the beauty of the place, which he insisted could only be God-given, and went on to found a monastery in the nearby woods. He stuck by the story even when it was pointed out to him that the village had never been anything to look at; that the only remains of a construction in the woods was a battered old hunters' shed, which concealed the frantic throes of adulterous affairs; and that had the village such a close association with Christianity its inhabitants would surely be of a far higher moral standing.

The truth was that Amour-sur-Belle was named after Marcus Damour, a Roman soldier who left the army claiming tempestuous bowels in order to fight for the Gauls, as he had heard that their food supplies were better. After fathering six ugly children, he went on to cultivate in the fields around the village a mysterious new crop that his compatriots had brought with them from Italy. It produced bunches of red or green berries which, when crushed, fermented and drunk, proved to have a remarkable ability to improve the inhabitants' mood. Recaptured by the Romans while working on his vines one morning, Damour was found guilty of desertion and crucified.

Damour's fatal mistake was to have settled in a village frequented by Romans marching between Angoulême and Périgueux. Intolerable numbers would stop, lured by its fountain which was widely believed to cure gout. The inhabitants, fed up of soldiers soaking their pestilent feet in their drinking water, eventually put the word out that it also cured lively libidos, which immediately put a stop to the visitors and their mouldy sandals. But the villagers' torment was far from over. For, when the area succumbed to Christianity, the miraculous fountain was dedicated to St Pierre, and once a year the place was overrun by pilgrims whose personal habits were even more pernicious.

There was one brief moment of glory in the village's ignoble history. Before Napoleon left for his Russian campaign, he asked the owners of the local forges, including that of Amour-sur-Belle, to produce his cannons, an honour so great it made the inhabitants who worked there tremble with pride. Before leaving, he handed out a scattering of IOUs and ennoblements to the forge owners. But, after failing in Russia, the emperor refused to pay his debts and they were ruined. The peasants returned to their crops cursing the short general and wrapped themselves in their familiar cloaks of misery.

The inhabitants trembled once more, this time with fear, when men arrived in 1936 with their horses and carts to install the first electricity pylons. They trembled again, with excitement, when they returned in their vans in 1967 to lay the pipes for running water, after which turning on a tap remained a novelty for several years.

Amour-sur-Belle's questionable looks worsened with time. A community with four times its current population a generation ago, eleven of its deserted houses had since slumped to their knees in despair. Several stone barns, their doors long rotted away, stood throttled by an infestation of weeds, their walls gripped with bone-coloured ivy that had long ago given up the will to live. The village no longer even had a stone cross, it having been removed the previous century by the diocese who thought the place no longer worthy after a morose resident knifed her husband to death, unable to bear the agony of seeing his contentment.

However, its humble appearance worked in its favour, for the English considered the place far too ugly to colonize. As a result, Amour-sur-Belle enjoyed the distinction of being the only place for kilometres inhabited solely by natives. Visitors were also scarce. Most tourists who happened to come across its forlorn château, which had changed hands eight times between the French and English during the Hundred Years War, and whose ramparts with their missing sections of crenellations were too scandalous to warrant the place a mention in the guidebooks, simply carried on driving.

There was a time when the residents of Amour-sur-Belle tried to pass the place off as a town in the hope of securing more amenities from the local authority. Yves Lévèque, who had always fancied a municipal swimming pool, despite the fact that he was the only person who could afford one of his own, wrote a letter to the council stating that following a particularly cold winter the village had experienced a popu-lation explosion. Not only that, but many outsiders had suddenly noticed the unrivalled charms of Amour-sur-Belle and had made it their home. Within weeks the dentist received a reply stating that the first stage of any alteration to the status of the village would be a population headcount, for which a date had been set for two months' time. Letters were hastily sent across the country to relatives who hadn't received a Christmas card for years, inviting them for a visit and indicating the precise date when the offer was open. A note was also despatched to a great-aunt in Newfoundland and a telegram to a second cousin in Swansea.

When the day of the headcount arrived, however, the population had swelled by just two people. His plans in tatters, Yves Lévêque rushed to the barber shop and asked Guillaume Ladoucette for all the wigs, false beards, moustaches and sideburns that he possessed. The dentist struggled out with a large cardboard box and distributed its contents amongst the villagers. When the man from the council arrived, he discovered a surprisingly hirsute population. As he walked around the village with his clipboard, he suddenly came across a resident standing on the church steps, panting. He had exactly the same features and attire as the man who had just been sitting outside the Bar Saint-Jus. The only difference between the two was that the first man was totally bald. But what astonished the official most was that some of the gentlemen with the longest beards undeniably had breasts. By the time he had finished his count, the population of Amour-sur-Belle, many of whom, he noted, were desperately short of breath and suffered from chronic perspiration, stood at 897. That evening, a victorious Yves Lévêque started asking around the bar for volunteer lifeguards.

The following Tuesday, however, a second inspector arrived, unannounced. Yves Lévêque, who happened to be attending to his roof at the time, was the first to spot him stalking around the village with his clipboard. Horrified, the dentist shot down his ladder. But in his panic he was unable to remember who had the box of hairpieces that were waiting to be combed out before being returned to the fastidious barber. By the end of the week, a letter arrived at the dentist's house stating that after two official audits of the population of Amour-sur-Belle, its status would remain unchanged.

Guillaume Ladoucette had just emerged from the woods with the biggest Caesar's mushroom he had ever picked and was striding back home enjoying the envious glances at its rich orange flesh when he was woken from his dream by the sound of a door banging in the breeze in the street below. The barber remained in exactly the same position, his arms down the sides of his body as if already dead in his coffin, and his eyes closed, desperately trying to get back to the rue du Château so he could arrive back home, put some butter and garlic into a frying pan and allow the flavour to take him to fungal heaven. But it was no use. When he fell back to sleep he found himself standing in front of his barber's which had been bought by Jean-Baptiste Rigaudie. Stretching out of the door was a queue made up of all his customers who had gone bald, whose hair had suddenly grown back. Those waiting on what was now a red leather banquette were not passing round Petit Beurre Lu biscuits, but were being served little cakes made by Stéphane Jollis, who ignored his friend's mournful tapping on the window.

Jolted awake by the horrifying spectacle, the barber swung his legs out of bed, settled his feet on the floor and peered cautiously between his ankles. Satisfied that he was alone, he stood up and made his way to the bathroom naked. Slowly, he nudged at the dark wooden door with his toes. Pressing an eye up against the crack between the door and the frame, he surveyed the room. Above the bath taps was a set of shelves bearing a collection of exquisite gentlemen's soaps. The bottom row was reserved for those he deemed too splendid to use, which were simply taken out of their boxes and sniffed. Next to the taps was a large loofah and a natural sponge containing two chest hairs. Lined up on top of the small marble-topped table by the sink was a razor in its box, a blue shaving mug that had belonged to his father and a badger-hair shaving brush with an ivory handle.

Seeing nothing untoward, he poked his head round the door as an extra precaution. Satisfied that she wasn't there, he walked in, rested both hands on the sink and raised his eyes to the mirror. The reflection was far from that of a Living Example. The right side of his moustache was thirty degrees higher than the left and urgently needed rewaxing into position. His finger wave had taken on the appearance of a rolling tempest as a result of a night of constant tossing; a portion of it hung down over his left eye and another was stuck to his forehead.

But Guillaume Ladoucette did not pick up the tiny spirit level he used to line up his moustache every morning. Neither did he open the jar of wax, or indeed his pomade the colour of figs. Instead, he put his fingers under the tap, ran them through his hair and wasn't in the least bit concerned about the lamentable results. Nor did he lift both arms above his head and bring them down majestically in front of him until his palms were flat on the floor, a feat of flexibility he performed daily to stave off the ravages of middle age, and on occasion to impress his contemporaries in the Bar Saint-Jus. Instead, he shuffled back into the bedroom and sat on the edge of the bed, his back rounded like the sagging walls of the old rabbit hutches in the back garden. Eventually, he looked around for his clothes, but his trousers hanging in the wardrobe seemed terribly far away. So too did the pile of white cotton underpants next to the rows of neatly paired socks in the top drawer of the dresser. An hour passed before he summoned sufficient will to clamber into a fresh pair of underwear. But once they were in position, his motivation abandoned him again and he pulled on the rest of the clothes he had worn the previous day, which were slumped on the wooden chair next to the wardrobe. He sat down again on the edge of the bed in his work trousers, pierced with tiny fragments of hair that never came out, though he had no intention of going in that day, or any other for that matter. When he could no longer brave the hurricane of his mind stirring up insufferable thoughts of what would become of him, he decided to distract himself with breakfast.

In his bare feet, the barber walked slowly down the creaking wooden stairs, but stopped on the last one. Craning his head forward, he surveyed the sitting room with its boisterous wallpaper, which had once, for a brief and unfortunate moment, been very much in vogue. On top of the back of the brown settee was a plump green velvet cushion against which he rested his head while watching television. Sitting on one of the chair arms was a small glass containing the sticky red residue of homemade *pineau*. The great pale stone mantelpiece bore a wooden framed clock whose ticking had driven one relative to suicide; above it was mounted his father's shotgun, which had claimed three wild boars. On the windowsill was the handbell his mother rang in the street during the war whenever De Gaulle had been on the radio from London in order to irritate her neighbours, who were Pétainists. Hanging on the wall next to the door to the kitchen was the calendar the fire brigade sold door-to-door at Christmas, which the barber always bought, hoping it would secure their prompt arrival in the event of a fire. And sitting on the coffee table was nothing more sinister than an old copy of *The Lunar Gardener* magazine.

Grabbing the handrail, Guillaume Ladoucette slowly crouched down, tipped over to one side and looked underneath the table. Satisfied that he was still alone, he walked through to the kitchen and poked his head round the door. He scanned the tops of the cupboards bearing the casserole dishes in which he hid his valuables; the huge pale stone mantelpiece with its row of old Peugeot coffee grinders; the bamboo coat rail by the door on which was hung his jerkin and a torch; and the cellar door handle which bore a necklace of dried red chillies. Crouching down again, he leant to one side, peered underneath the table and saw nothing other than a fallen walnut kernel.

Unable to eat as his throat was still choked with the bilious fumes of anxiety, he pulled out a chair from under the table and sat down to drink his coffee. Immediately the barber felt something collapse underneath him. He shot horrified to his feet and inspected the red cushion that his grandmother had made. There, crushed into the fabric, were pieces of shell, and smears of egg yolk were rapidly seeping into it. It was then that Guillaume Ladoucette felt something wet against his buttocks. 'That infernal chicken!' he cried.

Violette, the infernal chicken, who belonged to Fabrice Ribou the bar owner, had never dared set a scaly red toe in the house while Madame Ladoucette had been living there. But since the old woman had moved to a smaller place, after no longer being able to cope alone in the family home, the bird had taken to entering the house as if she owned the place. Guillaume Ladoucette had tried everything he could think of to get rid of her, short of blasting the bird off his garden wall where she would sit warming her fluffy under-carriage while staring at him. He had even tried locking all the doors and windows whenever he went out, but it was no use. He would return home to find peck marks in his butter, tell-tale four-toed footprints in the talc on the bathroom floor and black-and-white droppings on his freshly washed cotton underpants airing in the cupboard.

After scraping as much egg off the cushion as he could and changing his trousers, the barber left the house, taking care to double lock the front door behind him. He had no idea where he was going. All he knew was that he had to escape the fog of panic swirling around his ankles. But as soon as he started walking, his hurried footsteps simply whipped it up further. As usual Madame Serre, hair the colour of pigeon down and fingers crooked with age, was sitting on a picnic chair in the morning sun outside her front door. But the barber, engulfed in doom, failed to notice his next-door neighbour and walked on by without his usual greeting or enquiring whether there was anything she needed. She watched him disappear up the street, wondering what she had done to offend him and whether wonky moustaches were now the latest fashion.

Eventually he came to the rue du Château, one of four in the village. Only one, however, led to the castle. The peculiarity had come about following a complaint by Gilbert Dubuisson the postman that some of the street signs had become illegible with age, which was troublesome for his replacement whenever he was on leave. An administrative blunder resulted in a job lot of 'RUE DU CHÂTEAU' signs being sent to Amour-sur-Belle. Well aware that it would take years for the mistake to be admitted and rectified, the residents simply took down the faded old ones and replaced them with the new delivery. To avoid confusion, the three streets that didn't lead to the château were also known as 'The Street that Needs Resurfacing', 'The Street where Henri Rousseau Drove into the Back of Lisette Robert's Car' and 'The Street that Doesn't Lead to the Château'. But the system rarely worked as all of the streets needed resurfacing, Henri Rousseau had bumped into Lisette Robert's car in two of them and all three failed to lead to the château.

As Guillaume Ladoucette continued on his walk, his hands deep in his pockets and his moustache an alarming thirty degrees out of true, his mind was buffeted in one direction after another as he sought a solution to the catastrophe. He had very few savings left, and his mother was certainly in no position to bail him out. He would have to find new employment and fast. But what could he do? His skills lay in executing a magnificent short back and sides, fitting false sideburns and not breathing a word about the adulterous affairs that his customers claimed to be having. While they were all useful skills in their own right, they were hardly transferable.

Turning a corner, he headed past the Romanesque church which had been stripped of all traces of beauty during the Revolution.

'Morning, Guillaume. Everything all right with you? Haven't seen you in ages,' called Marcel Coussy, the old farmer, who was shuffling up the road in his work slippers.

'Fine, thanks,' the barber lied.

'Have you heard about the shower?' he asked.

'No,' Guillaume Ladoucette replied and carried on his way. As he passed the empty pharmacy the barber's heart suddenly sprang. 'That's it!' he said out loud, cupping his hands against his temples as he peered into the window at the shelves of exotic-looking bottles covered in a silent shroud of dust. 'I'll become a pharmacist!'

The business had remained closed ever since the famous mini-tornado of 1999. Many assumed it had struck Amour-sur-Belle because of its curious weather pattern. But none of the meteorologists who poured into the village from all over France with their foul-smelling waterproofs and smudged spectacles could agree on the cause.

Certainly none of them had predicted it. Or if they had, they hadn't let on. At first, the villagers assumed that the persistent breeze was just blowing a little stronger that morning. By the afternoon, Guillaume Ladoucette had telephoned his customers who wore hairpieces warning them not to venture outdoors. When evening fell, residents still in the streets, arms stretched out in front of them and unable to move forward, had to be lassoed inside by the nearest home-owner. The curved salmon-coloured roof tiles rattled up and down like pan lids and the wind screeched so loudly the villagers could no longer hear their neighbours' arguments over what to do. Not expecting to live to see the morning, they descended into their cellars and brought out their best wines, jars of foie gras, wild boar terrines, bottled truffles, preserved duck legs, pickled walnuts, ceps in vinegar and dried venison sausages and confessed their sins between mouthfuls.

No one realized that Patrice Baudin was still out in the worst of it until it was too late. Nor was it clear why he hadn't sought shelter sooner. Some suggested that with no woman in his life there was no one to urge him to put down his pestle and mortar when it started to look grim. What was certain was that he never made it further than the grocer's.

For, suddenly, the skinny vegetarian was swept clean off his feet into the air, never to be seen again.

The following day, the first everyone realized that they were still alive was the violent twisting of their innards followed by a desperate urge to vomit. After bringing up the pestilent contents, their stomachs twisted again as they remembered the secrets they had divulged. When the sound of retching eventually subsided and the wood pigeons could be heard again, shutters started to open and pale faces appeared. Several more barn roofs were missing, two uprooted oak trees had been thrown against the front door of Yves Lévèque's house, preventing him from getting out, and the château had lost yet another section of its crenellations.

Patrice Baudin's absence was first noticed by Lisette Robert when she came to the pharmacy seeking the morning-after pill. When the midwife found the shop shut, she went to the one in Brantôme but was so caught up in her own predicament that she failed to mention his absence. Two days later, when numerous villagers went to the shop in search of relief from chronic constipation, word spread that the pharmacist was missing. Expecting him to have landed somewhere around the village, there was a cursory check of potagers and flowerbeds. At the end of the week, by which time several were in need of prescriptions, a search party was mounted. The surrounding fields were combed, but nothing of note was found except a tin bath, four dead ginger Limousin cows and a walnut-oil press. They then scoured the woods, which a number simply used as an opportunity to collect fallen sweet chestnuts while marvelling at the whole sweet corn kernels in the gigantic wild boar pats. Only then were the police called. But all the officers found were the pharmacist's cracked gold-rimmed spectacles hanging from the church guttering. Over the following weeks, each time it rained, the villagers looked up to the sky wondering whether he was about to descend. But soon they got used to his absence. And, by the time that thousands of cranes had flapped their way noisily over Amour-sur-Belle signalling the start of winter, they had stopped looking at the clouds expectantly and mothers had started to use his unfortunate disappearance as a warning to children to finish their meat.

Not long after the mini-tornado, Henri Rousseau's wife, who had a mania for order, demanded that the number of residents on the village sign be reduced to thirty-two. Many believed the suggestion was rooted in spite, as Patrice Baudin had strongly opposed her husband being fitted with a hearing aid when there was no evidence that he was deaf. However, it was decided that the sign be left as it was out of respect for the pharmacist, who had always resisted gossiping about the ailments of his customers, no matter how many drinks he was bought in the Bar Saint-Jus. Modeste Simon, who never spoke again after witnessing his unfortunate disappearance from her bathroom window, kept his broken spectacles in her bedside drawer, along with the photograph she had secretly taken of him the previous year at the Donkey Festival in Brantôme.

But almost as soon as the idea to take over the pharmacy came to Guillaume Ladoucette as he stared inside the darkened shop with its abandoned pestle and mortar, he dismissed it. For while Patrice Baudin's views on eating meat were unfathomable, he was otherwise highly intelligent and the barber knew only too well that he could never comprehend the mysterious subjects the man had had to study, despite having left the Périgord Academy of Master Barbers with a distinction.

Turning away from the empty shop, he returned his hands to his pockets and continued up the street, the sun starting to warm the folds at the back of his neck. Suddenly, he heard a voice from behind.

'Hello, Guillaume! Dawdling a bit today, aren't we?' asked Sandrine Fournier, the assistant ambulant fishmonger.

The barber turned and stopped. 'Hello, Sandrine,' he replied. 'Hot, isn't it?'

'Very,' replied the barber, who hadn't noticed.

'Have you heard about the shower?'

'No,' he said, forgetting to say goodbye as he turned the corner.

As he trailed past the monument dedicated to the *Three Victims of the Barbarous Germans*, Guillaume Ladoucette told himself that there must surely be something that he could do. But he could think of nothing. Amour-sur-Belle already had all the tradespeople it could sustain, and they were all reliant on the custom from the surrounding hamlets. There was no role for a man of forty-three who had dedicated his life to conquering the cow's lick, the double crown and dandruff.

By the time he turned into the rue du Château, the barber's trousers began to feel loose around his waist as he thought of all the luxuries he would no longer be able to afford. There would be no extra packets of Cabécou when he ran out midweek; no little walnut cakes from the Friday market in Brantôme; no dozen oysters from the man who set up his stall in the village every Saturday morning; and only two bottles of Château La Plante a week. As he imagined the exquisite gentlemen's soaps he would no longer be able to purchase from his favourite shop in Périgueux, Guillaume Ladoucette was certain his armpits had begun to reek.

As he passed the ancient communal bread oven, Guillaume Ladoucette began to stoop. By the time he had dragged himself over the bridge, he'd envisioned his hair hanging in matted dust-grey clumps down his back, growing from a scab-encrusted scalp. Shuffling along the banks of the Belle through the patches of wild mint, he thought of the repugnant beard he would have to grow to keep him warm, which would stretch to his useless loins and harbour nesting sparrows. As he passed the washing place, a shallow

41

square of water where the women did their laundry until 1967, he imagined his ears so full of hardened wax that he was unable to hear Yves Lévèque shouting from the other side of the bank: 'Hey, Guillaume! Have you heard about the shower?'

He dragged his way around the outside of the château, his feet unsteady on the crisp pigeon droppings because in the fog of his imagined destitution they had both developed gout. As he passed the doors to the Romanesque church, from which oozed the smell of violent green mould, he found himself hitching up his trousers because his mind told him that they were held up with string that had rotted. He spent the next hour trailing around the village staring at the ditches in which he would undoubtedly end, wondering how long he had left to live and why everyone kept talking to him about showers.

By the time he reached the Bar Saint-Jus he had barely enough energy to take the five paces to the bar and hoist his skeletal frame up on to a stool. Through his overgrown eyebrows he could just about make out Fabrice Ribou behind the bar cleaning between the syrup bottles.

'Hello, Guillaume!' said the bar owner. 'You're looking well. Nice trousers by the way. Are they new? What can I get you?'

'A glass of red, please,' said the barber, who still hadn't forgiven him for his treachery, despite the fact that he hadn't charged him for a single drink since his new haircut.

'On the house,' said the barman, pushing the glass towards him.

The barber picked it up and brought it to a table by the window. After taking a sip, which he didn't taste, he looked out at the place du Marché and wondered whether he'd rather be cremated or buried.

'Hey, Guillaume! Have you heard about the shower?' asked Denise Vigier, the grocer, stopping at his table.

'No,' replied the barber, suddenly remembering his manners and getting up to kiss her on both cheeks.

'You haven't?' she asked, sitting down opposite him.

'No,' he replied.

'The whole village's talking about it. Where have you been all day? Someone said you didn't open the shop today.'

'Oh, I've been busy.'

'You'll never guess what the council has decided to do,' she said.

'What?' he asked out of politeness.

'Well, you know how it hasn't rained for ages?'

'Yes.'

'From next month they're banning everyone from taking a bath and installing a communal shower in the village!' she said triumphantly.

'They're installing a what?' he asked.

'A communal shower.'

'We'll all have to take a shower together?' Guillaume Ladoucette asked, horrified.

'No! One at a time, but they'll fine anyone who takes a bath.'

'How on earth are they going to regulate that?'

'God only knows.'

'Where else are they doing it?'

'It's just here.'

'Just here?'

'Apparently they want to see how it works before introducing it elsewhere. Everyone's saying they picked Amour-sur-Belle because of that headcount business. Apparently they were furious and that first inspector got suspended.'

'If Yves Lévèque had given me back those wigs and beards immediately after the first headcount as I asked him to, none of this would have happened,' replied the barber. 'The box went missing for weeks and when he eventually returned it, they were all twisted into funny shapes. I couldn't sell them.'

'Where do you think they'll put it?' asked the grocer.

But the barber, too disturbed at the memory of how much

money he had lost over the box of hairpieces, didn't want to speculate about the location of a municipal shower. He drained his glass, forgot to kiss Denise Vigier the grocer goodbye and left. When he returned home, he retired to bed without eating or bathing and remained there for six days, four hours and nineteen seconds. At that point, he raised his head from his pillow, looked out of the window and caught sight of his mother in the distance, recognizable by the tomato splat on the back of her pale-green dress. It was then that Guillaume Ladoucette had his Brilliant Idea.

4

AS HE SAT WAITING IN HIS CAR, GUILLAUME LADOUCETTE PULLED
down the sun visor to kill time. Turning his head to the right,
and then to the left, he critically surveyed his morning's
handiwork in the mirror. It was indeed a splendid creation,
he noted with immense satisfaction. He admired how it
stretched out beyond the edges of his mouth, rising at both
ends with an elegant lift which he'd fashioned fifteen degrees
higher than usual on account of his ebullient mood. A
number of white hairs had been skilfully camouflaged with
the aid of a black moustache crayon. The fact that it still
reeked of duck fat was tempered by the sight of the ends,
masterfully twisted to such a fine point they looked as if they
could spear cockroaches.

After snapping the visor back up, he looked around the car
for something else to do. Licking the end of his thumb, he
wiped off a brown smear he suddenly noticed on the dash-
board. He then took out a tissue from his pocket and dusted
the rim above the radio. Leaning over, he opened the glove

compartment and peered inside. Instantly bored by the sight of its contents, he shut it again. After staring blankly in front of him for several minutes, he sighed and looked at his watch for the fifth time.

Despite the time, Guillaume Ladoucette forgave Stéphane Jollis for keeping him waiting. It was a habit the baker had never broken even though the pick-up time for their fishing trips hadn't changed for more than twenty years. But the barber's compassion had nothing to do with tolerance, for he regarded tardiness as being almost as shameful as protruding nasal hair. Nor was it simply a matter of lassitude after spending so many years outside the baker's house, killing time by appraising the contents of his glove compartment. The reason for Guillaume Ladoucette's ability to pardon his best friend's abominable time-keeping was sitting on the back seat underneath a white tea towel to shade it from the worst of the heat. For whilst the two men were fiercely competitive when it came to fishing, their unspoken rivalry was not over what one another caught, but the contents of their picnic baskets. And the barber, who had been labouring in the kitchen since five that morning, was convinced that victory would be his.

The passenger door suddenly opened and a strong, hairy arm reached in and placed an equally large basket made from sweet chestnut on the back seat. The limb momentarily disappeared and returned with a red tea towel, which was carefully placed over it. The car suddenly tilted towards the right as the baker held on to the roof with one hand and manoeuvred his substantial frame inside, followed by his head.

'Hello. Sorry I'm late,' he said.

Guillaume Ladoucette looked at the baker. Having showered as he always did on a Sunday lunchtime after shutting the shop for the day, his friend appeared a decade younger owing to the absence of flour in his thick black curls. The barber had been cutting them for years in exchange for a daily loaf. It was a system that worked more in his favour since Stéphane Jollis only bothered to surrender his scalp every few months, by which time the barber could slide a whole finger down the middle of a ringlet, much to his exasperation.

'Not to worry,' he said, starting the car. 'Got everything?'

'Yep,' replied the baker, winding down the window.

The pair drove out of the village and turned right at the field with the ginger Limousin cows that winked. After passing a series of maize fields, they slowed down to a precise 49 kph as they trundled through the village of Beauséjour, where the traffic police waited for their prey in collapsible chairs in the sun. Each time the barber changed gear, his knuckles rubbed against Stéphane Jollis's thigh, which bloomed over the passenger seat as if baked with too much yeast.

'Bring any lunch with you?' Guillaume Ladoucette enquired, trying to sound as casual as possible.

'Just a snack,' the baker replied, staring straight ahead of him. 'You?'

'Just a snack,' said the barber, wrinkling up his nose dismissively.

When they arrived at Brantôme, the two men, each carrying a family-sized picnic basket, made their way along the bank of the Dronne, which flowed around the town known as the Venice of the Périgord. They passed the metal steps where swimmers clambered out of the slothful water and continued until they reached the *No Fishing* sign. They then put down their baskets at their usual spot, both filled with the comforting knowledge that a splendid afternoon lay ahead of them.

After Stéphane Jollis had wiped his sweating forehead on both shoulders, he joined the barber sitting on the edge of the bank in the shade of the tree which neither could name.

The baker then took out a baguette from his basket, broke off an end, pulled out some of the soft white innards, rolled it into a ball with his artisan fingers and pierced it with his hook. Once the barber had impaled a worm on his, they both took off their shoes and tied their lines around their right ankles. Carefully rolling up both trouser legs to the knee, they plunged their feet into the cool water and felt the weighted lines spiralling down towards the bottom of the river.

'That's better!' said Guillaume Ladoucette, wriggling his hairy toes in the water. A clump of talc slowly rose to the surface and started to shift gently right with the current.

'Bliss!' agreed Stéphane Jollis, raising his right trouser leg slightly higher. 'Hot, isn't it?'

'Scorching,' replied Guillaume Ladoucette. He peered down between his legs. 'Plenty down there.'

'It's definitely the best spot,' replied the baker.

They sat in contented silence, freckles of sunlight warming their knees through the leaves, watching the turquoise dragonflies land on the dusty water that slowly creaked by.

'Remember that trout Yves Lévèque caught?' asked the baker.

'I've never seen anything that size before.'

'I couldn't believe it,' the baker said.

'Nor could I.'

'It was huge.'

'Massive,' agreed Guillaume Ladoucette. 'It was so big he said he couldn't eat it all in one go.'

'I'm not surprised. Where did he say he caught it?' asked the baker.

'Somewhere near Ribérac.'

There was a pause.

'I bet he bought it from the ambulant fishmonger's,' said Guillaume Ladoucette.

'I bet he did too,' Stéphane Jollis agreed.

Silence fell again as both men leant back on their hands. Occasionally, one would lift a foot to change his bait or to pick out a piece of green weed that had slithered between his toes. After a while a male duck started chasing a female across the water. The pair watched as it landed on the back of its target, where it stayed despite the hysterical flapping.

'That's rape, that is,' said Guillaume Ladoucette, horrified.

'It's just how ducks do it,' replied the baker.

'Do you think we should do something?'

'You can't interfere with nature.'

'But she doesn't like it. Listen to that racket she's making.'

'They could be quacks of ecstasy for all you know.'

'She wouldn't be trying to get away if she liked it.'

Stéphane Jollis paused. 'Well, in the absence of a duck phone to ring the duck police, if you're really concerned why don't you swim over and separate them?' he suggested.

'Do you think she'll be all right?'

'Guillaume! The dragonflies have been doing the same thing ever since we got here. I haven't seen you rushing valiantly to their defence.'

'They don't sound in pain like that poor duck does.'

'That's because dragonflies are mute. They've probably been emitting silent screams of terror all the time we've been here and you just haven't noticed. You'd better separate them too while you're out there. I'd be careful of the wings, though, they look a bit on the delicate side.'

Guillaume Ladoucette ignored the baker as he secretly started to panic about the welfare of the dragonflies.

'Look, she's flying off now,' said the baker, pointing to the duck. 'You worry too much about things.'

'I don't,' replied the barber.

'You do.'

'At least I use proper bait.'

'Everyone's using bread again these days. Pick up any

fishing magazine and there'll be an article about it. It's only natural. Fish, like humans, can't resist the work of a true artisan.'

Silence fell again. Suddenly Guillaume Ladoucette decided that it was time to get the upper hand. 'I suddenly feel a bit peckish,' he announced.

'So do I,' said Stéphane Jollis, who, unbeknownst to the barber, had spent the whole of the previous evening cooking. They shuffled backwards along the grass on their bottoms towards their respective baskets. Stalling for time, Guillaume Ladoucette pretended to look for his penknife as he waited to see what would appear from the rival basket. He watched as a bunch of tomatoes-on-the-vine surfaced, which were inhaled before being placed on the red tea towel. Next came a jar of *cornichons*, followed by a bunch of pink radish and another baguette. Then, with what was unmistakably the hint of a sly smile, a large earthenware container was brought out and placed on the grass. Guillaume Ladoucette, who recognized the look, was instantly worried.

'Bit of pâté from the grocer's?' he enquired, unable to stop himself.

'No, actually,' replied the baker, tearing off a piece of bread and loading it up. 'I made it myself. I had a few minutes to spare and already had the duck foie gras so thought why not? The recipe says to add two soupspoons of cognac, but I always use four. I find you get a much richer taste. But they're right about the truffle juice – you wouldn't want any more than fifty grams.'

Guillaume Ladoucette watched while Stéphane Jollis opened his mouth at the same time as raising his eyebrows and crammed it in. 'Oh, delicious,' came the muffled verdict. 'Oh, yum! Fancy any?'

'No thanks, otherwise I won't manage this!' he replied, drawing out a large flask from his basket and unscrewing the lid. 'I tell you, nothing beats vichyssoise glacée soup on a hot day. It's the leeks from the garden that really makes it, I think. Want to try some?'

'No thanks, otherwise I won't manage this!' replied the baker, carefully lifting out a bowl from his basket with two hands. 'What I really love about this particular salad is the way you cook the potatoes in their skins. Delicious. Then, of course, ham, red peppers and lobster tail are always such a great combination. It makes all the difference, of course, if you picked the lobster yourself while it was still alive so that you knew you were getting a good one. Let me give you a little taste,' he said, searching in his basket for his serving spoons.

'No thanks, otherwise I won't be able to manage this!' cried Guillaume Ladoucette triumphantly, holding up a goat's cheese tart. Stéphane Jollis glanced at it unconcerned and then turned away, plunging a fork into his salad.

'Can't wait to try it,' continued the barber, cutting a slice with his penknife. He paused for dramatic effect and then added before taking a mouthful: 'I milked the goat myself.'

Stéphane Jollis made what was undeniably a choking sound.

'I was round at Marcel Coussy's farm a few months ago and we got milking the goats, and then I thought I may as well help him make the cheese,' continued the barber before taking another bite. 'Mmm, really goaty! Fancy some?'

'No, thanks, otherwise I won't manage this!' the baker announced, lifting a walnut and apple cake out of his basket with a flourish. But they both knew it was useless: nothing could have beaten Guillaume Ladoucette's caprine masterstroke.

As they ate their lunch, the baker started plotting his menu for the next fishing trip while the barber wriggled his hairy toes with delight, until Stéphane Jollis pointed out that he was disturbing the fish.

Emboldened by his victory, Guillaume Ladoucette decided

to broach the subject that had been curling around in his mind ever since he lifted his head from the pillow after his six-day repose. 'Stéphane . . .' he began.

'Yes,' the baker said, biting into a tomato and squirting his white T-shirt with seeds.

'You know I've closed the barber shop . . .'

'Yes,' he replied, flicking at his chest. 'I haven't mentioned it in case you didn't want to talk about it.'

'I've decided to set myself up as a matchmaker.'

'A what?'

'A matchmaker.'

'A matchmaker?'

'Yes.'

'Why a matchmaker?'

'Well, how many people do you know in the village who are in love?'

Stéphane Jollis momentarily stopped chewing as he considered the question. His friend did indeed have a point. For, despite its name, love was something that Amour-sur-Belle was sorely lacking. The majority of the inhabitants were single, not helped by the number of divorces which had taken place following the famous mini-tornado of 1999, during which infidelities, crimes and other depravities were drunkenly confessed on the assumption that no one would live to see the morning.

A number of residents weren't even speaking to each other. Stéphane Jollis himself and Lisette Robert hadn't passed the time of day since the episode of extreme weather, during which Patrice Baudin wasn't the only thing to disappear. The tornado had also elevated the entire contents of Lisette Robert's pond and the resulting shower of frogs landed in the baker's garden. While it never became clear precisely what had happened to them, it was widely believed that the baker, who smelt fiercely of garlic the following day, and who was spotted by five witnesses buying large quantities of butter in the grocer's, had eaten the lot. This was despite the man's vehement protests to the contrary, which included the fact that the only people who ate frogs' legs were tourists, having fallen for a joke started in 1832 by a mischievous French merchant, while in London, who claimed that it was a national delicacy.

Then there were those who said as little as possible to Denise Vigier the grocer, having never forgotten that her grandmother had been found guilty of horizontal collaboration at a tribunal in 1944 and, after a swastika had been drawn on her forehead, had been given a 'Number 44' haircut in front of a spitting crowd in Périgueux. The villagers raised their eyebrows at the tins of frankfurters on Denise Vigier's shelves, and nudged each other whenever she joined the annual memorial service at the monument to the *Three Victims of the Barbarous Germans, Shot on 19 June 1944.*

Fabrice Ribou had refused to serve Sandrine Fournier at the Bar Saint-Jus ever since the death of his father. The old man had pestered the assistant ambulant fishmonger so often to tell him where in the woods she found such marvellous ceps that she eventually blurted out 'by the hunters' shack'. While the remains of the omelette were rushed to the hospital as quickly as possible, it was not fast enough to identify which poisonous mushroom he had mistakenly consumed. Everyone naturally sided with Sandrine Fournier, for the locations of such prodigious yields were a jealously guarded secret passed down through families, but no one supported her publicly for Fabrice Ribou's was the only bar for kilometres.

Stéphane Jollis swallowed his mouthful. 'Brilliant idea, Guillaume,' he said, pausing before adding: 'Please don't take this the wrong way, but you're not exactly married yourself. And never have been. Some might question what you know about love.'

Guillaume Ladoucette looked at his knees. He and the

baker had grown up together after Madame Ladoucette had breast-fed Stéphane Jollis when his own mother's milk had finally dried up with the arrival of her ninth and last child. The boys' friendship had been sealed through afternoons spent by the Belle trying to see whose pee could reach the far bank first, a competition eventually won by Stéphane Jollis at the age of six and a half, whose victory was put down to a stolen bottle of lemonade. But despite their bond, the baker knew nothing of the tumultuous state of Guillaume Ladoucette's heart. The affliction was such that his doctor had taken one look down his ears and gasped at the decades' worth of unwept tears. He sniffed just below his chest and winced at the smell of rotting flowers coming from his spleen. He shook his head at the man's freakish flexibility, another tell-tale sign. And he baulked at the surfeit of hormones that had leaked from his japonicas, cascaded down his legs and collected at his toes where they produced such dense hairs he found within them a discarded watermelon pip.

'Monsieur Ladoucette,' he began after his patient had dressed again. 'I think we both know what your problem is. And it is a severe case of lovesickness at that. You may recover. You may not. I'm afraid that there is no medical intervention that can ease your suffering. If it gets any worse – and it may well do – you are, of course, welcome to come back, but really there is nothing that I can do. I'm sorry.'

The barber picked up his coat and shuffled towards the door. Just as he was about to shut it behind him, the doctor called out: 'Whoever she is, I hope she's worth it.'

There were many in Amour-sur-Belle who would have thought that Émilie Fraisse was indeed not worth it. It would have been a different matter, of course, during her youth. While not the prettiest in the village – Lisette Robert carried that particular burden – there was certainly no end to the approving glances she received as she was growing up. When still a child, the expertise she had displayed at shooting blackbirds one winter, following an atrocious snowfall which left the village with nothing else to eat, attracted a stream of schoolboy admirers. When she was ten, she started charging them fifty centimes to stroke the butter-coloured hair which so annoyed her, the proceeds of which she spent on gunpowder for her father's shotgun, which he lent to her when his wife wasn't looking. When she got older, and attempts were made to touch other parts of her, they were smartly rebuffed. The only boy she let anywhere near her was Guillaume Ladoucette, who had never tried. But their proximity never went further than their heads touching as they gazed in wonder at the still quivering kidneys of a hare they had just caught.

When, at the age of seventeen, Émilie Fraisse left Amour-sur-Belle, she gave Guillaume Ladoucette her Nontron hunting knife with its boxwood handle and ancient poker-work motifs and asked him to look after it while she was away. He never got to say goodbye because he was helping his father collect firewood and was too embarrassed to explain why he wanted to suddenly leave. When he came back to the village, Émilie Fraisse had gone. Several weeks later, a letter arrived from Bordeaux in which she recounted how much she was enjoying working in her uncle's butcher's, asking him not to tell her mother that she was behind the counter rather than on the till as promised. But Guillaume Ladoucette, whose mind was already afflicted, couldn't think of how to reply. After he read and reread the letter, he simply folded it up, put it inside an empty tin of Docteur L. Guyot throat pastilles and buried it underneath a flowering hellebore in the garden. Such was his regret at not having had the courage to reply, he turned his eyes away each winter when it bloomed.

The girl's remarkable talent with a knife at first shocked her relatives. But soon they forgot her age and sex, and the girl with the long plait who would sing strange songs as she hacked up ribs of bloodied beef and plunged her hands into bowls of glistening, purple entrails to cure homesickness became a local curiosity.

It wasn't long before Émilie Fraisse attracted the attention of Serge Pompignac, a local landowner who came into the shop to buy a brace of pheasant. When he asked, as a joke, whether she had shot them herself, the girl replied, 'Of course,' as if he had just asked the most foolish question imaginable. By the time he had reached home, he found that his mind still hadn't left the girl. That evening, he decided against serving the pheasants to his dinner guest. Instead, the following day, he ate them alone in his grand dining room, picking from his tongue the pieces of shot that broke one of his teeth, and placing them around the side of his plate as he chewed. When he had swallowed the final mouthful, he held up each tiny bullet to the light and inspected it carefully. Getting up from his seat, he fetched a small wooden box and dropped them inside one by one. They rolled around as he walked to his writing desk and placed the box in a secret compartment. It was only then that he rang his dentist.

Unable to get the thought of the girl with the long plait and bloodied apron out of his mind, he returned to the butcher's the following day but found that she was not there. Too embarrassed to ask her whereabouts, he bought a couple more pheasants anyway. Passing by the shop three days later, he caught sight of her thin frame between the coils of black pudding and was inside before he realized he had moved. He hung around the shelves of preserves and mustards, avoiding the other staff until she was free to serve him and then asked for another brace of pheasant. When, as she was wrapping them, he asked where she had shot them, she replied, 'No,' as if he had just asked the most foolish question imaginable. When he took the birds home, he left them in the kitchen and forgot about them, until the stench grew so bad even the dogs vomited.

The following week, he walked straight up to the counter and ordered everything that was for sale, including all the jars of mustard and preserves. Once all his purchases were eventually loaded into the van waiting outside, he turned to Frédéric Fraisse and said: 'I presume your niece's work is over for the day. Do I have your permission to take her out for an afternoon walk?'

Frédéric Fraisse, still astounded by what had just taken place, glanced at his niece and mistook her look of horror for assent. Six months later, exhausted from the disappointment of coming downstairs every morning to find letters only from her mother at her place at the breakfast table, Émilie Fraisse agreed to marry Serge Pompignac.

It wasn't long after she had left her aunt's house and moved into her marital home that her husband suggested that she stopped working in the butcher's. Émilie Fraisse, who had refused to change her name, at first ignored her husband's repeated requests, which were born of his fear of someone else loving her as much as he did. She finally gave in on the tenth day of him not speaking to her. Her mother thought it was for the best. 'You don't need to work in a shop any more,' she wrote. 'Not with a husband as rich as he is. You should count yourself lucky.'

Émilie Fraisse spent her early days wandering around the vast house staring at the ugly oil paintings and grotesquely carved furniture, thinking about Amour-sur-Belle. Once, she considered writing again to Guillaume Ladoucette, but took his lack of response to her first letter as a sign of indifference. When, a year later, her mother asked why she still didn't have any grandchildren, Émilie Fraisse counted the number of times she and her husband had made love and found that she didn't need more than one hand. She had first suspected that something was wrong when it took almost three months to consummate the marriage. But the problem was never discussed, and the longer it continued, the more Serge

Pompignac held it against the woman he had thought would finally be able to cure him.

With no children to look after and her position in the butcher's long since given to an apprentice, Émilie Fraisse spent her days cleaning the house, locking herself in each room so as not to be disturbed by the maids who had already done them. After dusting the furniture, she would set about polishing it, her efforts all the more determined for her desperate desire to make a difference despite the lack of dirt to begin with. When she had exhausted herself cleaning one room, she would set upon another until she had finished the whole house, and would then begin again. When the maids started complaining that there was never enough polish, Émilie Fraisse started buying her own so as not to raise their suspicions, and burnt the holey dusters in secret. At the dinner table, which had shrunk by three centimetres after years of rabid polishing, Serge Pompignac would look at his wife with her long hair that had turned prematurely grey and try and remember the girl who had fired the shot which he still kept in the tiny wooden box in the secret compartment of his writing desk. And she would try and remember the man who wanted her so badly that he had bought the weight of sixteen people in fresh meat and 2,312 pots of mustard.

It came as a relief when, after almost twenty-six years of marriage, Serge Pompignac handed her more money than the butcher shop could have made in a decade. 'I'm sorry,' he said. 'I thought it would be different. Please forgive me.'

'I do,' she replied.

'What will you do?' he asked.

She thought for a moment and then replied: 'I'm going to buy the château in Amour-sur-Belle. It's filthy.'

During the years she was away, Guillaume Ladoucette had had a number of romantic liaisons, but nothing had come close to what he felt for Émilie Fraisse. He would catch glimpses of her on the rare occasions she would return to the village for the weekend to see her parents. But he never spoke to her, lacking the courage to approach. Once, when she arrived at the barber's for a haircut for old time's sake, she found the door closed with a note on it saying: 'Back in five minutes. Scissors on the table for those who can't wait.'

When, a week ago, she returned permanently to Amour-sur-Belle and brought up the château's drawbridge behind her, whispers started about her long grey hair and lack of children. Versions of how she came to afford the mournful building with its scandalous ramparts were buffeted around Amour-sur-Belle with the perpetual breeze. Guillaume Ladoucette refused to believe the one that blew through his keyhole and simply tried to think of what he would say to his first and only love when he eventually bumped into her.

'I may very well still be a bachelor, Stéphane,' conceded Guillaume Ladoucette, staring at the far bank, 'but it doesn't disqualify me from being a matchmaker.'

'Yes, you're completely right. You'll be marvellous,' replied the baker. 'Any help you need, just ask. Where will it be?'

'Where the barber shop is.'

'Splendid.' They sat in silence as the fish refused to bite and Guillaume Ladoucette wondered what to call his new venture. After a while, Stéphane Jollis, so convinced that his friend's lunatic plan was doomed to failure, asked for a piece of goat's cheese tart as a gesture of solidarity.

5

IT WAS MONSIEUR MOREAU WHO FIRST SPOTTED THE STRANGER walking around Amour-sur-Belle one Wednesday morning. The villager was in his usual position on the wooden bench by the fountain said to cure gout absorbed by a procession of ants transporting the horse chestnut tree to his right in forensic portions to a mystery location on his left. He had followed them on numerous occasions, but never once during his years of amateur sleuthing had he been able to discover the whereabouts of what would now constitute 13 medium-sized branches, 323,879 leaves and 112 conkers complete with shells. Despite his advancing years, entire afternoons had been spent on his belly in the dust following his subjects, only for the scent to go cold at a hole alongside the south-facing wall of the home of Sandrine Fournier. The one time he had mustered up the courage to ask if he could inspect her cellar 'for the presence of a sizeable amount of foliage', the assistant ambulant fishmonger accused him of having been out in the sun too long and closed the door.

When not staring intently at the ground by his feet, Monsieur Moreau, who was used by many as a local landmark when giving directions, could be found slumped on the bench, the back of his head resting against a clump of weeds growing out of the stone wall behind him like a green beard. The old man's flaky closed eyelids, dry open mouth and stagnant air caused many to assume that he had died, which resulted in the widespread habit of people poking him as they passed in order to be the first with the news of his demise.

On this occasion he didn't see the stranger's face, just his highly polished left shoe that was threatening to crush an ant he had named Arabella, which already that morning had survived being almost flattened by two tractors, a bicycle, three cats and a pigeon as it rattled across the street with an outsized piece of twig.

'Watch where you're stepping!' Monsieur Moreau yelped, sticking an arm out in front of him to prevent the carnage. The man quickly stepped aside, turning back several paces later to look at the ground, still unsure of what he had almost stepped on

The next person who saw him was Denise Vigier the grocer, who was outside her shop arranging some oak-leaf lettuces, her colossal bosom poking out either side of her white apron. 'Half-price lettuces,' she lied, when she spotted him approaching. But the offer failed to detain him and the opportunity to find out what he wanted was gone.

Yves Lévèque had just settled himself at a table in the Bar Saint-Jus, rejoicing that a patient had just cancelled, when he looked up from his newspaper across the place du Marché. 'Good God!' the dentist exclaimed. 'It's the man from the council who carried out the first headcount!'

There was a painful sound of scraping of chairs as the customers abandoned their seats and stood as close to the window as their stomachs would permit.

'You're right!' declared Fabrice Ribou, running a hand through his pine cone. 'He's put on a bit of weight, hasn't he?'

'Right old porker,' said Henri Rousseau, his forelock covering one eye.

'Are you sure that's him?' asked Marcel Coussy the farmer.

'Positive,' replied Yves Lévèque. 'He's still got the same pair of trousers on. I used to have a pair. I'd recognize them anywhere.'

'I wonder what he's doing here,' said Didier Lapierre the carpenter, whose partially flattened pine cone bore the telltale sign of a mid-morning snooze in his van.

'Whatever it is, he hasn't come to measure up for a municipal swimming pool, that's for certain,' said the dentist. 'Watch out, he's coming over!'

By the time the door opened, all that could be heard was a hideous ensemble of exaggerated slurping and Fabrice Ribou's whistle, which his customers had repeatedly informed him was a unique form of torture.

Fortunately the man walked straight up to the bar, forcing Fabrice Ribou to unpurse his lips and ask him what he wanted to drink. Introducing himself as Jean-François Lafforest from the council, he informed the owner that he had come on official business. Clutching his soft leather briefcase to his stomach, he took a deep breath. It had taken him three weeks to memorize the speech he had to give, on account of the nervous breakdown he had suffered following the wicked taunts of his colleagues when he had returned to the office with his preposterous headcount.

'Ladies and gentlemen,' he announced, facing the room. 'You will all receive the following information in the post within the next few days, but I am here to inform you of the decision myself in the event that there may be some immediate questions. I'd like to make it clear from the start that the following announcement is a council matter and decided by a committee.' He paused. 'Not by me,' he added, looking round quickly.

With a raised hand, Fabrice Ribou, whose mind was never far from his takings, interrupted the man, telling him that if he was about to make a public announcement it was only fair to round up the other villagers. To his immense satisfaction, after a series of phone calls, his clientele had doubled.

On seeing by how much his audience had swelled, Jean-François Lafforest hugged his briefcase closer towards him until the left buckle was pressing painfully against his umbilicus. 'As you are no doubt aware, it has not rained for some considerable time, before which the reservoir was already at a worryingly low level,' he continued. 'It is my duty to inform you that a municipal shower will shortly be installed in the place du Marché. From that time the taking of baths will not be permitted in Amour-sur-Belle and anyone caught infringing the regulation will be fined. We are well aware of how much water is being consumed at the moment and expect the amount to fall dramatically when our preventative measure has been introduced. I will briefly answer any questions you may have, but it will all be explained in the letter that you will duly receive.'

'How much is the fine?' asked Gilbert Dubuisson the postman.

Jean-François Lafforest rubbed his upper lip as he muttered a figure.

'How much did he say?' asked a voice from the back.

'How much did you say?' asked Lisette Robert.

'One hundred euros,' repeated the man from the council.

'One hundred euros!' exclaimed Marcel Coussy the farmer.

'For having a bath in our own homes!' said Madame Moreau.

'As I said before, it's not I who decides these matters,' said Jean-François Lafforest, wiping a tickle of sweat from the side of his face. 'If you would like to take the matter further I have a list of names of people you could get in touch with. As you will see, mine isn't on there.'

'How will you know if anyone's had a bath?' asked Lisette Robert.

'Spot checks will be carried out,' replied Jean-François Lafforest, 'the details of which will be determined. By others. Not me.'

Quite what happened next, Jean-François Lafforest was never certain. All the man from the council knew was that one moment he was in the bar and the next he had been deposited back at the far end of the square, his soft leather briefcase arriving seconds afterwards. When he had recovered sufficiently from the shock to get back on to his feet, he hurried back to his car. But just as he turned the key, the fear in his stomach curdled its contents. Opening the car door, he stuck his head out and showered a patch of nettles with vomit.

Guillaume Ladoucette didn't attend the meeting, having resisted Fabrice Ribou's sales tactics with the insistence that he was busy. After putting down the phone, he took the key to the barber shop from its nail by the kitchen mantelpiece, dropped it into his trouser pocket and locked the front door behind him. For several minutes, he stood in silence with his back against the door, his palms feeling the warmth of the wood. Suddenly, without warning, he unlocked it again and burst back in. But the room was still empty.

It was warm inside the barber shop. As he pushed open the door a pile of letters skidded across the floor. He stood looking around, noticing the dust that had flourished on the mirror in just over a week. Below it, in the sink, was a withered lizard still bearing the grimace of a prolonged and painful death from dehydration. The grey nylon gown had slipped from its hook on the wall and lay slumped on the floor like a body felled by a firing squad. When, eventually, he mustered the courage to touch something, he reached out and ran his hand along the back of the black leather chair, sending millions of fragments of hair twisting and sparkling in a sliver of sunlight.

Reminding himself that today was the start of his new life, Guillaume Ladoucette set to work. As he picked up the post and put it in a neat pile by the door to take home, he thought: No more dandruff. As he folded up the cape, he muttered: 'No more pretending to customers that they're not going bald.' As he pulled forward the bench and reached down to pick up two empty packets of Petit Beurre Lu biscuits, he said to himself: 'No more inhaling trimmings which would eventually have formed a hairball in my stomach and killed me.' Cheered at the thought of having saved himself from certain death, he dropped all the products that had been for sale into a plastic bag, including the combs in three different colours, the pots of pomade the colour of figs and the bottles of hair tonic bearing a picture of a perfectly groomed gentleman.

Into a box he packed his small, yet curious collection of old barbering utensils, including the shaving bowls, the wooden balls which were placed inside the cheek to facilitate shaving, the sets of little brass moustache tongs and the assortment of cut-throat razors. On top of them he carefully rested the framed original advert for Dr L. Parker's electricity cure for baldness, bearing a picture of a faithful customer with a treatment cap strapped to his head. He then went to the other side of the room and looked up at his certificate from the Périgord Academy of Master Barbers, but something in his stomach stopped him from taking it down.

When Stéphane Jollis arrived to remove the barber's chair and sink, Guillaume Ladoucette disappeared into the back garden unable to watch, reminding the baker to turn the water off at the mains. Once the task was done, the two men stood back and contemplated the empty room.

'Why don't you just whitewash it?' suggested the baker.

'It's been white for nineteen years. What about pale pink?'

'Pale pink? What would you want pale pink for?'

'It's romantic.'

'They use it in hospices.'

'What would you have, then?'

'White.'

'I don't want white,' said Guillaume. 'What about blue?'

'Too cold.'

'What about cream?'

'If you're going to have cream you may as well have white.'

'What about green? I like green.'

'It's the colour of schoolrooms,' said the baker.

'What about red, then?'

'It would look like a bordello. That's an idea, why don't you open a bordello?'

'Stéphane, would you mind concentrating on the issue at hand? I'm running out of colours.'

'White,' he replied before leaving to return to the bakery.

The morning Guillaume Ladoucette opened his new business, the sun was firing with such ferocity the pigeons had gone mad. Unable to remember how to fly, they tottered after Madame Ladoucette in a feathery grey shadow, recognizing in her a similar suffering. A number of them, a spark having suddenly fired in a prehistoric part of their brain, thought that they were fish again. Monsieur Moreau found six drowned in the fountain said to cure gout, their pink scaly feet cleansed of droppings. He was dissuaded from giving them to his wife to cook immediately he saw the crazed look in their eyes, which frightened him so much that when night fell he buried the lot in the graveyard as close to the Romanesque church as possible.

In preparation for his grand opening, Guillaume Ladoucette had bathed with a bar of Geo. F. Trumper Milk of Flowers soap, which his favourite shop in Périgueux imported from the famous London barber's for their special customers, who were, in fact, anyone willing to pay such a price. He had never expected an occasion grand enough to warrant its use, and had spent the last four months simply gazing at his purchase on the bottom shelf above the taps from his recumbent position while being buffeted by the noisy foam of cheap bubble bath. Such was the depth of pleasure it had given him, after washing he lay for thirty-seven minutes in the water fragrant with English wild flowers, the bar sitting in the curious dip in his sternum that his grandfather had told him was an excellent place to keep salt while eating a boiled egg.

As Guillaume Ladoucette approached the shop, he admired once again the fancy lettering of the words 'Heart's Desire' above the door. It had cost him more than he expected, but he was so delighted with the result that he invited the signmaker home for a bowl of cassoulet afterwards. After unlocking the door, he turned round the plastic sign hanging on the inside so that the word 'Open' faced the street in swirling red letters. After hanging his new navy suit jacket on the peg where the grey nylon cape used to be, he gave it an affectionate brush with his hand even though there was not a speck on it. Savouring the moment, he then slowly sat down at the oak desk facing the window. He had bought the desk from the cave in the limestone cliff at Brantôme that sold bric-à-brac. Slightly battered with a prominent ink stain that had secured its free delivery, an afternoon of polishing and buffing had vastly improved its appearance. It wasn't its pretty brass handles that had seduced Guillaume Ladoucette, however, but the narrow drawer which sat just above his stomach containing numerous compartments for small things as well as long things.

After lacing his fingers on the edge of the desk behind a clean sheet of white paper, he bared his most welcoming of smiles and waited. A few moments later, when nothing had happened, he slowly moved his pen from the right-hand side of the piece of paper to a horizontal position above it. He relaced his fingers and smiled again.

Not long after jaw-ache had set in, he looked down and, feeling a twist of excitement, slowly slid open the narrow drawer. There, each in its own little compartment, was a rubber, a pencil, a stapler, a selection of pens and the contents of a large packet of multi-coloured rubber bands which had been divided between two sections because of their quantity. After moving the stapler to a different compartment, he slowly closed the drawer again.

Guillaume Ladoucette resumed his original pose of unfettered expectation. When, several minutes later, he was still alone, he glanced out of the window to check that no one was looking. He then moved his tie to one side, pulled open his shirt between the second and third button, lowered his head and inhaled deeply, savouring the exquisite blend of musky floral aromas still trapped in his chest hairs. Once his tie was back in position, he dropped a hand down the side of his new swivel chair. As he did so, his fingers brushed against a lever which he lifted. An instant later his curiosity was sated when he found himself plummeting towards the floor like a runaway lift. After several fruitless yanks, followed by a lifting of his bottom, the seat eventually rose to its original height and he cautiously sat back down.

Looking around the newly painted walls, he silently congratulated himself on having opted for pale pink after all. He then got up, walked round to the other side of the desk and sat on the chair with the peeling marquetry, which he had also bought from the bric-à-brac cave in Brantôme, seduced by its cushion bearing a hand-embroidered radish. 'Most comfortable,' he concluded again, rubbing the ends of the arm rests. Before returning to his swivel chair, he looked in his old barbering mirror, which he had decided to leave where it was, and fiddled with his tie, which was already in the correct position.

Two hours later, Guillaume Ladoucette had made the

gratifying discovery that if he put one hand on the edge of the desk and spun himself round, he could, on average, achieve three revolutions before the chair came to a standstill. In his final best of three, his sense of achievement was complete when he managed such propulsion that he whipped round a staggering four-and-a-half times.

When midday finally came, he took his new navy jacket off the peg, put it on and went home for lunch. Returning after his pig's head soup, medallions of pork, green beans fried in garlic and a round of Cabécou, the matchmaker looked around for a sign that a customer had dropped by – a little note on the door perhaps – but everything was just as he had left it. After hanging up his jacket, he returned to his seat. After several minutes, he tried to match his record of four-and-a-half revolutions but had to stop as it was giving him the urge to vomit. He then lifted the receiver of the phone, which he had placed over the ink stain to hide it, and found that, despite the absence of calls, it was indeed working. Sliding open the narrow drawer above his stomach, he surveyed the contents with as much satisfaction as before and slowly slid it shut again so as not to disturb anything. Chin in his left hand, he then gazed across the road to the home of Gilbert Dubuisson and inspected the man's meticulous window boxes, which were a particular source of pride to the postman. Two hours later, the matchmaker realized that it was time to go home when he found himself considering knocking on the loquacious postman's door and asking him whether he fancied popping in for a chat, an invitation the man had never previously needed. Telling himself it was still early days, he straightened the cushion with the hand-embroidered radish and returned home for another bath while he still had the chance.

By the third day, the matchmaker had decided to leave his jacket at home, twirling around on his new chair had lost all its allure and the most significant event that had taken place in Heart's Desire was that the stapler was now back in its original position. Just before lunch, he discovered the proper purpose of elastic bands and managed to fire seven that landed directly on the doorknob. By the afternoon he started to wonder where all his customers were. Everyone knew he had opened for business, surely. The previous week he had called the *Sud Ouest* and a charming young reporter had come to see him, expressing considerable interest in his new venture. His picture had even appeared alongside the article, but the photographer had taken it from a crouching position south of his chin, resulting in a shot that the matchmaker believed revealed too much of the contents of his nasal cavities and, much to his horror, gave the impression that a giant fruit bat had just landed on his top lip. But despite the publicity, the only person who had opened the door since was a workman carrying a piece of piping who asked the way to the place du Marché as there seemed to be more than one rue du Château.

By the seventh day, Guillaume Ladoucette was tieless and back in his short-sleeved checked shirts and comfortable trousers that he had worn for barbering. Instead of being shod in a pair of new, hard, black lace-ups, his feet were now stark naked, having been slipped out of his supermarket leather sandals, and were enjoying the cool of the red tile floor. The contents of the narrow drawer hadn't been inspected for days as the thrill had long since worn off, and the stack of plain white paper in the top right-hand drawer had gone down by half, having been snipped into a variety of creations with a pair of scissors he'd retrieved from his cardboard box of barbering utensils in the cellar. Just when he told himself to stop, his fingers reached for another piece and within seconds had produced the Hanging Gardens of Babylon. Unable to control himself, by the time that he looked at his watch again, he had created all Seven Wonders of the World.

By the thirteenth day, the matchmaker had come to detest the colour of the walls. As he sat with his elbows on the desk, which now seemed far too big, he suddenly recalled the pale-pink walls of the room in the hospice that had entombed his father for the last two months of his life. Madame Ladoucette had replaced the picture of a vase of flowers over her husband's bed with the portrait of the Virgin Mary from their bedroom in an effort to make the room more homely. As his father was unable to see it from his recumbent position, Guillaume Ladoucette had suspected that it was rather more for her comfort than for his. Whether it worked or not, he couldn't tell. Certainly, she seemed bright enough whenever she was there, tucking in his sheets which were already tucked in, and combing his hair which was already combed. And she continued licking her thumb and plastering down his eyebrows, fearful that breaking the habit that had irritated him to the point of fury throughout their marriage might alert him to his terrible prognosis.

Each evening when mother and son left, the spiteful cold air would take their breath away just as the sight of the patient did each morning when they returned. After crossing the car park for the silent journey home, Guillaume Ladoucette would hold open the passenger door for his mother, but she would insist on climbing into the back, unable to bear the thought of sitting in the front without being able to place her hand on her husband's thigh.

When the news was quietly broken that there was only a matter of hours left, Madame Ladoucette finally gave up the pretence and sank to her knees at her husband's bedside. Taking his hands in hers, she wiped her scalding tears on his knuckles which had already started to chill. And it was then that she asked: 'Do you remember how we met, Michel?'

'Of course, Florence,' he replied with his final smile, still able to see her through the veils of death. It was a question they had regularly asked each other during the many good periods of their marriage simply for the pleasure of hearing the other tell the story that still warmed them both. There was no chance of the script being embellished over time, for the words they had first spoken to each other were as sacred as those Madame Ladoucette muttered in the Romanesque church every Sunday through the spores of violent green mould. And their son, who had heard them so often, could verify that they were still the same version he had first heard at the age of eleven months from within his cot.

The couple had met at a travelling circus when she was twelve and he fifteen. Michel Ladoucette's father had relieved the cursed monotony of farming by hiring himself out as a part-time acrobat to the shows that ventured near to Amour-sur-Belle. His greatest trick, which he practised in the privacy of the cowshed, was to jump down his own throat, an audacious disappearing act involving a backwards somersault. He never permitted his children to see him perform, fearing that they would not be able to resist the lure of the high wire or the girls with the silver headdresses and stow away in the llama cages. He had not the slightest idea that all seven attended every performance, sitting in the shadows of the far reaches of the tent so as not to be spotted.

Florence Fuzeau arrived one night on foot with her mother from the village of La Tour Blanche. They sat with blankets on their knees in the front row, thrilled by the fact that there was no safety net between the high wire and the sawdust. When the farmer and part-time acrobat asked for a volunteer, Florence Fuzeau's mother pushed her daughter forward in the hope that it would stop her complaining about the cold and strengthen her personality, which she feared was feeble. However, her mother's hopes were far from met. Not only did the girl's temperature plummet the higher she was obliged to climb, but the three minutes and fifty-six seconds she spent sailing back and forth in the air, her wrists gripped by the upside-down showman whose legs were hooked over the trapeze, was the root cause of her fear of death that stalked her for the rest of her life.

When the show was over, Michel Ladoucette, who had witnessed the girl's terror from his seat in the far reaches of the tent, ran after her to apologize for his father's antics. He spotted her easily in the night as her face was even paler than the moon. But when he caught up with her, he was so struck by her charm, he was at a loss as to what to say. Despite her wretched performance, he could think of nothing else but to enquire as to how long she had been a professional. The girl, her head still lurching back and forth, accepted his compliment and agreed to see him again, believing she would have to eventually marry him as he had already seen her knickers.

She started preparing herself for her husband's death on their wedding night. When he finally fell asleep, she lay on her back, tears coursing down her temples into her ears at the ghastly thought of ever losing him. It was a habit that became as much a part of her nocturnal ritual as saying her innumerable prayers. At times, when her husband woke in the middle of the night and groped in the darkness for the comfort of her warm body, which smelt of brioche, a finger would find its way into her ear. He spent the whole of his married life believing that his wife had chronic glue ear problems, but that she was too embarrassed to mention it.

However, during their years together, there were times when Florence Ladoucette cursed the day they had met at the travelling circus. Her husband, who had not inherited the slightest bit of talent from his showman father, drove her to a state of wrath whenever he tried to copy his father's greatest trick in the confines of the kitchen, insisting that the tiles provided just the right purchase for the perfect lift-off. Never once was he successful, however, to which the broken pots and scuffed cupboard doors attested. She reached the end of her tether when her husband, who became a waiter after the disused quarry flooded, bringing an end to the cultivation of button mushrooms, was threatened with the sack for attempting to juggle with the plates. It happened to be the same day she had caught his fingers inching towards the carving knife, knowing that he was going to attempt to swallow it as soon as her back was turned. When she threatened to leave him he reminded her that it was acrobatics that had brought them together. 'And it will be acrobatics that drive us apart!' she cried, marching out of the kitchen towards the woods where she hid, waiting for him to come and find her as night fell.

Monsieur Ladoucette found his wife's protestations over his attempts to emulate his father entirely unreasonable and would sit in his chair by the fire mentally cataloguing all her offences and shortcomings, including checking his tongue twice a day for sign of disease; refusing to allow him to eat apples, claiming that they had caused enough trouble with Eve; and insisting that their son wore a clove of garlic around his neck to prevent him from getting worms. When, finally, however, in order to save the marriage, he consented to give up all attempts to perform his father's greatest trick, his efforts continued in his dreams, his body flipping and jerking underneath the sheets despite the family Bible his wife would place on his chest to weigh him down.

Despite decades of dread, when the frightful moment eventually came, Madame Ladoucette was no more prepared for her husband's death than she had been on her wedding night. The wail she let out pierced her son's stomach with the ease of a hot blade. He was never sure what had wounded him more that night: losing his father or the harrowing anguish of his mother.

When Guillaume Ladoucette could no longer bear looking at the pink walls, his eyes turned to the framed certificate from the Périgord Academy of Master Barbers that he had been unable to take down, and he thought of his life's passion that had come to an end because of his stubborn refusal to change. He saw himself in his four-year-old short-sleeved checked shirt that failed to disguise his winter plumage, his supermarket leather sandals which he had bought because they were cheap, and his moustache which he had to colour with a crayon to cover the grey. He looked down at the desk with the ink stain standing in mockery of the venture that had failed before it had started. But most of all he thought of the woman he had lost, his idiocy in not replying to her letter and the twenty-six years they could have spent together, now gone and dusty. And when he concluded that he had failed at the one thing that mattered most in life, the hot blade pierced his stomach for a second time.

Just then the door opened.

6

GUILLAUME LADOUCETTE LED HIS FIRST CUSTOMER TO THE CHAIR
with the peeling marquetry with the same care he would
have taken helping an invalid traverse a frozen lake in un-
suitable footwear. When finally satisfied that he was
comfortably settled on the cushion with the hand-
embroidered radish, the matchmaker, who had taken on the
semblance of a mother penguin obsessed with her solitary
egg, padded round to the other side of the desk with the ink
stain where he sat down carefully on the swivel chair, his oil-
drop eyes not leaving his new arrival for a second.

'Welcome to Heart's Desire!' he announced with a smile of
such breadth his moustache swept an inch closer to each ear.
'A little coffee, perhaps?'

'Yes, please.'

Guillaume Ladoucette trotted off to the back of the shop
and poured a couple of cups from the percolator on the small
table with the lace tablecloth. He placed one in front of his
customer, settled himself back on the swivel chair, pulled off

his pen top with a flourish and declared: 'Now, just a few formalities to go through before we get down to business.' Pointing his nib towards the paper, he raised his eyes and asked: 'Name?'

'You know very well what my name is,' the man replied. 'We've known each other all our lives.'

'Name?' Guillaume Ladoucette enquired again.

Silence ballooned between them.

'Yves Lévèque,' came the eventual reply.

'Address?'

'I'm your next-door neighbour!'

'Address?'

'Amour-sur-Belle. And that's in the Périgord Vert in South-West France in case you've forgotten that too.'

'Age?' Guillaume Ladoucette asked, his head lowered.

'Thirty-five,' the dentist replied.

'Age?' the matchmaker repeated with the weariness of a courtroom judge who had heard one too many deceits during his career.

'All right, forty-four.'

'So, how can I help you?' asked Guillaume Ladoucette, lacing his fingers in front of him and resting them on the desk.

'Well,' he said. 'I heard you'd set yourself up as a match-maker and I just thought I'd just come and see what it was all about. Just as a neighbourly gesture, of course.'

'Splendid! We offer three levels of service—'

'We?' asked the dentist, looking around the room.

'Heart's Desire offers three levels of service,' Guillaume Ladoucette continued, 'all uniquely tailored to suit your individual needs. We have the Unrivalled Bronze Service, the Unrivalled Silver Service and then of course the Unrivalled Gold Service.'

'And what do they involve?'

'The Unrivalled Bronze Service enables you to help

yourself in your quest to find love. We offer tips on where you might be going wrong, suggest ways in which you could improve your appearance, perhaps, and point out any unfavourable personal habits that need to be confronted. The rest is then up to you. Customers who choose the Unrivalled Silver Service are matched up with the utmost thought, care and consideration to someone of unparalleled suitability on our books. And finally, those who opt for the Unrivalled Gold Service can stipulate the person to whom they wish to be introduced, providing that he or she lives within a certain radius and that the object of their affection is single. Those who opt for the Unrivalled Silver or Unrivalled Gold Services automatically get the benefits of the Unrivalled Bronze Service free of charge.'

Guillaume Ladoucette sat back in his chair and started rolling his pen between his fingers as he waited for the dentist's reaction. Yves Lévèque adjusted his spectacles with his long, pale instruments of torture.

'So, how many people have you got on your books?' he enquired.

The truth bolted before Guillaume Ladoucette had a chance to rein it back in. 'None,' he replied, placing the pen back on the desk, already smelling defeat.

'I see,' said Yves Lévèque, frowning. 'And how much are you charging for all this?'

His hopes rising again and his fingers fluttering, Guillaume Ladoucette pulled the brass handle of the top left-hand drawer of the desk with the ink stain. Pushing aside several paper Wonders of the World, including a particularly splendid Mausoleum at Halicarnassus, he took out a price list printed on cream card and slid it across the surface of the desk with his index finger. Yves Lévèque looked at it, then looked at it again to make sure he had not misread it. As he did so, Guillaume Ladoucette slowly opened the narrow drawer above his stomach and took out his rubber and stapler. Silently, he placed them on top of the desk in the hope of seducing his customer with his arsenal of professionalism.

'So let me get this right,' said Yves Lévèque, sitting back in the chair with the peeling marquetry, the price list in his hand. 'I could pay you a small fortune and opt for the Unrivalled Bronze Service to be advised on such matters as clipping my nails regularly. Or I could pay you an even bigger fortune and choose the Unrivalled Silver Service and you'll match me up with myself, as things stands. Or, thirdly, I could plump for the Unrivalled Gold Service and pay you an unsightly fortune for you to sidle up to someone and tell them that I fancy them.'

'Come, come, Monsieur Lévèque ...'

'You can call me Yves, Guillaume, as you have done all your life. We went to the same school, remember?'

'Yves. The fact that there is currently no one else on our books is a mere formality. It is only a matter of time before things pick up. And, as my first customer, you would, of course, be eligible for a ten per cent discount. Now, I must point out that the Unrivalled Bronze Service is not designed for a man of the world such as yourself. Heavens, no. Naturally, you know how to comport yourself in the company of women. I, myself, have seen you with several over the years and your behaviour appeared entirely proper. Neither are there any nasty habits that I feel need addressing. Your problem, as I see it, is simply lack of opportunity. What have you done to improve your chances of finding love? There must be many suitable women who come into the surgery. You're the only dentist for kilometres.'

'Well,' said Yves Lévèque, looking beyond the matchmaker as he thought. 'I keep myself clean and tidy, which can't be said for everyone around here. You'd know all about that, having had to get as close to them as I do. I always flatter them on their brushing technique. But the problem with getting romantically involved with a patient, of course, is that when you eventually split up and they come back for treatment, they assume that whenever you tell them that they need a filling you're just trying to cause them more pain.'

'I see,' said the matchmaker. 'Is there anything you might have done recently to improve your chances that hasn't perhaps worked, or, worse still, is hampering your efforts?'

As Yves Lévèque shook his head, the spikes of his pine cone rattled against each other. 'Nothing I can think of,' he replied.

'Something to do with your appearance, perhaps?'

The dentist looked blankly at the matchmaker for several minutes.

'Well, maybe that's a little something to think about,' said Guillaume Ladoucette quickly. 'So, what will it be, the Unrivalled Bronze Service, the Unrivalled Silver Service or the Unrivalled Gold Service?'

'I'm still not convinced about any of them.'

'I suppose you could always carry on as you are, but what you've tried so far clearly hasn't worked, which is a shame because there's nothing quite like the soft mounds of a woman's breasts against your back at night, is there?' said the matchmaker, whose breathtaking salesmanship over the last nineteen years had shifted 15,094 combs, 507 wigs, 144 false moustaches, 312 nasal hair clippers, 256 pairs of false side- burns, 22 pairs of false eyebrows and 3 merkins.

Yves Lévèque remained silent.

'There's a woman out there waiting to find you, as you are waiting to find her,' Guillaume Ladoucette continued. 'My job is to unite the pair of you before she finds someone else.'

'But your prices are extraordinary!' protested the dentist.

Guillaume Ladoucette leant back in his chair and looked out of the window. 'I bumped into Gilbert Dubuisson on his rounds yesterday,' he said. 'He had really bad toothache and said he was going to have to make an appointment to see you.'

The matchmaker paused before adding: 'Sounded to me like he needs root canal treatment.'

Silence billowed again. Guillaume Ladoucette picked up his rubber and started inspecting it as he waited for a decision. But Yves Lévèque was unable to speak. Yet again he felt the sharp edges of the loneliness that had been rattling around inside his stomach for half a decade. It had caused such chronic constipation that not even a piece of Le Trappe Échourgnac cheese laced with walnut liqueur, made by the sisters of the Notre-Dame de Bonne Espérance Abbey, left on his bed sheet at night was able to entice the blockages out. As he sat rubbing his palms on the stained wooden arms of the chair, slowly the loneliness rose and became wedged in his throat. The more he tried to speak the more it strangled him and his cheeks lit up with the struggle. Gripping the edges of the cushion, he shut his eyes and with one final gulp he swallowed the obstruction back down. But the coppery residue of five loveless years had coated his tongue. When he finally opened his mouth, he let out a squeak like a rusty weathervane, coughed, and whispered: 'The Unrivalled Silver Service.'

Over an hour later, having divulged more about his ill-fated love life than he even realized he knew, Yves Lévèque got up. Before leaving, he poked his head out of the door to check that no one was around to witness his exit. In his pocket was an elastic band given to him by the elated match-maker as a goodbye present, which he'd accepted with bewilderment, assuming its relevance would come to him later. Once the dentist had gone, Guillaume Ladoucette put his arsenal back in the narrow drawer with the compart-ments. After turning over the sign on the door, he locked up and headed home.

The sun had lost the worst of its grip and bobbing in the wake of the perpetual breeze was the scent of wild mint growing along the banks of the Belle. Not that the matchmaker noticed. He had in fact failed to take in anything of the short journey home, for such was the extent of his jubilation at finally having a customer on his books, a sudden onset of delirium had blanked out the curved salmon roof tiles, the ancient stone walls on top of which wild irises grew and the pigeons that had forgotten how to fly and had converted to pedestrianism. In their place was the image of Yves Lévèque sitting on the terrace of one of the exquisite riverside restaurants in Brantôme holding the hand of a woman opposite him. By the time he had reached halfway home, the woman, who had perfect teeth, had fallen for the dentist's hitherto disguised charms. When the matchmaker turned into his street, the couple was standing before the priest in the Romanesque church with the violent green mould that clawed up to the stations of the cross, he was best man and the groom had finally apologized for returning his box of hairpieces in such a state of turmoil.

Arriving at his house, the matchmaker cupped his hands against the kitchen window and peered inside. Stepping lightly towards the front door, he slid the key silently into the lock and gently turned it. Slowly pushing the door ajar, he then took a small hand mirror from behind the flower box on the windowsill, slid it inside and tilted it in various directions as he tried to see every angle of the kitchen.

'Good evening, Guillaume! What on earth are you doing?' came a voice. The matchmaker jumped and turned his head to see Madame Serre holding a watering can with fingers twisted with age.

'Ah! Good evening, Madame Serre. Err, nothing. That's what I'm doing, absolutely nothing. Nothing at all. Not a single thing. And if I were doing something, which I'm not, it certainly wouldn't be what it looks like. Not a bit of it. I'd better go, actually, because I'm not doing anything and it's about time that I was. Bye!' replied the matchmaker and closed the door smartly behind him.

Once inside, he poured himself a glass of still mineral water from a bottle in the fridge and sat down at the kitchen table with a nectarine, which he had carefully washed to avoid getting worms. As he cut into it, he wondered what to have for his victory supper. When he had finished the fruit, he dabbed his mouth with his favourite white napkin with his initials embroidered in red in the corner, let the nectarine stone slide off the plate into the bin and put the plate into the sink. He then walked over to the cellar door, turned the handle on which hung a necklace of dried red chillies and slowly descended the stairs.

At the bottom, he pulled a cord which lit up a naked bulb furred with dust. One of his favourite places as a boy, the cellar still held its allure. While the majority of the fruit and vegetable conserves were now his own, there were still a few at the back of the shelves that had been made by his mother, their contents rancid to the point of explosion, which he kept for the comfort of seeing her handwriting on the labels.

There were other treasures down there too, including a large collection of his ancestors' clogs, their soles shod with what appeared to be tiny horse shoes. As a child, he would put them on and drag them around the bare earth floor with his tiny pink feet, which had not yet gone to seed. His favourite was the ornately carved pair made of poplar which had belonged to his grandfather, who reserved them for Sundays and funerals. They had fitted Guillaume Ladoucette perfectly for a period of eleven months when he was fourteen. But he had been forbidden from taking them up into the house as his parents couldn't trust his Bedouin-like tendency for giving away his possessions to whoever expressed a liking for them.

But they were not the only delights. There was also the 'monk', a large wooden frame in which a pot of embers would be placed to warm the bed, so called because of a monk's obligation to lie in the bishop's bed to warm it up. Then there were the yokes and a pair of enormous bellows used to inflate the skins of calves in order to remove them more easily. Filling the corners were ancient, largely unfathomable, wooden and iron implements laced with cobwebs, the purpose of which no one could deduce. Every now and again, the young Guillaume Ladoucette, convinced that some good should come of them, would take one out into the garden, clean it up and try and find a use for it, which one afternoon led him to trying to fashion a garden sieve out of a chastity belt.

Ignoring the bite of his grandfather's Sunday clogs, which he still put on when in the cellar despite the aggression of their nip, the matchmaker moved along the shelves of jars, and with the obsessional scrutiny of an alchemist, inspected his bottles of *pineau*. In various stages of fermentation since the previous year, their contents resembled ghastly specimens of human tissue and bodily fluids. First, he had crushed the grapes in a food mixer and then sieved the results through a pair of tights, the purchase of which had caused numerous smirks in the grocer's, and which had led to the much-repeated comment by Denise Vigier that if they were for him, he would be much better off with the extra-large size. He had then added enough cognac to create a concoction of 40 per cent alcohol and 60 per cent grape must. He looked with satisfaction at the clarity of the liquid in the top three-quarters of several of the bottles, and calculated that it would only be a matter of weeks before he would try it.

Passing the pickled tomatoes, their flushed cheeks pressed up against the glass, he then turned his attention to the bottles of walnut wine that he had made the previous August. He had spent a happy afternoon picking the green nuts from the tree in the garden, breaking them up, mixing them with eau-de-vie, sugar, the zest of an orange and a cinnamon stick, which was a new addition last year. It had all been filtered with another pair of tights, purchased this time from

Brantôme to avoid Denise Vigier's tongue. He peered at the murky liquid, wondering whether he should have used more cinnamon sticks.

But the biggest change to the cellar since Guillaume Ladoucette had returned to live in his childhood home was the astrological maps and planetary charts that now covered the walls above the wooden shelves. For, as his years advanced, he had followed the inevitable path of a man who had discovered a white hair in his moustache and embraced his potager with the enthusiasm of a new lover, intoxicated by its alluring yields and tormented by its capricious failures in equal measure.

The coloured maps and charts were the cornerstone of his seduction technique. For Guillaume Ladoucette was of the conviction that plants were as responsive to the cycles of the moon as the tides. A high priest in the cult of lunar gardening, he undertook no task in the potager, no matter how small, unless the moon was passing in front of the correct zodiacal constellation. Preparation of the soil, sowing, thinning out and hoeing, for example, were only performed while the moon was passing in front of Capricorn, Taurus and Virgo. The optimal time to concern oneself with leaf crops such as lettuce and spinach was when it was passing in front of Cancer, Pisces or Scorpio. And if the moon was in Gemini, Libra or Aquarius, it was the turn of artichokes, Brussels sprouts and broccoli. He naturally endorsed the teaching that there were four days a month when only a fool would work in his potager: when the moon was closest to the earth, which made stems grow long and skinny like useless adolescents; when it was at its furthest point from the earth, which produced plants that were susceptible to illness; and the twice-monthly occasions when it passed through the plane of the earth's orbit around the sun, causing such celestial perturbations that seeds would fail to sprout.

Guillaume Ladoucette wasn't alone in his adherence to this

religion, which was practised during daylight hours. Since he had the most detailed and up-to-date maps and charts available – some of which repeated themselves but brought him the comfort of knowing that everything was covered – he was often pestered with zodiacal queries from new disciples who had also been rudely confronted with their middle age by finding a white hair in the least expected of places.

Having checked the position of the moon, the matchmaker struggled out of his grandfather's clogs and found relief in his supermarket leather sandals. After clicking off the light, he creaked back upstairs and headed towards the back door. Once he had unlocked it, he poked his head round, scanned the top of the garden wall, the lawn and underneath the frilly pink hydrangea and stepped out with confidence towards his potager.

Thwacking his way across the grass, he passed the well with its pointed stone roof and the old white sink with its cheery red geraniums. First he admired his row of garlic, which he had planted four days before a full moon and around which he had loosened the ground when it was passing in front of Capricorn to ensure plump bulbs. He decided not to dwell on his artichokes, which, instead of standing straight as soldiers, had more the air of a group of conscientious objectors about them, despite having been planted when the moon was in Gemini. But their mournful sight, and the nagging regret at not having added more cinnamon sticks to his walnut wine, suddenly reminded the matchmaker of his capacity for failure and his mind turned to Yves Lévèque. As he reached for a weed and tossed it into a basket, he wondered whether he really would be able to find a woman who would overlook the dentist's much-discussed parsimony, his annoying habit of looking at people's teeth when spoken to, and his unspeakable efforts at growing *cornichons*. Bending over to pick some spinach, his heart began to slip. But as he reached for another handful, he was suddenly reminded of his stroke of good fortune when he had pulled apart the large floppy leaves during his cursory search for Patrice Baudin following the famous mini-tornado of 1999. 'That woman exists and I shall find her,' he told himself, turning his back on the quicksand of despair and marching back to the house with his pickings to prepare his celebratory supper.

Instead of finding a displaced skinny vegetarian pharmacist lying amongst his spinach, Guillaume Ladoucette had, in fact, discovered an exquisite oil painting of a young woman whose lack of refinement suggested a person of little means. While of no apparent value, its charm was undoubted. It was the rapture expressed by the anonymous artist's palette that held the eye. There was no mistaking the tenderness in the blush of her cheeks, the adoration that nestled in each of the curls that hung around her shoulders and the devotion which shone from her eyes, which defied nature. Her common white blouse had been afforded the purity of Egyptian cotton, and its cheap buttons the lustre of a Venetian courtesan's.

Not knowing whom it belonged to, and failing to recognize his own mother, Guillaume Ladoucette brought the portrait inside, carefully removed the soil from the canvas and repaired the damage to the gilt frame. For the next few weeks, he asked everyone he came across whether they had lost an oil painting during the recent severe weather. Unable to find its owner, he eventually hung it in the sitting room to the right of the mantelpiece where he would gaze at it from his armchair wondering who the girl was.

It never occurred to Monsieur Moreau that his painting had taken flight from the wood shed when its roof was blown off during the mini-tornado. He immediately assumed that a thief had stolen it, which had been his constant fear ever since hanging it there almost six decades before. There had never been any question of him bringing it into the house lest his wife recognized the woman who later became her greatest adversary.

Monsieur Moreau's unrequited devotion had lasted so long its discoloured pages were almost too fragile to turn. He too had been sitting in the darkened recesses of the great white circus tent that night and witnessed the devastating spectacle of Florence Fuzeau's knickers. His ardour had been ignited two years before when the girl suddenly turned to him one afternoon in the school playground and licked him on the cheek. The boy took the gesture as a sign of affection. But it was nothing of the sort: Florence Fuzeau was simply suffering from a chronic lack of salt.

That night, as he sat watching a dwarf cleaning up a steaming pile of llama droppings before the next act, he decided he could wait no longer to make his declaration of love. But when the lights finally went up, he was distracted by the sight of one of the Pyrenean bears; it had escaped back into the ring and was being chased by a man in red velvet slippers, who only minutes before had been kissed by the animal while it was standing on its hind legs. When René Moreau eventually stood up to try and reach her, he found himself thwarted by the boisterous crowd, which didn't want to leave. And when he finally caught up with her, he discovered to his horror that someone else had got there first.

Blaming what he considered to be his life's greatest misfortune on failing to pay attention to the task at hand, he devoted the next few years to the study of oil painting to rid himself of the fault in his character. To his utter surprise, the results were remarkable, but he was never able to paint anything other than his lost love. When he married, he put down his brush, believing it to be an infidelity. Retrieving all the portraits from their hiding places, he built a fire at the bottom of the garden and burnt each one apart from his favourite. Unable to part with it, he hung it behind a pile of logs in the wood shed; he stacked them in a fashion that permitted him to gaze at it simply by removing a couple. Each year, he longed for winter and the frequent calls of his wife to fetch more logs for the fire.

The only person to whom he spoke of his secret passion was himself, while walking in the woods. He uttered his longing with such desperation that it frightened the birds and nothing would grow along the pathways of his jumbled meanders. Madame Ladoucette's obsessional attempts at preventing illnesses from stalking her husband – a regular source of marital conflict – only served to increase Monsieur Moreau's affection. And when his wife took her very public exception to the woman, he tried everything in his powers to persuade her to let the matter go. He bought her all manner of frivolities as a distraction, including satin ribbons and shiny whistles from the itinerant salesmen, but the only purchase she was interested in was another kilo of ripe tomatoes. In the end he resorted to hiding her ammunition, but she simply bought more. It never dawned on him that his life's greatest misfortune was not that he had never married Florence Ladoucette, but that he had married the love of his life and never realized it.

When he eventually retired, he devoted his by now unparalleled powers of concentration to watching ants, but they never afforded him the same joy as his oils. But when he tried to pick up his brushes again, he found that he had developed a catastrophic allergy to turpentine.

Guillaume Ladoucette had always been embarrassed by his mother's prolonged and public war with Madame Moreau. Not long after the famous mini-tornado of 1999, when he had returned from taking yet another of her tomato-splattered coats to the dry-cleaner's, he invited Monsieur Moreau round for an apéritif in the hope that he might persuade his wife to desist, or at least to cut back on her ammunition, given his mother's frailty. After apologizing profusely for his wife's behaviour, Monsieur Moreau explained that in all his years of marriage he had never once managed to change his wife's mind over anything. The only consolation he could offer his host was that such was the advancement of her years, his wife could now only hit her target in one throw out of every five. It was when the pair had just started their second glass of homemade *pineau* that Monsieur Moreau looked up and saw the portrait whose paint had been infused with his tears. Immediately, he assumed that Guillaume Ladoucette was the thief and was so taken aback that he put down his glass and declared that he had to leave.

Over the following months, Monsieur Moreau abandoned his study of the ants as he could think of nothing but the painting. He would sit on the bench in his brown nylon trousers and blue cap longing for another look at the lips over which he had laboured for months, such was his reluctance to leave the curves that reminded him of willow leaves. He would then imagine Guillaume Ladoucette slipping into the shed at night and discovering the portrait in its hiding place, although he could never fathom how the barber had managed to achieve such a feat. He would see him taking it down, lowering it into a large sack and sneaking out of the garden with it. What made matters worse was that the thief had then had the audacity to hang the stolen item in his sitting room for all to see. Yet he felt unable to demand its return, convinced that the felonious barber had recognized the sitter and would divulge his secret.

Eventually the man could bear it no longer. Woken up one afternoon by a sudden downpour as he dozed on the bench, he ran to Guillaume Ladoucette's house and thumped on the door. Ignoring the offer of a kitchen chair and towel, Monsieur Moreau walked straight through to the sitting room where he settled himself on the armchair in front of the portrait, his hair dripping. He took the glass of *pineau* he was offered, but never once raised it to his lips as he instantly forgot it was there. Guillaume Ladoucette found himself pursuing a conversation that was largely one-sided with a man who smelt like a damp goat. Eventually, frustrated by his visitor's distraction, he followed the man's eyes to the portrait and asked: 'Do you like it?'

'With a passion you wouldn't believe,' he replied, taken aback by the thief's effrontery.

Guillaume Ladoucette immediately got to his feet, took down the portrait and gave it to him saying: 'Then you should have it.' Monsieur Moreau left with it wrapped in a plastic bag under his arm, happy that the thief had finally absolved himself, and Guillaume Ladoucette closed the door warmed by the happiness that giving brings.

7

THE ONE PERSON IN AMOUR-SUR-BELLE WHO WELCOMED THE FACT that the pigeons had suddenly forgotten how to fly was Émilie Fraisse. A number of residents, infuriated by repeatedly tripping over them when they scuttled out of nowhere like feathered rats, had resorted to kicking them into oblivion with rage. Yet the châtelaine, for the first time since her arrival, was able to sleep past five in the morning without being woken by the tapping of dry, horny beaks on the ancient château windows by grey crowds jostling on the enormous stone sills, a sound which had driven one fifteenth-century owner over the ramparts in despair. His infuriation was complete when he discovered himself irrefutably alive in the pestilent waters of the moat below, wondering how he was going to get back inside the fortifications which he had spent a lifetime making impenetrable.

Despite its narrowness, Émilie Fraisse slept on the right-hand side of the four-poster Renaissance bed, the position she had assumed throughout her marriage. She had picked the side nearest the door on her wedding night to enable a swift exit should the worst of her fears come to pass. But instead of the pain she was expecting, her groom had simply kissed her on the forehead and gone to sleep, leaving her blinking with bewilderment in the darkness. It wasn't until almost three months later after several abortive attempts, that she finally lost her virginity, which increased her confusion. A year later, when still not pregnant, she started to attempt to increase the frequency of their love-making, while never once mentioning the subject of her husband's lack of success. Serge Pompignac initially welcomed her efforts. But as the problems continued, her endeavours were eventually rebuffed and he would turn his back on her in a miasma of self-hating frustration. The longer the issue remained unspoken, the more they felt unable to talk of other matters, and eventually, the stitches binding them together came undone. Émilie Fraisse's isolation was complete when she no longer felt able to talk to the maids, lest they brought up the subject of the shrinking furniture.

It was during her first night in the château of Amour-sur-Belle that she rediscovered the joy of sleeping alone. Instead of lying on her side facing away from her husband, her arms drawn up against her breasts for fear that they might torment him, she lay on her back, her arms stretched out either side of her as if she had been dropped from a great height. And when, in the middle of the night, the unfamiliarity of her surroundings woke her, she experienced the delight of getting up, going downstairs and returning with a steak sandwich so rare the bread was stained red, which she ate from within the bedcovers. And when she opened her eyes that first morning, never once having been bounced from slumber by a murmuring body next to her executing a five-point turn, she realized that for the first time in over two decades she was not disappointed to be awake.

Eager to explore her new home, Émilie Fraisse covered her

slender nakedness with a white cotton dressing gown with dark-blue embroidered flowers, which she had hung on the back of the door. She hadn't bothered to inspect the château before purchasing it, relying on her memory of the place from the last time she visited it during one of her rare trips home to see her parents, who eventually moved from Amour-sur-Belle in search of a more rational climate.

The building had been on the market for almost five years, during which time it had crumpled into an even more pitiful state. André Lizard, the previous owner, had parted with all of his inheritance to buy it, with the intention of restoring it into a respectable tourist attraction that would finally secure it a mention in the guidebooks. He had been determined to repair the scandalous ramparts, which were missing so many sections of their crenellations, raze the nettles in the dry moat and coax the Belle back into it. There were plans to drive out the bats from the bell tower whose centuries of droppings had risen so high they prevented the door from opening; to replace the junk-shop furniture, which had been bought to fill in the gaps left by the ancient treasures sold by previous owners to feed a variety of disturbing addictions; and to prevent the rain from leaking through the roof into the King's Bedroom, which had been kept permanently ready for a royal visit that had never come.

It wasn't long before André Lizard discovered the folly of his dream. When, after four years of frustrated searching, he finally found some of the missing stones from the crenellations buried several metres deep in the banks of the moat, he attempted to hoist them back up the outside walls using a pulley system. But the rope frequently snapped, sending the enormous blocks hurtling to the ground again, once flattening a dog. When the stones were finally fixed into position, he discovered that he had got them the wrong way round and spent another six months prising them off and resetting them. Eight days after the work was complete, the famous mini-tornado of 1999 scattered them over the side again like seeds.

He then turned his attention to the moat, but had to give up his attempts to lure the Belle back into it after the local barber made a spectacular fuss about changes to the water table affecting his potager. The layers of encrusted bat droppings revolted him to such an extent that he was unable to enter the bell tower by the window to remove them. Tired of grappling with the roof above the King's Bedroom, he gave up, concluding that it was its destiny to permanently leak. And, as the years grated painfully by, bringing only a handful of visitors a week during the summer months, there was no income to fund the replacement of the junk-shop furniture. By the time André Lizard admitted defeat, the dry rot had risen up his shins, his skin had taken on the pallor of the stone walls in the dungeons and the damp had led to a fungal infestation which flourished in his armpits with unstoppable rapaciousness.

When news finally came of a cash buyer for the château and its contents, André Lizard immediately handed over the enormous iron key to his solicitor and left within the hour, his threadbare slippers crunching over the crisp pigeon droppings covering the drawbridge. A solitary suitcase in his hand, he had not decided upon a destination because anywhere else would be better. As well as the contents, he left behind him a large quantity of rare wine hidden from the Nazis in the dungeon, a tiny unmarked grave containing the remains of the dog that he had killed, and a colourful colony of moulds that the scientific world had long thought extinct.

In her bare feet, Émilie Fraisse walked slowly down the corridor, stopping to touch the rough stitches of the faded tapestries lining the walls. The first depicted a fifteenth-century wild boar hunt, its black prey surrounded by three baying greyhounds wearing wide collars. In the forefront beaters in blue and red tights held more dogs on leashes, while men hid amongst the trees aiming their crossbows. In the distance, sitting on a hill, was a smug-looking rabbit. Further down the corridor was another tapestry featuring a group of beautiful ladies-in-waiting posing in long, sumptuous gowns in a red apple orchard. Members of Catherine de' Medici's secret weapon known as the 'flying squadron', part of their duty included furthering the queen's ambitions by the use of seduction.

Pushing open the heavy wooden door to one of the bedrooms, the châtelaine was heartened to see that nothing had changed since her previous visit. Sitting on the bed and the ornately carved chairs was the same collection of hideous old dolls in discoloured lace, their unblinking eyes staring blindly in front of them. Running her hand along the top of the dressing table, she was instantly comforted by the sight of the grey powdery residue on her fingers. Shutting the door behind her so as not to disturb the dust, which she was saving for later, she visited every room, opening the heavy wooden shutters and then throwing open the tall lattice windows behind them as she went. In sprang arrows of hot light that pierced the ridiculous junk-shop furniture and made the authentic antiques glow. By the time she had inspected every room, Émilie Fraisse knew she had made the right decision to buy the place: it was just as filthy as she had remembered it.

Without stopping to get dressed, she retraced her steps, collecting all the garish red and pink plastic flowers that had been crammed into cheap vases and putting them into a black rubbish sack she found in a drawer in the kitchen. Opening the vast front door, which had been bleached fossil grey by the sun, she padded across the courtyard to the splendid late fifteenth-century chapel that had been rebuilt using leper labourers, and cut armfuls of the ivy that was growing up its stone walls. She refilled the vases with twists of the evergreen, and placed a single apricot rose which had been rambling for centuries in the water glass next to her Renaissance bed.

Finally daring to enter the bathroom, she inspected with curiosity the insect carcasses lying in the bottom of the heavily stained tub. Taking a bar of soap from her solitary suitcase, she then went outside, took off her white cotton dressing gown with the dark-blue embroidered flowers and happily showered under the cold water of the garden hose. As she strolled naked around the château to dry off, the soles of her feet beetle black within an instant, she came across a leather chest studded with brass in one of the upper bedrooms. Her curiosity stoked, she knelt on the floor, heaved up the lid with both hands and discovered a nest of antique dresses. Standing up, she pulled them out one by one and inspected them as they hung from her hands, crippled from years of confinement. After selecting one in iris mauve with lacework covering the bodice, she stepped into it and to her surprise found that it fitted. Looking into a mirror dappled with age, she twisted her long grey hair, which was annoying her, into a pile at the back of her head, and secured it with one of the jewelled pins she found in a tortoiseshell box on the dressing table. She rustled her way back along the corridor and descended the stone spiral staircase, the bottom of the gown rippling down the cold steps with their lamentable repairs. In a pot by the kitchen sink she found a large pair of scissors still covered in dried flecks of parsley and hacked off the bottom of the dress from the knees down. She then set about looking for dusters.

When, within an hour, she had exhausted them, the châtelaine climbed into her car and drove to the nearest supermarket where people glanced in confusion at the woman in the antique shorn-off dress, whom many failed to recognize, purchasing an enormous quantity of cleaning materials, along with a week's supply of food. When she returned to Amour-sur-Belle, Émilie Fraisse wound up the car window and kept her eyes straight ahead of her so as not to have to stop for conversation. Arriving at the château, she stuck a note over the opening times saying 'Closed for the Week' and pulled up the drawbridge behind her.

In the vaulted kitchen with its tarnished collection of copper pans and utensils covering shelves on three sides of the walls, she stuffed a pair of calf's ears with veal, ham and mushrooms and tied them securely into bundles. After putting them into some stock, she left them to cook slowly for three hours while she got down to business. Her treat for the day, which had pirouetted in her mind as she drove back, was the llama skeleton that stood in the hallway and had developed an ashen pallor. Working methodically on each of its seventy-nine bones, after several hours she had returned it to its natural colour of unripe brie.

Over the course of the week, the châtelaine navigated steadily through the rooms with her warship of dusters, brushes and scented polishes, sustained by the comfort of knowing that as soon as she had finished she would immediately have to start again. As she wiped and rubbed she found beauty in the decay of the place, which she had no intention of restoring, and looked in awe at the vast palette of the moulds and the tenacity of the woodworm. When her back and neck could take no more, she would climb to the roof and sit by the scandalous ramparts admiring the curves of the Belle, the bright yellow irises in the dry moat below and the flight of the buzzards, their big floppy feet hanging below them. At night, before sleeping, she would walk naked across the courtyard and lie on the uncut grass watching the shadowy swoop of the bats, enjoying the rich stench of their droppings.

On her final day before opening, like a diner about to savour her most succulent prawn which she has left until last, Émilie Fraisse slowly opened the door to the empty *grand salon* and looked inside. There, stretching towards the enormous stone fireplace, was the reversible floor, one side oak, the other walnut. According to the visitors' guide, an incomplete collection of badly typed pages in a ring-bound folder that generated more questions than it answered, the floorboards, originally installed in 1657, were turned every two hundred years. Émilie Fraisse took a bucket and first lightly washed down the oak boards which were uppermost. When the sun's fingers had dried them, she got back down on her hands and knees and polished each one until the floor reflected her shadow. Once she had finished she returned to the vaulted kitchen, fried several rounds of black pudding and ate them with a piece of bread sitting on one of the carved pews in the splendid fifteenth-century chapel, rebuilt using leper labourers. On returning to the *grand salon*, she stood at the doorway to admire her handiwork. Getting back down on her knees again, she released a small, spicy belch, and, ignoring the fact that the boards weren't due to be changed for another fifty-one years, turned them all over as she had been longing to do ever since she moved in. By the end of the day the rippling walnut was so dazzling that the house martins which flew in couldn't find their way back out.

Rising early the following morning, Émilie Fraisse lowered the drawbridge and removed her hand-written note from the board. Halfway through the afternoon, while picking quince from the overgrown orchard, by which time she had forgotten that she was open for business, a German tourist in becoming shorts appeared at her side asking for a tour of the château. After offering him a couple, she put down her basket and led him to the hall. When she and her guest arrived at the llama skeleton, and he enquired where it had come from, Émilie Fraisse said nothing of the fact that, according to the visitors' guide, its body had been found in the moat seventy-two years ago after it had escaped from a travelling circus. Instead, she found herself telling him how the animal had been ridden back from Persia by a thirteenth-century troubadour as a gift for his beloved after she had rejected both him and his previous offerings, which included a purple nightingale and one of his kidneys. The llama, a species that wasn't even known to exist at the time, appeared to do the trick. For a period the three lived in harmony in the château, with the animal enjoying a bedroom all to itself with views of the garden and a place at the dining-room table despite its unsavoury habit of spitting. But, after a while, the woman began to pay more attention to the llama than the trouba- dour, since it wasn't afflicted by a need to recite atrocious poetry in deadening quantities. Twisted with envy, one night when his lover had retired early to bed, the ungrateful poet killed his winning mode of transport, heaved it on to the spit and ate it. It was never known precisely what happened to the man, but his headless ghost still haunted the cesspit, and on a windy night snatches of atrocious poetry blew in through the cracks in the château windows.

When Émilie Fraisse had finished her story, the German, who was enraptured (although slightly confused because he thought that llamas came from South America), immediately asked her to take his photograph standing next to the skeleton.

Arriving at the *grand salon*, the tourist naturally enquired about the splendid reversible floor. The châtelaine then found herself recounting how it had been copied from a similar one at the nearby château of Bourdeilles in an escalating seventeenth-century war of neighbourly one- upmanship. It developed into such a vicious feud between the two owners that they each kidnapped the other's daughter and locked her in one of the towers to increase the other's misery. When, after a week, neither could bear their prisoners' incessant wails, which made the engraved muskets rattle in their holders and the copper pans in the kitchen hum, they both unlocked their tower doors, hoping the girls would flee. But it took several months for the captives to realize that they were no longer imprisoned, by which time, like caged birds, they had become attached to their surroundings and refused their freedom. Each father was then stuck with a daughter he found even more infuriating than his own. Such was the pity the men developed for each other's plight, they took up falconing together, during which they spent most of the time bemoaning the curse of fatherhood.

The German, who couldn't disguise his delight, immediately bent down and stroked the lustrous wooden floor. When the pair reached the dining room, Émilie Fraisse pointed to the sixteenth-century Annunciation scene carved in mahogany above the door, which depicted a naked man with three testicles and a pelican feeding her three chicks. But instead of explaining that it was a reference to Gabriel's announcement to Mary of her forthcoming child, the châtelaine told the German that the man's parents had been so horrified when he was born with the deformity that they abandoned him to a passing street merchant. While the boy was much loved, he never got over his sense of shame. When he reached his teenage years, he joined the Wars of Religion to prove his manhood, taking up arms to defend Catholic Périgueux from assaults by Protestant Bergerac. While the town suffered countless embarrassing defeats, the man with the three testicles managed to kill more Protestants than most, which wasn't many. In the absence of a real hero, and in desperate need of one to keep up morale, he was afforded such a status. One night, when he and his comrades were celebrating his having slaughtered double figures that week, the man put down his goblet, pulled down his trousers and revealed what he insisted was the secret of his success. Such was the positive reception, he decided to display his abnormality with pride, and took to walking around naked at every opportunity. It was during one of these moments of bravado that a mother pelican landed at his feet looking for food for her three chicks. There then ensued a battle even uglier than any the man had fought against the Protestants, and he lost his entire collection of testicles. But rather than diminish his heroic standing amongst his comrades it increased it, as lost body parts always did in warfare, and he became a constant source of curiosity for the ladies.

When the châtelaine finished her tall story, which slipped out without a thought, her cheeks flushed at the sudden realization of the indelicacy of the subject matter. But by then the German, who had at first assumed that the pelican was a symbol of Christ and that the three testicles represented fertility, was standing transfixed in front of the carving asking whether there was a postcard of it.

And so it was for every piece of furniture or detail whose history Émilie Fraisse either didn't know or found too pedestrian, and each embellishment was balanced with phrases such as 'it is believed', 'so the legend goes' or 'some say'. Her motives were in no way pecuniary. She had enough money to sustain her for the rest of her life without a single visitor, and she had no interest in increasing their numbers. Neither was it mischief, for the woman had still not yet recovered that trait. Nor, indeed, was it boredom, for she couldn't remember the last time she felt so engaged with the world. She simply didn't want to disappoint him.

When the German tourist left, as charmed by the decrepit château as he was by its owner, he handed her four euros, which, according to the noticeboard outside, was the entrance fee. But she waved it away, grateful for the longest conversation she had had in years. Later that day, she found the coins in an envelope in her letterbox along with a thank-you note and a recipe for quince jelly handed down from his grandmother.

Inspired by her visitor's letter, Émilie Fraisse slipped her feet into a pair of vast gentleman's wellington boots to protect her legs from scratches and slopped over to the garden, which was knitted with weeds. Near the wall on top of which bearded irises grew, she discovered a plot of heirloom vegetables and marvelled at the ancient, long forgotten varieties: the blue potatoes, the hyacinth beans with their startling purple-red pods, the strawberry spinach and the round black radish. She spent the evening in a state of utter contentment, her bare feet padding back and forth across the kitchen, making jams, jellies and chutneys in the enormous copper pans. The most exquisite was the black radish jam made with honey and a whisper of fresh ginger. When they had cooled, on each of the jars she stuck a hand-written label stating the contents, the date and the words 'From the Ancient Gardens of the Château at Amour-sur-Belle'. After filling the larder with half of them, she tied around each of the others a piece of antique lace from the bottom of the dresses she had shortened and put them for sale in the window of the wooden hut at the entrance to the château, erected years ago to house the ticket-seller for the crowds who never came.

The following morning, she explored the contents of the armoury, which she had already cleaned but not lingered over. Slowly, she drew a finger along the mother-of-pearl inlay on the crossbows and noticed how the tiny flowers glinted lavender in the light. She lifted down one of the smaller breastplates, all of which were dented, strapped it on and knocked on it at her navel. She then chose the smallest of the engraved muskets, grabbed a handful of shot and closed the door.

After changing into a pair of breeches, a long-sleeved shirt which she found hanging in a wardrobe and some gentleman's buckled leather boots, she crunched her way over the drawbridge and headed for the woods. Slipping between the branches, she was immediately comforted by their skeletal embrace and the sight of her feet amongst the tarnished leaves still lying where they had dropped dead the previous autumn. Immediately, she recognized the trees of her childhood and stood disbelieving the height they had reached as they creaked in the breeze.

Curiosity set her following the wild boar track to see whether it still passed the old hunters' shack. With a natural lightness of foot, she moved quietly across the littered floor, pushing away branches which snapped at her back and listening to the calls of the birds she had once been able to imitate. After a while, to her surprise, she saw in the distance the outline of the hut that she had been expecting to have tumbled down long ago. As she got closer, she was struck by the fact that it was no longer as desolate as she remembered. Indeed, it appeared that someone had set about transforming it, for the hut no longer tilted perilously to the left. There also seemed to have been repairs made to the roof, and, as she approached further, she noticed that someone had even bothered to replace the glass in the tiny window, which had always been broken.

Slowing down as she arrived in the clearing, she stopped to listen to the demented hollow tapping of a woodpecker; she hadn't heard one for years. As she continued on her way, she glanced inside the hut. There, on the floor, were two villagers whom she instantly recognized. But what perplexed her more than their nakedness was the fact that, as far as she knew, one of them was very much married to someone else. The couple was so engrossed in their physical pursuit, which, judging by the sounds they were making, seemed to be an agony to them both, they failed to notice the woman with the musket and gentleman's trousers standing dumbfounded at the window.

The châtelaine made her way out of the clearing as quickly and as quietly as possible, and headed for the far reaches of the woods. The spectacle turned her thoughts to the corrosion of her own marriage. Wounded by envy, she stopped and leant against a tree felled by the famous mini-tornado of 1999, and for the first time since she had returned to Amour-sur-Belle felt the familiar drizzle of melancholy. She stood getting wet until her eye was caught by the roots of the tree, which were exposed to the elements like disgorged entrails. She walked round to look at them more closely. Trapped within, she spotted a fallen leaf whose colour reminded her of her newly lustrous walnut floor, and she put it in her pocket. Her mind then slid to the other pleasures the château had given her, including the llama skeleton, the exquisite black radish jam she had made and the warmth of the handshake of the nice German tourist. Before she knew it, the smell of rain had passed and she was aiming at a large hare which she felled with a single shot.

As she carried it back to the château by its ears, she thought of the two terrines she would make from it, one of which she would put out for sale with the other jars in the disused ticket hut. Stepping over a fallen branch, she suddenly wondered what had happened to her Nontron hunting knife with its boxwood handle and ancient pokerwork motifs. Then she remembered the last afternoon she had spent in the woods with Guillaume Ladoucette before leaving Amour-sur-Belle. She had tried to pretend that the occasion was of no importance, but had not been able to sustain her indifference. Handing him her knife for safekeeping, she had hoped that he would recognize the significance. But the teenager took it without a word and slid it into his pocket. For an instant she wondered whether he was going to kiss her, and she remained still. But the moment never came and she filled the silence by wondering out loud whether the mushroom at her feet was poisonous, when they both knew that it wasn't. She then thought of the following morning and how she had put her suitcase in her father's car early and waited on the wall for Guillaume Ladoucette to come and say goodbye. But he never came. Eleven months later she learnt from a neighbour on her first visit back to the village that he had been cutting firewood with his father and had arrived running shortly after the car had pulled away. He had then sat on the garden wall, head bowed, hands in his pockets, for hours.

Her mind turned to the countless mornings she had come downstairs in her aunt's house in Bordeaux to find that there was still no reply waiting at her place at the table. She wondered again, as she had all those years ago, why he had never written back. Squeezing through the branches, she came to the same conclusion as always – that he hadn't felt the same way as she had. And, as she had learnt to do as a teenager, Émilie Fraisse put all thoughts of Guillaume Ladoucette out of her mind and headed back towards the château to disembowel the hare.

8

THE INSTALLATION OF THE MUNICIPAL SHOWER TURNED OUT TO BE a far more wretched procedure than Jean-François Lafforest had predicted, and having worked for a local authority all his life he had already been tripped up by most of the pitfalls of human nature. When he arrived at Amour-sur-Belle to inspect the work, having vomited twice along the route at the thought of returning, he saw to his surprise that the shower had actually been sited in the correct place next to a wall on the far side of the place du Marché. But when he looked further, he discovered that instead of the door facing the wall, which would have afforded the villagers a degree of modesty, it was in fact facing the square. And, as the drainage work had already started, the mistake could not be rectified.

Having suppressed any natural instinct towards per-fectionism over the years in order to maintain an essence of sanity, Jean-François Lafforest simply accepted it, reasoning to himself that if it was the only thing that was to go wrong then the project would be a spectacular success. But as the plumbing work continued, it soon came clear by the amount of water billowing up from the trench and crawling across the square towards the Bar Saint-Jus that the wrong size pipe had been ordered. When, three days later, he returned to the site and asked the two labourers, whom he eventually tracked down to the bar, why the work had not progressed, he was told that the new part had still not arrived. He then went in person to the council's purchasing department where he was informed that the pipe would have to be ordered from Spain, which could take up to four weeks. He nodded in silence, knowing full well that no parts were ever ordered from outside France owing to national pride, and that any mention of 'Spain' was simply an indication of yet another colleague having been infected with inertia, a highly contagious malady stalking the corridors that could cripple in an instant.

Aware that there was no cure, Jean-François Lafforest noted down the precise measurements of the pipe that was needed, drove to a large DIY store on the outskirts of Périgueux and bought one. After waiting several days, he then took it to the purchasing department and explained that one of his friends had just been to Spain and managed to pick one up. Knowing that the man in front of him would now claim that the pipe of unknown origin would have to be thoroughly vetted before being deemed acceptable, which actually meant that it would be placed in a cupboard and forgotten about, Jean-François Lafforest silently placed on his desk a large serrano ham and bottle of Rioja which he had bought in a supermarket to help alleviate his colleague's frightful symptoms. They worked in an instant and the pipe was immediately approved.

Returning to Amour-sur-Belle, the man from the council handed the part to the two disappointed workers who were in the same place as he had left them. When, the following day, he made a surprise visit, he found them yet again sitting at Fabrice Ribou's highly polished counter. Correctly suspecting that the bar owner with the curious haircut that resembled a pine cone was giving them free drinks in order to disrupt the work, Jean-François Lafforest then gathered up his courage and made the decision to stay every day at the site, sitting on a collapsible chair he kept in the boot of his car while clutching his soft leather briefcase to his fleshy stomach. The only time he abandoned his post was for his twice-daily trip to the nearest field where he would shower the prepubescent maize with the curdled contents of his stomach.

When the installation was finally complete, notices were sent to each household informing the occupants that the taking of baths was forbidden from midnight onwards, and that the shower would be ready for use the following morning. That night, Guillaume Ladoucette filled up his bath, took off his clothes, put them on the chair and stepped in. He remained recumbent for several hours, gazing with premature nostalgia at his knees rising like islands out of the water.

Yves Lévèque, who had a pressing reason to smell his best the following day, had set his alarm for 5.30 a.m. hoping to beat the early-rising baker to the shower. When it went off, the dentist instinctively turned over, unwilling to leave the comforting valley of his sleep. Just as he was sinking back down again the haunting image returned of a long, curly, black hair, normally covered in flour, wrapped around his big toe as he showered. He immediately bolted out of bed, pulled his green-and-white-striped dressing gown on over his navy pyjamas and twisted his feet into his slippers. Grabbing his drawstring washbag, he checked to see that his bottle of shampoo was inside, and slipped out of the front door.

As he strode down the road with a white towel over his shoulder seeing the village for the first time so soon after dawn, he thought how marvellous it was to be the first to crack open the day. But on reaching the rue du Château, he

suddenly heard footsteps. He turned round to see the unmistakable bulk of Stéphane Jollis in a voluminous white
T-shirt and tartan boxer shorts clutching a blue towel coming
up behind him. The baker was moving at a much faster rate
than normal, stirred from his bed by the thought of catching
a glimpse of Lisette Robert in a state of undress. The dentist
immediately quickened his step. Several paces later, he
looked over his shoulder again and coming up behind
Stéphane Jollis was the midwife in a short red satin nightdress with a towel tucked under her arm, who had been
driven from her sheets by the fear of having to shower after
the early-rising postman who was infamous for his
despicable habit of urinating behind trees whenever caught
short on his rounds. Not only did Gilbert Dubuisson believe
that no one ever saw him, but never once did it occur to
him that his attempts at concealment were thwarted by the
resulting copious clouds of rising steam and the wetness of
his toecaps.

Not far behind Lisette Robert, Yves Lévèque spotted the
postman, naked apart from his blue towelling dressing gown,
which was flapping open indiscreetly. Scurrying along with a
turquoise towel hanging around his neck, he had decided to
take a shower before work to avoid going in after Monsieur
Moreau, who he feared would engulf the cubicle with the
aroma of goat. Not far behind Gilbert Dubuisson was indeed
Monsieur Moreau, who had forgotten his towel and was
wearing a pair of light blue cotton pyjamas that stopped at his
knees. While not used to a daily toilette, he was determined
to beat the felonious matchmaker in case he stole all the hot
water. On his tail was Guillaume Ladoucette in an elegant
burgundy silk dressing gown, with two towels and a fiercely
guarded piece of soap from his favourite shop in Périgueux
in his pocket, who had been roused from his sleep by the
torturous sound of a chicken egg slowly rolling across the
wooden landing floor. Driven to a state of fury and unable to

get back to sleep, he could think of nothing else to do at that hour than to try out the new shower. But sprinting past them all was Sandrine Fournier, the mushroom poisoner, who had been woken by the shuffling of slippers underneath her window. Looking out, she noticed all the towels and washbags, and while she couldn't understand why there was such an urgent need to get to the shower so early, decided to try and beat them all just in case.

When Yves Lévèque finally returned home, he lay on his back on top of his bed still wrapped in his green-and-white-striped dressing gown fuming at the indignity of being seen by his neighbours in his nightclothes. As he tugged the pillow further under his head, his eyes fell to his feet and he saw to his horror a cigarette butt stuck to the bottom of his shiny maroon backless slippers. He immediately suspected Didier Lapierre the carpenter, who had not only insisted on smoking in the queue despite the dentist's protests that it was making him feel nauseous at such an early hour, but who had also made a sly attempt to push in by coming up to ask him whether he could borrow his soap. But the dentist was having none of it. As soon as he realized that the carpenter was still standing there long after his request had been turned down, Yves Lévèque sent him to the back of the line of humiliated villagers shooting furtive glances at each other's state of undress while complaining bitterly about the council.

The dentist kicked off his slippers in disgust. He had told the carpenter countless times that smoking restricted blood flow to the gums, but like all his patients who indulged in the pernicious habit, the stained results of which he was obliged to remove, the man never listened. He removed his glasses, carefully folded them and placed them on the bedside table. However, despite the fact that it was still almost two hours before the time he usually woke, he was unable to drift off again. It wasn't his affront over the municipal shower that kept him awake, but the undulation of his innards and the grip around his heart as he thought about what lay ahead of him at lunchtime. As he lay looking at the ceiling, he remembered when, two days earlier, Guillaume Ladoucette had formally telephoned him, despite having just greeted him over the garden wall, and asked if the dentist could come and see him at Heart's Desire. His mind crawled over every detail, from sitting down on the cushion with the hand-embroidered radish, to watching the matchmaker take out a stapler and rubber from a drawer above his stomach and line them up on the desk as Yves Lévèque wondered what he was about to be told. The man with the formidable moustache had then got out a file, which struck him as rather thin, and announced with a degree of fanfare that he now had 'a number' of clients on his books, and that he had found him a most suitable match. The dentist had watched as Guillaume Ladoucette then sat back and did nothing further than smile. When he asked for more information about the woman, the matchmaker had stirred himself from the comfort of his contentment, apologized and then read out her particulars. She was a woman in her late thirties with splendid teeth and an array of other notable attractive features. She had a love for nature and was financially solvent, having worked in retail ever since leaving school. 'So she won't be after your money,' the matchmaker had remarked, raising his eyes from his notes. 'Nor are there any children to support.'

Such was his desire to end his years of loneliness, and the resulting curse of constipation, Yves Lévèque had immediately suggested that they went for lunch.

As he continued to look up at the ceiling, spotting a new spider web that he had never noticed before, the dentist wondered what he was going to wear. He soon decided on a white shirt and a pair of jeans, which he hoped would give him a youthful, casual air. But what worried him most was not his appearance, but what he was going to say to his match.

There was, after all, only so much conversation to be had about the many benefits of flossing.

Yves Lévèque had no idea why people chose to become dentists. It was a question that perplexed him on a daily basis as he stared into yet another mouth harbouring a set of ramshackle teeth, the enormous challenges of which held no allure. His had never been a conscious decision, but a matter of honour that came to him as instinctively as breathing. It was three days after his fifteenth birthday when he learnt the family secret. Tortured for days by toothache and intoxicated from the amount he had drunk to distract his mind from the agony, his father had suddenly raged: 'I wish my bloody parents were around!' Unable to defend himself adequately against his son's battery of questions, he then confessed that far from being a farmer who had received a fatal bolt of lightning while working in the fields one day, Yves Lévèque's grandfather had in fact been an itinerant piglet dentist. He would follow the fairs and markets, where he would break the young animals' pointed teeth so they were unable to bite each other while being transported by train. Despite the grubbiness of his trade, his grandfather had always been exceptionally well turned out, instantly recognizable by his elegant straw hat and silk necktie.

It wasn't chance that had brought Yves Lévèque's grand-parents together, but fate, which made their eventual parting even more mournful. An illegal tooth-puller, his grand-mother also followed the fairs and markets. Travelling in a red-and-white-painted horse-drawn wagon, she attracted crowds even bigger than the most accomplished magician. A trumpet and trombone player would sit on her roof; their role was not only to attract customers with their rousing music, but to drown out the wails of those who came on board, rested their heads between the illegal tooth-puller's formidable thighs and submitted to her pliers. Whenever they happened to turn up at the same venue, she and the piglet dentist would make love in the back of the wagon well into the night, the band having to play even louder to drown their howls of delight. It wasn't long before she fell pregnant. But before they could marry, the piglet dentist was struck down by a disease that was sweeping the pens, and within days he had turned the same curious shade as the animals and was dead. Fearing for the life of their baby, as well as for her own reputation, the mother gave the infant to her parents who lived in Amour-sur-Belle. The child – Yves Lévèque's father – never saw his mother again.

When he had finished the story, he poured himself another glass of red, instructed his son never to repeat the tale and refused to talk about his parents ever again.

Despite his youth, Yves Lévèque could see that his father had passed through life crippled by the weight of his illegitimacy. When, several months later, his father asked him what he wanted to do with his life, he replied without hesitation that he wanted to be a dentist in the hope that it would restore his father's dignity. The man watched his son flourish in his profession until he became the richest person in Amour-sur-Belle. Yves Lévèque's success was not, however, down to inherited talent, but a consequence of the fact that there was no other dentist for kilometres because his contemporaries had set up in towns and cities to seek their fortune. But with the relative wealth had also come the burden of keeping it, and his father also heard the whispers about his son's meanness, which he disputed loudly until his death, his self-respect long since restored.

Having cancelled his patients in order to prepare for his lunchtime appointment, the dentist got up and moved slowly around the house so as not to generate a sweat. In the hope of weighing down his undulating innards, he cooked himself a breakfast of two soft-boiled eggs and six plump asparagus spears from Gilbert Dubuisson's garden. The postman had given him the vegetables by way of a bribe to treat him gently whilst in his chair. It was a gift the dentist had been hoping for, ever since smelling their distinct scent in the vapours of Gilbert Dubuisson's urine rising from behind an oak tree.

As he dipped a spear into the yolk with his long, pale instruments of torture, his mind turned to the last woman he had truly loved. There had, of course, been others since. But, despite five years of searching, none had provoked in him the same ferocity of affection that he had felt for his ex-wife. It wasn't the thunderbolts of life that had felled their marriage but an infestation of termites that had gnawed silently away at it. The petty grievances stacked up one on top of the other until they were so high they became insurmountable. By the time the couple parted, the dentist was so enraged he could not believe his foolishness in having married her in the first place. But as the years passed, and the tethers of anger worked loose, Yves Lévèque was able to see her for who she was rather than for who she wasn't, and he bitterly regretted his foolishness in having let her go. Hoping that they could start again, he spent eight months trying to track her down. But when he eventually found her, she had grown her hair and was happily married to a man who didn't mind her speaking for long periods on the phone and whom she tolerated putting empty bottles back into the fridge.

Yves Lévèque spent the rest of the morning sitting on the bottom stair trying to conceive inspiring conversation. Defeated, he picked up a book and started to read, but was unable to take in the meaning of the words. He then rearranged what few ornaments he had before returning them to their original positions. When, eventually, it was time to get ready, he ironed his jeans and white shirt, put them on and inspected himself in the mirror on the front of his wardrobe. But instead of the young, casual reflection he was hoping for, he saw a forty-four-year-old bespectacled dentist with a haircut which, although the height of fashion, still gave him a start whenever he caught sight of it.

Aware that there was nothing more he could do with his appearance, he dribbled some aftershave on to his long, pale instruments of torture and patted his neck in the hope that he would at least appeal to one of his match's senses. Pulling the front door shut behind him, he got into his car and, as he drove through the village, told himself that the date would go splendidly. But any sense of calm he had manufactured was immediately dispelled when Madame Ladoucette suddenly stepped into the road from behind the crumbling communal bread oven, followed by a tottering entourage of demented pigeons drawn to a fellow sufferer. The dentist's heart pinched with shock. Immediately he stood on his brakes and watched the procession until the last bird had reached the other side. He then slowly pulled away, shaking his head. As he turned right at the field with the ginger Limousin cows that winked, his thoughts turned to the advice that Guillaume Ladoucette had given him. He was not to talk about himself incessantly, a male trait which women apparently found particularly irksome. He should demonstrate interest in his match not only by asking her questions, but also by listening to the answers. At the end of the meal he was expressly forbidden to ask her to split the bill. And while the dentist couldn't understand how vegetable counsel came into the remit of the Unrivalled Silver Service, as he got up to leave the matchmaker had put his hand on his shoulder and informed him gravely that of all vegetables, *cornichons* were the most sensitive to the cycles of the moon, and that if he really wanted to get anywhere with them he ought to sow them when it was passing in front of the constellation of Aries.

As he turned off the road to Périgueux and pulled into the restaurant car park alongside a field of green, stubby maize, Yves Lévèque recalled the disagreement they had had over his choice of venue. The matchmaker had insisted that Le Moulin de la Forge, renowned for the fact that its six-course set menu only cost eleven euros, including wine, was far too modest a place for a first date. But Yves Lévèque had been adamant. Why, he argued, would he want to invest any more in a woman when there was no guarantee that he would like her? After trying to cajole him Guillaume Ladoucette had finally given up. Not only was the customer always right, he reasoned, but it was better for the woman to know what she was getting herself into from the start.

The dentist pushed open the restaurant door and looked around at the labourers and artisans in their jeans and short-sleeved shirts, resting their enormous hands on the white paper tablecloths. Choosing a table in the far left-hand corner, he pulled back a chair and sat down facing the diners. After moving his knife and fork slightly further apart, he surveyed the room again, congratulating himself on his choice of venue. While it couldn't be described as elegant, there was undoubtedly a degree of charm about the place, he thought. In a recess was a washbasin with a large bar of hand soap jutting out of the wall like a cream marrow where customers could wash before eating. And while the choice of décor wasn't to everybody's taste, you had to admire the owner's courage. Marie Poupeau had selected a wallpaper depicting the interior of a wood which engulfed diners in a perpetual state of autumn. Whenever newcomers asked where the lavatory was, she would always reply: 'Up the path,' while pointing to a section of the back wall which showed a leaf-strewn track disappearing into a boisterous orange horizon. It wasn't until they approached that they noticed a handle and then a door. The proprietress had advanced the motif further by hanging on the walls the mounted heads of deer and wild boar, caught by regulars.

Yves Lévèque watched as Marie Poupeau in her straight black skirt and tiny pink blouse darted around the room like an erratic breeze, never forgetting at which stage of the six courses her customers were. But her vigilance wasn't only needed in the dining room. Each time she went into the kitchen she had the added burden of having to fend off the gropes of the chef, who was not only her husband but also a Companion of the Dish of Tripe. For the ardent promoter of cow stomach recipes was unable to resist the tantalizing curve of his wife's belly.

As he poured himself a glass of water, Yves Lévêque noticed Sandrine Fournier, the mushroom poisoner, come in and start talking to Marie Poupeau, who was on her way back to the kitchen with an empty carafe of wine. He remembered the sight of the woman speeding past him in the early hours with a white cotton nightdress hitched up to the knees and a pair of towelling slippers, which she had stopped to take off as they were impeding her trajectory. The assistant ambulant fishmonger had beaten him easily to the shower, despite his last-minute sprint which brought him in second. Not only had he had to wait in the place du Marché in his nightclothes while she worked out how to turn the thing on, but he'd been further inconvenienced by the protracted seventeen minutes and twenty-three seconds she had spent under the water. Then, when she finally emerged, still wearing a floral shower cap, she'd stuck up loudly for the postman and baker during the ensuing row, both of whom were insisting that they went in after her as they had to get to work. The dentist reluctantly waved them through, unable to bear the thought of having to wait for either his bread or post. He stood outside the cubicle complaining bitterly to Lisette Robert, a sympathetic ear as she should have been third, insisting that if it hadn't been for Sandrine Fournier he would already be at home smelling of sandalwood.

After counting all the leaves on the wall to his left, the dentist then looked at his watch and saw that his match was eleven minutes late. As doubt over her arrival swelled up inside him, he started to count the leaves on the wall to his right to distract himself from his unease. When he had finished, he realized that he had forgotten the total for the first wall, and started counting them again so that he could compare the two. Once he had come to the useless conclusion that there were more leaves on the right wall than on the left, he looked at his watch again and surveyed the room with a short sigh. Apart from the workmen and artisans with their enormous hands, the only women there were Marie Poupeau, who was bringing in a platter of quiche, and the assistant ambulant fishmonger, who was sitting alone on the table in the adjacent corner looking directly at him. It was then that Yves Lévêque realized to his horror that Sandrine Fournier was the woman he was waiting for.

The dentist tried to avoid her eye, but it was useless. Within seconds she was standing at the side of his table and he could think of nothing else to do other than get up, kiss her on both cheeks and gesture to the chair opposite him. The mushroom poisoner sat down and the pair looked at each other, both wondering what on earth Guillaume Ladoucette had been thinking. They spent the first few minutes talking about the man they couldn't get out of their minds, such was their desire to throttle him, who at that very moment was sitting underneath his walnut tree with a large bowl of cassoulet, silently congratulating himself on his brilliance. They praised his enterprising spirit, the colour of his walls and his hand-painted sign. And when they had run out of things to say, they suddenly remembered the comfort of the cushion with the hand-embroidered radish.

Much to their relief, Marie Poupeau then arrived with a large steel bowl of communal soup which was passed from table to table. Putting it down in front of them, she complimented Sandrine Fournier on her hairstyle, telling her that she should pin it up more often as it suited her. And when she asked whether her sleeveless blue dress was new, Sandrine

Fournier, who had bought it only the day before, replied firmly that it wasn't.

After they had helped themselves to a bowlful of the clear liquid steeped with tiny pasta stars, they immediately started eating without wishing each other a good appetite. It was then that Yves Lévèque noticed that his match had a tendency to slurp.

'Guillaume Ladoucette said that you loved animals,' said Sandrine Fournier after several minutes of silence.

'I fish,' the dentist replied, presuming it was what the matchmaker had been referring to.

'I like fish too,' replied Sandrine Fournier. 'But admittedly they're dead ones.'

'So how long have you been working on the fish van now?' he asked.

'Twenty-two years. As we travel around so much I tend not to get bored.'

'You like it then?'

'I'm allergic to shellfish, so it keeps me on my toes.'

When the second course arrived, the dentist was unable to enjoy his quiche, which was widely exalted, such was the strength of the noxious waves of perfume lapping his nostrils. Instead, he spent the time explaining – at considerable length – the dos and don'ts of fishing, during which Sandrine Fournier noted his habit of pointing at her with his fork.

'Quite a few of our customers are fishermen, actually. I'm sure some of them try and pass off our fish as their own. Not, of course, that I'm suggesting you would, even though you do always ask for the biggest trout we've got,' she replied evenly.

By the third course, fat slices of moist roast pork with haricot beans, Sandrine Fournier found that she was no longer hungry as her stomach had clamped shut at the overpowering stench of aftershave seemingly floating amongst the autumnal foliage. As she attempted to force it down, to pass the time she asked the man described by the matchmaker as a highly successful entrepreneur who worked with his hands about his job. The dentist gladly obliged, until he noticed her picking her teeth with her thumbnail, and before he could stop suddenly found himself asking her whether she was still remembering to floss.

During the fourth course, the only sound from the table in the far left-hand corner of the restaurant was the furious crunching of walnuts and lettuce as both tried to bring the misery to a swift end.

When the communal cheese board arrived, passed from the table behind them by Marie Poupeau, Sandrine Fournier watched the dentist's long, pale instruments of torture gripping the knife as he cut himself a piece of Brebis. She then imagined them tracing the length of her bare thigh and was so overcome by repulsion that Yves Lévèque felt obliged to ask her whether she was feeling all right.

When Marie Poupeau finally brought the sixth course, a small basket bearing two small tubs of ice cream, they simultaneously reached for the chocolate one. Yves Lévèque felt Sandrine Fournier's nails, which he was convinced still harboured traces of smoked haddock from her morning's work, lodge themselves into the back of his hand. And such was his feeling of nausea, he immediately gave up his claim to the dessert.

As soon as the mushroom poisoner had finished it, the dentist asked for the bill, insisting that he had to get back to work. And when it arrived, he immediately suggested that they went 'halvies-halves'.

Once in the car park, they turned and faced each other.

'I've had such a marvellous time,' lied Yves Lévèque.

'Me too,' lied Sandrine Fournier.

'We really ought to do it again,' lied the dentist.

'Can't wait,' lied the assistant ambulant fishmonger.

As they drove off in different directions, they both vowed that it would never happen.

The pair's mutual dislike was not solely the result of having grown up in the same village and witnessed the worst of each other's nature, but the natural antipathy of brother and sister of which neither was aware. One overcast October afternoon, Yves Lévèque's mother had finally succumbed to the hands of Sandrine Fournier's father, who, despite being married himself, had constantly preyed on her, having spotted a chink in the family's armour. Yves Lévèque was not the only result of that secret union in a field of dried-out sunflowers, which had lurched back and forth in the perpetual breeze like ghastly wizened cadavers. The episode had also made her fall back in love with her husband who she knew was not capable of such grotesque deception as the man on top of her. She never spoke to her one-off lover again. The only time she ever thought of him was when someone commented how much her son looked like his father, and she would honestly agree.

9

WHEN LISETTE ROBERT ANSWERED HER DOOR TO FIND GUILLAUME
Ladoucette clutching a bouquet of artichoke stems she
immediately assumed that he had come to discuss one of his
little matters. He always arrived on her doorstep unannounced on such occasions, armed with meticulously
clean root vegetables in the winter and thoroughly rinsed
frilly lettuces in the summer, which he would hand to her at
the door insisting that he grew far too much for a bachelor.
While his comestible offerings were greatly appreciated,
there was one particular period in autumn when Lisette
Robert dreaded his knock at the door. With a smile that she
hoped concealed her secret horror, the midwife would take
the plastic carriers filled with figs to the kitchen and place
them next to those already given to her by other villagers
equally overcome by their trees' bountiful yields. Selecting
first those with the soft give of a testicle, which were always
the sweetest, she would spend the next few days coura-
geously trying to get through them. But despite the

bewitching taste, after several days of gorging her guts would take no more. Unwilling to cook with them – for countless fig tarts and jars of jam would also come her way – yet reluctant to throw them out, she would hand out the remaining bags to anyone who happened to be passing her door who was not quick enough to realize their contents. Already overloaded themselves, they in turn would give them to their neighbours, each of whom would express delight at the unexpected gift yet curse as soon as their door was closed and the bag was opened. On several occasions, much to his utter consternation, Guillaume Ladoucette had found himself being offered his own figs still in the same bag which had been passed along a chain of no fewer than seventeen people.

His visits to Lisette Robert, which had been going on for years, rarely varied. Depending on the weather, the pair would sit either at her kitchen table or outside on the old faded red sofa against the back of the house underneath the vine-strangled trellis. They would chat for several hours, for, after so many years as a barber, not only was Guillaume Ladoucette as accomplished at small talk as he was at levelling sideburns, but he was also highly experienced in the art of listening. Over the years Lisette Robert had learnt to accept his reluctance to pass on the gossip served up by his customers, and satisfied herself with the odd titbit that happened to tumble from his fiercely defended plate. A slave to patient confidentiality herself, and cursed with an unnatural abhorrence for passing on scandal, the midwife would simply pick it up and place it inside her mind's cabinet of curiosities with the other tittle-tattle she collected. From time to time during moments of boredom, she would open the door, take out a specimen, hold it up to the light and run a finger over it. She would then place it back inside and turn the lock until next time.

As they talked, Guillaume Ladoucette would gallantly try to resist glancing at the midwife's underwear in such tantalizing proximity either on the washing line or airing in front of the fire. Then, during a pause in the conversation, he would announce as if the thought had suddenly struck him: 'Oh, by the way, Lisette, I was meaning to ask you something . . .' and offload whatever medical anxiety was troubling him.

Guillaume Ladoucette had been suffering from a mild form of hypochondria since childhood. His mother, convinced that he had caught the disease at school, refused to allow him to return to the classroom for a month to avoid further contamination. She immediately insisted that her husband planted a medicinal herb garden next to the potager to provide the boy with the necessary compounds to cure him. Such was the clamour of her anxiety it woke the other terrors inside her. She then demanded that the herb garden be surrounded by boxwood because of its alleged ability to ward off storms, as ever since the young Yves Lévèque had told her of his grandfather's tragic fate while labouring in a field she was convinced that her husband would be struck by a fatal bolt of lightning. It was a story Yves Lévèque continued to relate even after he was told the real circumstances surrounding his grandfather's death when he was older. When, an hour after her request, Monsieur Ladoucette had still not moved from his seat by the hearth, she informed her husband that he would not be welcome in the marital bed until the task was done. She refused to speak to him for the rest of the day, and set about planting angelica in the borders to protect her charges against ghosts and plagues.

Monsieur Ladoucette, who as a rule tried to resist humouring his wife's lunatic notions, had fully intended to plant the medicinal herb garden that very afternoon simply for the pleasure the activity would bring him. But as soon as the threat was made he immediately changed his mind out of vexation, and spent the next three nights sleeping in the bathroom underneath the damp blue mat. His wife finally called him to bed when she could no longer bear the sound of his bones knocking against the wooden floor as he flipped and jerked in his sleep without the weight of the family Bible on his chest.

Usually after raising his medical perturbation, Guillaume Ladoucette would be satisfied with Lisette Robert's insistence that he was still a considerable distance from death. Only once had she suggested that he visited his doctor, which was the time when she secretly suspected that he was suffering from an acute form of lovesickness, a strain more atrocious than any she had read about in her medical textbooks. For several months after his visit to the doctor, who confirmed the midwife's fears, Guillaume Ladoucette avoided coming round to see her, afraid that she would ask him who was the object of his affections. He only started speaking to her again when he bumped into her in the market and was unable to stop himself from asking her whether his eyes looked unusually yellow. After reassuring him that they were as white as the eggs he had just bought, and not once mentioning his trip to the doctor, he resumed his visits. The next time he arrived he was so overloaded with pumpkins and gourds that he pulled an obscure muscle in his back, requiring her immediate medical assistance.

Lisette Robert welcomed the matchmaker in and stood back to let him pass with his bouquet of artichokes, the vicious pointed tips of which were threatening to befuddle his meticulously composed moustache. Now that he was in the confidence of the lovesick, the midwife was even more pleased than usual to see him and followed him into the kitchen hoping for another specimen for her cabinet of curiosities. She immediately got out a glass for his customary *pineau*. Guillaume Ladoucette had suffered the indignity of the shop-bought confection made in the neighbouring department of the Charente for so many years that he felt it was far too late to admit to his loathing of it and took the glass with a smile that he hoped concealed his secret dread.

Both agreed that it was too hot to sit outside; the match-maker rested the vegetables on the table, pulled out a wooden chair and sat down. After tapping his heels against the floor to loosen his supermarket leather sandals, which had stuck to him in the heat, he flipped them off and cooled his feet on the tiles.

'You're lucky to catch me in, actually,' said Lisette Robert, sitting down opposite him with a glass of red. 'I've only just got back.'

'Where from?' he asked, squinting as he tried to read the label on the back of a jar of purple mustard made from grape must on the table.

'I've been to see Émilie Fraisse at the château.'

Guillaume Ladoucette was so taken aback at hearing the name, he immediately forgot his sudden concern about his eyesight. Despite his frequent strolls around the village in the hope of spotting her, and looking up each time someone passed the window of Heart's Desire, he had only seen Émilie Fraisse once since her return. She had been slowly making her way up the rue du Château – the one that did actually lead to the castle – carrying a basket of groceries and wearing a curious emerald taffeta dress that appeared to have been shorn off at the knees. As he watched her walk away, he noticed that something pinning up her quicksilver hair sparkled. It was an image that had pawed at him ever since, winding round his legs whenever he walked, almost tripping him up. Whenever he went to bed, it would turn round and round next to him and eventually settle on the covers until the morning when it would nudge him awake.

'I think she looks great, I don't know why everybody's going on about her having gone grey,' said Lisette Robert. 'She's done a great job of that château. Remember how filthy it was? It's spotless. It still smells of bat shit, though, but she says she likes it.' Lisette Robert then got up from the table and fetched a jar of hare terrine from the counter. 'Look! She even sells little pots of things she's made, although she wouldn't let me pay for it.'

The matchmaker silently took the glass jar and looked at the handwriting on the label, which he instantly recognized, having dug up her letter only the day before. It had been easy enough to find, several feet under the hellebores, a bulb of which his mother had once fed him as a cure for worms, resulting in an episode none of the family ever forgot for its near-fatal consequences. When the spade tapped the metal, he reached in and pulled out the old red tin, which was instantly familiar. Bringing it back to the kitchen, he covered the end of the table with an old copy of the *Sud Ouest* newspaper and sat down to clean it with a damp tea towel. After wiping off the soil, he saw again the words 'Docteur L. Guyot Throat Pastilles, First Class Pharmacist, Contains Tar, Terpin, Menthol and Benzoin'. It was stiff at first, but eventually the tin opened to reveal a picture of the great medic himself on the inside lid brandishing a formidable moustache, with the words 'Specialist in Illnesses of the Chest' emblazoned below. And there, folded inside, was Émilie Fraisse's letter just as it was the day he had put it there twenty-six years ago.

Eventually Guillaume Ladoucette summoned up the courage to take it out. He carefully unfolded it and read it again. And when the matchmaker reached the final line – 'hope to hear from you soon' – he felt the familiar ache of regret.

As he sat at the kitchen table, with more years behind him than there were in front, he thought of the day Émilie Fraisse had left Amour-sur-Belle and the hours he had spent sitting on the stone wall in front of her house having arrived too late to say goodbye. He thought of the tiny bunches of lily of the valley that he had left on the wall every May Day since to bring her good luck, having never dared present her with one, according to tradition, when she had been there. He thought of the day when her letter arrived, and how his mother had left it on his bedside table so he could open it in private. He thought of the joy it had brought him, as well as the unbearable fear of having nothing of interest to say that had prevented him from replying. He thought of the torment he felt at the end of that spring when the nightingales finally stopped singing, as it meant that they had found their mate. And he thought of the dread he felt every spring since when they started to fill the day and night with their song.

When the matchmaker eventually finished scolding himself for not having replied, he folded up the letter, put it back into the tin and closed the lid. Slowly, he went upstairs, sat on the edge of his bed and pulled open the drawer of his nightstand. He placed the tin inside next to the only other thing the drawer contained: a regularly oiled Nontron hunting knife with a boxwood handle and ancient pokerwork motifs, which hadn't been used for the last twenty-six years.

'It looks delicious, doesn't it?' asked Lisette Robert. 'I was just about to have some. Would you like to join me?'

'That would be lovely, thank you,' Guillaume Ladoucette replied, his mind elsewhere.

'Can't wait to try it. She said she caught the hare herself.'

And with that, Lisette Robert placed a baguette and a jar of *cornichons* on the table, followed by two plates and two knives. She then reached inside the fridge for the Cabécou and placed it near to her guest, knowing its capacity for acting like salt in the cement of his resistance against passing on tittle-tattle. Sitting back down again, she opened the terrine, smelt it, declared it delicious and offered it to her guest. His manners prevented him from refusing it. After helping himself, Guillaume Ladoucette gave the jar back to his host. He watched as she pressed a dark, coarse corner on to a piece of bread and put it in her mouth. 'Marvellous!' she declared. 'Do tuck in.'

The matchmaker silently loaded up a piece of bread and

reluctantly brought it to his lips. He hesitated for a moment before tasting the musky meat fused with garlic, thyme, red wine and onions, all touched by the hand he had wanted to hold for almost three decades. Before he had a chance to swallow, his earache returned and he quickly got up to open the back door so that Lisette Robert would not smell the sudden odour of fetid vase water coming from his spleen.

As they ate, Lisette Robert talked about the wretched municipal shower and how she had mistakenly left her new bottle of shampoo in the cubicle only to find it empty when she had returned to fetch it. It had such a distinct smell of apples, she added, it wouldn't be long until she had sniffed out all the culprits. Guillaume Ladoucette, who had only just turned his thoughts away from Émilie Fraisse, was immediately relieved that the bottle had been empty by the time he had squeezed it.

'I expect you've had some successes at work?' the midwife then asked, sliding the Cabécou closer to her visitor. It was only then that the matchmaker remembered why he had come. Suddenly he stood up, picked up the bouquet of artichokes and presented them to her with as much fanfare as he could muster with half a chewed *cornichon* in his mouth, which included an attempt at a small bow. 'These ...', he announced, pausing for effect, 'are for you.'

'Thanks very much, Guillaume, that's very kind of you,' the midwife replied, taking them. 'They look splendid. I thought you were having trouble with yours this year.'

'Who told you that?'

'No one,' she fibbed.

'They're not mine,' said the matchmaker as he sat down, annoyed that someone had been talking about his artichokes behind his back. 'Someone else grew them. Your secret admirer, in fact.'

'Secret admirer?'

'Lisette, I have to confess that I am here in an official

capacity. A gentleman came into my office and immediately signed up for our Unrivalled Gold Service. Now, that means that he has someone very specific in mind that he would like to be introduced to. And that, my friend, is you.'

'Why would anyone want to be introduced to me?' she asked, confused.

It was Lisette Robert's mother who recognized that her daughter was cursed the day she was born. Instead of a blue shrew like the rest of her children, her youngest had arrived as pink as a peony and it took just one look at the face feeding at her breast to see that the girl would carry the colossal burden that beauty brought for the rest of her life. Every night she included in her prayers the supplication that her daughter's looks would fade, while her husband, who knew nothing of the problems that lay ahead, kissed the top of the baby's head so often she was left with a permanent hollow. The girl's many siblings, whose looks at kindest could be described as theatrical, were far too young to know that their sister's allure was anything but a blessing and instantly started calling her 'ugly' out of spite.

It was easy at first to hide the affliction. When the baby was in the pram, her mother simply covered her face with one of her husband's white cotton handkerchiefs. But as she got older, the child would pull it off and the secret was out. On hearing of her unrivalled beauty, people came from the surrounding hamlets to marvel at the infant, until her mother could take no more. 'She's not a circus freak!' she eventually cried and bolted the door.

'They only want to look at her,' her husband said, alarmed at his wife's reaction.

'You just wait,' she replied without further explanation as she closed the shutters.

Her prayers were not answered. And to make matters worse, her daughter's physical charms appeared to increase the older she became. The moment her mother realized, she refused to set foot in church again, not even for the funeral of her great-aunt which she had been looking forward to for decades. She then got out her will and added in block capitals at the bottom her wish to be buried next to the chicken coop at the bottom of the garden as she found comfort in the birds' ferocious looks. She started dressing her youngest in the most gruesome of clothes, mixing her older sisters' worst fashion mistakes with her brothers' most hideous hand-me-downs. But it was no good. They simply highlighted the girl's beauty and afforded her her own unique style, which some of the younger girls in Amour-sur-Belle attempted to copy, much to their parents' horror.

When boys – and men – started showing an interest in her from an early age, Lisette Pauillac, who grew up believing her siblings' insistence that she resembled a truffling pig, assumed they were being ironic and ignored them. But one of the younger ones was more persistent than the rest and, by the time she was eighteen, Lisette Pauillac, exhausted from refusing him, finally married Pierre-Albert Robert. Whilst the bride assumed that the wedding would signal the end of her troubles, for neither he – nor anyone else – would pursue her any more, her mother correctly suspected that it was only the beginning of them.

For more than two years Pierre-Albert Robert couldn't believe his luck. At times when the couple were eating, the mobile butcher was unable to hear what his wife was saying so struck was he by the dark curls that tumbled to her shoulders, which she would attempt to tuck out of the way behind an ear. She only had to look up at him, her eyes shining like freshly opened horse chestnuts, for him to lose his appetite. When she got up to clear the table, he would look at the silhouette of her body through her frightful dress made transparent by the light from the window. And he would see more graceful curves than those of the Belle flowing outside, in which she would happily let him bathe to mutual exhaustion.

It was her husband who taught her how to dress, buying her ecstasies of silk and lace in fantastical colours to wear underneath her new frocks, which delighted her as much as him. But when he pushed his lips through her waterfall of curls and whispered into her ear the extent of beauty, she never believed him.

However, the attraction of a new possession never lasts and Pierre-Albert Robert eventually came to the realization that his mother-in-law had been dreading ever since the day her daughter was born: Lisette Robert was just like everybody else. He first suspected that his wife was imperfect when he noticed that the fatter of the two chocolate *religieuses* she had bought for them that morning had disappeared. Up until then she had always offered him the biggest of everything. Putting it down to a woman's natural craving for *pâtisserie*, he was further surprised to note a few weeks later that she had also beaten him to the lamb cutlet in the fridge which he had been greatly looking forward to. Having settled into her marriage, Lisette Robert had simply resorted to her natural familial instinct of getting to everything before the others. In an attempt to reduce some of the conflict, Pierre-Albert Robert resorted to hiding his little pleasures around the house. However, he had a tendency to forget where he had put them, much to Lisette Robert's fury upon finding donkey *saucisson* sweating its foul aroma amongst her clean sheets waiting to be ironed.

Not only could his wife not be trusted to share things fairly, but her piano playing irritated him beyond measure. The musical instrument, the only one of its kind in the village, had been her family's only treasure and was given to the couple on their marriage, so relieved was her father at finally getting rid of the last of his enormous brood. But as time wore on, Pierre-Albert Robert soon realized that his wife, like a cuckoo, only knew one tune, which she justified by pointing out that her siblings never let her practise. And what had seemed so charming to him at first eventually became a source of utmost annoyance, surpassed only by her elephantine attempts at learning another.

Pierre-Albert Robert rode swiftly through the reality phase of his marriage until he arrived at the inevitable staging post of disappointment. While most eventually move on to acceptance, the mobile butcher lingered for so long that he lost all sense of direction. He would suddenly find himself in the naked arms of customers who instantly recognized the bitter taste of disillusionment on his tongue. But they didn't complain, happy in the knowledge that for the next eight minutes and forty-three seconds he had chosen them over Lisette Robert, and grateful for the *gigot* of lamb he would leave on their kitchen table to ease his guilt while they were doing up their buttons.

His wife never suspected a thing, and was merely confused when her husband's takings suddenly went down. But she never thought to question it. His dalliances continued during her first pregnancy and their mutual grief when their son died during his arrival. They continued during her second pregnancy and their subsequent joy at the birth of another son. They continued until the boy was brought home from hospital, when one of Pierre-Albert Robert's special customers came to the conclusion that Lisette Robert had had one blessing too many in life and slipped a stocking into the mobile butcher's pocket.

But the woman had overestimated her rival's concern for domesticity and it was Pierre-Albert Robert who found it. He recognized it instantly and when he challenged its owner he realized he was dealing with a woman who would stop at little to destroy what he had. Unable to bear the look in his wife's eyes if she ever found out, he went to the Bar Saint-Jus to decide what to do. When he could drink no more, he drove to the customer's house hoping to persuade her to keep their secret. His van was found the next morning by Gilbert

Dubuisson while the postman was on his rounds. It took the firemen more than forty minutes to get it upright and pull it out of the ditch. And it took them less time than one of Pierre-Albert Robert's duplicitous liaisons to conclude that his neck was broken in two places.

His death spared Lisette Robert the realization of his shortcomings and she buried her husband with the natural pain of a widow. It didn't take long, however, before the mourners became suitors, and she was back to where she started.

The matchmaker looked at the midwife and replied: 'Lisette, you have a wealth of charms that you don't even know about, which only adds to them. That you are in demand comes as no surprise to me.'

'Who is it?'

'I'm afraid customer confidentiality forbids me to say.'

'Do I know him?' she asked, nudging the Cabécou even closer.

'Forgive me, but I can't divulge that either.'

'Well, what's he like?'

'He's a solvent bachelor with a love for the outdoors who has his own transport.'

'Would I like him?'

'Love is often unpredictable,' said Guillaume Ladoucette.

'He might not like me.'

'Lisette, he likes you very much, which is why he wants me to introduce you to him.'

She licked her finger, stabbed some crumbs on her plate and sucked them off as she considered his proposal.

'Why not?' she replied.

Shortly afterwards, Guillaume Ladoucette stood up, kissed Lisette Robert goodbye on both cheeks and left. On his way home, he waved to Modeste Simon tying up her white hollyhocks with blue string, who still hadn't uttered a word since the unfortunate disappearance of Patrice Baudin, the skinny vegetarian pharmacist, during the famous mini-tornado.

Of all the villagers to bump into he was grateful that it was she, for he had no time to chat. The reason for his haste was the sudden appearance of Stéphane Jollis's head round the door of Heart's Desire the day before. It wasn't the sight of the baker that had unsettled him, for he regularly dropped by for a chat, often with the remains of a hastily eaten quiche resting on the slope of his chest like rock fall, which, much to the matchmaker's infuriation, usually cascaded on to the floor and was then trodden on with a pair of floury shoes. It was Stéphane Jollis's suggestion that they go fishing the following afternoon that had confounded him.

As their next scheduled trip had not been until two Sundays' time, and the baker never took time off on a Wednesday afternoon, Guillaume Ladoucette immediately smelt a rat. Suspecting that the baker had something of un-rivalled succulence up his sleeve, as soon as his friend had left the matchmaker closed Heart's Desire and hurried home, despite the fact that it was only three in the afternoon and business wasn't exactly brisk. He flung open all his cupboards, fought his way to the back of the fridge, rifled through his cookbooks and shot down into the cellar where he clattered around in his grandfather's Sunday clogs that nipped trying to find something extraordinary amongst the preserves. He then stood in the middle of the kitchen in despair, engulfed by the thunderous ticking of the clock on the sitting-room mantelpiece that had driven one relative to suicide. Suddenly he grabbed his keys, fled to his car and drove for two hours to Bordeaux. On his return, he set to work and didn't retire to bed until well after one, by which time his snores were so monstrous they woke the birds in the woods and set off the dawn chorus several hours too early.

Arriving home from Lisette Robert's house, the match-maker took out a plate and flask from the fridge and put them inside the picnic basket on the kitchen table, having first checked it for the presence of the infernal chicken.

Carefully carrying the basket to the car, he placed it on the back seat and covered it with a white tea towel. He then drove to the baker's house, turned off the ignition and immediately pulled down the sun visor to kill time. But before he had time to critically assess the elevation of the tips of his moustache, or bore himself by looking at the contents of the glove compartment, the passenger door suddenly opened and a strong, hairy arm reached in and placed a basket made from sweet chestnut on the back seat. The arm momentarily disappeared and then returned with a red tea towel which was thrown over it. The car suddenly tilted towards the right as the baker held on to the roof with one hand and manoeuvred his substantial frame inside, followed by his head.

'Hello, Stéphane,' said Guillaume Ladoucette evenly, his suspicions raised even further by the fact that his friend hadn't kept him waiting.

'Hello, Guillaume,' replied the baker.

'Got everything?'

'Yep.'

The pair sat in silence as they drove out of the village and turned right at the field with the ginger Limousin cows that winked. As they slowed down to pass through Beauséjour, the matchmaker decided to test the water. 'Bring any lunch with you?' he asked, sliding his eyes towards his passenger.

'Just a snack,' came the reply. 'You?'

'Just a snack,' said Guillaume Ladoucette, wrinkling up his nose dismissively.

Silence slipped between them again as they continued their journey along the fields to Brantôme. Once they arrived, the two men made their way along the bank of the Dronne away from the exquisite town until they reached the *No Fishing* sign. They put down their baskets in their usual spot, sat down and loaded up their hooks. A pair of supermarket leather sandals was then slipped off, followed by a ridiculously small pair of floury shoes. After each tying their line to an ankle, they rolled up their trouser legs and plunged their feet into the river.

'That's better!' said Guillaume Ladoucette, momentarily distracted by the unsurpassable pleasure of cool water seeping between his hairy toes. But Stéphane Jollis, who was mopping his forehead on his shoulder, didn't reply.

As he watched the turquoise dragonflies hitching a ride on the dusty surface of the shifting water, the matchmaker decided to leave the suggestion of lunch as long as possible, hoping to lull the baker into a false sense of security. But three minutes later, like a torture victim unable to take the agony any more, Guillaume Ladoucette suddenly squealed: 'I feel a bit peckish!'

'So do I,' replied Stéphane Jollis.

They shuffled back on their bottoms until they reached their baskets, pieces of emerald green weed dripping with water hanging from the fishing lines. The matchmaker pretended to hunt for his penknife as he waited to see what would come out of the rival basket first. He watched as a loaf of six-cereal bread appeared.

'Bake that this morning, did you?' asked the matchmaker, impressed by his friend's subterfuge with such a pitiful start.

'No, actually, I sold out. I had to buy it,' came the reply. 'Want some?'

'No thanks, otherwise I won't manage this!' said Guillaume Ladoucette, reaching inside his basket and pulling out a flask of chilled sorrel soup. He slowly poured a serving into a bowl, raised a spoonful to his lips, swallowed loudly and declared: 'Marvellous! I think it's always better when you thicken it with an egg yolk. But what really makes the difference, of course, is when you've grown the sorrel yourself. Want some?'

'No thanks,' replied Stéphane Jollis.

The matchmaker waited for the rest of his customary reply, but it never came. Suspecting that his friend was playing an even shrewder game than he had imagined, Guillaume Ladoucette took another mouthful of soup, watching over the brow of his spoon for the next revelation from the basket made from sweet chestnut. Just then, the baker reached inside it and brought out a packet of cheese still in its plastic supermarket wrapping.

'Emmental?' exclaimed the confounded matchmaker, wondering what ruse Stéphane Jollis was up to.

'Want some?' asked the baker.

'No thanks,' replied Guillaume Ladoucette, unable to disguise his horror. 'They make that in Switzerland. Anyway, I can't, otherwise I won't manage this!' As he spoke he carefully lifted out of his basket a plate on which was spread a dozen open oysters, followed by a dish containing four spicy chipolatas and a bottle of Bordeaux. After pouring himself a glass of wine, he bit into a sausage, then speared an oyster with a fork and slowly brought it to his mouth. After swallowing loudly he let out a sigh of immense satisfaction.

'Bordeaux oysters, what a sublime dish!' he concluded. 'Whoever thought of that combination was a genius. But you know, what I find is that it's never quite the same as actually going to Bordeaux to choose the oysters yourself, picking up the ingredients for the sausages and popping into a vineyard to select the best vintage to go with it. I sent you a postcard while I was there, actually. Fancy any?'

'No thanks,' replied Stéphane Jollis, biting into his bread and cheese.

Guillaume Ladoucette waited for his usual reply, but nothing else came from the baker's basket. Unsure of how to proceed, the matchmaker put a hand into his own, pulled out a jar and put it on the grass between them. 'Fruits in kirsch,' he said meekly, looking at his friend. 'I picked the fruit from the garden two years ago and it's been fermenting ever since. Should blow our heads off. Fancy any?'

'No thanks,' replied the baker.

Guillaume Ladoucette could take it no more. 'What's wrong, Stéphane?' he asked.

'Nothing,' replied the baker, staring ahead of him.

'Come off it. You're not your usual self.'

'Nothing, honestly.'

'You can't turn up with some Swiss cheese and pretend there's nothing wrong, Stéphane.'

The baker carried on staring at the opposite bank, his shoulders rounded.

'Is it something to do with work?' the matchmaker asked.

'No.'

'Are your varicose veins playing up?'

'Not particularly.'

Guillaume Ladoucette took another mouthful of soup as he thought. 'Fed up of not having caught anything in the last thirty-odd years?'

'Nope.'

The matchmaker put down his bowl of soup and joined the baker in staring at the bank opposite.

After a while, Stéphane Jollis swallowed. 'I was wondering . . .' he started.

'Yes?'

'If I might . . .'

'Yes?'

'Have a go.'

'Of course you can!' the matchmaker replied. 'What with?'

'You know,' said the baker.

'Not quite.'

'The gold one.'

'What gold one?'

'The unrivalled one.'

'I'm not with you.'

'The Unrivalled Gold Service. I'd like to sign up,' said the baker, keeping his eyes firmly ahead of him.

'What a splendid idea!' exclaimed Guillaume Ladoucette,

turning towards the baker. 'Whom do you have in mind?'

'Lisette Robert.'

'Lisette Robert? But you don't even talk to each other.'

'I know,' said Stéphane Jollis, his eyes falling to his knees.

'But what about the business with the frogs?'

'I didn't eat them.'

The matchmaker paused, looked at his friend and narrowed his eyes to accusative slits. 'Not even sautéed with garlic and butter?'

'No! It wasn't me! I've never eaten frogs in my life. Nobody in their right mind would. Have you?'

'Of course not! Only tourists do.'

'There we are then.'

There was a pause.

'So, can I sign up?' the baker asked.

Guillaume Ladoucette studied the Dronne as he considered the ethics of introducing two Unrivalled Gold Service clients to the same woman. It certainly didn't feel right, he thought. Just as he was about to turn his friend down, his eyes fell on the baker's ridiculously small floury shoes sitting on the bank next to them, and the baguette he had broken in two in search of the soft white innards for his bait. The matchmaker then thought of the pitiful lunch the baker had brought, and his worrying descent into the dubious world of Swiss cheese.

'Stop by tomorrow: there are procedures to go through,' said the matchmaker eventually, helping himself to another oyster. 'And expect a haircut.'

10

'DID YOU OR DID YOU NOT SUGGEST GOING HALVIES-HALVES?' ASKED Guillaume Ladoucette, studying the dentist closely from behind the desk with the ink stain.

Yves Lévèque moved uncomfortably on the cushion with the hand-embroidered radish, but remained silent.

'Well?' demanded the matchmaker, folding his arms across his chest as he waited for an explanation.

'There might have . . .' muttered the dentist looking at the red tiled floor.

'Might have been what?'

'There might have been a mutual agreement that the bill was split,' he said, sighing.

'A mutual agreement? Yves, I have three eyewitness accounts stating that you very much put it to Sandrine Fournier that she paid half. What do you say to that?'

Yves Lévèque kept his silence.

'Well?'

The dentist shrugged. 'I just didn't like her.'

'But you came here seeking professional advice, I gave it to you and one of the last things I said was not to ask her to split the bill. No wonder it didn't go well.'

'She's not the sort of woman I'm looking for.'

'Not everyone falls instantly head over heels,' said the matchmaker. 'Love is like a good cassoulet, it needs time and determination. Some bits are delicious, while others might be a bit rancid and make you wince. You may even come across the odd surprise like a little green button, but you have to consider the whole dish.'

'I don't even like cassoulet.'

'How can you not like cassoulet? You've obviously never had a good one. Have you ever tried mine?'

'No, but Patrice Baudin did and look what happened to him.'

'Patrice Baudin's unfortunate conversion to vegetarianism was a result of dark forces at play, which cannot be explained. Anyway, that's beside the point. I think you should give it another go with Sandrine Fournier.'

'Can't I just have my money back?' asked the dentist.

'I'm sorry, it's not possible.'

Suddenly the dentist felt the sharp edges of loneliness shift around in his stomach and Guillaume Ladoucette thought he could smell copper.

'You must have other people on your books,' insisted Yves Lévèque.

The matchmaker tugged at the brass handle of the top left-hand drawer, pulled out a file that struck Yves Lévèque as rather slim, waggled it in front of the dentist and put it back inside again. 'Of course I have other clients, but I don't think you've made enough of an effort with Sandrine Fournier,' he argued.

'But I told you, there's just something about her I don't like. She gives me the creeps. What has she said about it?'

'Much the same as you. But don't worry, I'll talk to her. As I explained earlier, time and determination: that's what you need. Whenever you feel hopeless, just think of a Toulouse sausage and some haricot beans.'

As the dentist got up to leave he asked: 'What were you saying about a green button?'

'Never mind.'

Just before he opened the door for his customer, the matchmaker put his hand on his shoulder and added: 'Remember: A man is only as good as his last meal.'

Once Yves Lévèque had left, Guillaume Ladoucette made his way back to his desk. Just before he sat down, he noticed a flaked almond on the floor and his thoughts turned to his first customer that morning. He had only just kicked off his supermarket leather sandals when the door opened. As his hairy toes started hunting around the floor underneath his desk to find them again, he looked up to see that it was Stéphane Jollis. For once, the baker had arrived with a little something: a brown paper bag containing two almond croissants fresh from the oven, which, in view of the landslide on the brow of his white T-shirt, would not be his first that morning.

'I don't wish to be rude, Stéphane, but would you mind giving yourself a bit of a shake before you come in?' the matchmaker called.

'I see what you mean,' said the baker, looking down at himself. He took a step back and gave a cursory sway of the hips.

'Think dog, rather than the hula-hula,' suggested the matchmaker.

After the baker had shed his gastronomic fallout, Guillaume Ladoucette gestured to the chair with the peeling marquetry. Once the baker was comfortably installed, the pair immediately got down to business. From his bottom drawer, the matchmaker took out two plates and two paper serviettes. They then helped themselves to a plump almond croissant each, which they savoured with a cup of freshly brewed coffee from the percolator on the small table with the antique lace cloth at the back of the shop. After they had finished, they dusted their mouths, during which Guillaume Ladoucette made the fortuitous discovery of a sizeable crumb on his chin, which he popped into his mouth. The matchmaker returned the plates to the bottom drawer, and they both sat as still as basking lizards in the warmth of their contentment. Eventually, Stéphane Jollis remembered what he had come in for. After checking that his client hadn't changed his name or address overnight, the matchmaker filled in his particulars and then disappeared down into the basement. He re-emerged with a grey nylon gown in which he swiftly captured the baker.

'But I don't want my hair cut!' protested Stéphane Jollis.

'I'm not introducing any client of mine who has signed up for the Unrivalled Gold Service looking as though a beaver has constructed a dam on his head. Really, Stéphane.'

Within seconds, Guillaume Ladoucette's fingers were fluttering and long black tendrils coated in flour were dropping to the floor.

'Right,' said the matchmaker after sweeping them up and walking his friend to the door, 'I'll make the necessary arrangements and keep you posted. Now, what aren't you to forget?'

'To make sure that I always shake before I come in?'

'Yes, there's that, but it wasn't what I was meaning.'

'That a gentleman never needs a haircut?'

'Yes, there's that too, but I was thinking of something else.'

'Not to pick my teeth with my fork?'

'Yes, yes, that too. Sorry I had to bring it up, but it's all part of the service. I was actually referring to your agreement not to bring up your research.'

'Research?'

'All that stuff about the French never eating frogs' legs and that it was all a joke started by a French merchant in eighteen sixty-two while he was in England.'

'It was eighteen thirty-two, actually.'

'Whatever. My advice is to leave all matters amphibious well alone.'

Insisting that he wouldn't forget, the baker left, enjoying the sensation of the perpetual breeze on his newly shorn head as he walked down the road, and bracing himself for the outrage from the inevitable queue of customers waiting outside his shop door.

Guillaume Ladoucette dropped the flaked almond he had just spotted into the bin, sat down on the swivel chair and stared blankly in front of him. Putting his elbows on the desk, he rested his chin on the palms of his hands and wondered what on earth would become of him. Heart's Desire had been open for several weeks now and what did he have to show for it? A parsimonious dentist (who smelt of copper, with a haircut that would put off the least discerning of women) and an assistant ambulant fishmonger (with an allergy to shellfish) who couldn't stand the sight of each other. Then there was the business with Lisette Robert. While the midwife deserved a chance at love just like everyone else, was it really fair to encourage two Unrivalled Gold Service customers to take up arms in the battle for her affections, considering the long roll call of casualties each year and their ghastly injuries? Even if it were, had he done a dishonourable thing by having two such suitors on his books at the same time? And did either of them stand a chance anyway?

The matchmaker then thought of the handful of clients who had come in the previous week, and the one who concerned him the most: Gilbert Dubuisson. The postman had needed little persuasion to forget about the Unrivalled Bronze Service and proceed immediately to the considerably more expensive Unrivalled Silver Service. But what woman would ever want such a loquacious man with despicable urinary habits? And while the postman undoubtedly had his talents – as everyone did – the matchmaker was in no doubt that a woman needed far more from a husband than an ability to grow asparagus, important though it was. The man had been driving him into an almost daily state of irritation by his frequent visits from his house opposite 'to see how things are going'. Like a cicada, the postman's presence could instantly be detected without him being visible because of the noise he produced, most of which was not worth listening to, particularly when he was talking with vigour about his window boxes. At times, he even had the cheek to arrive with a packet of Petit Beurre Lu biscuits and settle himself on the bench for the afternoon. If that wasn't bad enough, the matchmaker was certain that his presence was putting off potential customers, to say nothing of the crumbs he shed with the trajectory of a sneeze.

Maybe my Brilliant Idea wasn't so brilliant after all and I've made an awful mistake, thought Guillaume Ladoucette. What happens if I don't find my customers anyone to love? They'll all hate me. I'll be driven out of the village. Who will look after my potager?

He continued to stare ahead of him, seeing nothing. Who am I to give advice on matters of the heart, anyway? he wondered, remembering the letter he had dug up the day before to which he had never replied. Guillaume Ladoucette sighed and was just about to get up to make himself another cup of coffee when something on his left supermarket leather sandal caught his eye. He picked it up and held it under his nose. Just as he was inspecting with increasing fury what was undeniably a constellation of peck marks, the door opened. It was Émilie Fraisse.

Guillaume Ladoucette looked at her for what seemed several minutes, his open wound of mortification preventing him from moving. Eventually, he bent down, dropped his supermarket leather sandal on the floor, crawled his toes back inside and stood up. He must have made his way to the door, but when he tried to replay the moment in bed that night he couldn't remember how. Was it too fast like an eager fool or too slow like a decrepit old man? The next thing he remembered was holding the door handle in silence. He must have just stood there because Émilie Fraisse eventually asked him: 'May I come in?'

'Yes, yes, of course, come in, come in,' he replied and watched as she walked past him, stood in the middle of Heart's Desire and turned to face him. Suddenly remembering his manners, the matchmaker approached her and kissed her on both cheeks. As he did so, he breathed in the scent of her skin which, after twenty-six years, was instantly familiar. But when he tried to recall it in bed that night, he was unable to.

After showing the châtelaine to the chair with the peeling marquetry, and offering her coffee, he went to the small table at the back of the shop to make it. But as he stood in front of the percolator with his back to her, he found that he had forgotten what to do. And when he finally remembered, and had been standing waiting for the water to pass through the filter for several minutes, he suddenly realized that he had unplugged the machine at the wall, a habit learnt from his mother in case of an electrical storm. As he waited again, he imagined Émilie Fraisse sitting on the cushion with the hand-embroidered radish hating the pink walls and he wished that he had chosen a different colour.

Finally he brought the cups over and put them down on the desk with the ink stain, which he quickly covered with the telephone. He then sat down on his swivel chair and looked again at Émilie Fraisse, who looked back at him with eyes the colour of fresh sage, and smiled.

'It's lovely to see you,' he said, smiling back.

'It's lovely to see you too, Guillaume,' she replied.

'You're just as I remembered.'

'I've gone grey,' she said, embarrassed, her hand instinctively reaching for the back of her head.

'It suits you very well.'

'Thanks.'

The pair silently held each other's gaze.

'Lisette Robert said you've stopped barbering and set your-self up as a matchmaker.'

'That's right. And you've bought the château, I hear.'

'Yes, yes, I have.'

'How's that going?'

'I adore it.'

Silence bloomed again.

'Actually, I was wondering whether you might be able to help me,' Émilie Fraisse said.

'Of course. I'm sure you need all the help you can get sort-ing that place out. What is it you'd like me to do?'

'Oh, it's nothing to do with the château.'

'No?' asked Guillaume Ladoucette, surprised.

'I was wondering whether you could possibly help me to find love.'

Half an hour later, in an antique saffron dress that appeared to have been shorn off at the knees, and with a white dahlia tucked in the back of her hair which was pinned up with something that sparkled, Émilie Fraisse left Heart's Desire having signed up for the Unrivalled Silver Service.

After crunching her way back over the crisp pigeon droppings covering the drawbridge, the châtelaine pushed open the vast wooden front door bleached fossil grey by the sun, which she kept unlocked in the hope that someone would steal the collection of hideous old dolls in discoloured lace. She kicked off her ridiculous seventeenth-century shoes and padded past the llama skeleton along a corridor with a patch of florid yellow mould thought by scientists to be long extinct. In the cool of the vaulted kitchen, she surveyed the splendid collection of copper pots, pans and utensils now sitting on, or hanging from, freshly painted pale-blue shelves on three sides of the room. Looking forward to an agreeable afternoon polishing the few pieces still left to be done, Émilie Fraisse took down the largest brioche mould and settled herself on the seat with wild boars carved on its feet. In and out of the curves she rubbed until she could see her head distorted to hideous proportions. Returning the mould to its place on the shelf, she then took down the diamond-shaped turbot pan. Just as she was about to start on the flat lid, the bell rang. Resting the lid on the table, she padded back down the corridor in her bare feet past the llama skeleton and opened the door. There, squinting in the sun, was a man with a clipboard in one hand and a soft leather briefcase in the other, which he was clutching to his stomach. It took a moment for her eyes to adjust to the light, but when they did, she noticed what appeared to be a splash of vomit on his right shoe.

'Forgive me for disturbing you, madame. My name is Jean-François Lafforest and I work for the council,' he said.

'How lovely to see you,' said Émilie Fraisse. 'You're after a tour, I presume.'

'I'm afraid I'm here in an official capacity, madame.'

'Oh, I see. Well, let's get you out of the heat, otherwise you'll end up looking like that old door of mine. Come in, come in. Don't worry, the llama doesn't bite. Excuse the state of my hands, I've been cleaning the copper. Follow me to the kitchen so I can wash them and I'll be all yours.'

The châtelaine led Jean-François Lafforest along the corridor with its patches of rare yellow mould to the vaulted kitchen, where he stood in his unfortunate trousers that didn't fit, his hands on his hips as he marvelled at the pots and pans glowing like hot coals.

'I must congratulate you on your efforts, madame, it really is a beautiful collection. I visited the château many years ago and one wouldn't even have known they were made of copper.'

'Please, sit down,' she said, offering him the ancient wooden seat which slid open to hide the salt from the tax collector. When he showed reluctance, she reassured him that she would rather it be used than looked at. While she was washing her hands, the man from the council apologized again for disturbing her.

'On the contrary,' said Émilie Fraisse. 'It's nice to have some company. Not many people stop by as they're too horrified by the scandalous ramparts. Now, you must be thirsty. What can I get you to drink? A glass of rosé, perhaps?'

'Water would be fine,' replied Jean-François Lafforest.

After handing him a glass, Émilie Fraisse sat down and asked: 'How can I help you?'

The man from the council looked at the floor and then at the châtelaine. 'As you will know, madame, we have been obliged to install a municipal shower in the place du Marché because there is hardly any water in the reservoir and it hasn't rained for so long. It has been brought to my attention that, according to the ledger outside the cubicle that residents are obliged to fill in, so far you have failed to use it. And if those who have approached me are to be believed, nor does it seem to be simply an oversight because neither have you been seen using it. Now, it is not for me to pry into people's washing habits, but, as you will be aware from the letter sent to all the inhabitants of Amour-sur-Belle, the taking of baths is strictly forbidden.' He paused before adding: 'It embarrasses me to say this, madame, but I will have to inspect your bath.'

For several seconds Émilie Fraisse considered the request and then said: 'Of course you do. Of course you do. Oh dear me, come this way, you might not like what you see.'

Jean-François Lafforest followed the châtelaine up the stone spiral staircase, her bare feet silent on the steps with the lamentable repairs. They passed along a corridor hung with faded tapestries until they reached a door with an enormous iron handle, which she turned and stood to one side to allow the man from the council to enter. He walked up to the bath, peered inside and started with such violence that he dropped his soft leather briefcase.

'I didn't know where else to put it,' Émilie Fraisse explained. 'I found it in the garden pond while I was clearing it out. I couldn't resist it. It was a bit of a job getting it out, mind you. The pond was filthy, as you would imagine, so I thought if I kept it in some clean water for a while it would lose its brackishness.'

When the man from the council had recovered from his surprise, he congratulated the châtelaine on her beautiful eel and asked her how she was planning to cook it. Émilie Fraisse replied that she hadn't yet made up her mind, though she tended to prefer them stewed rather than roasted. As they walked back down the stone spiral staircase, she added: 'You must be wondering how I keep clean. I use the garden hose outside.'

Once back in the vaulted kitchen, Jean-François Lafforest immediately sat down. His hateful task over, he suddenly felt a fog of fatigue swirl up around him and snuff out his senses, for he had woken at the deathless hour of seventeen minutes past four, after which he had remained awake, dreading the sun crawling out of the ground.

'It's almost five, you must have finished for the day. I expect you're ready for an apéritif?' asked Émilie Fraisse.

Despite the fact that the contents of his stomach had only recently been violently expelled, the man from the council gratefully accepted. And, for the first time while in Amour-sur-Belle, he felt a fern of happiness unfurl inside him. His senses restored, he looked at the woman in the curious antique saffron dress that appeared to have been shorn off at the knees, whose hair was pinned up with something that sparkled, and asked whether it was possible to have a tour after all.

The châtelaine happily agreed and took her guest into the dining room where she proudly showed him the original *pisé* floor. He marvelled at the smooth stones in various shades of white and brown, the size and shape of potatoes, which were intricately laid out in rose-window patterns. When Jean-François Lafforest asked whether she knew anything of its history, Émilie Fraisse found herself telling him a story of how, during the sixteenth century, one of the château owners had fallen in love with a young villager, having watched her bathing in the Belle from the magnificent ramparts, which still had all their crenellations. In an effort to win her heart, he sent her love letters in the form of paper boats which he launched from the moat. The clandestine correspondence continued for several months until his wife discovered what he was up to and ordered that the river be diverted around Amour-sur-Belle. Not only was his hope of love thwarted, but the villagers had nowhere to bathe or wash their dishes and an abominable disease broke out. Many died a frightful death, including the young girl. The inconsolable château owner immediately ordered that the Belle run once more through the village. His wife naturally assumed that the new floor he had laid in the dining room was an apology for the little paper boats. In fact, the stones had been collected from the bottom of the river where the young woman used to bathe, and made into a floor so that he could walk over them in bare feet every day in order to be close to her.

When she had finished the story, Jean-François Lafforest smiled at his hostess, enchanted.

As they entered one of the bedrooms with its original ceiling made of sweet chestnut, the man from the council questioned the provenance of a little footstool the like of which could only be found in the most dispiriting of junk shops. Émilie Fraisse suddenly found herself telling him that it was stuffed with the hair of a famous horse, whose master had one day discovered its remarkable ability to predict the weather. He took the animal from fair to fair and stood it inside a little tent where people queued to witness its forecasts. Rain was signalled by a nod of its head, winds by a swoosh of its tail, hail by a pawing of its left hoof and sun by a baring of its colossal yellow teeth. The horse, which was always accurate, soon earned the man a fortune. One week, a terrible storm was on its way, the arrival of which the horse was all too aware. However, its master misinterpreted its whinnying, during which it bared substantially more of its colossal yellow teeth than usual, as a month of uninterrupted sunshine. Instead of quickly harvesting their crops, the farmers left them to enjoy the forthcoming good weather. But their corn and wheat were ruined. They immediately blamed the horse, even though it had been right all along. Having nothing left to eat, one night the farmers captured the animal and made it into sausages, which they sold at highly inflated prices on account of the horse's standing. Its master was so upset he decided to keep some of its hair as a memento, and had it fashioned into a footstool.

'It's said that whenever there's a storm on its way the room suddenly fills up with the smell of damp horse,' added Émilie Fraisse, closing the door behind them. Jean-François Lafforest, who had never heard that story either, was enraptured.

The only tale the man from the council didn't believe was when they reached the *grand salon* and he enquired about the putrid smell coming from one of the tapestries. The châtelaine then told him the very true account of how during the reign of Louis XIII the comte de Brancas, gentleman-in-waiting to Anne of Austria, had dropped the queen's hand on entering a room *pour aller pisser contre la tapisserie*. The previous owner of the château had read about this and taken it up as a new hobby with breathtaking devotion.

When Émilie Fraisse had finished peddling her fiddle-sticks, she picked up a basket from the hall and the pair left the cool of the château for the garden. They walked alongside the warm stone wall on top of which bearded irises grew until they reached a clump of knitted brambles and determined grasses reaching all the way up to their thighs. She pulled them apart revealing the rows of heirloom vegetables. 'You'll be staying for supper, I hope,' she said, picking some of the long-forgotten ancient varieties, including black tomatoes, square-podded peas and violet sweet potato.

When they returned to the vaulted kitchen, Jean-François Lafforest crouched down and peered at one of the copper bowls used for beating egg whites which was hanging from a hook on the blue shelves, while Émilie Fraisse refilled their glasses. 'Now, where's that pig's bladder?' she asked out loud as she looked inside the fridge. Eventually it was found, cleaned and stuffed with a plump duck which had been swiftly and expertly plucked. She lowered it into one of the copper pans on the stove containing veal stock to cook until it was tender. The man from the council sat watching her from the ancient seat that slid open to hide the salt from the tax collector, another fern of happiness uncurling inside him.

'Let's eat in the dining room,' said the châtelaine. 'Every guest is a special occasion.' At her suggestion, he went to open the lattice windows to let the coarse damp air out and the velvety evening in. While he struggled with the stiff handles, she descended the death-cold steps of the dungeon to fetch a bottle of red which had been hidden from the Nazis. They brought their plates through and sat opposite each other in the middle of the long oak table which had been stolen from a monastery. As the sun slithered away, and they finished their first bottle, they were both seduced by the anonymity of strangers. It wasn't long before Jean-François Lafforest told his host about the first time he had come to Amour-sur-Belle to carry out a headcount when the village was trying to pass itself off as a town. He told of the dastardly tricks the residents had played on him, and the subsequent trouble he had got into at work. He told of the merciless ribbing he had received at the hands of his colleagues, who had all suddenly taken to wearing wigs and false beards in the office. He told of the nervous breakdown he had suffered and how he had been determined to return to work, because without it, what was he? He told of the fits of vomiting he experienced each time he had to come to the village, but that at least they were helping him lose the weight he had put on during those terrible days when he refused to leave the house. He told of how he had always opposed the idea of installing a municipal shower, and how he sometimes felt that the committee members had decided to have one installed simply to make his life harder. He told of how he was saving for a house with a garden where he could erect a greenhouse like the English had, so that he could cultivate orchids in impossible colours because he wanted something beautiful to look after. And when Émilie Fraisse asked was his wife not beautiful, he replied that he had never married, having left his fiancée during the dark days because he didn't feel worthy of her. He added hastily that he was perfectly happy on his own and that he wasn't looking for anyone to share his life. Without realizing it, he then slipped off his shoes underneath the table stolen from the monastery and rubbed his feet on the stones said to be from the spot where the young villager had bathed in the Belle.

Émilie Fraisse then told of how she had recently returned from Bordeaux to the village where she had grown up. She told of how she had bought the château with no intention of restoring it, and that she liked the scandalous ramparts with their missing sections of crenellations just as they were. She then told him how she could well believe the dastardly tricks that the villagers had played on him, and that knowing them as well as she did, he had probably got off lightly.

The bats had taken up their circular swoops over the fifteenth-century chapel rebuilt by leper labourers by the time that Jean-François Lafforest asked Émilie Fraisse whether she had ever known love. She told of how she had once been married, and that although her former husband hadn't been a bad man, they had failed to make each other happy.

'Was that the only time?' the man from the council asked.

For a moment Émilie Fraisse watched the night silently pouring in through the open lattice windows. 'There was another time, but it was many years ago,' she replied.

'Would you like to have someone in your life now?' he asked.

'Oh yes,' she said, turning back to him. 'Without love we are just shadows.'

At the end of the evening, Jean-François Lafforest thanked his hostess for such a wonderful dinner, and Émilie Fraisse thanked him for being such a wonderful guest. They said goodbye at the front door, which glowed like mercury in the moonlight, and the châtelaine stood listening as he crunched his way over the drawbridge. When, eventually, he arrived home and opened his soft leather briefcase, the man from the council found inside a jar of black radish jam tied with a piece of antique lace.

Guillaume Ladoucette was already in bed with just a sheet over him, trying to remember every word that he and Émilie Fraisse had spoken and guessing at those he was unable to. He thought of how captivating she had looked with her sage-green eyes, curious antique dress which appeared to have been shorn off at the knees and hair pinned up with something that sparkled. He thought of how ridiculous he must have seemed peering at his supermarket leather sandal when she walked in, and he wished that he had been wearing a different shirt. And he thought what a fool he had been for taking her on as a customer and not telling her there and then of his years of undiminished love that made his ears ache with unwept tears.

In the early hours, when sleep still hadn't sniffed at him, he finally came to the conclusion that there was nothing he could have done except agree to take her on. The only question that remained was who would he match her with? Two hours, 14 minutes and 33 seconds later, just as he heard the first hurried scuff of slippers as a villager headed for the municipal shower, the perfect solution came to him.

11

YVES LÉVÈQUE STOOD IN HIS GARDEN CONTEMPLATING THE unspeakable state of his *cornichons*. As he studied the deformed green fruit, no bigger than peanuts, he wondered whether his neighbour had actually been right about something. Maybe he should have sown them when the moon was passing in front of the constellation of Aries after all. Certainly, they were a catastrophe, he thought, moving aside the leaves in the hope of finding something worth pickling. Unable to bear the humiliation any longer, particularly as Guillaume Ladoucette's upstairs shutters opened on to an uninterrupted view of his garden, he wrapped his long, pale instruments of torture around the base of the stems, tugged them out of the ground and threw their crippled frames on to the compost heap next to the Mirabelle tree.

Maybe the matchmaker was right about Sandrine Fournier the mushroom poisoner as well, he thought, wandering back inside and slumping on to the brown leather sofa he had inherited from a late uncle. He stared at the wall opposite with its stone ivy carving which his ancestors had prised from the Romanesque church during the Revolution and used when building the house. Sandrine hadn't looked that bad in her strapless blue dress with her hair up, he reasoned. And if a relationship did develop, there was always the tantalizing prospect of getting a discount on his purchases from her fish van. But with the alacrity of a cut poppy shedding its petals, the dentist abandoned his delusions. The woman was an abomination, he concluded. Her new sleeveless dress had cut into her over-sunned flesh, sending it cascading over the top like burnt brioche. Her hair should have been left down to camouflage what should never have been on public display. And as for a discount on his purchases at her van, he had always managed to confuse her sufficiently with his orders so that she gave him too much change anyway.

The dentist looked at his watch. There was still half an hour before he would have to leave the house to meet her. Maybe he could just not turn up, he thought, suddenly filled with the fire generated by a good idea. He could make up an excuse that would silence both her and the matchmaker. He could say that a patient had suddenly appeared at his door tormented by toothache, and that he had had no option but to take him in and tend to him. Such a story would also serve as a warning to Sandrine Fournier about the horrendous consequences of not flossing, he thought, sunning himself in the warmth of his ingenuity.

But just as Yves Lévèque was trying to decide which of his patients he could blame for his absence, his breath was caught by the sharp corner of loneliness shifting around his stomach, and he knew that if he was ever going to be cured of his cursed constipation he would have to try harder in his quest for love.

Reluctantly, he climbed the stairs to the bathroom and looked into the mirror. As usual, his haircut caught him by surprise. After adjusting it, he inspected it from every angle, but wasn't convinced that he had gained any benefit from the tweaking. Taking his glasses off, he peered further into the mirror and removed a yellow crust from the corner of his left eye. His glasses back in position, he considered his reflection again and tried to seek out the slightest hint of allure. With no success. He then bared his teeth and comforted himself with the knowledge that his grandmother, the illegal tooth-puller, and his grandfather, the piglet dentist, would be proud of them.

Standing in his barren bedroom, he changed his shirt to a green short-sleeved check affair which was already ironed and hanging on the front of the old family wardrobe that was too big and too ugly. He walked to the dressing table and dabbed himself with cologne usually reserved for Christmas and bank holidays in celebration of a day free from peering into the abandoned graveyards of people's mouths. He then got into his car, drove out of the village and turned right at the field with the ginger Limousin cows that winked.

Yves Lévèque hadn't been entirely truthful when he gave the matchmaker his reason for choosing Brantôme as the location for his next encounter with Sandrine Fournier. Guillaume Ladoucette had immediately agreed with the dentist when he declared that there was no better a setting to find love than the exquisite town. However, the dentist had in fact chosen the place for its infestation of tourists, amongst whom he hoped to lose the mushroom poisoner should she prove as insufferable as the last time.

As he pulled into the car park near the Monks' Garden, his heart sank when a space became available next to a vehicle he instantly recognized as that belonging to the assistant ambulant fishmonger on account of the rust that she consistently failed to remove, much like the debris trapped between her teeth. Before he had time to change his mind, however, she appeared as if from nowhere. This time, he noted, the tops of her arms were fortunately covered by a short-sleeved white blouse, which, having had to mount and descend the contours of her bosom and stomach, only just reached the top of her severely fitting denim skirt. As they kissed each other on each cheek the dentist held his breath. But it was no use. As soon as he inhaled again, he was flooded with the putrid tide of her perfume.

'It's lovely to see you,' lied Yves Lévèque.

'It's lovely to see you too,' lied Sandrine Fournier.

It was no accident that Yves Lévèque had chosen Friday morning as their next rendezvous. What little space the tourists had left was taken up by the weekly market. One behind the other, the pair squeezed their way past the stall with its neat display of mottled pink *saucisson*, speared with labels denouncing such contents as donkey, bull and bison. Eventually, they reached the bridge and were herded along the rows of bloated sand-coloured foie gras, skinned rabbits, plucked pigeons and trussed-up chickens turning on spits, their eyes closed to their grim fate. They struggled past the garlic-seller crying out the virtues of his mauve bulbs, then found themselves standing outside the splendid abbey, which now served as the town hall. The dentist then suggested that they visited the caves behind it to escape from the heat and the crowds, to which the mushroom poisoner readily agreed.

As the pair went in search of the ticket office, Yves Lévèque drew Sandrine Fournier's attention to the eleventh-century detached bell tower, with its stone pyramid roof and complex tiers of windows and arches which reached four storeys high.

'Did you know that that's the oldest bell tower in the Périgord Vert?' he asked.

'It's actually the oldest in France,' she replied.

When they reached the kiosk in the cloisters, the dentist bought a single ticket for the self-guided troglodyte tour, and then stepped aside so that the assistant ambulant fishmonger could purchase hers. As they passed into the courtyard to commence the tour, he insisted that it started on the right, but deferred to the assistant ambulant fishmonger who was convinced that it started on the left. When they approached the nearest information panel, and discovered that it was numbered 33, Yves Lévèque, his fury ignited, silently blamed Sandrine Fournier for their starting the circular tour at the end. And, as they continued in the wrong direction, neither had the slightest notion that they were in a corridor of limestone caves once used as a place of pagan worship by hermits, and later by monks.

As they wandered through the dank, grey monotony, repeatedly having to step out of the way of visitors coming towards them, they came across a grotto into the walls of which had been cut a series of square holes. It was then that Yves Lévèque, who had been following Sandrine Fournier, noticed to his utmost irritation that they were now at information panel Number 24, and had missed out the preceding half-dozen. His horror was complete when the mushroom poisoner then attempted to read its English translation out loud and at considerable volume. So unfathomable was her delivery that when the torment was finally over, the dentist, despite his reasonable grasp of the language, had not the slightest idea that he was standing in a dovecote. Nor had he been able to ascertain that pigeons had not only been greatly appreciated by the monks for their meat, but also for their droppings, which were used as fertilizer, in which there had been a flourishing trade.

Passing deeper into the caves, sleek with luminous slime, Sandrine Fournier suddenly felt a chill judder down her spine. The cause was not the sudden drop of temperature, however, but the touch of Yves Lévèque as he grabbed her arm, startled by the sudden ringing of the bells.

When they reached the Cave of the Last Judgement, with its grotesque carving on the back wall depicting a divine figure surmounting Death who was hovering over a line of severed heads, Sandrine Fournier declared that it represented 'good over evil'. However, Yves Lévèque saw in it something quite different.

'I see it more as the triumph of Death,' he muttered, his long, pale instruments of torture twitching.

And when they arrived at the ancient fountain cut out of the rock face with its tiny ferns and dripping moss dedicated to Saint-Sicaire, they stopped to run their hands under the cool water. But both recoiled in terror when they read that it used to attract thousands of pilgrims on account of its miraculous ability to bestow fertility.

As they left through the entrance, they resisted the lure of the town's restaurants whose terraces overlooked the slothful Dronne into which willows dipped their branches. Neither did they stop to admire the blue-shuttered houses on the other side of the river, nor the faded words on a wall above the teak-coloured water indicating it once served as the *Bains Publics*. Instead, they immediately headed back to the car park. Once there, they turned to face each other for only the second time that morning.

'I've had a marvellous time. Those caves were fascinating,' lied Yves Lévèque. 'We really should meet up again.'

'I couldn't think of anything nicer,' lied Sandrine Fournier. And as they kissed one another on each cheek, the assistant ambulant fishmonger held her breath. But it was no use. As soon as she inhaled again, she was flooded with the putrid tide of his cologne.

Two days later, Émilie Fraisse sat on the curiously unworn steps of the Romanesque church in Amour-sur-Belle fiddling with a lizard baked like a biscuit in the sun that she had picked up from the ground. The châtelaine had no idea whom she was waiting for. She had received a phone call from Guillaume Ladoucette, who sounded in a particularly gleeful mood, telling her that he had found her the most perfect match. The gentleman was an outstanding communicator, with a particular interest in trees, who had suggested that they go to the *floralies* at Saint-Jean-de-Côle. The matchmaker then explained that the annual flower festival had been delayed by a couple of weeks while the village recovered from the scandal caused by its mayor getting caught with his fingers in another woman's Venus flytrap.

While Émilie Fraisse failed to understand the matchmaker's euphemism, of which he had initially been proud but later deeply regretted, she happily accepted the suggestion, immediately remembering the village as a rival to Brantôme on account of its beauty. As soon as she put down the phone, she abandoned the heavy, dusty tapestry she had been repairing and raced up the stone spiral staircase, her bare feet slapping on the lamentable repairs. Opening her wardrobe, she scanned the row of antique dresses, hanging like captured butterflies, which she had found in the leather chest studded with brass. But suddenly she was no longer certain of their appeal. She then heaved open the gentleman's chest under the window, but when she tried them on, she feared that the doublets and hose would be too hot in such weather. Returning to the wardrobe, she searched again through the silk and taffeta and came across a cream organza gown which she had never worn. And when she tried it on, to her surprise it fitted. She hurried back downstairs, the hem of the dress rippling down the lamentable repairs, found the kitchen scissors and hacked off the bottom third, as well as the arms that had been ravaged by moths. She then ran upstairs again, looked into the mirror dappled by age, put up her hair and secured it with a jewelled pin from the tortoiseshell box on the dressing table. Before leaving, she rubbed the llama's tailbone for good luck and crunched her way across the pigeon droppings on the drawbridge.

As she waited on the church steps, the châtelaine noticed Madame Ladoucette approaching on the other side of the street. Émilie Fraisse had not seen her since her return. But the old woman failed to hear her greeting and the châtelaine watched her slow crane-legged procession, wondering what the red splat marks were on the back of her green dress, and why she was being followed by a shuffling crowd of pigeons, which had grown morbidly obese since forgetting how to fly.

Soon after Madame Ladoucette came Fabrice Ribou sporting an unfathomable haircut, and for a moment Émilie Fraisse thought that it was he she was waiting for. But the bar owner simply returned her greeting, cursed the heat and continued on his way. She then spotted Denise Vigier coming from the other direction wearing a pink dressing gown and matching slippers, a white towel slung over one shoulder. Several minutes later, Didier Lapierre drove up and parked underneath one of the lime trees. Émilie Fraisse couldn't help but notice that his haircut was equally as baffling as that of the bar owner, and wondered whether Guillaume Ladoucette had been forced to give up his job because he had lost his discerning barber's eye. She was just about to get up to greet him, assuming that he was her match, when the carpenter approached the village noticeboard outside the church, pinned something on to it and walked back to his car.

Once he was out of sight, Émilie Fraisse immediately got up to inspect it. 'CLANDESTINE COMMITTEE AGAINST THE MUNICIPAL SHOWER' it read. Underneath were detailed the date and time of the next meeting, as well as the location. It was signed 'Yves Lévèque, Chairman.'

The dentist had formed the group partly out of residual bitterness that his efforts to pass off the village as a town in order to secure a municipal swimming pool had failed. Having now to appear in public in his pyjamas was one humiliation too many. Twenty-seven people attended the first meeting held at the old washing place by the Belle, a square of shallow water on the edge of the river where women traded gossip until running water arrived in 1967. Sitting under the tiled pitched roof, with the scent of wild mint fluttering through the open sides, it took over an hour to sort out the squabbles over code names. Yves Lévèque then declared that it was time for the *pot d'amitié*, but when he turned to Fabrice Ribou, the bar owner confessed that he had forgotten the drink. Ordered back to the bar for four bottles of red and four of rosé, the chairman then asked Denise Vigier to fetch some plastic cups from her shop. But she insisted on being paid for them, and only started walking down the riverbank to fetch them after the dentist assured her she would be reimbursed from committee funds. Sandrine Fournier then turned to the chairman and enquired: 'What committee funds?' It was then that Yves Lévèque asked for a donation of five euros each 'to further the cause'. The protests were not only loud, but impolite. And by the time they reconvened at the washing place the following week, numbers were already down by half.

Bored of tracing designs in the ground with the stiffened lizard, Émilie Fraisse got to her feet to look round the twelfth-century church. She pushed against the studded, wizened door and immediately inhaled incense laced with mould spores. Descending the stone steps into the crypt, she was surprised to see that the bones of priests who had once served in the church, which had been desecrated during the Revolution, were still scattered on the floor. Back upstairs, where all traces of beauty had been plundered during the same raids, she contented herself with admiring the flourishing emerald fungus which was crawling up to the stations of the cross.

Startled by the viciousness of the sun when she came out, the châtelaine didn't immediately recognize the person who was standing with his back to her on the steps. It was not until he turned round that she saw that it was Gilbert Dubuisson the postman. Seizing the chance to ask him about a package she was expecting, the châtelaine approached him. It was then that she noticed his unusually smart trousers and a fresh blob of shaving foam the size of a lark's egg behind his ear lobe, and she suddenly realized that the man she had been waiting for was him. The postman, who looked momentarily taken aback, then kissed her on both cheeks. They then worked out that during the time that she had lived away from Amour-sur-Belle, they had seen each other at three weddings, one cancelled funeral and two annual fêtes in honour of the village patron saint, whose name no one could remember.

'Don't worry, I'll fill you in on what's been going on,' said Gilbert Dubuisson, walking towards his car underneath one of the lime trees and opening the passenger door.

As they drove out of the village Émilie Fraisse looked at the memorial to the *Three Victims of the Barbarous Germans* and asked how Madame Serre was. The postman replied that the old woman still lived next door to Guillaume Ladoucette, and always attended the annual commemoration service at the memorial, as did most of the villagers. He then reminded Émilie Fraisse of how the three villagers had been killed, even though she could never have forgotten. There was one detail, however, that he didn't tell the châtelaine because neither he nor anyone else outside the Serre family was aware of it. Unlike the other two men who were shot in Amour-sur-Belle by a group of young German soldiers on 19 June 1944, Madame Serre's twin had never been a member of the Resistance. Too fearful of becoming a *maquisard*, and too young to be conscripted, Christophe Serre slept in one of the troglodyte caves behind the village during the day and worked on the family's farm at night to ensure that they had something to eat. It was never known who had whispered to the enemy that he had been involved in subversive activities, but their reward of a plundered ham was guaranteed. On one of the rare occasions that Christophe Serre ventured into the village during daylight, the young German soldiers spotted him talking to the two Resistance members they had come in search of. All three were felled in an instant by a bullet in the head.

For a while Émilie Fraisse sat in silence as she thought of the terrible fate of Madame Serre's twin, and the savagery of the perpetrators, whom the village had never forgiven. Her mind then turned to the nice German tourist who had visited the château and she found that it was too much to comprehend.

'Do you remember the mobile butcher?' asked the postman as they turned left at Brantôme and passed through the avenue of plane trees.

'Didn't he die in a car accident?' asked Émilie Fraisse.

'Oh, I don't mean Pierre-Albert Robert, but yes he did, poor soul. It was me who found his car in the ditch at the side of the road. Shocking business. Anyway, watch out for his replacement. They took his licence away for two months earlier this year because he was putting *trompettes-de-la-mort* mushrooms in his pâté and trying to pass them off as truffles.'

As they passed along the flat-bottomed green valley, the postman then asked: 'Remember where we were standing on the church steps?'

'Yes,' Émilie Fraisse replied.

'They found Patrice Baudin's spectacles in the guttering above,' continued Gilbert Dubuisson. 'Remember him, the pharmacist? He became a vegetarian after eating Guillaume Ladoucette's cassoulet, although the matchmaker claims he must have joined a secret cult for his mind to have become so horribly twisted. Anyway, Patrice Baudin blew away during the mini-tornado and Modeste Simon hasn't spoken since. Fancied him rotten. Some say she's even hired a private detective to try and find him. But I keep telling them that if she has, the company must use plain envelopes. Of course, Guillaume Ladoucette uses his disappearance as yet more evidence for his ridiculous cult theory. But for God's sake don't mention anything to do with pharmacies, severe weather or sudden weight loss the next time you see him as you'll only get him started.'

Eventually, they reached Saint-Jean-de-Côle and found a parking space on the side of the road, which was unheard of. They walked up the narrow lane that led to the château, across which were strung garlands of tangerine and red paper flowers made in the village hall for the past fortnight by locals thrilled by the recent scandal involving the mayor. When they stopped at the table to pay, Émilie Fraisse got out her purse, but Gilbert Dubuisson politely told her to put it away and that the pleasure was all his. After the back of their hands were stamped with a dark blue tulip, they continued up the narrow lane, past the man with the beard selling honey and candles, and stopped to look at the first flower stall. As they gazed at the battalion of geraniums and pelargoniums in astonishing colours lined up on the ground with the precision of a Roman army, the postman admitted to taking considerable pride in his window boxes. He then pointed out the 'Madame Nonin' pelargoniums with their red petals and pink and white centres, and said that he found them most pleasing. Émilie Fraisse, who agreed that they were indeed charming, then pointed to the ones in front, say-ing she particularly liked their star-shaped leaves, which Gilbert Dubuisson correctly identified as 'Distinction'. They then both agreed that you should never buy anything from the first stall you come across, and that you should look around first. But as they left, the postman glanced longingly at the 'Madame Nonin' pelargoniums and the châtelaine glanced longingly at the 'Distinctions', and they considered the worrisome prospect of the stallholder selling out. Within moments, there were two carrier bags of plants behind the

170

counter already paid for to be picked up on their way out.

Bonded by the warmth of an early purchase, they turned right at the end of the narrow lane. Émilie Fraisse instinctively headed towards the stall selling laurels as Guillaume Ladoucette had told her that her match had a particular liking for trees. But when she mentioned this to the postman, he was at an utter loss as to what the matchmaker could have meant.

Stopping for a moment in the main square, they looked at the splendid Château de la Marthonie. The words *monument historique* were hand-painted on the sign in case anyone doubted its fifteenth-century provenance. They gazed at the marvellous pointed roofs, which clearly did not leak, and took in the floral scented air, which carried no hint of bat droppings.

They then strolled into the open market hall with its ancient wooden pillars and steep tiled roof, but quickly came out, agreeing that the striped petunias were too vulgar for their taste. Instead, they stood and looked at the church behind it and admired the hideousness of the monsters, wrestlers and fearsome beasts carved in the stone beneath the eaves.

As they approached the main street, the postman pointed towards the roofs of the pastel colour houses and asked whether they were the ones referred to as 'the finest in the Périgord Vert'. And when the châtelaine replied that she thought they had been called 'the finest in France', the postman said: 'I'm sure you're right.'

Wandering along the stalls, they stopped to gaze at the pepper plants, and when Émilie Fraisse read out their curious names – Bulgarian Carrot, Hungarian Hot Wax, Banana Early Sweet and Jamaican Hot Chocolate – Gilbert Dubuisson asked her where she had mastered her English.

Shortly afterwards, they came across a collection of tiny flowered geraniums underneath a vast umbrella, with a small hand-written sign saying 'Touch and Smell!' Émilie Fraisse stretched out a hand, rubbed one of the leaves and brought her fingers to her nose. 'It smells of walnuts!' she exclaimed.

The postman then rubbed the leaves of another plant, and smelt his fingers. 'It smells of eucalyptus!' he said.

She then rubbed the leaves of another plant. 'It smells of carrots! How funny,' she remarked.

As they crossed the Gothic humpback bridge over the river Côle, with its bulbous cobbles the colour of bruises, the postman took the châtelaine's arm lest she tripped. But there was nothing much to see on the other side since the succulents failed to interest either of them, and when they made their way back over the bridge, Émilie Fraisse took Gilbert Dubuisson's arm again when it was offered.

'Shall we have something to drink?' suggested the postman.

'What a good idea,' replied the châtelaine, and they sat down at the bar opposite the rose-seller with her butter-scotch, vanilla, raspberry ripple, marmalade and cassis blooms.

Gilbert Dubuisson returned with a bottle of red Saint-Jean-de-Côle, and when they had filled their glasses, they looked around and suddenly noticed how busy it was.

Émilie Fraisse then asked Gilbert Dubuisson about his job, and he told her how much pleasure it gave him. While it meant having to get up early, it left him the rest of the day to please himself. His vines took up a fair bit of his time, he added, and then, of course, he felt morally obliged to pop in to see Guillaume Ladoucette in his shop opposite as he seemed so lonely, and it was only fair that someone should provide him with a little bit of conversation during the day.

'He's lonely?' Émilie Fraisse asked.

'Sometimes I look in the window and he's staring into space and I know he's just willing me to come in for a chat. It's not always convenient, of course, but you have to think of others.'

'And is he lonely in his personal life?' she asked.

'Well, he's had his share of interest, but, like the rest of us, he just hasn't met the right one, which is a bit ironic considering he's set himself up as a matchmaker. But he obviously saw a gap in the market and went for it.'

'And what about you, Gilbert? Have you ever found love?'

'Once,' he said. 'But it was a long time ago.'

The postman refilled their glasses and, for the first time ever, found himself recounting the true story of Sandrine Fournier the mushroom poisoner. He had loved her throughout school, he explained, and her lack of popularity only inflamed his passion, because in some curious way he thought she was keeping herself for him. It was when she took him to the old hunters' shack one afternoon several years after they had both left school that he discovered she hadn't kept herself for him at all. But he was so grateful he didn't care. She taught him things there that he didn't even know existed, and while he often felt defeated by her energy, he never complained. She shared with him the best places in the woods to find mushrooms and sometimes they would go out with a little frying pan and some butter and cook their harvest right there amongst the trees. But Gilbert Dubuisson feared her carnal appetite was too much for one man to satisfy, and he let her go, convinced she would venture elsewhere. Still bearing a full head of hair, he managed to capture the attention of Fabrice Ribou's younger sister, Yvette. Such was Sandrine's jealousy that when Yvette Ribou's father next begged her to tell him the best place in the woods to find ceps, she told him that it was by the hunters' shack as she knew that he would find his daughter there in a state of undress with Gilbert Dubuisson and put a stop to the relationship. But when the young couple heard him coming, they hid underneath the blanket which had covered generations of illicit lovers. As it was, Monsieur Ribou was far too taken with what he thought were fungal delights to bother looking inside. After a while, Gilbert Dubuisson looked out of the broken window to see who it was, and saw him picking some mushrooms which he instantly recognized as being poisonous. Fearful of being discovered with the man's daughter, he silently pulled the stained blanket back over his head. When the postman heard that Monsieur Ribou had taken ill, it was he who rushed the offending omelette to the hospital. But it was too late. Fabrice Ribou blamed Sandrine Fournier for his death as it was easier than acknowledging his father's stupidity, and banned her from his bar. Despite his pleas, the assistant ambulant fishmonger never took Gilbert Dubuisson back. Nor, indeed, would she serve him from the fish van again whenever he came for his weekly prawns, as she had suddenly developed an allergy to shellfish.

'Oh Gilbert, I am sorry,' said Émilie Fraisse when he finished his story.

'And now, from what I understand, she's seeing the dentist. Someone spotted them in Brantôme together. Apparently they were all over each other.' The postman continued to look ahead of him for a moment, then patted the châtelaine's arm and said: 'But that's all in the past. I must say, I've had a marvellous time.'

'So have I,' agreed Émilie Fraisse.

When they had finished the bottle, they both agreed that it was time to go. 'I'll just be a minute,' said the postman, suddenly getting up. When he returned, he was carrying a white plastic bag, which he presented to Émilie Fraisse with the words: 'A little gift.' She looked inside and, immediately recognizing what it was, rubbed the plant's leaves, brought her fingers to her nose and breathed in the aroma of carrot.

It was then that Émilie Fraisse decided to pass on the little bit of gossip she'd learnt that morning from Guillaume Ladoucette. 'You know how they normally hold the flower festival at the beginning of May?' she said as they stopped to pick up their purchases on the way back to the car. 'Well, they had to delay it by a couple of weeks because the mayor got his hand trapped inside a Venus flytrap.' She paused before adding: 'They had to cut his wrist off.'

12

UNFORTUNATELY FOR LISETTE ROBERT IT WAS MADAME Ladoucette who first noticed that there was no hot water in the municipal shower. The old woman came across the contraption during one of her daily meanders. Her son had never bothered to explain its arrival because of her sudden and obstinate preference for washing in a cauldron. Her curiosity tweaked, she circled the cubicle twice and then tried the door, which opened immediately. After peering around, she stepped inside and invited her feathered shadow to join her. Once satisfied that everyone was aboard, she closed the door. Forty-seven minutes later, once the novelty had worn off, Madame Ladoucette looked around her and decided to turn what appeared to be a handle. Much to her amusement, she suddenly found herself drenched in water. Her companions, however, were not so amused. Such was the violence of the commotion, the door suddenly burst open and the expelled participants quickly left the scene.

When the old woman was subsequently spotted wandering

around the village, her sopping blue dress clinging to her crane's legs and still commanding bosom, a crew of soggy birds trailing in her wake, everyone naturally assumed that she had been up to her usual tricks. Several popped their heads around the door of Heart's Desire and said: 'Your mother's been in the Belle again.' When Guillaume Ladoucette eventually found her, he managed to corral her behind the nectarine display outside the grocer's and took her home to get dry. After pouring out the water from her black shoes into the sink, he slipped out to pick some honesty to replenish the vase by her bed, knowing that his mother took comfort in the belief that the plant protected against everything that hovered over the surface of still waters and galloped with cleft hooves. As he arranged the stems of flat green seedpods, he questioned again his decision to move her into the small house in the centre of the village, in the hope that it would be easier for her to manage and provide fewer opportunities for mischief. But whenever he dared mention the retirement home in Brantôme, with its cheery staff and benches in the sun where she could sit and watch the ducks swimming in the Dronne, she instantly regained all lucidity and squawked: 'Not on your nelly.'

Once dry and on the streets again, everyone naturally assumed that Madame Ladoucette's repeated comments about the temperature of water referred to that of the river. It was not until several hours later when Lisette Robert turned on the shower, after first having to remove seven grey feathers and a large amount of black and white droppings discharged in fright, that news of the absence of hot water spread. The uproar was instant and the council received 127 calls about a matter concerning a population of just thirty-three, the vast majority of which were from the Clandestine Committee against the Municipal Shower putting on an array of accents to boost the number of complaints.

As soon as Guillaume Ladoucette had made sure that his

mother was safe and dry, he hurried back to Heart's Desire as fast as a pair of supermarket leather sandals would permit, anxious to hear how Émilie Fraisse and Gilbert Dubuisson had fared in Saint-Jean-de-Côle. By the time he opened the shop door again, there were two pieces of correspondence on the doormat, one of which was another demand for payment from the signwriter, and the second a letter clearly marked for the house next door. The mistake immediately recalled the clot of a postman, who had been on the matchmaker's mind to such an extent the day before that he had gone to the Romanesque church twice to distract himself. The tiny congregation was so surprised at his appearance, it immediately assumed that he must have sinned in the most heinous of fashions and spent most of the service wondering what he had done, and with whom. Gilbert Dubuisson then followed him into his dreams, where the postman strode around in his heavy boots all night, with Émilie Fraisse on his arm wearing an antique wedding gown which appeared to have been shorn off at the knees.

Once back at work, the matchmaker found that he was unable to sit still on the swivel chair, and, despite his headache from the weight of the postman's footwear, immediately set about cleaning the place. As he dusted his framed certificate from the Périgord Academy of Master Barbers, he imagined Gilbert Dubuisson's unremitting conversation, which would have surely driven Émilie Fraisse to distraction. As he dusted the four ornate blue and white coffee bowls he had placed upside down along the huge stone chimney breast to cheer the place up, he thought of the man's obsession with his window boxes, which would surely have bored her as rigid as a week-old corpse. Wiping the bars of the old spit on to which ancient soot still fell, he thought of the man's despicable habit of urinating behind the nearest tree when caught short on his rounds, and was convinced that his bladder would have failed him at some stage. Certain that their time together would have been a disaster, he then plumped up the cushion with the hand-embroidered radish, which sent a tiny cloud of hair shards pirouetting into an arrow of sunlight coming in from the window. After decades of barbering, the trimmings were a continual presence despite Guillaume Ladoucette's fastidious cleaning. Once the floor was swept, he made himself a cup of coffee, sat down at his desk and picked up the phone to take down the messages left while he was out. But there were none.

In his favourite short-sleeved light-blue shirt, which he hoped camouflaged the winter plumage that he had still failed to shed, the matchmaker waited for Émilie Fraisse. When she failed to arrive, he reached into his briefcase and pulled out a bottle of mineral water. After pouring himself a glass, he swallowed two of the headache tablets he kept in his bottom right-hand drawer next to the jar of cherry stalks which were an excellent diuretic. He then moved his feet to a cooler patch of tiles below the desk.

In an effort to cheer himself up, Guillaume Ladoucette slowly pulled open the narrow drawer above his stomach. Peering down, he admired the selection of pens all neatly lined up in their own little compartment, as well as his fine collection of multi-coloured plastic bands split into two according to colour – red and green on the right, and yellow and blue on the left. Just as he was about to move the stapler to another compartment the door opened. It was Émilie Fraisse.

Sunset-pink, he closed the drawer, crawled his toes back inside his supermarket leather sandals, then ushered her towards the chair with the peeling marquetry. While he was making coffee, his embarrassment left him as he began to smell the delicious news upon which he was about to feast.

'So!' he said, passing her a cup and getting himself comfortable on the swivel chair. 'How did it go? Gilbert

Dubuisson is such a charming fellow, I expect you had a marvellous time.'

'We did indeed,' replied Émilie Fraisse, smiling.

'You did?' asked the matchmaker, horrified.

'Yes, I can't thank you enough. And he was exactly as you described him – really chatty and we caught up on old times and he told me all about what's been going on.'

'Not too talkative?'

'No! Between you and me my husband and I didn't talk very much in the end, so it's refreshing to be with someone who has something to say.'

'I expect he told you at considerable length about his window boxes?' he enquired.

'Oh, yes!' Émilie Fraisse then turned round and pointed to the postman's house. 'See those flowers with the pretty red petals – aren't they lovely? We bought them together at Saint-Jean-de-Côle.'

Panic rising, the matchmaker slowly followed the sage-green gaze.

'He didn't happen to dash off suddenly at any time, did he?' he asked. 'Because if he did I can explain precisely what he was doing.'

The châtelaine stopped for a moment to think.

'Yes, now that you come to mention it, he did,' she said. 'We were sitting having a drink in the bar next to the plane trees—'

'There's just no hope for the man—' started Guillaume Ladoucette.

'And he nipped off and came back with a lovely geranium with leaves that smelt of carrots for me as it had made me laugh. Wasn't that lovely!'

'Well, I expect it's too early to say whether you'll be seeing each other again,' said the matchmaker, reaching into his top left-hand drawer for his file of customers. 'Maybe we should set you up with someone else in the meantime.'

'Oh, we've already arranged something. He's coming round to the château for dinner. He wants to see my heirloom vegetables.'

'I didn't know you grew heirloom vegetables,' whispered Guillaume Ladoucette from underneath the stone that had rolled on to him and crushed him.

'Oh yes, I've got quite a collection. Gilbert's particularly interested in the white carrots. Anyway, I'd better go. I wouldn't want to take up any more of your time and you never know, there might be a visitor wanting a tour. I just wanted you to know that everything went splendidly and to thank you.'

Émilie Fraisse, who appeared to be wearing an antique gown of deep nutmeg shorn off at the knees, and a pale pink rose in the back of her hair where something sparkled, got up to leave.

'What a lovely rose,' was all that Guillaume Ladoucette could think of to say to delay her.

'Thank you. Gilbert left it for me on the drawbridge this morning with a little note explaining that it was from his garden. Do smell it. I've never known anything like it.'

Guillaume Ladoucette slowly got up and approached Émilie Fraisse. He stood behind her and leant in on the pretext of smelling the rose, hoping instead to draw in the exotic scent of her bare neck. But the flower's spicy aroma was too overpowering. And it was only as she walked out that he remembered the flower's name, and his horror was complete: Bride's Bouquet.

After closing the door, the matchmaker returned to the swivel chair. He sat with his chin in his hands staring out on to the street, but whenever he tried to look elsewhere, his eyes kept returning to the six 'Madame Nonin' pelargoniums in the window boxes opposite. He then opened the narrow drawer with the compartments, but it offered no comfort. Reaching down to his briefcase, he took out a red net bag of mini *saucissons* and tore it open. By the time they were finished he hadn't tasted one of them. He slipped his hand again into his briefcase, brought out the *Lunar Gardener* magazine and started to flick through it. But he was not rewarded with the slightest bit of pride upon noticing that his letter had been printed correcting a statement from the previous month's edition that peas should be planted during a waning moon, which he had pointed out would make them susceptible to a monstrous onslaught of worms.

Unable to bear the torturous sight of the postman's pelargoniums any longer, the matchmaker decided that his day's work was over, despite the fact that it was not yet even lunchtime. Not bothering to lock the shop, he walked home, oblivious to the full force of the sun's arsenal. He muttered: 'Hello,' to Madame Serre, who was sitting outside her house like a sentinel, but forgot to ask her whether she needed anything. Instinctively, he opened the fridge, though his appetite eluded him. After fetching what was needed from his potager, he prepared himself a sorrel omelette and tomato salad, which he ate, oblivious to its delights, at the kitchen table so as not to be tormented by the sight of the roses growing against the garden wall.

After washing up, he returned to the hard-backed kitchen chair, where he sat for almost two hours, his arms resting on the table, listening to the ticking of the clock on the sitting-room mantelpiece that had driven one of his ancestors to suicide. As he sat, the seeds of despair took root and started to flourish. And when he noticed a ginger feather sticking out of the butter dish next to the radio, so overgrown was his spirit that it failed to stir with anger.

It wasn't until he got up to fetch himself a glass of water and felt the second demand for payment from the signwriter in his pocket that he decided to return to Heart's Desire before he ruined that too.

*

Jean-François Lafforest assumed he was cured when he arrived at Amour-sur-Belle that afternoon with his shoes still clean. For the first time he had taken some pleasure in the journey, remembering the kind châtelaine who had slipped a jar of black radish jam into his briefcase. He thought about the sixteenth-century château owner who had sent love notes down the Belle in the shape of tiny boats, and the *pisé* floor he had had installed to be closer to his love. He thought of the talented horse which could predict the weather, and the shabby footstool which was all that remained of it. And he thought about the house he would one day buy with a garden big enough to erect a greenhouse like the English had, which he would fill with orchids in impossible colours.

He was spotted as soon as he parked and, within moments, an uppity crowd had formed. It followed him to the place du Marché and, as he walked, he drew his soft leather briefcase closer to his fleshy stomach. Once at the cubicle, he circled it several times inspecting it from every angle. He then turned on the shower and put his hand in the spray. When he asked to speak to the villager who had discovered the problem, Lisette Robert was called for. But the midwife was attending a delivery and it was another three hours before she was seen parking outside her house and received her immediate summons. By the time she arrived, Fabrice Ribou had brought over some of his bar chairs, arranged them in a grandstand formation around the cubicle and was selling drinks to the crowd. Lisette Robert, whose figure, both the men and women noticed, curved more gracefully than the Belle, was then asked to explain to the man from the council what had happened. She recounted the fact that the water had been cold from the moment she had turned it on, and included the detail of the seven feathers and black-and-white droppings. Jean-François Lafforest listened intently, declared the ornithological findings irrelevant and picked up his briefcase.

'So what's wrong with it?' asked Yves Lévèque, chairman of the Clandestine Committee against the Municipal Shower.

'There appears to be no hot water,' said the man from the council.

'We know that, that's why we called you out,' the dentist replied.

'There's nothing I can do, I'll have to get someone on to it.'

'Why did you bother coming out if there's nothing you can do?' asked Denise Vigier the grocer.

'I had to check first that there was no hot water,' replied Jean-François Lafforest, fiddling with one of the buckles on his briefcase.

'Did you think we were making it up?' asked Monsieur Moreau, who had been stirred from his contemplation of the ants in the hope of seeing Madame Ladoucette's still-commanding bosom in a wet dress again.

'Not at all,' replied the man from the council.

'He thought we were making it up!' said Henri Rousseau, fiddling with the hearing aid that he didn't need.

'I did not!' insisted Jean-François Lafforest.

'So what are you going to do about it?' asked Didier Lapierre the carpenter. 'If we have to suffer the indignity of walking around the streets in our pyjamas, you can at least pay us the courtesy of providing us with hot water.'

'I'm going to get someone to sort it out,' said Jean-François Lafforest. 'You'll just have to put up with it for the moment, I'm afraid.'

'Put up with it?' exclaimed the dentist. 'We're not going to endure cold showers while you try and sort it out. It could take months at the rate you lot move. We'll have to go back to having baths in the meantime.'

'I'm sorry. That's not an option. The fine will still stand,' said the man from the council uneasily.

'The fine will still stand?' repeated Yves Lévèque, dumb-founded. But by then the man with the trousers that didn't quite fit had already backed his way out of the chairs and fled for the nearest field to discharge the half-digested remains of a *merguez* sausage.

It took considerable time for the crowd to dispel as Fabrice Ribou prolonged the post-mortem by coming up with as many theorems, postulations and untruths as possible to increase his takings.

Once the place du Marché was empty again, Lisette Robert returned to the municipal shower. She flinched under the stream of cold water, and when she left, checked twice that she hadn't left her new bottle of shampoo behind. Walking home, she was grateful for the continued assault from the sun, which had yet to lay down its weapons for the day, and, as she passed Monsieur Moreau, who was back on the bench, poked him to see whether he was dead or asleep.

Standing in front of her wardrobe, she tugged at the door handles that always stuck and sent the glass bottles on her dressing table trembling when they finally opened. Reaching in, she took down her new periwinkle-blue frock. She had forced herself to buy it against her instinct, acquired in the days when her mother dressed her, which attracted her to the most repellent of colours. Stepping into it, she wondered whether the man she was going to meet would like it. She then combed her rivulets of damp hair into which her husband whispered things she never believed and went downstairs. After pouring herself a glass of *pineau*, which she kept in the house for Guillaume Ladoucette, she took it outside and sat on the faded red sofa against the back of the house underneath the vine-strangled trellis. Taking a sip, she wondered how on earth the matchmaker could like the sweet ruby liquid so much. She persevered, nevertheless, and, as she watched the day finally lose its bloody battle with the evening, she thought of the man she hoped he had set her up with, imagining the touch of his hand and the smell of his chest. But most of all, she tried to imagine herself ever loving him as much as her husband. When, at last, it was time to meet her mystery suitor, Lisette Robert brought her glass back inside and shut the door. And on her way out, she looked in the mirror in the hallway and saw the reflection of a truffling pig.

Arriving at the Bar Saint-Jus, the midwife was surprised to find that no one was waiting outside. Unsure of what to do, she opened the door and looked quickly around. Walking up to the bar, she ordered a kir, then sat down with her glass at an empty table in the window. She pulled towards her a copy of the *Sud Ouest*, plumped up from having been read so many times, and looked at the front page. Having taken none of it in, she then turned the page and, as she did so, scanned the room again. Assuming that her match was late, she continued with her feigned absorption. As she turned another page, she heard the sound of the chair opposite her being pulled back. She looked up to see Marcel Coussy, the farmer.

'Hello, Marcel, how are you?' she asked.

'Fine thanks, how are you?'

'Very well, thanks. I hope you don't mind, but I'm actually waiting for someone.'

'I know,' he replied.

'You know?'

'Yes. It's me.'

Lisette Robert tried to match the image the matchmaker had painted of the solvent bachelor with his own transport and a love for the outdoors with the man who was now sitting down in front of her. While the farmer may well have been a bachelor, it was clear to most that the reason he had reached his eighty-second year without having married was because no woman would have tolerated his reluctance to bathe. While it was true that he was solvent, it was also well known that he preferred the familiar comfort of misery than luxury. And as for his own transport, the only vehicles Marcel Coussy ever bought were tractors.

As she took another sip, Lisette Robert noticed that the elderly farmer had buffed himself up to a state of refinement normally only witnessed on Christmas Day. He had clearly washed, a process not usually endured by the farmer unless he was in hospital recovering from a fall from his tractor, on account of the fact that he didn't possess a bathroom. His habit of defecating in his fields could be witnessed by anyone unfortunate enough to be looking in that direction at the time. He was also clearly wearing shoes, rather than his work slippers, as the midwife could hear the tapping of his soles on the floor below the table. And it appeared that the wig many claimed he wore had recently been sent to the dry-cleaner's.

Unsure of what to say, Lisette Robert asked after his ginger Limousin cows, in particular why they winked whenever people passed. 'Because they're happy,' he replied. 'Like me.' She then asked after his dog, an equally scruffy affair (though with its own hair), which was skilled in the art of rounding up geese and had won numerous trophies. Next she complimented him on his artichokes, which had not only looked beautiful, but tasted outstanding. The farmer answered distractedly, so taken was he by the vision before him. Then, for several moments, they stared at each other.

'Would you like a drink?' Lisette Robert suddenly asked to rebuff the silence.

'I'll get them. Same again?' asked Marcel Coussy.

'Yes, please,' replied the midwife. But by the time the farmer returned from the bar, Lisette Robert was nowhere to be found.

When she returned home, she immediately phoned the matchmaker. Guillaume Ladoucette was already in bed asleep, the persistent breeze from the bedroom window curling round his considerable japonicas. Defenceless after having been pulled so violently from his dreams, he agreed to meet her at once at Heart's Desire. As he dressed, he tried to think what on earth could be wrong, and as he slipped his hairy toes into his supermarket sandals, suddenly realized.

The midwife was already waiting for him by the time he arrived. She said nothing as he opened the door. But as soon as they were inside and the door was closed behind them again, she demanded: 'Guillaume, how could you?'

'Please, take a seat,' he said, ushering her towards the chair with the peeling marquetry. 'Glass of wine? Or perhaps a little something to eat? I've got a spare set of keys to the bakery. I could nip round and get us a couple of *choux Chantilly*, perhaps. I'm sure Stéphane Jollis won't mind.'

'Guillaume, stop trying to divert my attention with little cakes.'

The matchmaker walked round the desk with the ink stain, sat down on his swivel chair and held up his hands. 'What was I supposed to do?' he asked. 'He came in here, signed up for our Unrivalled Gold Service and then asked to be introduced to you. I could hardly say, "No, you're too old and too malodorous, you don't stand a chance." He's an old customer of mine. And anyway, he doesn't know how ugly he is and you don't know how beautiful you are. You have that in common. It could have worked.'

Lisette Robert continued looking at him in silence.

'I did my best with him,' insisted the matchmaker. 'As you've probably noticed from the ledger, he hasn't used the municipal shower once since it's been installed. A friend of mine in Nontron lent me his bath. We soaked him for three days. And I got that wig of his sorted out. It was in an awful state.'

'He didn't even have anything to talk about!'

'That shouldn't have happened,' replied the matchmaker frowning. 'I told him plenty of interesting things to say. We had practice sessions while he was in the bath. He had it word perfect. He must have forgotten in the stress of the moment. You can't blame him for that.'

'I can't understand why we had to have a drink in the

Bar Saint-Jus, either. Everyone was looking. I thought we were going to meet outside and then go somewhere else.'

'Well, that was the plan. He must have kept you there to show you off, the scoundrel.'

Lisette Robert remained silent.

'Everyone deserves a chance at love, Lisette,' said the match-maker. 'You can't blame him for trying.'

'I'd bought a new dress and everything.'

'Well, the good news is that it won't go to waste.'

'Why not?'

'I have another Unrivalled Gold Service customer who wishes to be introduced to you.'

'Another one?'

'Yes.'

'I'm not going through that again.'

'Come on, Lisette, it wasn't that bad. Well, it wouldn't have been if Marcel Coussy had stuck to the game plan.'

'Who is it?'

'I can't tell you that.'

'Why not?'

'I'm bound by client confidentiality.'

'What's he like?'

'I'd describe him as a well-built gentleman – he's got a lovely haircut, by the way, not like the horrors some people have around here – with a refined palate. And by that I mean he wouldn't eat the sort of food that tourists do.'

'I don't know, I've already fallen victim to your powers of exaggeration once.'

'Lisette, it was a perfectly accurate description. And you won't have to meet him in the Bar Saint-Jus. It'll be out of Amour-sur-Belle, I promise you.'

'Where?'

'I'll make sure it's one of your favourite places. How's about that?'

'All right. But this is the last one I'm agreeing to, Guillaume

Ladoucette,' said the midwife, getting up from the cushion with the hand-embroidered radish.

After the matchmaker had walked her home, he returned to bed where he lay for several minutes in his usual position on his back, his arms down the sides of his body as if already dead in his coffin. He then switched on his bedside light and took another headache tablet lest the postman elbowed himself back inside his dreams and clattered around in his commodious footwear.

13

MUCH TO HIS DISMAY, GUILLAUME LADOUCETTE ARRIVED AT WORK early. The ruthless temperature of the water meant that he hadn't delayed in the municipal shower, despite the heavenly scented purchase from Périgueux he had slipped into the pocket of his burgundy silk dressing gown before leaving the house to improve his mood. For once he had turned off the water in his own time, without his normally protracted ablutions being interrupted by a series of thunderous knocks on the door followed by cries of 'Get a move on!' Such was his brevity under the water, he even had time to sit down on the short wooden bench in the tiny changing area just inside the door and dry between each of his hairy toes, a luxury he had never enjoyed since the shower's installation and which had made creeping fungus a constant anxiety.

Heart's Desire was the last place he wanted to be, and it wasn't just because of his deafening headache. It was only a matter of time before the postman would breeze in, install himself on the bench with a packet of Petit Beurre Lu biscuits and tell him in torturous detail about his time with Émilie Fraisse at Saint-Jean-de-Côle while showering the place with crumbs. Bending down to pick up a letter on the doormat, the matchmaker was further irritated to find that it had actually been delivered to the correct address, denying him the opportunity to feel superior to the man. He put the electricity bill in the top right-hand drawer of the desk with the ink stain to attend to later and made himself a cup of coffee. After moving the chair with the peeling marquetry so that it obscured the view of the six 'Madame Nonin' pelargoniums, he sat down on his swivel chair, dreading the sound of the door opening.

Several hours later, just as the matchmaker had decided that the red and green elastic bands would actually look better on the left-hand side of the narrow drawer with the compartments, and that the blue and yellow ones would look better on the right, he looked up to see Lisette Robert driving past wearing her new periwinkle-blue dress. Not long afterwards, having changed his mind about the elastic bands and returned them all to their original compartments, he noticed Stéphane Jollis driving past at speed in what was undeniably a new white T-shirt. He got up and stood in the doorway watching the car disappear, hoping that the perpetual breeze would transport his wishes of good luck to his friend.

After more than two hours' deliberation on his swivel chair over what to have for lunch, Guillaume Ladoucette finally settled on pig's trotters, one of the few things he didn't have in the house. If he left work early, the matchmaker reasoned, he could get some from the butcher's in Brantôme before it shut at twelve-thirty. While he was there, he may as well pick up a few things he needed from the pharmacy, he thought. And how could he go to the exquisite town without stopping to have an apéritif in one of the delightful cafés overlooking the Dronne, or indeed a stroll to appreciate the beauty of the abbey and the monks' garden? Having convinced himself that it was time to leave immediately, the matchmaker crawled his toes, which had been cooling on the red tiles, back into his supermarket leather sandals and straightened up the blank piece of paper in front of him. Just as he had got to his feet, the postman opened the door.

'Guillaume, my old friend! I'm so glad I caught you. I've prepared a little lunch to thank you for you know what.'

'That's very kind of you, Gilbert, but I couldn't possibly. I've already got plans.'

'Nonsense! Come on. It's all prepared.'

'Really, I was going to have some pig's trotters . . .'

'Well, you can have them tonight. They'll keep. Talking of trotters, I saw some lovely ones in Brantôme the other day, scattered with tiny slivers of *cornichons*. Come on, shut the door! That's it. I've got so much to tell you. You won't believe how well we got on. I admit I had my doubts when you first set yourself up as a matchmaker – as the whole village did – but it seems you really have a talent for it. Have you seen these? Just look at those leaves. Aren't they beautiful? They're called "Madame Nonin". I bought them at the *floralies* with Émilie Fraisse.'

If the over-sautéed veal in cep sauce and the potatoes under-fried in goose fat weren't painful enough, Guillaume Ladoucette had to endure them while listening to an enumeration of the many virtues of Émilie Fraisse, of which he was all too aware. When that was over the postman asked him whether he had heard the rumour that the council had discovered that the municipal shower's hot-water pipe had been sabotaged. Displaying not the least bit of interest, his guest replied that he had indeed. Although they were alone and indoors, the postman looked over each shoulder, leant forward and whispered that it was without doubt the work of the Clandestine Committee against the Municipal Shower on a highly secret mission. He then sat back again and asked Guillaume Ladoucette what he had heard. After stating that it was very much along the same lines, the matchmaker wiped his moustache, placed his serviette on the table and insisted that he really had to get back to work as he was run off his feet. But it was useless. Lowering his voice to a whisper again, the postman demanded to know the reason why he wasn't a member. Unsatisfied with the reply that he had too much on his plate at the moment, Gilbert Dubuisson then tried to lure him into joining with the promise of a uniform and pin badge, adding that there was always a *pot d'amitié* at their weekly meetings at the old washing place by the edge of the Belle. But Guillaume Ladoucette could not be seduced. The matchmaker got up to leave, but was swiftly headed off in the kitchen and ushered out to the back garden where he was subjected to a guided tour of his host's horticultural triumphs, followed by an even more protracted contemplation of the man's window boxes at the front of the house. Just when Guillaume Ladoucette had thought his torment finally over, and had made it halfway across the road, Gilbert Dubuisson called him back saying that he had forgotten something. The postman momentarily disappeared and returned with a deep-pink flowering plant that he presented to him, saying that he had grown it from seed. Guillaume Ladoucette, who insisted that it was all part of the service and there was really no need, reluctantly accepted it and returned to Heart's Desire, where he placed the unwanted gift in a corner, lacking the will to water it.

When Lisette Robert arrived in the small dusty car park outside the town hall in Bourdeilles, she turned off the engine and looked around. Unable to see anyone fitting the matchmaker's description, she stayed put, resting her hands on the bottom of the steering wheel. But the heat soon drove her out and she headed for the grass and sat down on a bench on the riverbank opposite the château, where she watched the

Dronne sloping by through the feathery willows. After a while she felt the weight of someone sitting down next to her. Much to her surprise, she turned to see Stéphane Jollis without his black tendrils and wearing a new white T-shirt.

'Hello, Lisette,' he said.

'Hello, Stéphane,' she replied.

They kissed each other on each cheek.

'Guillaume said that . . .' started the baker, but stopped.

'That we'd be spending the afternoon together?' asked Lisette Robert.

'Yes, if that's OK with you.'

'Yes, of course.'

'Lisette, I just want to say before we start. About the frogs. It wasn't me.'

'I know,' she replied.

'You know?'

'I never thought it was. It wasn't me who started the rumours.'

The baker looked confused. 'So why haven't we been speaking for all these years?' he asked, his eyes hunting the grass in front of him for the answer. But he failed to find it and nor did Lisette Robert provide one.

Eventually he smiled, his eyebrows soaring like two startled blackbirds. 'Well, it seems like it was all just a silly misunderstanding,' he concluded. 'Never mind. These things happen. Now, I thought we would go to Les Tilleuls for lunch and then visit the château. How does that suit you?'

'I'd love to, I haven't been here for ages,' she replied. But Stéphane Jollis was only half listening because he was trying to work out which of the midwife's curls had brushed his cheek when they kissed.

As they walked over the Gothic bridge, they stopped to admire the seventeenth-century ivy-clad mill house in the shape of a boat in the middle of the river, with its painted staircase leading down to an elegant garden. After taking a moment to watch the shaggy green river weeds being combed flat by the current, they continued up the road, past the *tabac* where the baker would have stopped for cigarettes if he hadn't forgotten that he smoked. Arriving at Les Tilleuls with its awnings and shutters a fresh shade of lichen, they were immediately shown to a table under the lime trees. The matchmaker had had the foresight to make a reservation as the baker, on hearing that Lisette Robert was available that day, had been too preoccupied with chasing the customers from his shop, much to their fury, and ridding his shoes of several decades of flour.

It wasn't long before the waitress brought a basket of bread and took their order for a bottle of rosé, which Stéphane Jollis automatically chose because he had been studying the colour of Lisette Robert's lips. The waitress then returned with the menus, which thrilled them both, but the baker took so long to decide, such was his befuddlement, that she had to come back three times.

When Lisette Robert's Périgourdine salad arrived, the baker complimented her on her choice. And when Stéphane Jollis's salad of three warmed Cabécous arrived, the midwife complimented him on his choice. After offering her the breadbasket, he helped himself to a piece, tore it in half and put it into his mouth. But so caught up was he with the sight of a duck's gizzard slipping into Lisette Robert's mouth that for the first time in his career he failed to evaluate the work of a fellow artisan. He then brought a mouthful of goat's cheese to his lips, but they were still echoing with the touch of Lisette Robert's cheek, and he put down his fork to prolong the heavenly sensation.

When Lisette Robert's pot-roasted pigeon stuffed with figs arrived, the baker complimented her on her choice. And when Stéphane Jollis's pikeperch in Pécharmant sauce arrived, the midwife complimented him on his choice. As they continued chatting, so taken was the baker with the sound of her voice that he was unable to hear a tourist sitting behind him ordering frog's legs. And when he asked the waitress for a bottle of mineral water, he instinctively chose the saltier brand because of the tears of desire he wanted to weep.

After being offered the dessert menu, the baker was in such a state of delirium that he kept forgetting to choose. Lisette Robert, who could wait no longer for her delight, had to tap the menu to get him to concentrate and he instinctively opted for the dish graced by her touch as he could see nothing else.

When Lisette Robert's warm chocolate pudding with vanilla ice cream arrived, the baker complimented her on her choice. And when Stéphane Jolliss's pear sorbet arrived, the midwife complimented him on his choice. But so struck was he by the fit of her periwinkle-blue dress that he forgot a woman's wholly natural desire to try all the desserts on the table, and when she asked: 'Can I have a lick of yours?' he turned a shade of burgundy. When, finally, he understood her true meaning, his hand was trembling to such an extent that he didn't think himself capable of the task. He loaded up his spoon and, clenching up his feet in his shoes that had been cleaned twenty-seven times, he held his breath and started its journey towards her mouth. But when the spoon was finally between her lips, the baker was in such a state of rhapsody that he forgot to pull it out again and the midwife had to recoil her head to disengage it. When Lisette Robert eventually swallowed, her face was such a picture of ecstasy that the overcome baker summoned the waitress and, when he eventually found his voice again, ordered another bowlful.

Once the baker had recovered from the spectacle, he asked for coffee. But when it arrived, so lost was he in Lisette Robert's eyes, which shone like freshly opened chestnuts above the rim of her cup, that he forgot to give her the little chocolate that the waitress had placed in his saucer along with the cubes of sugar. After having unwrapped and eaten hers, Lisette Robert waited patiently for what was the duty of a gentleman. But it never came. When she finally asked him whether he wanted his chocolate, the baker berated himself for having forgotten the natural order of life and immediately offered it to her. And when she returned from the lavatory, she found a further fifty-seven on her place mat as a result of the bribe he had slipped the waitress.

After Stéphane Jollis had paid the bill, they heaved themselves up from their seats and, such was the weight of their delighted stomachs, could only ease their way slowly up the hill towards the château. At the ticket office, the midwife insisted on paying the entrance fees, in gratitude for the fifty-seven tiny chocolates which she had swiftly scooped into her bag. When the ticket-seller handed the baker a guide to what was in fact two châteaux standing next to each other, he immediately passed it to Lisette Robert to hide the fact that he had suddenly lost his ability to read. After admiring the gingko tree, they made their way up the path to the medieval fortress. As they entered the cobbled courtyard, Lisette Robert read out the history of the thirteenth-century château, including its flits between French and English owners during the Hundred Years War. But Stéphane Jollis wasn't listening, such was the racket of his thundering loins. Clueless as to his surroundings, he followed Lisette Robert up the wooden steps to the splendid banqueting hall with its vast inglenook fireplaces. When the midwife went to sit on one of the stone window seats and peered down at the Dronne below, the baker followed her, his shoes squeaking violently on the polished wooden floor as his knees were no longer his own. And when she remarked that the room still smelt of musty old hearths, Stéphane Jollis couldn't reply as flames of desire had singed his voice box.

As the midwife headed to the stone staircase encrusted with pigeon droppings which spiralled up the magnificent octagonal keep over 30 metres high, the baker trotted after her. Pointing to the round wooden trapdoor on the ground, she remarked that the dungeon underneath was thought to have once held members of the Order of the Knights Templar when it was destroyed by the King of France. But Stéphane Jollis didn't look, so imprisoned was he by the sight of the periwinkle-blue bottom swaying up the stone steps in front of him. And when they got up to the roof with its wondrous view of the town and surrounding fields, and Lisette Robert leant up against the crenellations to take it in, the baker had to stop himself throwing himself over them, such was the grip of his mania.

After climbing back down again, they walked the short distance to the Renaissance château, and before they went inside, Lisette Robert read out loud its history. But Stéphane Jollis was unable to hear that its foundations had been laid in the sixteenth century by Jacquette de Montbron, widow of André de Bourdeilles, the ruler of Périgord, where she had hoped to receive Queen Catherine de' Medici in suitable splendour, because such was the commotion of his heart, he had turned stone deaf. They then walked down the hallway admiring the ancient oak chests covered in iron rivets fashioned in the shape of flowers. And when Lisette Robert pointed to the sign stating they were marriage chests, the baker suddenly regained his hearing, which was even more acute than when he had lost it.

As they entered a vaulted room to their left, Lisette Robert consulted her guide and announced that it had once served as a kitchen, but had since been converted into a chapel. And while the midwife was studying the scene of Jonah and the Whale carved on the base of the sixteenth-century Gothic and Renaissance tomb, Stéphane Jollis turned to the crucifix on the wall over the door and uttered the first prayer he had offered in decades. Wandering out, he then found himself in the armoury. The baker was just about to take down the impressive eighteenth-century German sword mounted on the wall to put an end to the unbearable ache in his loins when Lisette Robert walked in and her incredible beauty momentarily shocked him back to his senses.

After climbing the elegant steps to the first floor, Stéphane Jollis gazed at the bizarre wooden cupboards on the landing which were used to store food that was waiting to be checked for poisons by the taster before it was served. But Lisette Robert had disappeared into one of the rooms, and, with no explanation for the furniture's grotesque carvings, half human/half animal, half man/half woman, the baker assumed that desire had driven him mad, when in fact it was the only brief moment during that afternoon that he was in full charge of his faculties.

He then wandered into the ravishing Golden Drawing Room, where he found Lisette Robert. The midwife marvelled at the beams lavishly painted with intoxicating bouquets, sphinxes, family initials and fantastical animals, which continued along the edge of the room. She pointed out the splendid panels on all four walls painted with land-scapes, ruins, parks and châteaux. She led him to the oil paintings of the goddesses Abundance and Flora hanging above the fireplaces at either end of the room, which were thought to have been clothed when modesty came into fashion. She took him to gaze at the five French and English tapestries from the seventeenth and eighteenth centuries, including a glorious hunting scene depicting a mounted François I with his falconers and dogs. But Stéphane Jollis saw none of it as her beauty had distorted his vision.

When they reached the second floor, the baker guided by the musical sound of Lisette Robert's footsteps up the elegant stone staircase, they both turned right into the first room. But neither of them saw the exotic seventeenth-century Spanish strongboxes with their multitude of locked drawers intricately inlaid with ivory, gold leaf and tortoiseshell. Nor did they see the Parisian seventeenth-century tapestry of Renaud and Armide. Nor did they note the large metal Spanish braziers into which hot charcoals were tipped as an additional source of heating. Instead, they both stared, the baker's vision instantly restored, at Charles V's bed on the left-hand side of the room. It wasn't its sumptuous gilding that held their gaze. Nor was it the fact that it had come from the Palace of Saragossa, or indeed that it was called the Bed of Paradise. The reason for their arrest was that they were both suddenly confronted with the memory of the tumultuous night they had spent in bed together during the mini-tornado, which Lisette Robert had hoped would evaporate, but in which Stéphane Jollis had bathed every night since.

Later that afternoon, Guillaume Ladoucette was still staring at his gift from the postman, which hadn't been moved from the corner of the room, when the door opened. It was Lisette Robert.

'Lisette! Come in, come in. Sit down. Glass of wine?' asked the matchmaker, hoping for some good news to raise his spirits, which had slumped to his ankles.

'That would be lovely, thank you,' she replied, sitting on the cushion with the hand-embroidered radish. The match-maker opened his bottom left-hand drawer, poured out a couple of glasses and handed one to the midwife.

'Walnut?' he asked, offering her a bowlful.

'No thanks,' replied the midwife, who had her own to get through.

'Now tell me, Lisette. How did it go in Bourdeilles?'

Lisette Robert told him about their delightful stroll across the Gothic bridge with its view of the little mill house in the shape of a boat in the middle of a river. She told him about their most enjoyable lunch at Les Tilleuls, including the fifty-seven tiny chocolates she had left with in her handbag. She told him about the impressive gingko tree near the kiosk where they had bought the tickets. She told him about the marvellous tour they had taken of the medieval fortress, including their climb up the magnificent octagonal keep over 30 metres high. She told him about the wondrous treasures they had marvelled at in the Renaissance château, including the marriage chests, the tapestry of François I hunting, and the scene from Jonah and the Whale carved on the base of the sixteenth-century tomb. She told him of the ravishing Golden Drawing Room that had thrilled them both with its sumptuous ceiling, and how Jacquette de Montbron had wanted a room of great size and splendour with which to impress Catherine de' Medici, but the queen had never come. She told him how they had stopped on the Gothic bridge on the way back to admire yet again the little mill house in the shape of a boat. And she told him how they had said goodbye to each other in the car park opposite the town hall, both agreeing that they were delighted to be talking to one another once again. But what Lisette Robert didn't tell Guillaume Ladoucette about was the tumultuous night they had spent together during the mini-tornado, brought back with such vividness when they had been confronted by Charles V's bed.

The residents of Amour-sur-Belle had grown so used to the perpetual breeze that few noticed when the wind was up that afternoon in 1999, and by the time it was remarked upon it was blowing with considerable force. Most took it as a novelty and crowded at their windows hoping to see it blow off Marcel Coussy's wig. But no such spectacle ever took place because that morning the old farmer had noticed that, instead of lying down as they did when rain threatened, his cows had suddenly started to walk backwards. A phenomenon that his grandfather had talked about but never witnessed, it frightened the farmer to such an extent that, not trusting his decrepit barn, he locked himself in his house with all his cows. When the crops became uprooted and turnips started to come crashing through their windows, the horrified residents tried to close their shutters. But for some it was too late. The gusts simply got hold of the panels, wrenched them from their brackets and hurled them into the air like playing cards. Lisette Robert had opened her windows hoping that the wind would blow round the house and spare her the job of dusting. It wasn't until she tried to shut them that she realized something much stronger than her was pushing in the opposite direction. As her collection of old foie gras pots left their shelf and came smashing down on to the kitchen floor, and the furniture was shunted from one corner of the house to the other, her immediate thought was for her son, and she thanked God that he had gone away for the weekend. Her second thought was for the only possession that meant something to her: the family piano. At first she sat on top of it, keeping the lid down with her feet. When she travelled with it down the side of the sitting room and the curved salmon roof tiles started rattling like pan lids, Lisette Robert thought she wouldn't be long for this world, and decided she couldn't possibly die having mastered only one tune.

It was her elephantine attempts at learning another that alerted Stéphane Jollis to her plight. He had just closed his shutters, called his parents to bid them farewell, and was sitting in his kitchen drinking a bottle of champagne. The baker recognized the poisonous sound the minute it came down the chimney accompanied by a roar of wind which was perfectly in tune. He had suffered the bothersome noise often enough, but it was an irritation too far in his final hours. Getting to his feet, he put on his jacket and opened the front door.

After more than two decades of utmost dedication to his craft, if anyone in Amour-sur-Belle was sure to remain on their feet in such atrocious conditions it was Stéphane Jollis. Gripping the window ledges and drainpipes, he followed the snatches of music transported by the murderous wind, which tipped near lethal doses of it into his ears. When he saw Lisette Robert through the open window of her sitting room squinting at a musical score, he climbed in, put her over his shoulder and carried her out without a word. Clutching on to the drainpipes and window ledges, he made his way back to his house, her red skirt flapping like a sail above them. After standing Lisette Robert up in his kitchen, he started on the monumental task of heaving the front door shut. Once it was closed, he disappeared into the sitting room, returned dragging the sofa, and pushed it up against the front door as an extra precaution. He then calmly got out another glass, filled it with champagne, offered it to Lisette Robert and sat down.

By the time they had finished the second bottle, the baker had decided it was much more pleasant to die in company, and, grateful for his guest, suggested that they had their final meal together. The midwife thought it a splendid idea and only regretted not having brought a few nibbles with her. Suspecting that they didn't have enough time to cook, the baker emptied the fridge and cupboards, descended into the cellar, then spread his delicacies on the kitchen table, including a confit of goose, several game and rabbit pâtés, a partridge terrine, four wild boar *saucissons* and three cheeses rolled in cinders. They picnicked on the sofa with a couple of baguettes from the bakery, retrieved through the adjoining door, as the wind screamed through the keyhole behind them and a goat somersaulted past the window.

While they were on their seventh bottle of champagne the baker suddenly remembered his manners and announced: 'A woman cannot die without pudding!'

Lisette Robert, who was already well aware of the fact, followed him into the bakery and stood next to him by the counter filled with little cakes. Given first choice, and fearing that time was short, she automatically picked her favourite, a chocolate *religieuse*. First she pulled off the nun's head, bit into it and licked out the chocolate *crème pâtissière*. Once the head was gone, she then started on her plump choux pastry body and sucked out her chocolate innards. When the nun was dispatched, she then turned her attention to a coffee *religieuse* which she put to a similar death. Meanwhile, Stéphane Jollis was enjoying a couple of apricot tartlets.

It was while they were on their ninth bottle of champagne that they both noticed that only one little cake remained. The baker naturally offered the *Paris-Brest* to Lisette Robert, who in turn suggested that they share it. She scooped up some of the cream with her finger, held it to the baker's lips, and watched as he licked it off. He then scooped some up with his finger, held it up to her lips and watched as she licked it off. Within minutes Stéphane Jollis had lifted Lisette Robert on to the counter next to the till. Her legs still wrapped around him, he carried her to the table covered in flour at the back of the bakery where racks of little cakes were in easy reach. He then carried her upstairs and continued to knead her for the rest of the night and such was the height of their ecstasy they thought they had finally reached heaven.

Lisette Robert slipped away the following morning when she was finally able to stand, and discovered that, despite her suspicions, she was not in the land of the living dead after all. After ridding herself of *crème pâtissière*, she drove to Brantôme on discovering that the pharmacy in Amour-sur-Belle was shut and purchased the morning-after pill. Such was the depth of her embarrassment, she was unable to speak to the baker again. He assumed her silence was as a result of the rumours circulating that he had eaten her frogs. Assuming she had started them, the baker then refused to speak to her as his gastronomic honour had been slighted, and before long their only communication was silence. But whenever the villagers shuddered at the memory of the night of the mini-tornado, Stéphane Jollis shuddered with delight.

It was then that Lisette Robert told Guillaume Ladoucette the reason why, despite having had such a marvellous time with the baker, she was unable to pursue a romance with him. 'I love another,' she said.

'Another? So why did you agree to go on these dates?' the matchmaker asked.

'Because I kept hoping it would be him,' she replied meekly.

'Who is it?'

'The man from the council.'

After insisting on signing up there and then for the Unrivalled Gold Service, the midwife got up from the cushion with the hand-embroidered radish and left. But a new customer gave the matchmaker no pleasure, for all he could think of during his walk home was how he was going to break the news to his best friend, particularly after he had cleaned his shoes so thoroughly. Guillaume Ladoucette went straight back to bed hoping slumber would offer an escape from reality. Still awake several hours later, he prayed for sleep – accompanied by the postman if that was what it took – but it failed to show itself. It wasn't until night had faded with the first flushes of morning that he finally sailed away. But less than an hour later, he was battered awake by waves of anxiety. Convinced that he was going to die in his sleep of a broken heart, he went downstairs and for the first time set the table for breakfast as his mother had always done once the family was in bed to encourage their safe passage through the night. But it did nothing to calm him. For, as soon as he went back upstairs and returned to his raft, which was salty with worry, the matchmaker finally remembered the name of the flowering plant the postman had given him: love-lies-bleeding.

14

ÉMILIE FRAISSE WOKE UP IN HER FOUR-POSTER RENAISSANCE BED feeling the natural joy of having slept alone and immediately wondered what the cold, hard object pressing into her ribs was. Reaching down, she pulled it up towards her and instantly recognized the plate still covered with the smears of sautéed kidneys. It wasn't hunger that had driven her naked down the cold stairs with the lamentable repairs to the kitchen in the early hours of the morning, but her excitement over Gilbert Dubuisson coming to dinner, which at such an hour could only be dampened with offal.

Lying in the middle of the ancient white sheet, her hair coursing over the pillow like molten silver, she remembered the marvellous time they had had at the *floralies* and the pleasure it had been to spend time with a man who actually liked to talk. Again, she relived all the courtesies he had shown her: opening the car door, insisting on paying their entrance fees and above all not mentioning the reason why he offered her his arm as they crossed the bridge, whose cobbles they both knew would have felled her in an instant on account of her ridiculous seventeenth-century shoes. Her mind then turned to the wine he had treated them to, which pleased her because she liked a man who appreciated his palate; and she thought of his passion for his window boxes, for which she was grateful as it diverted his attention from such heinous pastimes as watching football. While his baldness had at first surprised her, she reasoned that if he could accept the fact that despair had turned her hair prematurely grey, then she could accept that age had stolen most of his. And she then considered his job as a postman, which was an entirely suitable profession for a future husband. Not only did it serve as a vital community function, but it also kept him moving and less likely to cultivate a stomach the shape of a pumpkin that so many husbands wore as a badge of honour, but which left their wives dead in their beds with disinterest.

It wasn't long, however, before the smell of stale buttered kidneys drove the châtelaine from her sheets, and she padded down the stone spiral steps with the lamentable repairs in her bare feet to the front door. Peering round it hoping not to be caught in a state of undress by an early-morning tourist, she then shot across the courtyard thick with the aroma of fresh bat droppings. As she showered with the garden hosepipe, she debated again whether to stew or bake the eel which had been writhing around inside her bath long enough to have lost its brackishness. And, as she washed her hair, she thought of the poor man from the council who had admired her find, and hoped that he had enjoyed his jar of black radish jam.

Once dressed, she stripped the thick white monogrammed sheets from her bed and replaced them with fresh ones. While she had no intention of allowing Gilbert Dubuisson to slip between them at this early stage, he would undoubtedly want a tour of the château and she wanted everything to look its best. But, despite having rejected the notion, the thought of sharing her bed with a man after so many arid years with her husband remained thrashing around inside her head, thrilling and terrifying her in equal measure. With no more offal in the fridge to calm her, she resorted to her compulsion for cleaning.

After flinging open the heavy shutters on the inside of the windows normally kept closed to protect the few genuine antiques from the bloodsucking sun, she prepared a battalion of cleaning materials and advanced her way with ruthless determination through the rooms. After scrubbing what didn't need scrubbing, she polished what didn't need polishing and then dusted what didn't need dusting. And when she stood back to survey her efforts, what already shone, shone and what already gleamed, gleamed.

When her slender arms ached as if they had been punched, and her knees were the shade of an obstinate raspberry stain, she untied the cord that the previous owner had put across a Regency tapestry armchair to prevent visitors from sitting on it. As she rested, Émilie Fraisse wondered whether she should go and speak to the matchmaker to calm her nerves. She then thought how ironic it was that Guillaume Ladoucette, whom she had grown up assuming she would marry but who hadn't replied to her letter, had introduced her to a man who had spent his life delivering them. Her mind turned to the last time they had seen each other the day before she moved away, and she remembered giving him her precious Nontron hunting knife with its box-wood handle and ancient pokerwork motifs while they were in the woods. And she wondered whether he had kept it.

When her energy returned, she sank her bare feet into an old pair of wellington boots, which were several sizes too big, to protect her legs from the brambles, and slopped her way across the courtyard to the garden. After filling her basket with apricot roses that had been rambling for centuries, she went back inside and arranged them in the vases in the dining room that had once been filled with frightful red and pink plastic flowers. After consulting her recipe book, she returned to the garden to pick the herbs she would need later for supper, and, before closing the door bleached fossil grey by the sun, bent down to rub the leaves of a geranium in a tub by the step. She then smelt her fingers and inhaled the scent of carrots.

On her way to the vaulted kitchen, she stopped in the corridor to admire the florid yellow mould long thought extinct which was slowly turning violet. Like the other patches around the château, its incredible beauty had prevented her cleaning it off. She then sat down on the ancient seat which slid open to hide the salt from the tax collector and thought about how she was going to despatch her eel.

When Guillaume Ladoucette's alarm went off, it wasn't the insufferable noise that brought him to his senses, but the shock that he was still alive. Hauling himself out of bed, he made his way to the bathroom, looked at his reflection in the mirror above the sink and failed to see the slightest hint of a Living Example of either a former barber or a matchmaker. He hoisted the tips of his moustache to a cursory 180 degrees and when they immediately returned to their crumpled position he left them as they were, since he no longer cared. Out of habit, he started performing his morning stretches, but as he did so, suddenly noticed to his horror that his freakish flexibility was such that his elbows now reached the floor. Remembering the words of the doctor who had warned him that his symptoms might become more acute, he immediately wondered whether the undergrowth rampaging across his toes had also worsened, but was too fearful to look. Lacking the will to brave the torturous temperature of the municipal shower, which still hadn't been fixed, he went to get dressed but found himself reaching for the previous day's clothes. As he sat on his bed aiming his arm into a shirt already limp from wear, he remembered the last time he had lost the spirit to put on fresh clothes: the day he had realized he would have to shut his beloved barber shop. And what had he achieved since? Yes, he had set up the matchmaking business and even had some clients. But the only match that had worked so far involved the one woman he wanted for himself.

Guillaume Ladoucette went to work that morning simply because it was easier than having to explain why he hadn't opened. He brought a coffee to his desk with the ink stain and, after drinking it, picked up the plant with the tiny pink heart-shaped flowers that the postman had given him and put it out of sight on the table at the back of the room next to the percolator. Just as he returned to his swivel chair, the door opened. It was Yves Lévèque.

Fortunately for the dentist, the matchmaker didn't have the will to upbraid him again. He had already admonished him once that week when he came to tell him about the odious time he had spent with Sandrine Fournier on the troglodyte tour, and was forced to confess that he had failed to pay for the assistant ambulant fishmonger's entrance fee after Guillaume Ladoucette had threatened to ring the abbey to find out the truth. Such was the matchmaker's infuriation, he had insisted that Yves Lévèque came into Heart's Desire just before he went to meet his next match.

'Are you all right?' enquired the dentist, sitting down. 'You look a little ... how can I put it? Shipwrecked ...'

'I'm fine. Just feeling a little off colour,' Guillaume Ladoucette replied.

'Don't I get offered a cup of coffee this time?'

'Sorry, do excuse me. My mind was elsewhere. Actually, what time is it? I've forgotten my watch.'

'Twenty-seven minutes past nine,' replied the dentist,

wondering what on earth had befallen Guillaume Ladoucette's moustache.

'Bugger coffee,' said the matchmaker, pulling open the bottom left-hand drawer of the desk and taking out a bottle of Pécharmant and two glasses. He filled them both and handed one to his client.

'Walnut?' he asked, offering him a bowl.

'No thanks,' replied the dentist, who had his own to get rid of.

'That's better,' said the matchmaker after taking a sip. 'Now, listen carefully. Which two words are not to come from your lips today?'

'Halvies-halves,' replied the dentist.

'Correct. Or any derivatives thereof. What do you do when standing at a ticket kiosk?'

'Buy a ticket.'

'And?'

'Buy the woman one as well.'

'Correct. What are the other two words you are not permitted to say this afternoon?'

'Dental floss.'

'Correct. Also banned are any dental procedures you think your companion might be in need of. Now, why do you compliment a woman on her dress?'

'Because you're more likely to get it off?'

'No! No! No! Because she has spent hours shopping for it, hours standing in front of the mirror in it and then hours wishing she'd bought the other one.'

'I see.'

'Now, can you think of anything that I could do to help your appearance before you go?'

'No.'

'Nothing at all?'

'Can't think of anything.'

'Sure?'

'Yes.'

'Positive?'

'Yes.'

'Right then. She'll be waiting in the square in front of the château in Jumilhac-le-Grand at ten-forty-five. You'd better get a move on. I've told her you plan to take her gold-panning and she said she'd always wanted a man with a sense of adventure, so you're well ahead already. It'll be so much nicer being out in the sunshine this time, rather than in some musty old caves. I have great hopes for you both. Now, remember to treat her as you would a good cassoulet: ignore the rancid parts, delight in the duck leg and shrug your shoulders at the little green button. Good luck.'

Yves Lévèque emptied his glass, shook the matchmaker's hand and got up from the chair with the peeling marquetry. He walked home as quickly as he could without breaking into a sweat so as not to spoil his freshly ironed shirt. Before starting the car, he checked his reflection in the mirror, and, after failing to find the slightest trace of allure, comforted himself by baring his teeth. As he turned right at the field with the ginger Limousin cows that winked, he tried to imagine the woman he was about to meet, and wondered whether she would be the one to finally release his cemented innards.

The dentist enjoyed the drive to Jumilhac-le-Grand as he wound through the mottled shadows of oaks and pines which offered a moment's relief from the sun's vicious assault. He hadn't been entirely truthful when he explained to Guillaume Ladoucette why he wanted to take his new match gold-panning. While it would indeed demonstrate that he had initiative, a characteristic he knew to be greatly admired by women, the real reason was that if she turned out to be as abhorrent as the mushroom poisoner, there was always a chance of recovering the sixteen euros the activity would cost him if he happened upon a little gold nugget.

Arriving at the square in front of the wondrous château, he

parked underneath a plane tree and got out to admire the fairytale skyline of pointed roofs and watch towers surmounted by bizarre figurines. Just as he had recognized Justice armed with a tiny sword and scales, and was trying to work out what sort of weapon Authority was holding, he sensed someone standing behind him. He turned round to find that it was Denise Vigier, the grocer.

The dentist had put up with a lot from the matchmaker over the years. There was the time when Guillaume Ladoucette bored a hole into their teacher's *gros pain*, squeezed a toad inside and then blamed him; the occasion when he convinced him that false sideburns were all the rage and sold him a pair which he had never worn, having come to his senses as soon as he left the shop; there was the filling in 1987 that he still hadn't paid for; there were the complaints he still made about the state of his box of hairpieces after the community headcount; there was his unwanted advice about his *cornichons*; and then, of course, there was the business of matching him up with the monstrous assistant ambulant fishmonger. And if all that wasn't enough, he had now set him up with the abhorrent grocer.

After greeting Denise Vigier, who appeared equally taken aback, Yves Lévèque complimented her on her blue-and-purple-patterned dress, which made him shudder.

'It's so much nicer than the other one,' he added.

'Which other one?' asked Denise Vigier.

'The one you wished you'd bought instead.'

'There wasn't one I wish I'd bought instead,' she replied, confused.

Silently cursing Guillaume Ladoucette, and wanting to get the agony over as quickly as possible, Yves Lévèque suggested that they made their way immediately to the nearby village of Le Chalard where the gold-panning was to take place. When the grocer suggested going in one car instead of two, the dentist strongly opposed the idea as he was hoping to lose her along the country lanes. But each time he looked in his mirror, he was tormented by the sight of the abhorrent woman crouched over her steering wheel.

When they arrived at the village, Denise Vigier thanked God that the café was open and quickly disappeared inside to use the lavatory. And the dentist, who was waiting on the terrace, cursed Him when he came face to face with the instructor holding his cash box. The dentist's long, pale instruments of torture reluctantly found their way into his pocket and pulled out enough money for both of them.

After the instructor's demonstration in the dancing waters of the river Isle, Yves Lévèque immediately grabbed a sieve and pan and waded away from the group. After a spurt of furious panning, he cast a look at Denise Vigier, whom Guillaume Ladoucette had described as an 'astute business-woman with a zest for life', who was still on the riverbank tucking the sides of her purple-and-blue-patterned frock under her knicker elastic to make it shorter. Her dress was an abomination, he thought again, and did nothing to help disguise her colossal bosom, the weight of which made her stand as if pitched against permanently driving rain.

Not long after, the grocer, a strand of black hair having escaped from her bun, waded towards him, exclaiming what fun she was having. As she stood next to him peering into her pan for specks of gold, the dentist instantly moved away, claiming that it looked more promising upstream. As he clambered across the rocks, trying not to slip over in his neatly pressed shorts, he thought about the unspeakable prices Denise Vigier charged in her shop and her effrontery at holding the village to ransom over a jar of mayonnaise.

Shovelling a new load of sediment into his sieve, Yves Lévèque hoped that the grocer wouldn't approach. As he put the sieve on top of his pan and swirled them both in the water, he thought of the tins of frankfurters and sauerkraut the woman kept on her shelves, which caused numerous pairs of eyebrows to raise, and he remembered the remarks people made every time she dared show her face at the annual memorial service held at the monument to the *Three Victims of the Barbarous Germans.*

Much to the dentist's fury, Denise Vigier then came splashing towards him, bunions the size of onions thrashing in and out of the water, yelping that she had got something. After wiping the river water from his spectacles, the dentist took a look at the object in the palm of the hand that had fleeced him on so many occasions. And when the beaming grocer insisted that he kept the sizeable nugget, all Yves Lévèque could think about was her treacherous grandmother who had been found guilty of horizontal collaboration at a tribunal in 1944 and, after a swastika had been drawn on her forehead, given a 'Number 44' haircut in front of a spitting crowd in Périgueux.

Guillaume Ladoucette turned the sign on the door round to 'closed' and headed home after a day that had never progressed beyond wretched. For over two hours Stéphane Jollis had sat inconsolable on the cushion with the hand-embroidered radish.

'But I can't understand it, we had such a wonderful time,' he had wailed, running his fingers through his hair, from which escaped a tiny puff of flour. 'And I'd cleaned my shoes.'

All the matchmaker could do was agree that his shoes were certainly unrecognizable, and that the fifty-seven tiny chocolates had been a masterstroke. In an effort to cheer his friend up, he even suggested that they both closed for the day and went fishing, despite the fact that he had nothing remotely victorious in his fridge. But the only thing that the baker wanted was Lisette Robert.

Eventually a search party made up of incandescent customers arrived to escort Stéphane Jollis back to the bakery. As he stood up from the chair with the peeling marquetry, a tiny piece of quiche crust fell from his chest and landed on the floor, which he trod in on his way out. But the matchmaker couldn't be bothered to pick it up, and it remained there for the rest of the afternoon, only to be crushed once more at the end of the day by a supermarket leather sandal.

When he arrived home, Guillaume Ladoucette found a bunch of borage hanging from the front door handle. He recognized it instantly as a gift from his mother, as the tiny blue flowers and leaves put into wine were believed to cure sadness. After untying it, he brought it inside and put it in a vase of water to make her happy. Gazing out of the back window, he couldn't bring himself to mow the lawn, even though it was the last favourable day in the month to do so as the moon was waxing and passing in front of a water sign. Nor could he face anything to eat, as the thought of the eel Gilbert Dubuisson had told him Émilie Fraisse was preparing for them that night had driven away his appetite. Drawn to the sound of the clock on the vast stone mantelpiece whose ticking had driven one of his ancestors to suicide, he sat down on the sofa and, to the cataclysmic thuds of the minute hand, imagined what the pair might be up to.

By the time the postman arrived at the château, Émilie Fraisse had already despatched the eel. After consulting various manuals she dismissed driving a knitting needle through its head as too cruel, and opted instead for the more traditional method of knocking it against the table to stun it, then cutting off its head. Skinning the fish had also been tricky, but once she had got a good hold of it by wrapping its neck in a tea towel, the skin rolled down as easily as a sock using the suggested pair of pliers.

When the châtelaine opened the door, Gilbert Dubuisson immediately offered her a posy of flowers from his garden, which surprised Émilie Fraisse because it had been so many years since a man had made such an effort to please her. As they walked past the llama skeleton and along the corridor with the mould that was still turning violet, he complimented her on her cinnamon-coloured antique dress which appeared to have been shorn off at the knees. And once they reached the vaulted kitchen, he stood and admired the splendid collection of copper pans and utensils illuminating three of the walls.

After offering her guest the seat that slid open to hide the salt from the tax collector, Émilie Fraisse poured them both a glass of wine. But as she sat down, she found that nerves had made off with her voice. Fortunately, Gilbert Dubuisson was as talkative as ever, so she simply leant back on the oak chair with wild boars carved on its feet and listened. By the time she had finished her first glass, her voice had been returned and she chatted back feeling as content in the postman's company as she had been at the *floralies*. And when he asked whether he could have a tour of the château as he hadn't been round it for years, she was only too delighted.

Wishing she was barefoot as she clattered her way down the corridor in her ridiculous seventeenth-century shoes, the châtelaine passed a modern wooden chest poorly encrusted with mother-of-pearl bought by the previous owner on a visit to Turkey to avoid getting into a fight. When Gilbert Dubuisson stopped to ask her about it, Émilie Fraisse found herself saying that it was the bottom half of a Renaissance armoire which had been in the château for centuries. She then told the story of a man who had spent so many years travelling the Pacific islands that he eventually cast aside his breeches, ruffled shirt and plume-topped velvet hat and went native. He spent his days fishing with the locals and learnt to hold his breath underwater so he could dive for pretty shells to please his fifty-six wives who found him exotic beyond measure. One day, a local with only thirty-two wives decided to dive even deeper than usual to find a highly prized shell to increase his standing in the village as his reputation had suffered since the newcomer's arrival. But the water was far too deep for the man to bear and he started to drown. The Frenchman, who was the only one still in the ocean, noticed that he was in difficulty and managed to rescue him. The local was so grateful that he gave him the beautiful shell that was still clasped in his hand. Such was the immensity of his gratitude, he also insisted that his rescuer took all his wives, who were only too happy for a change. But before long, the Frenchman was dead with exhaustion. On his deathbed he sent the beautiful shell to his brother, who lived in the château at Amour-sur-Belle, along with a letter asking that it be made into a piece of furniture to serve as a warning against doing people favours.

When Émilie Fraisse finished, the delighted postman pulled open one of the doors and said that he couldn't understand why the previous owner hadn't told him the fascinating story when he had showed him around.

After taking him up the spiral staircase with the lamentable repairs, the châtelaine opened one of the bedroom doors and invited Gilbert Dubuisson in. He looked around and then strode to the window where he stood admiring a Louis XV marble-topped chest of drawers. Explaining that it was, in fact, a vanity trunk, Émilie Fraisse pulled out the second drawer, lifted up the hinged mirror and showed him the compartments on either side used to store perfume bottles. Once she had closed it again, she pulled the left-hand handle of the fourth drawer which swivelled open to the right to reveal a white bidet. When Gilbert Dubuisson exclaimed how marvellous it was and asked whether she knew anything of its history, Émilie Fraisse found herself telling him that it once belonged to a woman of exceptional charm who took it with her as she travelled all over the Périgord Vert visiting her numerous lovers. One day, a former owner of the château discovered that he was not the sole object of her affections. Scandalized, despite having numerous lovers himself, the next time they had exhausted their passions, he smothered her with a pillow. It was then the man realized that he had not only killed the only woman he had ever loved, but also the only person willing to fulfil the more extreme of his carnal pleasures. Knowing that he would never reach such heights of ecstasy again, the man became a eunuch and set about destroying every vanity trunk in the country. However, he was unable to bring himself to destroy the one that had belonged to his accommodating mistress and it was the only one that survived to this day.

When she had finished the story, Émilie Fraisse suddenly became conscious of its sexual nature and blushed. The postman, who failed to notice the fire in her cheeks, said that the story was remarkable and ran his hand along the marble top in wonder.

On entering the *grand salon*, Gilbert Dubuisson immediately admired the reversible floor and enquired about the putrid smell coming from one of the tapestries. Émilie Fraisse told him the true account of how during the reign of Louis XIII the comte de Brancas, gentleman-in-waiting to Anne of Austria, had dropped the Queen's hand on entering a room *pour aller pisser contre la tapisserie*, which the previous château owner had read about and taken up as a new hobby with breathtaking devotion. Émilie Fraisse then wandered out, and had got halfway down the corridor before realizing that her guest was no longer following her. When she retraced her steps and met the gleeful postman striding quickly out of the room, she was convinced that she caught the smell of fresh urine.

Gilbert Dubuisson, who was having as splendid a time as his hostess, then asked to see her heirloom vegetables. In the battle-weary, bloody evening sun, they followed the ancient stone wall on top of which bearded irises grew. Pulling apart the overgrown brambles and wild grasses, she showed the postman the strawberry spinach, with its tiny red fruit which she made into jam and put out for sale in the ticket-seller's hut built for the tourists who never came. The leaves, she added, tasted like hazelnuts and should be cooked like spinach.

The châtelaine then walked over to the rows of asparagus lettuce and pointed out that instead of a heart they had a central stalk which was sufficient for one person. It was eaten raw in salad, she added, or steamed like asparagus, and its frilly leaves were to be ignored.

And finally, she showed him her slender perpetual leeks, with tiny new vegetables already growing out of them. The transfixed postman showed so much rapture that Émilie Fraisse immediately picked some of everything for supper.

The châtelaine and her guest then returned to the kitchen, where she completed her dish of eel stewed in Burgundy. However, she forgot to warn Gilbert Dubuisson that she was going to ignite the dash of cognac she had added after bringing the dish to the boil with cubes of bacon, which made him jump in terror. Once the postman had regained his composure, she then showed him into the dining room with its *pisé* floor, where candlelight fluttered across the vases of rambling apricot roses.

Eventually roused from the sofa by the cacophony of his empty stomach, Guillaume Ladoucette got up and wandered upstairs. After taking a regretful look at the dry bath, he made his way to his bedroom and pulled open the drawer of the nightstand. He then sat with his back against the bed head, his legs out in front of him, and carefully oiled Émilie Fraisse's Nontron hunting knife with its boxwood handle and ancient pokerwork motifs. Forgetting to take off his two-day-old clothes, he then turned off the bedside light and braced himself for another terrifying night on the high seas. Less than an hour later, such was the height of the waves of anxiety lashing around the house, Violette the infernal chicken came out from her hiding place, climbed up on to the bed and spent the night on his pillow lest she drown.

After dinner, which had taken much longer than either had expected as neither could stop talking, Émilie Fraisse accompanied Gilbert Dubuisson to the door glowing like mercury in the moonlight. As the bats performed loops of the courtyard, they both said what a wonderful evening they had had. Gilbert Dubuisson then gently took the châtelaine's hand and kissed the backs of her fingers. Again he complimented her on her cinnamon-coloured antique dress, the unsurpassable dinner, the vigour of her heirloom vegetables and her efforts with the château which had always been so filthy. And he added that if she needed any help scrubbing the moulds off the walls, he would be more than happy to oblige. It was then that Émilie Fraisse went off Gilbert Dubuisson.

15

HEART'S DESIRE WAS CLOSED THE FOLLOWING MORNING. Guillaume Ladoucette had only managed bouts of sleep between the frantic gasps for breath of a man overboard. Buffeted all night, it wasn't until the sun had already gone into battle that he collapsed, marooned on his back, into the deepest of slumbers, arms and legs outstretched with exhaustion. The clamour of his monstrous snores prevented him from hearing the alarm, which eventually gave up. It wasn't until he slowly opened his eyes to search for the horizon and came face to face with the unfortunate features of Violette the infernal chicken that he fully woke. Such were his screams of terror that the shocked bird instantly laid an egg.

Hoisting himself to his feet, he cast off his sodden clothes and made his way to the bathroom, stepping in the viscous slime of broken yolk. He refused to look into the mirror above the sink fearing that his reflection would only disorientate him further. After tying his burgundy silk dressing gown across his small mound of winter plumage, he walked his feet into his slippers, collected his washbag and towel and left for the municipal shower. Unable to speak, he only managed a shake of the head when Fabrice Ribou approached him in the queue with a tray and asked him whether he wanted a drink. At first, he was unable to feel the ruthless temperature of the water driving on to his head and collapsing his moustache into a soggy horseshoe. But it quickly brought him to his senses until he could stand the discomfort no more.

Once home, his stomach, tormented from having eaten nothing the previous night, drove him to the fridge, and he cooked himself a breakfast of scrambled eggs in which he tossed a handful of *lardons*. But the salt in the bacon reminded him of his tempestuous night and, falling into despair again, he found himself unable to get up from the table. When he next looked over at the clock on the oven it was almost lunchtime. Convincing himself that it wasn't worth opening Heart's Desire for such a short period, the matchmaker stayed where he was while his mind forced upon him images he didn't want to see.

When he stirred several hours later, Guillaume Ladoucette immediately felt shamed by his behaviour, for it wasn't respectable for a grown man still to be in his dressing gown – no matter how elegant – while the rest of the world was working. By the time he arrived at the shop, he had managed to put on a clean set of clothes and, while there was no trace of its former glory, his moustache was waxed so as not to hang down to his chin. He turned round the sign on the inside of the door, made himself a cup of coffee and, as he sipped it on his swivel chair, told himself that the most important thing was that Émilie Fraisse was happy. But part of him wouldn't listen.

Just as he had got out his file of customers, which was rather slim, a head appeared around the door. It was Stéphane

Jollis, wanting to know whether everything was all right as a number of his customers had noticed that Heart's Desire had been closed all morning. When the matchmaker replied that he was just feeling a little under the weather, the baker came in, trod again on the quiche crust, and sat down on the cushion with the hand-embroidered radish.

'Sorry, I forgot to shake before coming in,' said Stéphane Jollis.

'It doesn't matter,' the matchmaker replied. 'Would you like a drink?'

'Yes, please.'

'Red?'

'If you've got some.'

The matchmaker brought out a bottle of Bergerac from the bottom left-hand drawer of the oak desk and poured two glasses. He then reached back inside and brought out a bowl of cracked walnuts which he put in front of the baker.

'Walnut?'

'No thanks,' replied Stéphane Jollis, who had his own to get through. 'So what's wrong?'

'I just didn't get much sleep last night.'

'Nor did I,' admitted the baker.

While Guillaume Ladoucette had been cleaning Émilie Fraisse's hunting knife, Stéphane Jollis had been sitting up in bed inspecting the hairclip he had kept in his bedside drawer ever since finding it on the bakery table the morning after the mini-tornado. Despite knowing every detail of it already, he held it under his nose with his artisan fingers studying it. First he gazed at the swirl of diamanté, several specks of which were missing, then at the little clasp on the back where the black paint had worn, and then at the swirl of diamanté again. Eventually, he returned it to the drawer, shuffled down the sheet and lay on his back while the perpetual breeze danced around the pale moon of his stomach.

Over two hours later, hours spent lingering over the

memory of that night, to which he had added a number of blushing embellishments, the baker was still too agitated to sleep. As always, he found it hard to believe that a man such as himself could have had the great fortune to share his bed with Lisette Robert, and at times he had had to get out her hairclip just to prove to himself that it was true. And while he was well aware that bakers, along with firefighters, held the highest place in the nation's affections, and that the job carried such prestige that for years the family bakery was the only place in the village with a telephone, he had never imagined that such a gift from heaven would come his way. It was then that Stéphane Jollis finally came to the conclusion that it was time to see it for what it was: a miracle the like of which only happened once for a man such as himself. The baker then fell into a peaceful sleep, and, for the first time since that incredible night, wasn't disturbed by the haunting memory of poisonous piano playing coming down the chimney.

After pouring them both another glass, Stéphane Jollis announced that he wanted to sign up for the Unrivalled Silver Service.

'What a marvellous idea!' replied Guillaume Ladoucette. 'Nothing like getting back on that horse, eh? And don't worry about Lisette Robert. Everyone wants to go out with her. That's just the way of the world.'

The matchmaker opened the file of customers on his desk. 'Now, let's see,' he muttered. 'Who have we got here? Not her. Not her. Good God, not her. No. Can't see you two together. Not her. Her! There we are, Stéphane! Oh, maybe not.'

'What's wrong?'

'She's looking for someone tall and slim.'

'I'm not that short,' protested the baker.

'No, but there's the other matter.'

'Guillaume, a baker of distinction cannot be skinny. As you always said when you were a barber, you have to be a Living

Example. What would it say about my bread and little cakes if I were able to resist them?'

'You're quite right, of course. But I'm not prepared to take the risk.'

The matchmaker carried on looking through his file. 'No. Too old. No. Now what about her? Let's see ... Yes, that's a very good match indeed. You two should get on splendidly. Why didn't I think of her before? Now, I expect you want to get moving right away. Would you like me to call her now?'

Stéphane Jollis nodded enthusiastically. The matchmaker dialled the number and indicated that the woman had picked up the phone by pointing at the receiver and raising his eyebrows at the baker, who was watching him closely. Guillaume Ladoucette introduced himself, exchanged several pleasantries and then announced that he had found her a most favourable match. The man in question, he said, was a dark-haired artisan who liked to seize the day by rising early, and then went into considerable detail about his splendid haircut. And when the woman enquired as to whether he was athletic, the matchmaker replied that he was a very keen fisherman and, suddenly remembering his historic fall into the Belle, added that he enjoyed swimming.

Guillaume Ladoucette put down the receiver. 'She's very keen to meet you,' he said triumphantly. 'However, there's one minor problem. She's going away after the weekend for a short holiday and the only time she can meet you is Sunday morning.'

'I'll be at work,' replied the baker.

'Can't you take the day off?'

'My customers would knife me. It's one of the busiest days of the week,' said Stéphane Jollis, suddenly looking fearful. 'And I've got problems this Sunday as it is. There's no one coming in to help serve.'

'I see your point.'

The two men sat in silence.

'I know!' said Guillaume Ladoucette. 'I'll look after the bakery while you're gone. You could get up really early and prepare everything so all I'd have to do is serve.'

'But, Guillaume, you can't add up.'

'I can.'

The baker raised his eyebrows.

'OK, so maybe I can't,' said the matchmaker. 'But I could work it out on the till. It can't be that hard. I had one in the barber's, remember. Come on, Stéphane! She sounds right up your street.'

With great reluctance, the baker finally agreed, but not before laying down certain conditions. Guillaume Ladoucette was not to do any sums in his head, nor was he to take advantage of the trays of little cakes. There were a number of customers who came in at the same time every week for the same order and he had to make sure that he didn't sell out before they came in. He then went through each one of them by name indicating their requirements. 'Whatever you do, make sure there are enough little cakes left for the women,' he added. 'They'll skin you alive otherwise. Hide them from the men if you have to. Oh yes, and Émilie Fraisse always comes in on a Sunday morning for a *mille-feuille*.'

'Émilie Fraisse always comes in on a Sunday morning for a *mille-feuille*?' repeated the matchmaker.

'Yes. And don't forget Madame Serre and her rum *baba*. She's the worst.'

But Guillaume Ladoucette couldn't think about Madame Serre and her rum *baba* because he was still thinking about Émilie Fraisse and her *mille-feuille*. And, as he imagined her eating it, he found himself wondering what dessert she had served Gilbert Dubuisson, and within moments he had fallen down the familiar shaft of misery. Again he saw the postman arriving at the door of the château with a bunch of flowers, no doubt from his garden. Again he saw them together in the dining room with the *pisé* floor eating eel, which would undoubtedly have been exquisite. And again he saw the kiss on the lips that he was convinced that Gilbert Dubuisson would have given her, along with the snake of his arm around her waist.

The baker then left, muttering something about being hunted down if he didn't get back to his shop. In no mood to face Émilie Fraisse coming in to tell him about her splendid evening with Gilbert Dubuisson, the matchmaker stood up, turned the sign over behind the shop door, and went to look for the man from the council.

He found Jean-François Lafforest at the municipal shower in his unfortunate trousers, which were now starting to fit, talking to two workmen. When the matchmaker approached and asked whether he could buy him a drink at the Bar Saint-Jus, the man from the council immediately became suspicious and politely refused. Undeterred, Guillaume Ladoucette hung around. Certain of a trap, Jean-François Lafforest could stand the suspense no longer and approached the villager asking whether he could help him. When the matchmaker suggested that they went for a little walk together instead, he willingly agreed, believing that the agony of what lay in store for him could not be as torturous as wait-ing for it to befall him.

Guillaume Ladoucette first took him to the bench by the fountain said to cure gout, but when he prodded Monsieur Moreau, he found that the old man was still alive, so he took Jean-François Lafforest to the Romanesque church for some privacy. But when they arrived, he looked inside and found several villagers lying flat on their backs on top of the marble tombs trying to cool down. Unsure of where to try next, he then took him along the banks of the Belle. They walked through the patches of wild mint until they came to the old public washing place. After inviting the man from the coun-cil to sit next to him on a stone slab underneath the pitched roof, Guillaume Ladoucette then told him all about Heart's Desire, the Unrivalled Gold Service and the very special woman who wanted to be introduced to him.

Clutching his briefcase to his stomach, his eyes on the shallow square of green water, Jean-François Lafforest listened to what the man had to say. And he was impressed. He had been aware of the existence of the Clandestine Committee against the Municipal Shower since its inception, as details about its first meeting had been posted on the village noticeboard. And he was in no doubt as to what lengths its members would go to, having discovered that a sabotaged pipe was the cause of the lack of hot water. But while he knew that the group was capable of direct action, he had no idea that their dastardly attempts to get rid of the shower would involve such connivance as inventing mystery suitors to torment him.

When the matchmaker had finished his speech, the man from the council told him that while it was very nice to know that a woman held him in such high regard, he couldn't possibly entertain the idea of meeting her. Guillaume Ladoucette was taken aback.

'Monsieur Lafforest, I must impress upon you that the woman in question is no ordinary one,' he insisted.

'I'm sure she's not,' Jean-François Lafforest agreed.

'Forgive me, but I don't think you quite understand. I'm talking about a woman of exceptional beauty.'

'I'm certain she's extraordinary.'

'I don't wish to give away her identity, but I would wager she's the most beautiful woman you've ever seen.'

'No doubt, Monsieur Ladoucette. But I'm afraid I am not interested.'

The matchmaker then plundered the depths of his considerable sales skills. He first tried to appeal to the man's nobility, describing her caring nature, generosity and discretion. When that failed to work he talked of the woman's figure that was widely known to curve more graciously than the Belle, her eyes that shone like two freshly opened horse chestnuts, and her hair that coursed down her shoulders like a waterfall. When there was still no sign of interest, he resorted to gross exaggeration and praised her musical and housekeeping skills. But the man from the council was having none of it. He simply thanked Guillaume Ladoucette for his interest, bid him good day and left.

The matchmaker walked back along the banks of the Belle alone and dumbfounded. As the scent of wild mint threaded through his ankles, he ran through his sales pitch and couldn't for the life of him see where he had gone wrong. How could a man refuse such a woman? It was unthinkable. And how on earth was he going to break the news to poor Lisette Robert?

Over an hour later, back on his swivel chair, the match-maker was still trying to work out how he was going to tell the midwife when the door opened. He looked up to see an elderly man looking in hesitantly. Guillaume Ladoucette immediately scuttled his hairy toes back into his super-market leather sandals and got up to greet him. After ushering him to the chair with the peeling marquetry, he offered him a drink, which was politely refused. Once back behind the desk with the ink stain, Guillaume Ladoucette introduced himself.

'I know who you are, you nit, it's me, Pierre Rouzeau,' said the man. 'I must say, what on earth's happened to your moustache?'

It was only then that the matchmaker recognized his old boss. He got back on to his feet, hurried round to the other side of the desk and kissed him on both cheeks. As he went to sit back down again, Guillaume Ladoucette said that he thought the retired barber had left the Périgord Vert, which was why he hadn't be in touch for so long. Resting his brown spotted hands on the arms of the chair, the old man told his former apprentice what had become of him during the years when they hadn't seen each other. The business had continued to do well, helped by his sideline of selling the hair that was swept up off the floor to the mattress-maker, along with the trimmings he found in the turn-ups of his trousers. He thought that his marriage to Francine Rouzeau was going equally well until one evening over supper she told him that now all the children had left home, she too was on her way. He was astounded, as she had never given any indication that her life had not turned out as she had hoped. She then told him that the only times he had ever told her that he loved her were the morning they had got engaged, the afternoon they were married and the night they conceived their first child. Pierre Rouzeau then put down his knife and fork and told her for the first time that she had given him the sort of happiness that he had never known. But it was too late. She finished off her stuffed cabbage, reminded him that they had run out of bin liners, and left with her bags, which were already packed.

Every day for the following year he expected her to walk back through the door. He learnt how to clean the house and kept it spotless for her return. The fridge was always filled with her delights and the radio tuned to her favourite station. Every evening he ran her a bath, and then placed a fresh glass of water on her bedside table. He even filled her wardrobe with pretty summer dresses. But his wife never returned. Exhausted from his heart wheeling each time the door opened only to plummet again when it was someone else, he retired and moved away from Nontron. But part of him still hoped that she would track him down and he always kept the doors unlocked just in case. After a succession of burglaries, he was forced to lock them. To distract himself from worrying about how she would get in, he finally entered the World Barbering Championships in Illinois. And, despite the fact that he won the Gold Medal for Outstanding Achievement in the short-back-and-sides category, the victory meant nothing as he had already lost life's biggest prize.

When he finished, Pierre Rouzeau then asked Guillaume Ladoucette how many children he and Émilie Fraisse had.

'We never got married,' replied the matchmaker.

'Never got married? So whom did you marry?'

'No one,' replied Guillaume Ladoucette.

The two men sat looking at the floor in silence.

Eventually, the matchmaker lifted his eyes and asked his old boss what had brought him to Amour-sur-Belle.

'I've just moved back to Nontron as I missed the place, and someone told me that you had set yourself up as a matchmaker. So I thought I'd not only pay my favourite apprentice a visit, but take advantage of his services. I'm not too old, am I?'

After signing up for the Unrivalled Silver Service and reminding the matchmaker to do something about his moustache, Pierre Rouzeau opened the door with his arthritic fingers and left. Guillaume Ladoucette watched him walk past the window and then sat staring ahead of him, the pleasure of having seen his old boss tempered by the reminder that he had never married Émilie Fraisse. Even more reluctant to face the châtelaine if she came in, the matchmaker decided to close Heart's Desire early. But he was too late. Just as he was putting his pen back into the narrow drawer with the compartments, the door suddenly opened. It was Émilie Fraisse wearing an almond antique silk dress which appeared to have been shorn off at the knees. The matchmaker, exhausted by his night of seafaring, forgot to crawl his toes back into his supermarket leather sandals before getting up to greet her and it wasn't until he felt quiche pastry between his toes that he realized he was still barefoot. After ushering her to the cushion with the hand-embroidered radish, he quickly sat down again. Just as he was preparing himself for the torment of listening to the details he couldn't bear to hear, he took a closer look at Émilie Fraisse and asked whether she was all right.

'I didn't get much sleep last night,' she replied. Guillaume Ladoucette tried to catch his heart as it sank, but missed.

After the postman had wished her goodnight, Émilie Fraisse didn't wait to hear him crunch his way across the drawbridge and immediately closed the door. Slipping off her ridiculous seventeenth-century shoes, she sat on the bottom step of the spiral staircase with the lamentable repairs, her cheeks resting on her fists. How could she possibly ever love a man who was unable to see the beauty of the moulds that decorated the château walls like priceless works of art? And as she thought about her wasted efforts – the roses she had picked, the eel she had skinned and the tour she had given him – the familiar flints of disappointment thudded down on to her, more painful this time because of the weeping sores left by her husband.

When, finally, she found the will to stand up, she climbed the cold stairs, walked along the corridor with the rough, faded tapestries and turned the enormous handle on her bedroom door. In front of the mirror dappled with age, she slipped off her cinnamon-coloured dress that she had cut off at the knees in a panic only hours ago. She then took out the pin that was holding up her hair, which dropped like cinders down her naked back. And as she looked at her body which hadn't been touched for years, she scolded herself for having thought that she had finally found the man who would love her until it had caught up with her aged hair.

After pulling back the white heavy cotton sheet on her four-poster Renaissance bed, she lay on her back, piles of ashes covering the pillow. As she looked up at the tapestry canopy, she thought how foolish she had been to think that one day Gilbert Dubuisson might have joined her in it as her husband. She then thought of the only man with whom she had shared a bed, and of the time when he had started turning his back on her until eventually he no longer reached for her foot with his. And when her mind returned to the man she should have married, but who had never replied to her letter, so many flints of disappointment dropped on to her she was unable to move for the weight of them.

She soon lost consciousness, but woke again in the early hours when the pain returned. Down the spiral steps with the lamentable repairs she crept and made her way straight to the vaulted kitchen. The copper pans, lit up by the moonlight, flickered like flames. She opened the fridge door, made herself a steak sandwich and brought it back to her desolate sheets. For a moment she felt relief. But the flints immediately fell again and she ran back down the cold stairs with the lamentable repairs. By then so much moonlight had flooded the kitchen, the room blazed like an inferno, and she fled back to bed again in terror.

When Émilie Fraisse woke the following morning, she immediately had an urge to feel the sun on her skin. She passed along the corridor with the faded tapestries and climbed the tower to the scandalous ramparts. Sitting on one of the crenellation stones that had tumbled from the wall, she failed to spot the buzzards soaring with their enormous floppy feet hanging below them, and when she looked down at the dry moat below she saw to her despair that the yellow irises had died.

After showering with the garden hosepipe, she went into the dining room to close the lattice windows against the house martins that kept flying in and carving desperate circles around the room unable to find their way out. Yet she looked in dismay at the remains of the eel, the vases of apricot rambling roses which had started to shed their petals, the candles scorched to stumps, the two stained serviettes on the floor, and the flints descended again.

Deciding after all to leave the windows open to get rid of

the smell, she ran back and forth to the vaulted kitchen until the table was cleared. After washing up, she went to wipe the dining-room table which had been stolen from a monastery. But before long, she found that she had got out her beeswax and was rubbing it furiously. She then turned her attention to the side table on which the spoils of hunting were once displayed, and before long was buffing its legs. Once the dining room was completed, she opened the door to the *grand salon* with its huge stone fireplace and gleaming reversible floor. On to her knees she descended and started polishing the walnut boards which were uppermost. And even though they were not due to be turned for another two hundred years, once she had finished, she heaved them over and started again.

She then went up the spiral staircase with the lamentable repairs and cleaned the whole of the first floor. When she had cleaned the whole of the first floor, she cleaned all of the attic rooms. And when she had cleaned all of the attic rooms, she then proceeded to sweep the scandalous ramparts.

It was then that she decided to go and see Guillaume Ladoucette, but when she arrived at Heart's Desire, she found that the door was locked. She returned home, heaving the boards over and over as she polished them until she started to get confused and half the floor was walnut and half was oak. The ghastly clamour of clattering wood woke the bats hanging upside down in the watchtower. They flooded out into the courtyard in a leathery black mist, and such was their confusion in the sunlight they flew round in different directions, bumped into each other and plummeted from the sky.

When Émilie Fraisse eventually sat down on the cushion with the hand-embroidered radish, her knees were so red they appeared to have been scalded.

'So you had a good time with Gilbert Dubuisson last night?' the matchmaker forced himself to ask.

'Very,' replied the châtelaine.

'Excellent. Did he bring you flowers?'

'Yes. From his garden.'

'Thought he might. Did you give him a tour of the château?'

'Yes. He liked it very much.'

'And you showed him your heirloom vegetables?'

'Yes, he was enchanted.'

'And the eel. How was that?'

'A triumph.'

Just as Guillaume Ladoucette could feel his feet touching the ocean bed, Émilie Fraisse added: 'But I couldn't possibly see him again.'

'Why ever not?' he asked. But he never fully understood her reply. He caught something about moulds, and there being a lovely blue one in the dungeon, to say nothing of the violet one on the way to the kitchen. There was also a concern about the postman wanting to restore the scandalous ramparts next. But the matchmaker had no idea what she was talking about as his mind was elsewhere. For it was then that Guillaume Ladoucette decided to reply to Émilie Fraisse's letter.

16

WHEN GUILLAUME LADOUCETTE OPENED HIS EYES THE FOLLOWING
Sunday his heart was already in flight. It wasn't the thrill of
knowing breakfast was to be one of Stéphane Jolliss's plump
almond croissants still warm from the oven that had woken
him, though such a thought had proved sufficiently
intoxicating in the past. Rather it was the excitement he felt
over what was lying on the kitchen table next to his yellow fly
swat.

The matchmaker had intended to write his letter to Émilie
Fraisse immediately after his Saturday lie-in, which turned
out to be such an unusually protracted affair that when he
eventually rose after eleven hours on his back, arms down the
sides of his body as if already dead in his coffin, his immediate concern was for bed sores. After showering in the ruthless
waters of the municipal shower, which still hadn't been fixed,
and treating himself to some award-winning pig's head black
pudding from the splendid butcher's in Brantôme, he sat
down at the kitchen table in front of a piece of writing paper.

But he found that his stomach was writhing like a bag of snakes and he was unable to sit still. After having written only the date, he was up on his feet again to make himself another cup of coffee, despite the fact that the cube of sugar in his first hadn't yet dissolved. Returning to his seat, he wrote the words 'Chère Émilie', but then found himself by the back door with his hand in the sack of the previous year's walnuts, though he was far from hungry. After cracking them open, he installed himself back in front of his letter and stared at it as words continued to evade him. It wasn't long before he convinced himself that his fingernails needed clipping, even though he had done them only two days before. When he returned from the bathroom, he looked at the piece of paper, scratched out 'Chère Émilie' and replaced it with 'Ma chère Émilie'. But the snakes continued to writhe when he searched for the words to follow, and he suddenly reached for his copy of *Antiquités Brocante* magazine on the counter next to the bowl of pecked apricots. As he flicked through it, he noticed a listing for a little antiques fair in the streets of Villars, and before he knew it he was in his car hoping to find another Peugeot coffee grinder to add to his collection on the pale stone kitchen mantelpiece.

After parking next to a front door either side of which hung a small three-legged cauldron filled with pink geraniums, he wandered up the lane alongside the locked church with its enormous carved scallop shell over the door. He stopped at the first stall to inspect the handmade lace tablecloths, and as he ran his fingers over the bundles of white monogrammed napkins tied up with pieces of red ribbon, he found himself looking for a set with the initials EF, but was unable to find one.

Turning his attention to the next stall, the matchmaker tutted to himself when he saw the clogs laced with cobwebs made by spiders from a previous century, and which had fed several generations of woodworm. And looking at the ancient farming utensils spread out on the ground next to them, he found himself wondering whether any of them would be suitable to tend heirloom vegetables.

As he made his way up the street, he bumped into a customer from his barbering days who enquired how the matchmaking business was going. 'It's a bit like the dozen oysters you buy on a Saturday morning from the stall in the place du Marché. There are always one or two that are a bugger to open,' he replied, and turned into the square. Rummaging inside a tin, he found an old doorknocker covered in rust in the shape of a woman's hand holding an orange. The stallholder noticed his interest and immediately informed him that it was an original, hence the price. But Guillaume Ladoucette wasn't struck by its expense, but by its similarity to the last woman's hand he had seen, which had been resting on the arm of the chair with the peeling marquetry. And by the time he had visited each stall, he realized that he had completely forgotten to look for a Peugeot coffee grinder.

As he pulled the car door shut, his mind flashed him the blank letter on the kitchen table, and the snakes twisted again. The matchmaker immediately decided that as he was in Villars, he may as well visit the famous grottoes with their glistening calcite formations. This was despite the fact that he had already been thirty-seven times as his mother had brought him as a child whenever she suspected he had a temperature and bribed the guide not to let him out until closing time. But instead of his fever dropping in the cold, he would run through the dripping caves in terror trying to escape from what he thought were frozen ghosts.

Climbing down the steep staircase into the caves, he felt the chilled, damp air rise deliciously up his trouser legs. He made his way slowly through the vast chambers, their treasures twinkling in spotlights, and stopped to admire the curiously thin stalactites that hung like spaghetti from the roof. As he passed deeper inside, he marvelled at the strange blue drawings of beasts made by prehistoric man. But when he saw the remarkable semi-translucent yellow and ochre draperies, which hung from the ceiling like bed sheets, all he could think about was the woman whom he wanted to hold as he slept.

Returning to his car, the matchmaker suddenly decided that the writing paper on the kitchen table was not in the least bit suitable, and he started driving in the opposite direction to Amour-sur-Belle. Forty-two minutes later, he arrived in Périgueux and immediately headed for the city's best *papeterie*, near to the pineapple-topped cathedral that always closed for lunch. He spent over an hour breathing in the wondrous aroma as he chose between the colours and weights. He then stopped at his favourite soap shop along a cobbled street in the old quarter, despite the fact that there was no more room on the wooden shelves above his dusty bath for any more exquisite varieties, and spent another thirty-seven minutes in deep inhalation. And, as all he had had to eat at midday was a *merguez* sausage in a piece of baguette at the antiques fair, he headed off for supper in one of the squares. But when the waiter brought him his dessert, and he looked at the *bavarois framboise*, all he could think of was the painful colour of Émilie Fraisse's knees.

By the time he arrived home, Guillaume Ladoucette was too tired to embark on any more delaying tactics, despite having thought of several on the journey home. As the night squeezed in through the gaps either side of the shutters, he installed himself at the kitchen table again, armed with a glass of homemade *pineau* from an old plastic Vittel bottle in the cupboard, as well as his fly swat. He untied the ribbon on his new set of cream writing paper, took out one of the tiny sheets and launched into the letter without stopping to write her name in case it stalled him again. As he wrote, he failed to notice the demonic whine of the mosquitoes and never once did his pen stop. By the time he signed the letter, he had finally told Émilie Fraisse how much he had loved her at school, how much he had loved her when she left, how much he had loved her while she was away, how much he had loved her when she came back, how much he loved her now and how much he would always love her. He then added that his biggest regret in life was not having had the courage to tell her sooner, but that his feelings for her were so overpowering they had weakened him. After finishing his *pineau*, the matchmaker put his glass in the sink, went up to bed and remained on dry land for the entire night.

Descending the stairs the following morning, he was suddenly struck by the ghastly image of a black-and-white dropping on his smooth cream letter. But when he entered the kitchen it was just as he had left it. Picking up the letter, he read it again, anxious that the night had made him too bold in his sentiments. He was relieved to find that its content and tone were just as he had intended. Knowing that no corner of the house was safe from the infernal chicken, he then folded the letter carefully, slipped it into his pocket and left for the bakery.

Stéphane Jollis had got up before some of the birds had retired to their nests in order to get everything done before leaving the bakery in the hands of Guillaume Ladoucette. Sunday was always the most tiresome morning of the week. Not only did he want to remain under his bedcovers until after mass like everybody else, but the demand for his little cakes was at its most fervent as people needed something sweet to ease the suffering of having to eat lunch with their relatives.

When he opened the connecting door to the bakery, wearing voluminous checked blue shorts and a white T-shirt, he immediately turned on the radio to take his mind off the fact that he was awake at such a heinous hour. He decided against coffee as it would only sharpen his senses to his torment, heading instead to the steel work counter. With his surprisingly small hands, which his schoolteacher had remarked would rule him out of ever becoming a concert pianist, he made his pastry for the *mille-feuilles* and the strawberry and raspberry tartlets. He then opened the ancient black oven door, which bore the words 'Périgueux 1880', and slid them inside, along with the apple tarts he had prepared the day before.

After loading up his piping bags he opened a plastic box containing choux pastries he had made the day before and filled half the heads and bodies of the *religieuses* with chocolate *crème pâtissière* and half with coffee. After heating up their chocolate and coffee icing, he then dipped each cake into its corresponding pan, smoothing the icing over with his tiny plump finger as he went. His mind still numb from having been wrenched from his dreams too early, it never occurred to him to lick it when he had finished; rather he busied himself with giving the nuns their little whipped cream collars and wimples before starting on the éclairs.

Once the oven was empty again, he opened the door to the cold room and fought his way round the sacks of flour he was obliged to keep in there as the insufferable heat was making his dough over-inflate. But it was hardly worth the effort. He had even tried using less yeast, but still the loaves and baguettes swelled to such unnatural sizes they frightened the customers. He wheeled out the racks of trays lined with lengths of dough which had bloated overnight and positioned them near the oven. Placing the tip of a wooden shovel which resembled an oar on the lip of the open door, he then rested the end of its long handle on a stand behind him so that it was horizontal. Placing one of the enlarged raw baguettes on the head of the shovel, he then slashed it five times with a razor blade kept between his lips, lifted up the shovel and then fed the loaf into the far reaches of the oven, which was lit up by a reading lamp. He continued slashing and shovelling until all the baguettes were inside, rivulets of sweat coursing down the side of his face and into his eyes, which stung. Once the oven door was shut he dampened his coughing, which he blamed on the flour rather than his cigarettes, with his first cup of coffee. He then returned to the cold room for the loaves which were to be baked next.

Having filled and glazed the strawberry and raspberry tartlets, he cut the *mille-feuille* pastry into three long strips, slathered two with rum-laced *crème pâtissière*, stacked them all up and painted the top with white icing. But when he cut them into portions and found, as always, a delicious little slice at the end which was too small to sell, his mind was still so unbalanced from the early shriek of his alarm clock that he simply dropped it into the bin.

Once all the bread was cooked, Stéphane Jollis went in search of the trays of *viennoiserie* that had been blooming overnight in the cold room. Out came the *croissants* – rolled-up triangles of pastry layered with butter; the *chocolatines*, which Parisians called *pains au chocolat*; and the *pains aux raisins* which for once didn't remind him of the swirl of his umbilicus as his early rise had snuffed out his imagination. He loaded them into the oven along with the brioches bulging obesely in their tins, wiping the flash flood of sweat from his head on alternate shoulders as he laboured.

But just as one mountain was scaled, another peak appeared, and he went in search of some flour to prepare the following day's bread. As he was waiting for the machine to finish rolling and stretching the baguette dough, he sat down for a moment on his battered white stool to ease the strain on his serpentine varicose veins which came with the job. It was then that his floury feet began tapping to the music on the radio, a habit which didn't usually start until he had had his fourth cup of coffee. But by then Stéphane Jollis had finally come to his senses, stirred from his somnolence by thoughts of the mystery woman he was about to meet at the annual Donkey Festival in Brantôme.

By the time Guillaume Ladoucette arrived with his empty stomach, all the breads were standing up on end in their correct baskets along the back wall of the shop and the little cakes were lined up in neat rows behind the glass counter. All he had to do, the baker explained, was to serve. He pointed out that everything was clearly priced, and then carefully showed him how the till worked. But the matchmaker wasn't listening because he had his eye on the oven which he could see through the door.

'If there's a lull, can I have a go at making a loaf?' he asked.

'The day I allow you near my oven with some dough is the day you allow me near your hair with a pair of scissors,' replied Stéphane Jollis, who was in no mood to humour his friend. The baker then ran through the orders again and reminded him to make sure that there were enough little cakes left for everyone, particularly the women. As he went next door to get ready, he instructed the matchmaker to acquaint himself with the till while he was gone. But Guillaume Ladoucette immediately wandered into the kitchen and gazed at the long wooden shovels, one for each size of loaf, lying on a bracket against the wall like oars in a boathouse. Slipping inside the cold room, he peered inside the sacks of flour, and was unable to resist putting his hand into each one to feel the different textures. He then noticed a bowl of freshly prepared *mouna* dough, into which he sank a finger and tasted the raw brioche flavoured with aniseed and filled with raisins fat with rum. And when the baker returned to ask the match-maker whether he looked all right, he was alarmed to see something already hanging from the man's whiskers.

'Have you had a practice on the till?' he enquired.

'Not yet,' admitted the matchmaker.

'I don't think you're taking this very seriously,' admonished the baker, his fatigue heightening his exasperation.

Stéphane Jollis then reminded Guillaume Ladoucette that not only was he a fifth-generation baker and so had the family name to uphold, but his traditional French baguette had come third in the previous year's Dordogne Federation of Bakers contest. He then showed him his fingernails, bitten to inflamed stumps with anxiety over the insufferable heat inflating his bread into shapes that frightened his customers. This was at a time, he continued, when the nation was only consuming a miserable 330 grams of bread a day, compared to 600 grams just after the war. He then added that while they had had a number of highly enjoyable dough fights in the shop over the years, during which they had finished off the rum intended for the *mille-feuilles*, this was not the time to be considering playing silly buggers as his livelihood was at stake.

Guillaume Ladoucette protested, insisting that he took the task very seriously indeed, and that if there was anyone the baker could trust with his shop it was he. He then congratulated his friend on the state of his shoes, admired the fit of his new white T-shirt and declared his hair a triumph. Reminding him not to pick his teeth with his fork if he and his match had lunch together, he then swiftly opened the door, insisting that it was always better to arrive early. But Stéphane Jollis stood his ground and reminded him that he was not to do any sums in his head or eat any of the little cakes. He then added that it was imperative that the bakery closed for the day at twelve-thirty, after which he was to shut the blinds and ignore any hammerings on the door, no matter how desperate, or indeed any bank notes stuffed underneath it, as people had to learn that bakers were entitled to a life too.

'Will do!' he replied, ushering the baker out. He stood by the door watching his friend drive off and, as soon as the coast was clear, Guillaume Ladoucette went in search of breakfast.

Sitting in the back on the baker's battered white stool, grounded by the weight of the largest warm almond croissant he could find, the matchmaker wondered how he was going to deliver his letter to Émilie Fraisse. He certainly didn't trust the clot of a postman. Neither did he wish to drop it into her letterbox himself as the gossip would be relentless if he was spotted. Nor did he have any intention of handing it to her when she came into the bakery lest she read it immediately and subjected him to the mortification of being rejected on the spot. At a loss as to what to do, he decided to have just one little cake to help him think.

It was while he was finishing off his third tartlet, and eyeing up the other delights amongst the trays that the thought struck him. He picked up a pair of tongs, went over to the rows of *mille-feuilles*, lifted one up and carried it carefully to the steel work counter. After inspecting it for size, he reached inside his pocket, brought out the letter and folded it several more times. Selecting one of the baker's sharpest knives, he then prised the cake apart and slid the letter between its pastry leaves. After closing it again, he inspected it from every angle. Satisfied that the letter was barely visible, he put it on a plate and carried it through to the front of the shop. He then added it to the row of *mille-feuilles* already on display, positioning it nearest to him so he would know which one it was. Standing for a moment admiring his own genius, Guillaume Ladoucette was suddenly brought out of his reverie by a thunderous rap at the door. The matchmaker looked at his watch and noticed to his horror that he was already thirteen minutes late opening the shop. It was another four before he had worked out how to raise the blinds, located the bunch of keys and discovered which one opened the door.

There was little he could say to appease the infuriated crowd waiting outside. With the startling agility elderly ladies muster when confronted with a queue, Madame

Moreau suddenly darted to the front. Having never forgiven Guillaume Ladoucette's mother for stuffing an eel down her cleavage several decades ago, she immediately demanded an explanation as to why the matchmaker was there. When he replied that the baker had urgent business to attend to and that he was just helping out for the morning, she requested a *gros pain* and five mixed fruit tartlets. The matchmaker immediately fetched a box for the cherry, Mirabelle and apricot wonders, but as he started to put them inside, soon found that only two would fit and had to start again with a larger one. After finally handing her the box and a deformed loaf, he discovered that he had no idea how to work the till as it was nothing like the one he had used in the barber's. He proceeded to calculate the sum in his head, but the figure he came to was immediately corrected by the old woman, who had the backing of the crowd. Unable to open the till, he was then obliged to furnish her with an IOU for her change. By his fourth customer, the stress was such that he was no longer capable of even attempting mental arithmetic, and he started to take suggestions for the totals from the queue. Eventually he worked his way through the crowd, a number of whom left with considerable bargains.

Taking advantage of the shop being momentarily empty, Guillaume Ladoucette wandered into the back to recover on Stéphane Jollis's battered white stool. But just as he sat down, the bell went. Hoping the customer would be scared off by the peculiar bread, the matchmaker didn't move. But after a while he heard a cough which he instantly recognized as that belonging to a woman who had waited long enough to be served some little cakes.

Heaving himself off the stool, he sloped back into the shop, hoping that whoever it was had the correct change so he wouldn't have to hand out yet another IOU. Standing at the counter was no ordinary customer, but Émilie Fraisse, wearing an antique amber dress which appeared to have been shorn off at the knees and something pinning up her hair that sparkled. The jubilant matchmaker immediately marched up to the counter, explained that Stéphane Jollis had left the bakery in his capable hands for the morning and asked what he could get for her.

'A *mille-feuille*, please,' she replied.

Guillaume Ladoucette, whose confidence only accompanied him so far before abandoning him, instantly felt his heart shrivel out of fear that he had already sold the cake containing her letter in the preceding panic. But leaning over the counter, he saw to his relief that it was still there, instantly recognizable by its unusual bulk.

'Certainly! Stéphane Jollis said you'd be in and asked me to save one for you specially,' he replied, picking up the bulging slice with his tongs and placing it carefully inside a box. So elated was he that his plan had worked, he then added another three, announcing that they were on the house.

As he tied the string, Émilie Fraisse asked whether he remembered the haircut he had once given her which made her look like a cockerel, much to the fury of her mother. Guillaume Ladoucette replied that he did indeed, and asked whether she remembered the mushrooms they used to pick together in the woods and cook over a fire in the caves where the Resistance hid during the war. When Émilie Fraisse replied that she did indeed, the matchmaker fetched another box and lowered several coffee *religieuses* inside to keep her there longer. As he was tucking in the lid, the châtelaine asked whether he remembered the accident they had had on his new moped when she fell on top of him. Guillaume Ladoucette replied that he did indeed and leant over the counter to show her that he still had the scar from her teeth. When Émilie Fraisse apologized again, Guillaume Ladoucette opened another box and placed inside four rum *babas* to show that there were no hard feelings. As he stacked

it on top of the other boxes, he asked whether she remembered the time when they had made a little mill wheel with a
bicycle tyre in the Belle to generate a light in their den in the
woods. Émilie Fraisse replied that she did indeed and asked
Guillaume Ladoucette whether he remembered his father
coming to her house to secretly eat apples after his mother
had banned them because of the trouble they had caused in
the Bible. Filling a box with apple tartlets so that she would
see that he hadn't inherited the prejudice, Guillaume
Ladoucette replied that he did indeed and asked her whether
she remembered the priest turning the village hall into a
little cinema every Saturday night and projecting a film of his
choosing that always shocked the audience. Émilie Fraisse
replied that she did indeed and asked whether he remembered
the time when he was an altar boy and urinated in the holy-
water receptacle before mass. In an effort to hide his hot
cheeks, Guillaume Ladoucette then bent over the counter and,
as he reached for four *noix charentaises*, admitted that he did.

By the time Émilie Fraisse walked out of the bakery, not
only had Guillaume Ladoucette boxed up all the little cakes
for her, including those in the back for the following day, but
he had waved away any attempts at payment as he didn't want
the châtelaine to know that he couldn't fathom out how to
work the till, nor that he was a mathematical incompetent.
She ended up with so much to carry, she was obliged to fetch
her car to take all the pâtisserie home with her.

The fury of Stéphane Jolliss's customers at finding that
there were no little cakes left did nothing to dampen
Guillaume Ladoucette's elation that his plan had worked. Nor
did he let their complaints about overcharging when he mis-
calculated the cost of their loaves upset him. For not only had
he managed to give Émilie Fraisse the correct *mille-feuille*, she
had in fact walked out with all of them so there was not the
slightest room for error. Such was his newfound ebullience,
Guillaume Ladoucette even shut the bakery half an hour

early when he could no longer face writing another IOU.

Walking home past the spot where the village cross used to be before the diocese deemed Amour-sur-Belle unworthy of it, he imagined Émilie Fraisse biting into her *mille-feuille* while sitting at the dining-room table, her pretty feet resting on the *pisé* floor. He saw her discovering his letter secreted between the pastry leaves and reading it enraptured. After having admired the beauty of his hand, as well as the letter's ingenious and unsurpassably romantic mode of delivery, she would look no further than the poet who wrote it in her search for love. After they had married, she would open the bedside table drawer, take out the tin of Docteur L. Guyot Throat Pastilles and place his reply inside. And the two letters, like their authors, would never be parted. So enchanted was he by the image that when Guillaume Ladoucette hoisted up his trouser legs to find the reason for his torment, he immediately forgave the mosquitoes who had left their satanic bites all over his ankles. And when he reached his house, and bent over to inspect an unsightly splat on the ground, he even felt pity for the bird which had gorged on his cherry tree and had had the uncomfortable task of then having to pass fourteen stones.

Stepping into the kitchen, he found that he was so full of contentment he had not the slightest room for an appetite. But he decided to have lunch anyway as it went against nature not to. After several slices of cow's muzzle, followed by a salad of oak-leaf lettuce and two rounds of Cabécou, he went upstairs for a nap after the morning's excitement. As he passed the spare bedroom, he went inside to close the shutters against the sun, which was in direct firing range. As he did so, he looked outside and noticed that Yves Lévèque's unspeakable *cornichons* had vanished. Magnanimous following his victory with the letter, upon waking the matchmaker decided to pop next door to offer the dentist his condolences. He was also keen to discover how he thought his date with Denise Vigier had gone, as the man hadn't been in to see him since their gold-panning expedition.

Reluctantly, Yves Lévèque let him in. They went to the bed where the *cornichons* had once been and, as they looked at their withered bodies lying on the compost heap, Guillaume Ladoucette resisted the urge to point out that they should have been sown when the moon was passing in front of the constellation of Aries.

Sitting at the white plastic garden table underneath the parasol, Yves Lévèque described his morning with the abhorrent grocer. Nonetheless, the matchmaker commended him for having paid for Denise Vigier, as well as for complimenting her on her dress. He even praised his skill at accepting gifts from others on learning that he had swiftly pocketed the golden nugget. Such was his joyful mood, he didn't even scold him for dismissing her out of turn because of what her grandmother had done during the war. He simply reminded him that he would get nowhere in his quest for love if he didn't concentrate on the duck leg, ignore the rancid parts and shrug his shoulders at the little green button.

'How did she say it had gone?' the dentist asked.

'Denise Vigier is blessed with optimism and said she would give it another go. I would suggest that you do.'

Eager to change the subject, Yves Lévèque went inside and returned with a tray upon which were two almond tartlets, one of which he put in front of his neighbour. The matchmaker was taken aback. Not only had the dentist never offered him anything to eat before, apart from his surplus figs and walnuts, but he hadn't seen him in the bakery that morning.

Guillaume Ladoucette immediately picked his up and took a bite. 'Delicious!' he declared, his mouth still full. 'Where did you get these from?'

'The château.'

'The château?' he asked, confused.

'Apparently you sold all the little cakes to Émilie Fraisse. She wasn't sure what do with them so she started giving them away. Word soon got around. All you had to do was go up there and she would give you a boxful.'

It was then that Guillaume Ladoucette realized that any one of the residents of Amour-sur-Belle could at that moment be reading his love letter to Émilie Fraisse, which had taken him twenty-six years to find the courage to write. He instantly put down his almond tartlet as all he could taste was horror.

17

UNFORTUNATELY FOR THE RESIDENTS OF AMOUR-SUR-BELLE IT WAS Madame Ladoucette who discovered that the hot water was back on in the municipal shower. She returned to the cubicle in the early hours of the morning, woken from her dreams by a troupe of edible dormice clattering their way between the rafters in the bathroom ceiling. But Madame Ladoucette, who had forgotten that her husband was long since dead, mistook the noise for his bones rattling against the floor-boards as he flipped and jerked in his sleep underneath the damp bath mat. When she got up to rest her Bible on top of him in order to put a stop to the racket, she found that she was not in the family home with its perpetual cassoulet on the stove, cellar lined with shelves of preserves and magnifi-cent walnut tree in the garden, but a tiny house in the centre of the village with nothing more for a garden than several pots of hostas at the back door, which had been so ravaged by slugs they resembled lace. Not only was she in the wrong house, but when she picked up the damp bath mat, there was not the slightest hint of her husband underneath it.

Assuming that he had got up in the night to secretly practise his acrobatic tricks, she rushed to the kitchen to safeguard her best dinner plates. However, the room was empty, and when she looked into the cupboards, in the place of her wedding china was a cheap set of crockery of which there were only four pieces each. She then opened the utensil drawer believing he had crept off to swallow her knives, but even the sharpest could be accounted for.

Suspecting that her husband was out somewhere picking apples, Madame Ladoucette quickly put on her pale-blue frock, shoes and stockings and stepped outside into the aromatic night. She wandered round the empty streets, poking her head over garden walls searching for him in the darkness. But there was not a trace. She then tried the disused quarry that had been turned over to the cultivation of button mushrooms. But instead of finding him at work amongst the piles of horse manure, she came across faded *Strictly No Entry* signs on the boarded-up entrance. Believing that he must be chatting to his brother as he fixed iron shoes on to the hooves of cows hanging from slings around their bellies, she headed for the blacksmith's. But when she arrived, she found that most of the roof had collapsed and what little remained sheltered four recently rolled bales of hay. Concluding that he had gone to see his friend at the abattoir, she set off to find him, but when she arrived she found rampant weeds which clasped at her crane's legs and stopped the door from opening. Convinced he must be in one of the bars, she then made a tour of all three of them, but discovered only the Saint-Jus was still in business, and its shutters were closed.

It was when she was making her way out of the place du Marché that Madame Ladoucette spotted the hilarious contraption next to the wall. Remembering its potential for amusement, she instantly abandoned her search for her husband and pulled open the door. Refusing to allow her feathered shadow to join her because of their previous poor behaviour, she stepped in alone. The pigeons stood outside, tapping their horny beaks mournfully against the plastic door as Madame Ladoucette stood under the warm water in a state of delight while her shoes overfilled. It wasn't until over two hours later, when the water had started to run cold, that they were finally reunited.

The second person to open the door of the municipal shower was Stéphane Jollis, who enjoyed two minutes and twenty-three seconds of tepid water before it reverted to its previous ruthless temperature for the rest of the day. The brief respite only infuriated the baker further, having had to get up earlier than usual to sort out the catastrophe created by Guillaume Ladoucette.

He had never felt entirely comfortable leaving the bakery in the hands of the matchmaker, particularly when he arrived at Brantôme two hours early for the Donkey Festival having been ushered out of his own premises by the man. But as he sat sipping his fourth coffee and having to eat another man's croissants in the *salon de thé* to kill time, he decided that it was a risk worth taking for a chance at love.

When the time eventually came, Stéphane Jollis paid his considerable bill and made his way to the curious sixteenth-century bridge, which, rather than straddling the Dronne in a straight line, was bent at an angle like a dog's leg. Unable to see anyone who fitted the matchmaker's description, he busied himself reading the information panel on the wall which explained that the *pont coudé* owed its unusual shape to having to resist the sometimes impetuous river. He then walked to the middle of it and stood looking at the ducks swimming in the reflection of the splendid abbey, now a town hall, where one of his friends had married only a week before. And, as the abominable sound of braying rose from the Monks' Garden, the baker wondered again why it was that out of all his eight siblings only he remained unmarried. He then imagined his own wedding and thought of the pine tree, which, according to custom, when the last child married would be erected outside the marital home, stripped of its branches and topped with a crown of leaves and flowers, from which plastic bottles of water would be hung. He pictured the cartridge he would be given to shoot them with, which would be filled with feathers that would flutter from the sky like snow. He then saw the bottle of wine that would be buried in the ground next to the tree and dug up to toast the birth of their first child, who would naturally be born with the same tiny hands as he. And while they would deny the boy a career as a concert pianist, they would bring him the unrivalled joy of rolling up croissants, folding over *pain au chocolat* dough with two sticks of chocolate, decorating little cakes and shovelling his own bread into the ancient oven built in Périgueux in 1880, all for which size didn't matter in the least.

After watching the tantalizing trout sashay their way down the Dronne, the baker looked up again to see if anyone else had arrived. He then noticed a small, dark-haired woman in shorts standing on her own near the information panel. When he approached and asked her whether she was waiting for someone sent by Guillaume Ladoucette, she replied that she was indeed. The woman then told the baker that she had seen him on the bridge, but assumed that he wasn't her match as he seemed so unlike the description the match-maker had given. And when Stéphane Jollis asked her whether she was disappointed, she replied: 'Not in the least.'

Once they had introduced themselves to one another they walked across the bridge to the Monks' Garden, the sound of the abominable braying growing ever louder. When the baker asked Vivienne Chaume where she was from, the cashier replied: 'St Félix of Mareuil or of Bourdeilles,' and explained that the row over the name had been going on for several centuries and that the council had settled for both while it continued for several more.

When she asked where he was from, the baker replied: 'Amour-sur-Belle', and pointed out that its ugliness worked to its advantage in that no English lived there. And he added that while, despite its name, there wasn't much love there either, the village matchmaker was doing his best. But when Vivienne Chaume asked whether Guillaume Ladoucette had had any successes yet, Stéphane Jollis had to admit that he hadn't.

After finding a spot on the grass in the shade of a large magnolia tree, they sat down to watch the contestants ride round in a circle in homemade chariots pulled by their pet donkeys, while the commentator admired the beauty of the beasts' legs, the sturdiness of their necks and the angle at which their colossal ears hung.

The cashier and baker chatted while they waited for the obstacle course to be set up, and clapped with glee with the rest of the crowd when the commentator announced that the competition was about to begin. They watched as the first contestant, wearing a black felt hat and waistcoat, walked his donkey, without its chariot, in and out of a line of barrels. But when man and beast approached a green plastic sheet stretched across the grass, instead of walking over it, the animal dug in its front legs and refused to budge. And no amount of tugging on its reins would shift it, because by now it had lowered its shaggy bottom to increase its resistance. After having to walk round the sheet, the pair then proceeded between the planks of wood without any trouble. Nor did the animal make a fuss when it was walked to the centre of the ring for each of its feet to be lifted. It was when they reached the low wooden seesaw that it revealed the true depth of its delinquency. After refusing to walk over it, the donkey marked its objection further by raising its tail and releasing a volley of undigested hay that tumbled down to the grass in unsightly chunks.

When the commentator announced the beginning of the

final round, during which the contestants had to drive their homemade chariots around the obstacle course, Stéphane Jollis and Vivienne Chaume, who were thoroughly enjoying themselves, shuffled forward on the grass to make sure of an uninterrupted view. They watched in admiration as a woman in a floor-length skirt made her way round with only minor glitches, and then nudged each other when it was the turn of the man with the black felt hat and waistcoat. They clapped as he wound in and out of the barrels, despite his being docked a point for missing one out. They clapped as he drove his pet over the green plastic sheet of which it now showed not the slightest hint of fear. They clapped as the man tried to perform a particularly difficult turn during which he was rebuked by the commentator for looking at a woman in the audience instead of his beast. And they cheered when instead of reversing for five paces before crossing the finishing line the donkey bolted over it as if in a corrida, much to the terror of its white-eyed owner rattling in the homemade chariot behind.

While the prizes were being given out, Stéphane Jollis suggested to Vivienne Chaume that they went to look around the cheese and wine fair that was also taking place in the park. When they approached the first stand, the young viti-culturist from Domaine Rivaton, whose vines grew all the way down in Languedoc-Roussillon, offered them a *dégustation*, which Stéphane Jollis readily accepted. The baker was so thrilled by the man's Rosée des Prés that he bought four bottles. They then visited the stand of the woman from Berry who was selling pieces of *casse-museau*, a non-sweetened cake made with goat fromage frais according to an ancient recipe, which was eaten either as an hors d'oeuvre or with salad. Stéphane Jollis was so intrigued he immediately bought a whole one for each of them to take home. While passing the stand of Château Haut Jean Redon, the young viticulturist from Bordeaux also offered them a *dégustation*, which Stéphane Jollis thought a splendid idea. The baker was so struck by the quality of his 2003 vintage, which had just won a bronze medal in the International Wine Challenge, that he bought four bottles. They then crossed to the stand of the cheesemaker from Broc, where the baker so admired the *dégustation* of Monsieur Baechler's Fleuron, which had been maturing in his cellars for twelve months, that he bought an entire round of it. And when they reached Michel Fallet's champagne stall, the baker could see no reason why not to buy a bottle and drink it right there and then with the delectable Vivienne Chaume, who not only appreciated a good-looking donkey when she saw one, but was splendid company.

As he handed his match a glass, the baker was in such a state of delight that he invited her to come to the bakery one day the following week for a *dégustation* of his little cakes. Vivienne Chaume then horrified Stéphane Jollis by thanking him, but refusing all the same on the grounds that she was on a diet. The baker, who could see no possible future with a woman who would wilfully deny herself the exquisite pleasure of choux pastry filled with *crème pâtissière* by his award-winning fingers, felt instantly that it was time to go home.

Guillaume Ladoucette sat at the desk with the ink stain, his bare feet hunting for cool patches on the floor as he dreaded the door opening. Whilst he knew he would be in serious trouble with the baker, his was the only arrival he didn't fear as he was one of the few people who couldn't have received his love letter intended for Émilie Fraisse. Having omitted to write her name at the top of it in case it stalled his out-pourings, there was no doubt that its recipient would naturally assume that they were the subject of his amorous declaration. As a result, he had risen early in an attempt to avoid bumping into anyone at the municipal shower, but had been caught out by Gilbert Dubuisson who landed a series of vexed knocks on the door when the matchmaker didn't dare come out, having heard someone waiting outside. Debating whether to make a run for it, Guillaume Ladoucette slowly opened the door. But the postman immediately blocked his path and asked whether there was anything the matchmaker could do to make Émilie Fraisse change her mind and see him again. Guillaume Ladoucette assured him that as far as he knew he had acted like a perfect gentleman throughout, but that she had made up her mind. He then added that there were several women on his books who would find his company nothing short of a delight, and that he should come by when he had a moment and he would sort something out. After the postman had thanked him, Guillaume Ladoucette set off home, hoping he wouldn't take it as an open invitation to install himself on the bench for the afternoon and bore him to frustration with unfounded gossip while spraying the room with Petit Beurre Lu biscuit crumbs.

The matchmaker had just retreated to the back of the shop, where he hoped he would be less conspicuous, when the door opened. It was Lisette Robert.

'Are you all right?' she immediately asked, sitting down on the cushion with the hand-embroidered radish.

'Fine, thanks. Why?' he replied, approaching the desk and trying not to show the least flicker of emotion, let alone twenty-six years of unremitting love.

'You're looking at me in a funny way.'

'Funny how?'

'Just funny.'

'You didn't happen to see Émilie Fraisse yesterday, by any chance?' he asked.

'Yes, I did, actually.'

'At the château?'

'Yes, why?'

'Just wondered. She didn't give you any little cakes, did she?'

'Well, yes, that's what I went up there for. Apparently you sold her the lot and she called me to see if I wanted any. I got a boxful.'

Guillaume Ladoucette paused, stalled by panic. 'There didn't happen to be any *mille-feuilles* in there, did there?' he asked.

'Two custard tartlets and two *choux Chantilly*. Why?'

'Just wondered! Now, Lisette, glass of red?'

After offering her a walnut, which was refused as she had her own to get through, Guillaume Ladoucette had the unfortunate task of breaking the news to Lisette Robert that, as incomprehensible as it may seem, the man from the council wasn't interested. The matchmaker told her about their long talk at the washing place and that while he hadn't revealed who she was, he had gone to great lengths detailing her considerable charms. He had even tried a couple more times since, he added, but Jean-François Lafforest was having none of it.

Lisette Robert listened carefully, blinked several times and then asked dolefully: 'Is there nothing more you can do?'

'I'm afraid not, Lisette. There are only so many times I can ask. The man is resolute. I've never seen anything like it.'

The midwife looked at the floor, and the matchmaker looked at the pen next to the blank piece of paper in front of him. After a moment deep in thought, he raised his eyes and said: 'While there is nothing more I can do in my professional capacity, let me ask you this, Lisette: What would any right-minded person do if they went to the woods to pick mushrooms and came across one of those signs which say *The Picking of Mushrooms is Forbidden*?'

'Carry on regardless,' she replied without hesitation.

'Exactly!' he said.

Guillaume Ladoucette was correct in his suspicion that Lisette Robert was responsible for the sudden lack of hot water in the municipal shower. When word got around that the pipe had been sabotaged, everyone assumed it was the work of the Clandestine Committee against the Municipal Shower, apart from the matchmaker who knew full well that such ingenuity was beyond them as they couldn't even remember their own code names.

Lisette Robert had fallen quite unexpectedly for the man from the council. She had noticed something about him the first time he came into the Bar Saint-Jus with his soft leather briefcase, which he had clutched to his stomach, wearing his unfortunate trousers that didn't quite fit. There was a gentleness in his being that attracted her, as well as the weight of a past pain that he carried. When, to her delight, he returned to oversee the installation of the municipal shower, she would sit at the window of the bar, glancing at him over a copy of the *Sud Ouest*, the content of which she was too disturbed to take in. At night, as the perpetual breeze rode up and down her curves that were more graceful than those of the Belle, she would lie awake, her mind stirred to its sediments with thoughts of him. One dawn, unable to bear the agitation any longer, she got up to compose him a melody. Instead of the villagers being roused from their dreams by the poisonous sound of her elephantine attempts at piano playing, the most angelic strains rose from the keys and fluttered around Amour-sur-Belle.

Such was her devastation that Jean-François Lafforest no longer had any reason to come to the village once the shower was completed, she slipped out one night with her spanner to provide him with one. When, the following day, she was summoned to the cubicle by the villagers to explain to him how she had discovered that there was no longer any hot water, she was delighted to have the opportunity to stand as close to him as possible. After he had declared the ornithological findings irrelevant, and handed her back the seven grey feathers, she put the one he had held the longest inside her bedside drawer and at night would brush it back and forth against her lips as her mind spun with thoughts of him.

After the midwife left Heart's Desire to start running her first of five baths that day, Guillaume Ladoucette looked at his watch, hoping it was lunchtime so that he could go home and hide for a few hours. But it was only twenty to eleven.

Reaching into the top left-hand drawer, he took out his slim file of customers and started to read through it hoping to be struck by an inspiring match, but his mind kept parading him ghastly images of his amorous declaration in the most inappropriate of hands.

Just as he was checking his watch again, only to be disappointed a second time, the door opened. It was Stéphane Jollis, looking more floury than usual.

'I can explain everything!' said the matchmaker as soon as he saw him.

'I was hoping you could,' replied the baker, heading for the chair with the peeling marquetry and sitting down.

'Émilie Fraisse came in and we got talking about the old days and before I knew it I'd sold her the lot. I got carried away. It must have been the salesman in me.'

'But you didn't exactly sell them to her, did you, Guillaume?' replied Stéphane Jollis. 'I've counted up the money you left by the till, which for some reason you didn't open, and it certainly doesn't account for the two hundred and forty-six little cakes I left in your custody. Not only were there none left for my customers yesterday, there aren't any for them today. And on top of that people have been coming in waving IOUs at me all morning, a significant number of which I suspect are forgeries.'

'Forgive me, Stéphane. I'll make it up to you, I promise,' insisted Guillaume Ladoucette. 'And, of course, I'll pay for all the little cakes.'

'Not only were there no rum *babas* left for Madame Serre, so she had to go and hunt one down at the château,' the baker continued, 'but apparently you were unable to correctly add up a croissant and a six-cereal loaf.'

'I'll waive the fee for the Unrivalled Silver Service as well. How's about that?'

'It's a start,' replied the baker.

'Anyway,' said the matchmaker, desperate to change the subject. 'On to more exciting things – how did it go with the charming Vivienne Chaume?'

'She's on a diet.'

'A what?'

'A diet.'

'How extraordinary!' replied the horrified matchmaker. 'No, no, that will never do. You want someone who will revel in your talent, not recoil in terror each time you whip out your piping bag. And what would happen if you got married and she decided to go on another diet and people got wind that Madame la Boulangère was refusing your little cakes? It hardly bears thinking about. Do accept my apologies, Stéphane, I had no idea. It just goes to show that you shouldn't judge people by their appearance. She seemed perfectly sane when she walked in here. I'll mark it on her file. The mobile butcher won't be interested either. Now let's see who else we can find for you . . .'

But Stéphane Jollis said he had to return to work and that he would leave it for a few weeks until things had calmed down. When the door closed, the matchmaker watched his friend walk past the window in his blue-and-white checked shorts, opal varicose veins which came with the job crawling down his ample calves, which finished in a pair of ridiculously small feet. Guillaume Ladoucette looked at his watch. It was a perfectly reasonable time to close, he concluded. It was only half an hour before midday and matters of the heart shouldn't be discussed on an empty stomach, so it would be in everyone's interest if he left now. He packed up his things as quickly as he could and congratulated himself on having shut the door behind him before anyone could sit down on the cushion with the hand-embroidered radish and thank him for such a wondrous declaration of devotion.

The matchmaker set out for home the long way round in the hope of avoiding bumping into anyone. But as he passed the old communal bread oven Fabrice Ribou came round the corner. 'Hello, Guillaume!' he said.

'Hello,' muttered the matchmaker, not looking him in the eye.

'I must say, you're a man of passion, aren't you?'

'I am?' asked Guillaume Ladoucette, horrified.

'And so romantic. I would never have guessed.'

'It was a mistake.'

'Surely not.'

'Yes, it was. Honestly it was,' insisted the matchmaker.

'Anyway, I'm not of that persuasion, if you get my drift.'

'Nor am I!'

'But if ever my marriage comes to an end, I'll be straight round.'

'No, don't!'

'Everyone's been talking about all these little romantic encounters you've been organizing. And we all saw Lisette Robert and Marcel Coussy having a drink together. Lucky sod. I feel a bit left out, to be honest with you, but I've already got a wife so I can't join in. Or can I?'

Guillaume blinked several times.

'Of course you can!' he said smiling with relief.

'Fantastic!' replied the bar owner, his pine-cone haircut quivering at the very thought. 'When can I start?'

'Actually, you can't,' said the matchmaker, his mind clearing of panic.

'No?'

'Sorry. It's just for single people, I'm afraid.'

'Shame. Never mind. The job must be keeping you busy. I haven't seen you in the bar for ages.'

'I've been feeling a bit under the weather.'

'You should come by. How else am I going to become rich?'

Guillaume Ladoucette locked his front door behind him to prevent the sudden arrival of unexpected guests. In an effort to remind himself that life still had its pleasures, he descended the creaking wooden steps of the cellar, clattered around for a while in his grandfather's Sunday clogs that nipped and emerged triumphantly with a jar of potted goose. But just as he took his first mouthful at the kitchen table, it suddenly occurred to him that Madame Serre hadn't been sitting outside her front door like a sentinel on his return. He instantly imagined Émilie Fraisse telling her that there were no rum *babas* left and her having to leave with a box of *mille-feuilles* instead. Unable to make out his letter because of her poor eyesight, he then saw her taking it to the grocer, who read it out to her in the presence of a particularly long queue of customers. And the reason why Madame Serre was no longer at her post outside her front door was because she was hiding from him in horror at his amorous outpourings.

Hoping to take his mind off his troubles, he went into the garden to make a start on the first of his walnut wines, which he would make according to the leaf method as tradition dictated that the green nuts shouldn't be used until after 14 July. But as he climbed his ladder, he thought what a fool he had been to have given Émilie Fraisse all the little cakes. As he put the leaves to steep in four parts of wine to one of brandy, and added the sugar and orange peel, he thought how ridiculous he had been ever to think he could win her back. And as he poured the mixture into bottles and carried them down to the cellar to stand for a year, he wondered, as he often did, what she was doing.

*

Émilie Fraisse was in the vaulted kitchen shunting around the contents of her fridge looking for a little something to quell her appetite. Pushing to one side a beautiful piece of liver purchased from the mobile butcher, she came across the last of the boxes from the bakery. The châtelaine still couldn't understand how she had managed to come away with quite so many, particularly when all she had asked for was a solitary *mille-feuille*. She hadn't been home long before she realized she couldn't possibly get through all of their contents on her own and started calling people in the hope of offloading them. Not, of course, that she had minded the embarrassment of *pâtisserie* because each time Guillaume Ladoucette had stopped to open up another box, discovered that he had the wrong size, found the correct one, filled it up and tied the string, she had gained a few more minutes in his company.

She brought the box to the kitchen table, along with a glass of sweet white Château Marie Plaisance Bergerac. Lifting up the cardboard lid, she took out the first *mille-feuille* that Guillaume Ladoucette had chosen for her which she had naturally kept for herself because of its size. It wasn't until several chews and swallows later that it struck Émilie Fraisse that Stéphane Jollis's baking was far from its usual glorious standard. Inspecting it to determine what had gone wrong, she suddenly noticed something wedged inside. Pulling the cake apart, she retrieved a lump sodden with rum-laced *crème pâtissière*. When, eventually, she managed to unfold it, she found what appeared to be a letter. While the ink had bled and parts, including the signature, had just been swallowed, she could just about make out the words. And as she read, she realized that she had received her very first love letter, which was of such rapturous sentiment her heart soared higher than the buzzards above the scandalous ramparts. But what Émilie Fraisse couldn't understand was how the baker could have loved her all these years and not given her the slightest inkling.

18

IT WAS WHEN GUILLAUME LADOUCETTE WALKED SLOWLY downstairs in his burgundy silk dressing gown with the same reluctance to face the world that he had felt for the last week and spotted Violette the infernal chicken sitting on the rim of his pot of cassoulet, her tail lifted over its contents in readiness, that he finally snapped. The bird matched his shriek of outrage with a squawk of similar volume and immediately took to the air, flapping round the kitchen in frantic ginger circles that sent the pans clattering into each other on their hooks and the row of Peugeot coffee grinders on the pale stone mantelpiece crashing to the floor.

Ducking down, he ran to open the back door, through which the bird immediately fled for the safety of the garden wall. After locking the door again, the horrified matchmaker rushed to the stove fearing that the family's perpetual cassoulet, which had outlasted ten prime ministers, had been ruined in the flick of a tail feather. After examining the surface, he took a wooden spoon and slowly poked through the contents, peering underneath the pieces of duck, scrutinizing the pieces of Toulouse sausage, sifting through the haricot beans and lifting out the grey goose bone for closer inspection.

Yet the relief at finding the dish unsullied was not enough to calm Guillaume Ladoucette. Neither was the novelty of warm water in the municipal shower able to improve his mood. After returning home to dress, he headed immediately to the Bar Saint-Jus with as much determination as he could muster in a pair of supermarket leather sandals. Ignoring Sandrine Fournier, the mushroom poisoner, who approached him wanting to know whether he had found her another match, he walked straight up to Fabrice Ribou who was cleaning the coffee machine and announced: 'Your chicken's stalking me.'

On seeing his fury, something he had never witnessed before, the bar owner immediately offered him a seat and a drink on the house. He sat and listened as the matchmaker related how for the last six months he had suffered the indignity of peck marks in his butter and apricots, feathers in his *pineau*, tell-tale four-toed footprints in the talc on the bathroom floor and eggs in the most unacceptable of places. When he told him that the final straw had been the sight of Violette the infernal chicken about to defile his cassoulet, Fabrice Ribou immediately leapt to the bird's defence, claiming that a creature of her nature couldn't possibly be responsible for the man's torment and that it was probably someone else's. But the matchmaker reminded him that having grown up with chickens he was more than capable of telling them apart. And in any case, Violette's unfortunate features were unmistakable.

'She must be very fond of you,' concluded the bar owner, leaning back in his chair. 'She never comes anywhere near us.'

'But I don't want the affection of a chicken! I assure you her feelings are totally unrequited,' replied the exasperated matchmaker.

When Fabrice Ribou suggested that he kept his back door shut so she couldn't wander in, Guillaume Ladoucette leant towards him. Not only did he keep his back door shut at all times, he insisted with quiet rage, but for the last six months he had locked it again every time he had come through it. Neither was she getting in through the windows as he tied them in such a fashion that there was only the narrowest of openings through which a bird of her figure would be unable to squeeze. And when he opened them at night, he kept the shutters closed. How she was getting in was an utter mystery.

Fabrice Ribou sighed and brushed an invisible crumb off the table. While he couldn't lock up the bird as, he reasoned, she too deserved her freedom, and nor was he responsible for whom she fell in love with, he would be willing to come round at some stage to shore up Guillaume Ladoucette's defences. But the matchmaker, who rarely put his foot down, insisted that he came that instant.

Leaving the bar in the hands of his wife, Fabrice Ribou accompanied Guillaume Ladoucette home. After checking the locks on the front and back doors, he then asked the matchmaker to show him how he tied the windows and agreed that a chicken of Violette's girth couldn't possibly squeeze through the gap. They then went down to the cellar with its shelves of preserves and ancient farming utensils laced with cobwebs. While the bar owner looked around, Guillaume Ladoucette sat on the bottom step watching the man in silent fury. Not only was he incapable of admitting to having had his hair cut in the most preposterous of fashions by a rival barber, he thought, but such was his disregard for others he let his hooligan of a chicken roam around the village willy-nilly. Fabrice Ribou then announced that with no openings to the outside, it was impossible that the bird was getting in from the cellar. Taking a quick look at the astrological maps and planetary charts covering the walls, he then asked Guillaume Ladoucette what he should be doing about his melons. While the matchmaker thought the man didn't deserve his expertise, he nevertheless replied that it was a most auspicious time to be planting them out, adding that he should make sure that he nipped off the stems that grew above the first two leaves only when the moon was passing in front of Leo.

As they trooped up to the attic, Guillaume Ladoucette pointed out the path the eggs took when rolling across the landing at night when he was trying to sleep. He then opened the airing cupboard in the bathroom and showed him a fresh black-and-white dropping on a pile of otherwise clean cotton underpants. As they turned the corner on the stairs, he picked up a ginger feather from the floor and held it silently underneath the bar owner's nose. Once in the attic, Fabrice Ribou inspected the three tiny arch-shaped holes under the eaves which used to serve as entrances for pigeons at the time when they were kept for food. But the bar owner found that, like all the others in the village, the holes had been blocked off with a pane of glass decades ago.

'That only leaves the chimneys,' he concluded. The two men then headed back down to the kitchen. After Guillaume Ladoucette had picked up the coffee grinders from the floor, two of which had cracked, they peered up inside the blackened opening above the fireplace. After inspecting the one in the sitting room, Fabrice Ribou then announced that he would go and pick up some wire meshing and cover the tops of the stacks so that not even le père Noël with his wily ways could get down them.

Showing him out, the matchmaker thanked the bar owner for his help, unaware that it was rooted solely in his fear that Guillaume Ladoucette would put Violette in a pot before he did. The matchmaker had intended to spend the rest of the weekend behind closed doors, but Stéphane Jollis was insistent that he helped him at the Fête de la Saint-Jean celebrations that evening. Guillaume Ladoucette had tried to get out of it as the last thing he wanted to do was attend a social function frequented by the entire village as well as the inhabitants of the surrounding hamlets. But the baker was adamant, reminding him that he still owed him a favour.

To take his mind off the misery that lay ahead of him, Guillaume Ladoucette went outside to lose himself in the cultivation of vegetables. He thwacked his way across the grass to his shed, which he ran with the same rigour as a captain did his bridge, and pulled open the table drawer. Inside, amongst a pile of seed packets arranged in alphabetical order, he found those for his winter radish, which would eventually be thinned out when the moon was in Virgo. As he started to prepare the earth next to a row of round courgettes, he heard the clattering of Fabrice Ribou's ladder. And for the first time upon spotting Violette the infernal chicken warming her fluffy undercarriage on the garden wall, Guillaume Ladoucette smiled.

Up on the scandalous ramparts, Émilie Fraisse picked her way past the buckets of dried cement and stacks of old tiles abandoned by the previous owner when his delusion that he could make a difference had passed. Finding a spot in the shade, she sat down with her back against the stone wall. In her hand was the partly eaten letter, which, after having wiped off the *crème pâtissière*, she had left out in the sun to dry. As she read it yet again, it spoke of such rapturous affection that her heart blossomed. It was only upon remembering that it wasn't from the man she had always loved that the petals dropped. As she sat looking at the discarded walnut shells left by squirrels, she wondered whether she could ever feel the same ardour for the baker as he did for her. But while his letter was such bewitching poetry, and she had the utmost admiration for his work as an artisan, she knew that his were not the arms in which she longed to shelter.

More aware than most that letters had to be answered, Émilie Fraisse decided to go and speak to Stéphane Jollis. After pulling out her ridiculous seventeenth-century shoes from underneath her four-poster Renaissance bed, she clopped her way down the spiral stone staircase with its lamentable repairs, opened the vast door and crunched her way across the drawbridge. But when she arrived at the bakery, in an antique tea-rose dress which appeared to have been shorn off at the knees, she found a queue reaching all the way to the spot where the village cross had been before the diocese deemed Amour-sur-Belle unworthy of it. When Émilie Fraisse asked a woman in the queue why so many people were waiting, she replied that a love note had been found in one of the baker's little cakes, and while the sender's identity ws uncertain, they were all hoping to find one of their own. The shocked châtelaine, who had told only two people of her discovery, both of whom had sworn to keep the matter to themselves, decided to return later.

It wasn't Lisette Robert who had let slip about the curious correspondence in Émilie Fraisse's *mille-feuille*. When the châtelaine knocked at her door asking for help in deciphering the words blurred by rum-laced *crème pâtissière*, the midwife had taken one look at the letter and instantly recognized the hand of Guillaume Ladoucette. However, her cursed inability to gossip had prevented her from pointing out the sender's true identity. And when Émilie Fraisse eventually left, the midwife never spoke of it again and simply stored the intriguing episode in her cabinet of curiosities.

The person responsible for the enormous queue at the bakery was in fact Sandrine Fournier the mushroom poisoner. When news spread that Émilie Fraisse had made off with all the bakery's little cakes, the assistant ambulant fishmonger had knocked at the château door in the hope of wresting a coffee éclair from her. When Émilie Fraisse explained that they had all gone, such was the woman's disappointment that she immediately invited her in for an apéritif to console her. It was when Sandrine Fournier got up from the seat which slid open to hide the salt from the tax collector in order to admire the view from the window that she noticed the letter on the table. Despite the châtelaine's bountiful imagination, she was unable to come up with an explanation for the soggy missive other than the truth, that she had found it in her *mille-feuille*. The assistant ambulant fishmonger told Madame Serre of the discovery while wrapping up her trout, and advised her to inspect her rum *babas* carefully as she didn't want the old woman to choke to death before she had paid her monthly bill. Madame Serre, who had failed to catch the name of the recipient, changed it each time she repeated the tale, confident that eventually she would land on the correct one.

As Émilie Fraisse was making her way back up the rue du Château that did lead to the castle, Yves Lévèque pulled over to thank her again for the almond tartlets. However, it wasn't courtesy that had made him stop, but a desire to put off as long as possible his rendezvous with Denise Vigier. He had just got as far as asking Émilie Fraisse about the provenance of the llama skeleton in the hall when he was obliged to move as Marcel Coussy had come up behind him with two bales of hay impaled on the front of his tractor. Driving out of the village, the dentist turned right at the field with the ginger Limousin cows that winked and headed for Sorges. As he entered the flat green valley with its tumbledown château on the hill, he tried to remember how on earth the matchmaker had talked him into meeting the repugnant grocer again. And, as he approached the village, he decided that it was time to give up his quest for love as it was proving even more painful than his confounded constipation.

After parking outside the church with its carved skull and trumpeting angels above the door, Yves Lévèque was disappointed to see a sign indicating the way to the Truffle Museum as it meant he would be unable to go home claiming that it was impossible to find. As he passed the charming stone houses with their closed blue shutters, the stone in his heart plummeted even further when he saw the grocer already standing in the shade of a plane tree outside the museum mopping herself with a handkerchief. Kissing her on each cheek from as far a distance as possible, he then complimented her on her atrocious dress, which was so devoid of allure he was in no doubt that it had come from the stall in the market.

Once inside, the pair stood together briefly at the kiosk until Denise Vigier could no longer resist the lure of the gift shop and darted off. When the woman behind the counter handed him two tickets, Yves Lévèque knew he was cornered and reluctantly his long, pale instruments of torture found their way into his pocket. Wanting to get the ordeal over as quickly as possible, he entered the exhibition devoted to the prized Périgord truffle, known as the black diamond, and walked up to the first panel. As he was reading that truffles had no roots, shoots, leaves or true fruits, which had often baffled scientists as to whether they belonged to the animal or vegetable kingdom, Denise Vigier came in holding a tiny paper bag containing a truffle-shaped nail brush and began to study a panel out of sequence. As she stood learning about how the celebrated fungus could be found in the circular bare patch of earth that surrounded certain trees, pitched forward by her colossal chest as if battling against driving rain, the dentist wondered again what in heaven's name the matchmaker had been thinking of.

When the grocer disappeared to look at the exhibits round the corner, Yves Lévèque hung back and approached a cabinet of what appeared to be scorched brains in specimen jars. But as he peered at the 570-gram *truffe du Périgord* found in Sorges on 19 December 1995 by Monsieur Jean-Noël Combeau, all he could think about was the monstrous price

Denise Vigier charged for her mushrooms compared to those in the supermarket.

As soon as he saw her returning, the dentist swiftly walked off to read about the train that ran twice a week on market days between Excideuil and Périgueux, which truffle-hunters boarded with full baskets, the aroma of which was so strong that the railway authorities were obliged to reserve them a compartment so the smell would not compete with the ladies' scent. But his mind was transported to the grocer's treacherous grandmother who had been found guilty of horizontal collaboration at a tribunal in 1944 and, after a swastika had been drawn on her forehead, given a 'Number 44' haircut in front of a spitting crowd in Périgueux.

Denise Vigier was well aware of what was still said about her grandmother behind her back. The grocer had never asked her the truth of it, or indeed the truth of anything, for her grandmother had died a year after the war giving birth to her only daughter. The doctors all agreed that her death was a result of the terrible assaults she had endured, which were of such severity they judged it best not to tell her husband. It was never known who had denounced her, as there had been so many contenders. Everyone in Amour-sur-Belle knew that the Nazi had come to her house for the hunting gun the first night, as he had fired it into the air as a warning. Everyone knew that he had come for the pig on the second night as they had been woken by its squeals. But no one knew that when he came for Denise Vigier's grandmother the subsequent nights he had held a knife to the teenager's throat to silence her whimpers. Nor did anyone ever know about the scissors she had plunged between his shoulder blades one night when he was on top of her, where they remained to this day, below nine feet of earth in the garden behind the family shop.

Yves Lévèque was just about to suggest to the grocer that it was time to leave when suddenly one of the panels caught his eye. He retraced his steps and started to read about how Venus, when mourning the death of Adonis, was consoled by Amour telling her that a new fruit had been created in her garden that would cause eagerness in couples, and that it would be attributed with Adonis' virility. Amour then buried Adonis' body in a field where it germinated and converted into black truffles. Once harvested, he served them for supper at Venus' house when Mars was invited. While Venus refused to eat them, Mars finished the lot. The blonde Venus was never so beautiful the following morning and Mars beamed with utter satisfaction.

The dentist immediately went in search of Denise Vigier and asked her whether she fancied a spot of lunch in the village's Auberge de la Truffe. The grocer, who had found the museum fascinating, and was still thrilled with her purchase of a truffle-shaped nailbrush, thought it a marvellous idea. Despite the restaurant's splendid reputation, the pair managed to get a table with a yellow tablecloth in the conservatory overlooking the terrace. When the gracious waiter arrived to take their orders, Denise Vigier said she was considering the confit of duck. However, Yves Lévèque suggested that they both tried the special five-course truffle menu at a hundred euros per head, and that she wasn't to worry at the staggering cost because it was all on him.

It wasn't long before the truffle consommés arrived. As they marvelled at the forestry flavour and found to their delight slices of truffle lurking in the bottom of the oaky water, the dentist discovered that Denise Vigier had the most exceptional sense of humour. And as they joyfully savoured their scrambled eggs flecked with truffles, served with a magnificent foie gras resting on a bed of apple in a succulent truffle sauce, the grocer suddenly noticed the intense blue of the dentist's eyes behind his spectacles.

As the waiter appeared with their cod stuffed with slices of truffle and wished them 'Bonne continuation' before turning silently on his heels, Yves Lévèque found himself patting the grocer's knee as he asked her whether she wanted some more bread.

When the fourth course arrived in the form of two large ovals of puff pastry, the gracious waiter carefully cut a circle in the top of the one he had placed in front of Denise Vigier and, with the words *'Voilà la merveille!'*, lifted it up to reveal an enormous truffle inside sliced with a potato. And when Yves Lévèque started to cut his open, he thought to himself that he had already found his marvel.

After the truffle ice cream arrived, and the dentist declared that he couldn't possibly eat any more, Denise Vigier found herself resting her hand on his arm as she told him it was too rapturous to miss. As she held up a spoonful to his lips, and the fungal ecstasy slipped down his throat, the dentist realized that a colossal bosom was nothing short of a triumphant asset. And when, later that afternoon, he felt the enormous soft mounds against his naked back, Yves Lévèque sent up a silent prayer of thanks to St Anthony, the patron saint of truffle-growers.

After receiving a second call from the baker asking where he was, Guillaume Ladoucette reluctantly made his way to the field on the edge of the village where the fête was taking place. The enormous bonfire was already stacked up with a young oak propped up in the centre, the result of several days of arguments as a faction of the Comité des Fêtes insisted that a pine was always used. Certainly, no one could remember why a fire was lit to mark John the Baptist's day, a man known for his propensity for hurling water. Most assumed that it was a Midsummer pagan ritual adopted by the Christians to make them appear more alluring.

Just as the matchmaker had feared, people were already arriving, though it was only five o'clock. For, despite the fact that the residents of Amour-sur-Belle had little regard for one another, there was nothing they liked better than a community feed-up. And if a little light entertainment was laid on as well, giving them the excuse to take to the dance floor or to sing at considerable volume before the hors d'oeuvres were served, so much the better.

The matchmaker found Stéphane Jollis behind the bar, wiping the sweat coursing down his temples on alternate shoulders as he served villagers pitchers of rosé while ignoring complaints that the crisps in the bowls on the counter were stale. Guillaume Ladoucette hovered, hoping that everything was in hand and that he could slip away, but the baker suddenly spotted him and told him that help was needed with the food. The matchmaker lingered a moment, expecting his friend to pass him a glass of *pineau* to help dull the pain of being there, but the baker disappeared again behind the mob waiting to be served.

As Guillaume Ladoucette approached the trestle table covered with bowls of salad and grated carrot, Monsieur Moreau, who had temporarily vacated the bench by the fountain said to cure gout, informed the matchmaker that he was needed to baste the mutton, which was already turning on the spit. Guillaume Ladoucette reluctantly picked up the paintbrush, dunked it into the marinade and started dabbing at the sheep's carcass. Despite keeping his head down so as not to be recognized, it wasn't long before he heard someone calling his name. He looked up to see Madame Serre approaching. Within minutes he had learnt that it wasn't in fact she who had received his letter, but Didier Lapierre.

The matchmaker continued prodding with his brush, wondering what he should do. Should he wait for the carpenter to bring it up, or should he go and tell him that it had all been a terrible mistake? He worked through the various options as the meat hissed over the fire. But before he had made up his mind, the man suddenly appeared before him. However, Didier Lapierre didn't want to thump him at all. Instead, the man with the pine-cone haircut wanted to know whether it was true that Madame Moreau had received a love letter from a secret admirer.

The matchmaker assumed that the carpenter was being mischievous by not naming him as the sender. He then looked at the woman's husband standing several feet away, picking out foil-wrapped potatoes from the ashes, and wondered whether it was bad manners to strike an old man in self-defence.

It wasn't long before the villagers were demanding to be fed. Much to the matchmaker's distress, as he thought his work was now over, Monsieur Moreau informed Guillaume Ladoucette, whom he still hadn't forgiven for stealing his painting, that he was needed to carve. First in line with his empty paper plate was Fabrice Ribou, who not only asked for a big slice in return for having blocked up the matchmaker's chimneys for him, but couldn't resist telling him that Denise Vigier had found a love letter in a little cake from a mystery admirer.

'I thought it was Madame Moreau,' hissed the matchmaker.

'It wasn't either of them,' interrupted Madame Ribou, who was standing behind her husband listening with the attentive ear of a woman who had worked in a bar for three decades. 'It was Modeste Simon.'

After carving them each a slice, Guillaume Ladoucette looked around the field, and then noticed to his horror that Modeste Simon had just joined the end of the queue. Slowly, she moved up the line towards him and eventually held out her plate, maintaining the silence she had kept since the unfortunate disappearance of Patrice Baudin, the skinny vegetarian pharmacist. After he had served her, keeping his eyes lowered, Guillaume Ladoucette then watched as she found herself a seat at one of the trestle tables underneath the lime trees.

He was still wondering what to do, as it was unlikely that

she would reply if he spoke to her, when one of the inhabitants from a neighbouring hamlet called his name, held out his plate and asked: 'Did you hear about the love letter Marcel Coussy received inside a chocolate éclair? Apparently it was a work of unparalleled poetry.'

As night squeezed out the day and the accordion player struck up, Guillaume Ladoucette started to head home. But Stéphane Jollis spotted him and insisted that he had something to eat for his efforts. Though his appetite had abandoned him, the matchmaker reluctantly helped himself and found a seat underneath the lime trees next to the postman as the bonfire blazed.

He stayed put as people left the benches, joined hands and started dancing in a circle round the fire. Eventually the flames began to die and young men started jumping over it for luck, something which the farmer who fell into it the previous year had clearly lacked. And when they returned to their seats to sing in outrageous disharmony to the old tunes played by the accordionist, Madame Ladoucette approached the embers. According to the old custom, she had been up at dawn to pick the herbs of la Saint-Jean. But when she arrived in the meadows she found that she was the only woman who had turned up, so she had to sing alone as she collected them. And when, before the fête began, she approached the Romanesque church, she found no priest or choirboys leading a procession to the bonfire to bless it. Neither could she see any harvesters turning their backs to the flames in order to prevent sickle-induced sciatica, or cows and sheep being herded around it to ensure their protection for the rest of the year. She nevertheless passed her bouquet through the flames, and the following day, unable to find where her own beasts were kept, would tie some on to the door of Marcel Coussy's cowshed to protect the animals from illness and evil spells, and pin the rest on to her bedroom door to guard against sorcery and lightning. She stood and watched as the flames finally gave up and didn't notice when Madame Moreau flicked a piece of sliced tomato in her direction, which missed and flared as it hit the embers. And, despite the fact that things were not as they should be that night, before leaving the field for home she nevertheless stooped down and picked up a blackened remnant of the fire to put up her chimney to ward off thunder.

As the singing became more monstrous, the postman turned to the matchmaker and said: 'I now understand why things didn't work out with me and Émilie Fraisse.'

'Why?' asked Guillaume Ladoucette, wiping his moustache on a paper serviette, the sudden mention of her name adding to his unease.

'It's Stéphane Jollis she's after. She's been hanging around the bakery all day. The last time I went past he had locked the door and was taking her into the back. He probably gave her a *dégustation* of his little cakes. I bet it works every time. If only it could be that easy for the rest of us.'

The postman then turned back to face the fire and added: 'It's still chucking out some heat, isn't it?'

But Guillaume Ladoucette was unable to feel the warmth of the embers because his heart had suddenly turned cold.

19

PIERRE ROUZEAU LOCKED HIS FRONT DOOR IN THE CERTITUDE THAT on his return he wouldn't find his ex-wife sitting on the doorstep unable to get in. The frightful anguish he had suffered when he finally realized that she was never coming back was eventually followed by relief. Before leaving the house he no longer visited each room to check that everything was just the way she liked it. He changed the station on the radio from the one she had always listened to whose presenters drove him into a daily state of infuriation. He stopped filling the fridge with rounds of Le Trappe Échourgnac cheese laced with walnut liqueur, made by the sisters of the Notre-Dame de Bonne Espérance Abbey, which he couldn't abide and always ended up throwing out. Carefully, he filled a suitcase with all the pretty summer dresses he had bought for her when she left and carried it up to the attic along with her straw gardening hat with the red, white and blue ribbon that she had forgotten. And at night, he brought only one glass of water upstairs with him and learnt to sleep in the middle of the bed.

Before starting the car, the retired barber checked in the mirror that his hair, an abundant January frosting, was as it should be. As he passed through woods where long, dusty yellow flowers hung lazily from the sweet chestnut trees, and spotlights of sun illuminated curls of green bracken, Pierre Rouzeau wondered whether at the age of seventy-four he was a silly old fool to be looking for love. Certainly, he couldn't remember how to court a woman as it had been over half a century since he had won the heart of his ex-wife and he had been too proud to accept any tips from the matchmaker. But what he did know was that however many years he had left, he wanted to spend them sharing the many pleasures he had discovered in life. For while he liked nothing better than finding a nice shady picnic spot along the Dronne, wading into the velvety water and drifting downriver on his back as turquoise dragonflies hitched a ride on his pale stomach, it was so much friendlier in tandem.

His anxiety that morning wasn't helped by the fact that he had no idea whom he was meeting. Guillaume Ladoucette had told him that his match would be waiting for him underneath one of the lime trees outside the church in Amour-sur-Belle. He had added that if she needed to sit down she would be inside, but not to mistake her for anyone lying on the marble tombs trying to cool down. Pierre Rouzeau didn't need to enter the Romanesque church with its curiously unworn steps. For, as soon as he pulled up, he spotted a stout elderly woman in a light-blue dress, wide-fitting laced cream sandals and a short crop of hair the colour of pigeon down standing in the shade of the branches. It was Madame Serre.

He got out to greet her, executing a hint of a bow in the process. While they both thought they had bumped into each other sometime over the years, neither could be certain. The retired barber then opened the car door for her and, as she sat down, Madame Serre thanked him for offering to do the driving. She no longer enjoyed covering long distances, she explained, and while she had got away with not having sat her test for the last six decades, she didn't want to risk imprisonment at her great age as she had heard that the food was terrible and she only had so long left to enjoy herself. And, as they motored out of the village past the memorial to the *Three Victims of the Barbarous Germans*, they both said how much they were looking forward to the Félibrée. The annual festival of immense repute had been held in the Périgord since 1903 to celebrate the language and culture of Occitan, which was spoken all over the southern half of the country in various regional variations for over 1,500 years.

As they headed for Port-Sainte-Foy and Sainte-Foy-la-Grande, a community on opposite banks of the Dordogne which had been chosen as the venue, Madame Serre looked out of the window and said that despite having witnessed the miracle each summer for seventy-nine years, the sight of a million sunflowers starting to bloom never failed to excite her. Pierre Rouzeau then told her of the field he had passed on the way to pick her up where a solitary sunflower was facing in the opposite direction to all the others. And they both agreed that even God had a sense of humour.

Eventually, as they started to pass neat rows of vines and ancient wooden barns in which tobacco had once been hung to dry, Pierre Rouzeau announced that it wouldn't be much further. Madame Serre then spotted a sign pointing to a village called 'Fraisse' and said that a woman of that name had recently bought the château at Amour-sur-Belle. She then added that she had had to go there in search of a rum *baba* as the matchmaker had sold the châtelaine all the little cakes while helping out in the bakery. The retired barber then told her that if ever the bakery ran out again, she wasn't to suffer in silence as he had taught himself to make them when he retired, for, much to his shame, he hadn't learnt to be the perfect husband until after his wife had left him. And

Madame Serre replied that she still hadn't learnt to be the perfect wife even though her husband had left her many years ago, but that it was never too late to try.

They parked in a field and made their way at their own pace to the gate at the entrance of Port-Sainte-Foy, which had been blocked off to traffic. After Madame Serre insisted on paying their entrance fees, they walked in and gazed in wonder at the garlands of flowers which stretched for fifty kilometres back and forth across every street filling the sky with paper blossom. And, although they had both seen the spectacle every year since they could remember, they stopped to marvel at the procession of people dressed in traditional costumes. The men, they declared, looked splendid in their black trousers, black waistcoats, black wide-brimmed felt hats, white shirts and clogs. While the women, some carrying lace parasols, others finely woven little black baskets, looked ravishing in their long skirts, aprons, white cotton bonnets and lace collars.

Once the parade had passed, the couple decided to go and watch the demonstrations of ancient skills. On spotting the steam-driven threshing machine, Madame Serre recalled the one which came to Amour-sur-Belle every July to be shared with the surrounding hamlets, and how the drinking started early in the morning and carried on way into the night. As they stood watching the two women in their bonnets hand-stitching an eiderdown, Pierre Rouzeau said he could remember his aunt sitting at a similar frame. Further down the road they stopped to admire a woman in a long skirt and pointed clogs sitting in a pen with a goose between her legs holding an instrument in its mouth. After dropping several handfuls of maize into the top, she then merrily turned the handle sending the food directly down the creature's throat to fatten its liver. As the woman stroked its neck to ensure the food's passage, Madame Serre remarked that she missed keeping ducks and geese as she had always liked the feel of their soft, plump bodies between her legs while she was feeding them. Watching the plump blacksmith in his black waistcoat turning a handle on his brazier to blow air on to his coals, Pierre Rouzeau asked Madame Serre whether she could remember seeing donkeys working the fields, which she could. And when they tasted the walnut oil dripping out of the press, Madame Serre recalled the yellow-stained fingers of her mother who spent each winter cracking open millions of nuts with a small hammer.

It wasn't long before their stomachs informed them that it was nearing midday and, arm-in-arm so as not to lose each other in what was approaching a stampede, they made their way to the enormous marquee for the set lunch. Both grateful for a chance to sit down, Pierre Rouzeau poured them each a glass of the Félibrée vintage and asked Madame Serre about herself. She told him that she had raised eight healthy children and so she had never regretted marrying her husband, who had eventually left her after she had had an affair, which saved her the bother of leaving him. And as they both valiantly attempted to make their way through the garlic soup, duck foie gras pâté, confit of duck, beans, walnut and Cabécou salad, raspberry tart, coffee and plum eau-de-vie, they both agreed that the biggest curse of getting old was not being able to eat as much as they used to.

After making their way to the main square, they carried chairs from in front of the stage to the shade of a plane tree and sat and watched the traditional dancing, accompanied by the diatonic accordion and the hurdy-gurdy.

Both thrilled by the polkas but exhausted by the devastating heat, they decided to rest for a while by the river. Once settled in a quiet spot in the shade, Pierre Rouzeau opened Madame Serre's can of Perrier for her as she said she no longer had the energy. They slipped off their shoes and sat for a moment side by side watching the mahogany Dordogne creak by. Later, at home, when she blushed at the memory of her antics, Madame Serre blamed the sun for cooking her brain. Whatever it was, the old woman suddenly handed her drink to Pierre Rouzeau saying she couldn't take it any longer. With fingers crooked with age, she hoisted off her dress, waded into the deliciously cool water and floated off downriver on her back in her voluminous flesh-coloured girdle.

Guillaume Ladoucette arrived outside the bakery to pick up Stéphane Jollis for their scheduled fishing expedition and switched off the engine. He didn't bother pulling down the sun visor to critically assess the splendour of his moustache in the mirror. Nor did he open the glove compartment to kill time. He didn't even curse the baker's abominable time-keeping. Instead, he sat staring straight ahead of him wondering what his friend and Émilie Fraisse had been up to. The same thought had been rolling around the matchmaker's head for the last week, reminding him of the catastrophe each time he moved. As he stared at the spot where the village cross had once been, he again tried to work out when the romance had started. If only he had tried harder to convince Lisette Robert of the baker's many virtues, instead of accepting that she loved another, then Stéphane Jollis wouldn't have needed to look elsewhere, he concluded.

As he glanced at the bakery, its cream blinds drawn, he imagined its owner visiting Émilie Fraisse at the château, presenting her with a box of *mille-feuilles* made by his award-winning artisan fingers and tasting her heirloom vegetables. He wondered which of her antique dresses that appeared to have been shorn off at the knees she would have worn, and saw her quicksilver hair pinned up with something that sparkled.

Looking down at his fingernails, once clipped to per-fection, he saw they were now as bitten as the baker's had been since his dough had begun to swell to frightening proportions. They were such a disgrace, he thought, he would have to hide them from his old boss when he came into Heart's Desire to tell him how he had got on at the Félibrée with Madame Serre.

The car suddenly filled with the smell of rotting flowers as he thought of the courage he had mustered to reply to Émilie Fraisse's letter; the inferno of desire it had ignited while he was composing it sitting at his kitchen table; the elation he had felt when she had returned home with it in the most romantic of hiding places; the unspeakable mess he was now in since it had gone missing; and the utter devastation he felt now that she loved another.

Suddenly, the passenger door opened and a strong, hairy arm reached in and placed a large basket made from sweet chestnut on the back seat. The limb momentarily disappeared and returned with a red-and-white-checked tea towel that was carefully placed over it. The car suddenly tilted towards the right as the baker held on to the roof with one hand and manoeuvred his substantial frame inside, followed by his head.

'Hello. Sorry I'm late,' said Stéphane Jollis.

'Not to worry,' replied Guillaume Ladoucette, starting the car. 'Got everything?'

'Yep,' replied the baker, winding down the window. 'Funny smell in here.'

The pair then drove out of the village and turned right at the field with the ginger Limousin cows that winked. As they headed towards Brantôme past acres of maize fields lashed by flicking water cannons, each time the matchmaker changed gear, his knuckles rubbed against the baker's thigh blooming over the passenger seat. And, for the first time, Guillaume Ladoucette felt uncomfortable.

'Bring any lunch with you?' the matchmaker eventually enquired.

'Just a snack,' replied the baker, staring straight ahead of him. 'You?'

'Just a snack,' said Guillaume Ladoucette, wrinkling up his nose dismissively.

As they arrived in Brantôme, they turned left away from the infestation of tourists and parked by the river. The two men, both holding family-sized baskets, then made their way along the Dronne into which children hurled themselves, much to the outrage of the ducks.

Once they reached the *No Fishing* sign, they put down their baskets in their usual spot. Sitting at the water's edge, they both took a piece of weighted fishing line from their pocket. The baker then searched in his basket for a baguette, broke off an end and foraged inside for the soft white innards. Once he had sufficient, he rolled it up into a ball and speared it with his hook, while Guillaume Ladoucette opened a tin and selected a worm. After the matchmaker had taken off his supermarket leather sandals, and the baker his floury shoes, they tied their lines around their right ankles. Carefully rolling up both trouser legs to the knee, they then sank their feet into the dusky water and felt the lines pirouetting down towards the bottom of the river.

'That's better!' said Guillaume Ladoucette, waggling his hairy toes, feeling the cool river slipping between them.

'Bliss!' agreed the baker, enjoying the swirl of the water around his serpentine varicose veins that came with the job.

The pair sat in silence for a while as they watched the leaves spinning on the surface of the water sauntering slowly by. But Guillaume Ladoucette couldn't enjoy his favourite spot along the Dronne, despite the ducks tipping themselves over head first to reveal their feathered bottoms. For he kept imagining the baker slipping off Émilie Fraisse's ridiculous seventeenth-century shoes, tying a fishing line around her ankle and then offering her the most delectable contents of his picnic basket.

'I suddenly feel a bit peckish,' the matchmaker announced, determined to get the better of him.

'So do I', replied Stéphane Jollis.

As they shuffled backwards towards their baskets, their lines emerged out of the water festooned with lurid green weed. Stalling for time as he waited to see what would appear from the rival basket, Guillaume Ladoucette pretended to look for his penknife. He watched from the corner of his eye as a jar of *cornichons* appeared, followed by another baguette. Then, with a sly smile that Guillaume Ladoucette instantly recognized, the baker brought out an earthenware bowl and slowly started pulling off the clingfilm.

'A little green salad with diced hard-boiled egg to begin with? Lovely', said the matchmaker with relief, peering at it.

'There's nothing more satisfying than eating a fresh egg from one of your own chickens', remarked the baker spearing a lettuce leaf. 'Marcel Coussy does a great job of looking after my birds at his farm. And he's always very grateful for the walnut oil I press myself which I give him in return. He says he's never tasted anything like it. I've used some in the salad dressing, actually. Fancy any?'

'No thanks, otherwise I won't manage this!' said Guillaume Ladoucette, reaching into his basket with both hands and taking out a shallow earthenware dish. 'Tomato salad marinated in eau-de-vie on a hot summer's day. My favourite!' the matchmaker continued, pulling off the foil. 'Of course, the tomatoes always taste better if you've grown them yourself. But what really makes this dish unsurpassable is if the eau-de-vie is made from your own plums. I took them to the man with the travelling still last year and watched it being made. Fancy any?'

'No thanks, otherwise I won't manage this!' replied Stéphane Jollis, needing both hands to lift out an enormous dish from his basket. He whipped off the lid with a considerable flourish and paused for a few seconds so as to unnerve the matchmaker, who was craning to see what was in it.

'Bit of pie?' asked Guillaume Ladoucette. 'Lovely. I think I've seen that one in the supermarket.'

'It's actually boned stuffed duck baked in a pastry crust. After I boned the duck, I sliced off layers of the breast and thigh, diced them up and placed them back inside having sprinkled them with cognac and port.' The baker paused before adding: "The recipe says that adding a truffle is optional, but I still had that whopper I found last winter with Marcel Coussy and that pig of his, and thought I may as well use it. Shame really, because apparently it's the biggest that's been found in the Périgord in the last ten years. I must say the oil preserved it perfectly. Now where's my carving knife?' Stéphane Jollis then cut a large slice which he speared with a fork and offered to Guillaume Ladoucette. 'Fancy some?'

'No thanks,' replied the matchmaker, bringing out another dish covered in foil. But he failed to mention that the quails had been cooked in the leaves of the vine which grew over his front door. Nor did he bother bringing out his walnut tart made with the honey he had collected himself from a hive wearing a beekeeper's helmet, because he knew he had been spectacularly defeated by the baker's fungal masterstroke.

'I must say, I really can't think of anything I'd rather be doing now. Isn't this marvellous?' declared the baker, his mouth full.

'Yes,' replied Guillaume Ladoucette without conviction.

Stéphane Jollis then poured them both a glass of Bergerac, handed one to the matchmaker and said: 'There's something I have to tell you. I can't keep it to myself any longer.'

'Oh yes?'

'I've met someone.'

'Thought so,' replied Guillaume Ladoucette, his despair complete.

'She kept coming in to buy little cakes because of a rumour going round that a love note had been discovered inside one of them. God knows how on earth that one started, but I can't tell you how good it's been for business. People are coming from all over. In the last two weeks I've taken more than I have in the last three months. I've started recommending that they pop in to see you. You're going to make a killing.'

'Thanks,' replied the matchmaker lamely.

'Anyway. So she kept coming in, and there's nothing more flattering than a woman who appreciates your little cakes, and we had a little chat each time. I assumed she was only interested in my *mille-feuilles*, and then guess what happened!'

The matchmaker didn't reply.

'Aren't you listening?' enquired Stéphane Jollis, looking at his friend.

'Of course. She came into the bakery and kept buying *mille-feuilles*,' the matchmaker replied, keeping his eyes on the far bank.

'Guess what happened next!' said the baker.

'I couldn't possibly.'

'Well, I'd just locked the door one evening after work and was on my way to the municipal shower when I heard a voice behind me.' The baker paused, waiting for Guillaume Ladoucette to ask him whose it was. When no reply came, he continued with his story.

'I looked round and there she was! It was a bit embarrassing, actually, because all I had on was my dressing gown and I had to hold it down as the breeze kept lifting it up. I thought she was after some more little cakes, but she didn't mention them. I've got no idea what she was doing there. Anyway, she accompanied me to the shower and noticed my varicose veins and said her uncle had just got his fixed and she'd find out where he'd had it done and would let me know. There wasn't a queue when we got to the cubicle, so I went straight in and she was still there when I came out. We then went over to the Bar Saint-Jus for a drink, though Fabrice Ribou sent me home to get dressed first because I'd forgotten I was still in my dressing gown and slippers. We've been seeing each other ever since.'

'Fantastic,' said Guillaume Ladoucette, his eyes not moving from the far bank.

'I really think she's the one, you know.'

'I'm not surprised.'

'You don't sound very interested,' said the baker, looking reproachfully at his friend.

'Sorry,' said the matchmaker, looking down at his bare knees. 'I am, honestly.'

'It's strange that I've never bumped into her before. She only lives in Léguillac. Mind you, she hasn't been there long.'

'Léguillac?'

'Yes. It's Sylvette Beau. Do you know her?'

Guillaume Ladoucette turned to look at Stéphane Jollis.

'I've heard her name,' he replied, confused.

'I must say, that Émilie Fraisse is a bit of a weird one, isn't she?' the baker continued. 'She came in to see me the other day and was going on about how she'd never read such unsurpassable poetry, but that we didn't have a future together as she had always loved someone else, who hadn't replied to some letter she'd sent him. God knows what all that was about. I took her round the back and gave her a *mille-feuille*, which calmed her down a bit. I think she's been spending too much time alone in that château of hers.'

It was then that Guillaume Ladoucette untied the fishing line from around his ankle and handed it to the baker with the words: 'Sorry, Stéphane, I've got to go.' He didn't stop to pick up his tomatoes marinated in eau-de-vie made from the plums he'd grown in his garden and taken to the man with the travelling still. Nor did he collect his quails cooked in the leaves of the vine growing above his front door, or indeed the walnut tart made with honey he'd collected himself wearing a beekeeper's helmet. Instead, he started running down the bank of the Dronne as fast as humanly possible in a pair of supermarket leather sandals.

The matchmaker only noticed that the wind was up when

he passed Le Moulin de la Forge and saw the green plastic tables and chairs travelling down to the end of the tiny pavement. By the time he turned left at the field towards Amour-sur-Belle he saw to his horror that the ginger Limousin cows had started to walk backwards. As he approached the village, the green-eared maize was lurching grotesquely from side to side as if riding a murderous sea. And by the time he parked outside his house, sunflowers wrenched from the earth were battering the windows.

If the authorities had known that another mini-tornado was going to strike Amour-sur-Belle, certainly no one informed its inhabitants. While the local *gendarmerie* was in the habit of telephoning a good citizen in each community to pass on severe weather warnings, none of the officers was aware of anyone fitting that description living in the village.

Lisette Robert had just run yet another bath when she heard the curved salmon tiles rattling on the roof like pan lids. Instantly recognizing the sound, she rushed round the house closing the windows and bolting the shutters, remembering the trouble she'd got into last time. Once everything was secured, the midwife decided to take advantage of the sunflowers that had sailed in through the sitting-room window. After snipping off their roots, she put them in a vase on the kitchen table to embellish her final hours. She then looked inside the fridge, wondering what to have for her last meal and regretted not having been to the supermarket earlier.

It was while she was standing on a kitchen chair hunting through the cupboards for something befitting an occasion as momentous as her approaching death that the midwife heard a sound at the door. Assuming it was just the thuds of maize stalks, which had started to take to the air like tribal spears, she ignored it. When she heard the noise again, she opened the door in the hope that it was someone with better-stocked cupboards than she inviting her round to share their dying moment.

When the midwife saw that it was in fact the man from the council, she immediately forgot her disappointment about not having gone food shopping and invited him in. But such was the force of the wind that Jean-François Lafforest, who was holding on to the door frame with only one hand as he refused to let go of his soft leather briefcase with the other, disappeared and it took several long minutes before he staggered back into view again. As soon as he re-emerged, Lisette Robert shot out an arm, grabbed him by the shirt, hauled him in and shut the door.

Once he had straightened his hair, tucked his shirt back in and apologized for disturbing her, Jean-François Lafforest announced that he had come on official business. Clutching his briefcase to his stomach, he went on to explain that he had received a large number of reports that she had taken to having baths. And while he could fully understand that showering in a plastic cubicle in the place du Marché could never equal the unrivalled joy of bathing at home, it was, nevertheless, forbidden.

Lisette Robert, who had informed as many people as possible of her lawlessness, owned up at once. She then took the official upstairs and showed him her most recent transgression. And, as she stood by the edge of the bath, a pink sponge brazenly skimming across the water, she asked for another dozen similar offences to be taken into consideration.

Once back downstairs, Jean-François Lafforest sat down at the kitchen table next to the vase of sunflowers which Lisette Robert had arranged to brighten up her final hours. Taking a form from his soft leather briefcase, he studiously filled it in in block capitals, not wanting to pass away without having first carried out his duty. As the wind let out a deathly screech down the chimney, he then asked her to sign and date the bottom. Once the form was safely back inside his briefcase, Jean-François Lafforest sat back and took his first sip of the *pineau* the midwife had poured for him. And, after they had shared two tins of wild boar terrine and half a baguette, accompanied by the best reds she could find in the cellar, the man from the council accepted Lisette Robert's offer of joining her in the bath.

Guillaume Ladoucette immediately went to check on his mother. He found Madame Ladoucette sitting on her kitchen floor, her crane's legs stretched out in front of her, happily milking a goat which had happened to blow in through the window. When finally convinced of her safety, he started down the rue du Château that did lead to the castle, heaving against the wind which pummelled his chest with such ferocity he could scarcely breathe.

He kept his head down as he attempted to cross the courtyard but the wind grabbed him by the legs and spat him against the door bleached fossil grey by the sun that had fled. Once back on his feet, he thumped on it with his fists, but there was no reply. Feeling the gale tugging at his thighs again, he let himself in, and once inside, backed up against the door in order to close it. As the gravel in the courtyard twisted up in rage and fired itself against the windows like gunshot, the matchmaker called out. But there was no reply. Following the corridor with the violet mould now the colour of fresh blood, he entered the vaulted kitchen where the collection of copper pans and utensils rattled on their hooks as if possessed. But when he looked around, the seat that slid open to hide the salt from the tax collector was empty. Retracing his steps, he found himself in the dining room with the *pisé* floor, but there was no one hiding underneath the enormous table stolen from a monastery. He then ran through a corridor past a chest poorly inlaid with mother-of-pearl, but when he tugged open the door to the *grand salon*, all that could be found was the still warm bodies of three dead house martins on the reversible floor.

As tiles started hurling themselves down on to the courtyard, the matchmaker pushed open the studded armoury door with its rows of dented breastplates, ivory-inlaid muskets and swords that took two hands to hold. But the only thing he came across was the stench of defeat. Descending the stairs of the dungeon, all that he could make out in the darkness were the chains and scratches on the walls. Discovering a hidden door, he found himself in a secret passage that led to the late fifteenth-century chapel, which had been rebuilt using leper labourers. But when he entered through a small door in the back of the fireplace not a soul was on their knees praying for salvation.

Pounding up the stone spiral staircase with its lamentable repairs, he headed along the corridor hung with faded tapestries, which trembled as snatches of wind clawed their way through the cracks around the windows. It was as he knelt down to look underneath Émilie Fraisse's bed that the matchmaker spotted his love letter, which had stiffened in the sun, lying on her night table next to a glass of quivering water. He saw the bite mark where his signature had been and reread what he could of his writing, which had bled because of the succulence of the rum-laced *crème pâtissière*. And as his eyes moved over the outpouring of adoration, the unwept tears of longing that had been trapped inside him for twenty-six years made him wince with pain. Grabbing the pen next to the bedside lamp, he signed the letter for a second time and left it to search the tower.

Once he had been through the entire château calling her name until he was hoarse, he staggered like a drunkard back across the courtyard as the wind tormented him and sections of the crenellations thudded to the ground around him. When he reached the drawbridge, an agonizing roar made him turn round and he saw to his horror the chapel roof opening up like a can lid. For several seconds it hung in the air, as competing gusts tried to snatch it right and left. Suddenly they both let go and it plummeted from the sky in haunting silence and crashed to the ground several feet behind him. It was then that Guillaume Ladoucette fled.

When the matchmaker pounded on the door of the Bar Saint-Jus to be let in, there was already a considerable crowd inside trying to forget the lives they had wasted and were about to lose for ever. When his knocking was eventually heard, the door was opened and he was pushed inside by the maniacal wind. As several villagers wrestled it shut again, and tables and chairs were hurled to the other side of the room, Guillaume Ladoucette immediately asked whether anyone had seen Émilie Fraisse. There was a moment's silence before Sandrine Fournier and Monsieur Moreau both said that they remembered seeing her heading towards the woods. The matchmaker ordered a drink and sat by the window watching the tables and chairs from the bar's terrace being thrashed around the place du Marché. And as the wind coming in underneath the door clawed at his legs, Guillaume Ladoucette knew that the châtelaine didn't stand a chance.

Just as the villagers were about to start the lengthy process of confessing their sins, there was a furious pounding at the door. His heart tightening, the matchmaker immediately got up to unlock it. However, it wasn't Émilie Fraisse who staggered inside, but a man with a beard like Spanish moss drifting down to his umbilicus who was of such girth that Fabrice Ribou immediately feared for his bar stools.

'It's Patrice Baudin the pharmacist!' cried Modeste Simon, suddenly finding her voice for the first time in seven years. 'He's recovered!'

20

MADAME LADOUCETTE WAS THE FIRST TO WAKE THE MORNING following the second mini-tornado. Never once fearing that she was going to die, she had slept peacefully throughout the night, the herbs of la Saint-Jean pinned over her bed, a vase of honesty on her night table and the comfort of fresh, warm goat's milk in her crinkled belly. After dressing in a green-patterned frock bought from the stall in the market, and a pair of black shoes that hid the fact that her left big toe pointed north-west and her right big toe north-east, she opened the front door and was shocked to discover that Amour-sur-Belle was even uglier than usual.

As she headed past the ancient wooden weighing platform where farmers were once charged a *franc* for each horned beast that stepped on to it, she noticed that two derelict barns had been relieved of their roofs. Several houses riddled with skeletal ivy that had collapsed on to their knees years ago now lay flat on their backs, belly up to the feeble sun. Pieces of broken tractor, a pair of mounted antlers and a bed into which was still strapped its sleeping owner blocked the rue du Château that didn't lead to the castle, and when she reached the Romanesque church Madame Ladoucette discovered that many of the headstones lay face down as if they had been shot in the back.

Picking her way through pieces of dresser and exploded hay bales, she passed the empty pharmacy and saw that a bicycle had come through the window and now lay in the middle of the shattered display of ancient potion jars. When she reached the fountain said to cure gout, she peered inside and discovered a swollen baguette, a pan for roasting chestnuts and a single bed sock which looked familiar. The bench, and its serial occupier, had completely vanished.

Further on down the road she pitied the grocer for her ripped awning and wondered what her son would say about the window box of pelargoniums now lying on the floor of Heart's Desire, it contents disgorged over the floor. And when she reached the place du Marché with its bar full of marinated slumbering bodies, she realized that the only thing untouched in the village was the wonderful contraption against the wall which had given her such untold pleasure.

Stopping for a moment on the bridge to inspect a piece of crenellation which had landed in the Belle, Madame Ladoucette noticed at her feet a dead duck whose liver her expert fingers told her had just been fattened. Delighted at her good fortune, the old woman picked it up by its neck and swiftly carried it home. After lighting a fire in the hearth with pieces of a broken barrel, she placed in front of it one of the ancient irons that her son had put on her mantelpiece for decoration. Once it was hot, she laid the duck carefully on the kitchen table, covered it with a damp tea towel and proceeded to iron it, according to the tradition. And, when she started to pluck it, she found, as always, that the bird's feathers came out much more easily.

Several hours later, when other residents began to open their shutters, their immediate feeling was not one of relief at having escaped Purgatory, but one of abominable nausea from having gorged so much the night before. Assuming once again that death awaited them, they had emptied their fridges, cupboards and cellars. First they picked their most tantalizing delicacies: venison pâtés, black puddings, preserved goose legs, truffled foie gras, potted duck and *saucissons secs*. When they wiped their mouths and found themselves still at the kitchen table, they went back to their fridges, brought out whatever meat they had and quickly made sauces with their preserved ceps. When, eventually, they put down their forks, looked around them and found that they still recognized their surroundings, they peered into their stores once more and brought out flour, sugar, butter and preserved fruit. As the wind uttered its wicked screams through the keyholes, livestock tumbled past the windows and unhinged shutters pirouetted into the sky, the women set about baking tarts, hoping that God wouldn't be so cruel as to end their lives before they had tasted them. The gastronomic delights had been washed down with the best of their wines, which had been laid down for happier occasions. And it all came up again upon waking in a vomitous chorus that stirred those who hadn't dared open their eyes for fear of coming face to face with the Devil.

While his pale wife was brushing her teeth for the fourth time that morning, Monsieur Moreau slipped out of the house to check on the wood shed with his hidden portrait of Madame Ladoucette. When, the night before, he had attempted to go and rescue it, his wife had refused to allow him out of the house as she didn't want him to die before he had painted the kitchen as he had promised to three months ago. But when, eventually, he had finished the task, the wind was coming up between the floorboards in such gruesome breaths that not even love with its intrinsic madness could make him venture outside.

When he reached the bottom of the garden, Monsieur Moreau saw to his horror that the wood shed was no longer standing. With a clamouring heart, he searched through the scattered logs, but despite picking up every one of them, he was unable to find the portrait. Distraught, he immediately set out to find Madame Ladoucette, believing that his life must have been spared for a reason other than to spend his remaining days with his wife. When he knocked at her door, Madame Ladoucette immediately welcomed him in and set about boiling a pan of water to make them both coffee. Needing to empty his nervous bladder before confessing his ardour, he passed her bedroom on the way to the lavatory and couldn't resist peering in through the open door to the place where he had always dreamt of lying. Noticing that the top drawer of her chest was open, he crept inside to steal a glance at her underwear. And there, tucked in a pair of rolled-up black stockings, was undeniably a peony leaf. Instantly recognizing its positioning as an old peasant method of contraception, for which his mother had blamed the birth of his countless brothers and sisters, Monsieur Moreau immediately assumed that Madame Ladoucette had a secret lover. In fact, the leaf had simply dropped from a bouquet hanging on the wall, another weapon in Madame Ladoucette's arsenal against storms. Daunted by the thought of a love rival, not only did the urge to urinate leave Monsieur Moreau, but so too did the desire to confess his adoration. Instead, he went home, looked at his wife, thought that she wasn't half as bad as he remembered, and set about picking up the scattered logs in the garden so he could keep her warm during the winter.

It wasn't until midday that those slumped on the floor of the Bar Saint-Jus began to rouse, stirred by the shrill call from their stomachs alerting them to the fact that it was lunchtime. The first to wake was Fabrice Ribou, who had escaped the confusion of legs and arms on the floor by sleeping on top of the bar, as was his privilege as owner. Assuming he was in bed, he immediately rolled over to reach for the glass of water on his nightstand, and instantly dropped on to Yves Lévèque, causing the only fracture of the last twenty-four hours. Once the villagers had settled their arguments over whose limbs were whose, they got to their knees and it wasn't long before they were able to stand. Eventually, they found that they could focus, and even remembered their own names. When they staggered out of the bar and saw the frightful state that the village was in, their hearts immediately soared, knowing that the chances of the English buying homes in Amour-sur-Belle were now even more remote. They returned to their houses, drank straight from their taps as if their thirsts would never be quenched, then set about trying to retrieve what they had lost and appropriate whatever had blown into their gardens.

Guillaume Ladoucette, who was not in the least hung-over, had been unable to move from the bar when he woke several hours earlier as he found himself pinned to the floor by the colossal weight of Patrice Baudin. As soon as he was released, he lay for a few seconds waiting for an onslaught of pins and needles, which duly engulfed him with such ferocity he scarcely dared breathe. When the agony was finally over, he stepped out into the new day and hurried off in search of his mother. Once he had got past the goat in the hallway, which was scattering droppings across the floorboards like marbles, he found Madame Ladoucette sitting at the kitchen table next to a tiny pile of duck feathers happily making an eiderdown, with a foie gras on the stove.

Satisfied that she was unharmed, the matchmaker immediately fled to the château and discovered its courtyard pitted with sections of the crenellations. Picking his way through the remains of the chapel roof and the broken body of the hut for the ticket-seller, he pushed open the door bleached fossil grey by the sun and called for Émilie Fraisse. But the only reply was silence. After three hours of fruitless hunting, to his utter despair all he could find of the châtelaine was her ridiculous seventeenth-century shoes next to the llama skeleton where they had been the day before. His stomach writhing, he then searched the woods, calling her name as he clambered over crippled trees, their intimate roots exposed to the world. Not knowing what to do next, the matchmaker returned to Heart's Desire. As he was lifting Gilbert Dubuisson's window box out of the shop, Didier Lapierre the carpenter walked past and told him that all the villagers had now been accounted for apart from Émilie Fraisse. The matchmaker, who hadn't eaten all day as despair had flooded his appetite, immediately returned to the château. After searching every room, he combed the fields and then set out into the woods again with a torch as the stag beetles took up their nocturnal flight around the sweet chestnut trees, their hideous black pincers silhouetted against a full pink moon. When he returned home in the pale early hours, defeated, Guillaume Ladoucette took out the Nontron hunting knife with its boxwood handle and ancient pokerwork motifs from his bedside drawer, placed it in the dip of his chest that his grandfather had said was an ideal place to keep salt when eating a boiled egg, and tried to sleep. But sleep never even touched him.

The following morning, the Comité des Fêtes announced that the celebrations to mark Patrice Baudin's recovery from vegetarianism would be held that afternoon. Many of the villagers hoped that now that the lunacy was finally over Amour-sur-Belle's miserable standing in Périgord Vert would improve. But it was not the only reason why the residents were grateful for the man's return. Not only would they no longer have to travel to Brantôme with their prescriptions, but the pharmacist's surprise arrival in the Bar Saint-Jus had distracted the drinkers from confessing their abominable sins.

For once, there were no arguments about the menu. The bodies of fourteen chickens had been found amongst the church gravestones, five dead cows had been picked up in three of the rues du Château, seven lifeless pigs had been dragged down from rooftops, numerous deceased ducks had been scooped out of the dry moat and seven sheep carcasses had been found dotted around the balding maize fields.

When word got round that help was needed for the ensuing feast, the villagers instantly abandoned the tending of the injured and started hunting out their spits and barbecues. Those who found that their gastronomic instruments had taken flight descended into their cellars to fashion new ones out of whatever they could find. They brought their apparatus to the field where members of the fête committee were decorating the fences with uprooted sunflowers. After their makers' ingenuity was admired, the spits, two of which turned with the aid of bicycle wheels, were loaded up with meat which had been marinating in useless baths overnight.

Guillaume Ladoucette, his brain furred from lack of sleep and his stomach rolling with anxiety, had not the slightest intention of attending. After thanking the glazier for coming so promptly, he picked up the cushion with the hand-embroidered radish, took it outside and shook off some soil he had just spotted. Returning inside, he decided to give the floor yet another sweep. As he was putting the broom away, the door opened. It was Stéphane Jollis.

After the two men embraced, the baker headed for the chair with the peeling marquetry. His shoes were more floury than usual as he had been at work since just after dawn to make enough bread and little cakes for the festivities. Guillaume Ladoucette, his bare feet hunting for a cool patch underneath the desk with the ink stain, apologized for suddenly dashing off during the fishing expedition. After pouring them both a glass of Bergerac, the matchmaker offered his friend a walnut which was refused as he had his own to get through. He then told Stéphane Jollis of his love for Émilie Fraisse; how he had eventually replied to her letter twenty-six years late; how, in the most romantic of gestures, he had slipped it inside one of the baker's *mille-feuilles*; and how she hadn't realized that it was from him because the succulence of the rum-laced *crème pâtissière* had made the letter go soggy and she had swallowed his signature. The worst of it, the matchmaker added, the weight of his heart reducing his words almost to a whisper, was that she was still missing, and some of the villagers were already talking about altering the number on the sign at the entrance to Amour-sur-Belle which told visitors to slow down because there were only thirty-three of them.

As the baker poured the matchmaker another glass, he assured him that Émilie Fraisse would be found at some stage, adding that even Patrice Baudin had turned up eventually. He then offered to make a search of people's gardens, and once he had scoured their potagers, he would head for the woods.

'I've already looked,' said the matchmaker flatly.

Announcing that he had to get back to work, Stéphane Jollis stood up. But before he left, he thanked the matchmaker for the part he had played in helping him to find the delectable Sylvette Beau, who would never have come into the bakery if it wasn't for the rumour that a love letter had been discovered in one of his little cakes. He then thanked him for all the new business his epistolary antics had brought him, and admitted that he had planted a little love note inside a chocolate *religieuse* to keep them coming. As for the village sign, he said, heading for the door, it would never be altered because not only had the châtelaine been excluded from the original count as she had moved to Bordeaux by then, but no one would ever agree on who should pay for the new paint. He then added that if he didn't see the matchmaker at the fête that afternoon he would come to find him and carry him there himself.

When the baker had left, Guillaume Ladoucette remained sitting on the swivel chair, staring at a maize stalk hanging from the guttering of Gilbert Dubuisson's house. Just as he was wondering whether he should search the fields again, the door opened. It was Pierre Rouzeau. The matchmaker immediately got up to greet him and, as they held each other, the retired barber said how relieved he had been to hear that his apprentice had survived. Guillaume Ladoucette then swiftly returned to the desk with the ink stain to hide his bitten fingernails. After he sat down, the old man smoothed down the back of his hair, an abundant January frosting, and placed a small, slim box on the desk.

The matchmaker didn't need to ask how it had gone at the Félibrée with Madame Serre because Pierre Rouzeau couldn't wait to tell him. He told him about the charming drive they had had, and how ravishing the place had looked decorated with millions of paper flowers. He told him about the splendid traditional costumes people had worn and the magnificent dancing they had enjoyed watching together. He told him about the fascinating ancient skills, which had reminded them of their childhoods. And he told him about the wondrous Madame Serre, who had been the most divine company and the perfect lady throughout. And when Guillaume Ladoucette asked whether he would like him to arrange another date with her, the retired barber said he would indeed and that he knew of the most delightful picnic spot along the Dronne where he would take her.

Pierre Rouzeau then pushed the small, slim box towards the matchmaker with the words: 'These are for you.'

Wondering what it could be, Guillaume Ladoucette

picked up the box and slowly opened it. Instantly, he recognized his former boss's barbering scissors.

'They have brought me so much pleasure over the years, I wanted you to have them to thank you for the joy you have just given me,' he explained. The matchmaker replied that he couldn't possibly accept them, but Pierre Rouzeau was insistent. The retired barber then left, and as he passed the window of Heart's Desire he gave the matchmaker a jaunty wave with his arthritic fingers.

Guillaume Ladoucette was still marvelling at the unexpected gift, which had been used to win the short-back-and-sides category of the World Barbering Championships, when the door opened. It was Yves Lévèque with his arm in plaster. The matchmaker immediately put down the scissors, crawled his hairy toes back into his supermarket leather sandals and got up to help him with the door. The dentist thanked him, walked to the cushion with the hand-embroidered radish and sat down.

As Yves Lévèque started to recount how he hadn't enjoyed his time at the Truffle Museum, Guillaume Ladoucette, who felt he had exhausted his cassoulet simile, immediately started searching for other culinary words of wisdom. But it hadn't mattered, the dentist continued, because they had had such a rapturous time at the Auberge de la Truffe that it had more than made up for it. Denise Vigier had been the most sublime company, he said, adding that he felt such a fool for not having recognized her countless virtues before. And when the matchmaker asked whether he wanted him to arrange another date with her, the dentist replied that he did indeed, and the sooner the better. It was then that Yves Lévèque reached his long, pale instruments of torture inside his sling, drew out a gold nugget and placed it on the desk in front of the matchmaker with the words: 'I'd like you to have it.' Guillaume Ladoucette replied that he couldn't possibly, but the dentist, who had clutched it throughout the night of the mini-tornado praying to St Anthony that the grocer would survive, was insistent.

Stéphane Jollis kept his word. As soon as he saw that the matchmaker hadn't turned up to the fête to celebrate Patrice Baudin's recovery from vegetarianism, he went in search of him. Finding Heart's Desire empty, he went to Guillaume Ladoucette's home and discovered him in the back garden inspecting his potatoes for Colorado beetle. It wasn't until the baker threatened to sit on the crop if he didn't come with him that the matchmaker reluctantly followed.

As they arrived at the trestle tables decorated with sunflowers in the shade of the lime trees, an unsavoury argument about the seating arrangements was taking place. Gilbert Dubuisson was trying to encourage Sandrine Fournier to sit next to him, but the assistant ambulant fishmonger was refusing. Fabrice Ribou, who was sitting next to the postman, was trying to shut the man up, insisting that he couldn't abide eating lunch in the vicinity of the woman he blamed for poisoning his father with a fatal mushroom. Modeste Simon, who hadn't stopped talking since regaining her power of speech following the unexpected return of Patrice Baudin, was trying to persuade Lisette Robert to swap places with her so that she could sit next to the pharmacist. But the midwife was refusing to move because she was saving the place next to her for the man from the council. Madame Serre wouldn't sit down because there was no room on her table for Pierre Rouzeau. Madame Moreau was demanding to be moved as Madame Ladoucette was directing eel impressions at her. Yves Lévêque was refusing to let Marcel Coussy sit down next to him and Denise Vigier, insisting that the stench from the farmer's work slippers would put him off his food. And Didier Lapierre the carpenter didn't want to sit next to Denise Vigier on account of what her grandmother had done during the war.

Things swiftly got worse when Patrice Baudin, his

malodorous beard resting on the table, asked whether anyone had found his glasses following the first mini-tornado. Sandrine Fournier, who had grown two dress sizes larger since starting her fruitless search for a love letter in Stéphane Jolliss little cakes, replied that they were discovered hanging off the church guttering and that Modeste Simon had insisted on keeping them. 'Apparently they're in her bedside-table drawer,' she added. Modeste Simon was so mortified by the public exposure of her secret infatuation that she fled from the field in tears. The villagers were suddenly distracted from their squabbles by the arrival of the man from the council, whose trousers now fitted. Not only did they fail to understand how he had been invited, but neither could they fathom how he managed to get a place sitting next to Lisette Robert. But what they were even more insistent upon knowing was when he was going to take away the municipal shower. Jean-François Lafforest, who was one of only a few people who hadn't thrown up that morning, replied that the decision wasn't up to him and they would probably have to wait until the end of the summer. He then added that any future enquiries would have to be taken up directly with the council as he had resigned that morning.

Jean-François Lafforest was spared further questioning by the announcement that the food was ready. The villagers instantly forgot whom they were bickering with and sat down: Lisette Robert next to the man from the council; Yves Lévèque next to Denise Vigier; Stéphane Jollis next to Sylvette Beau; Modeste Simon – who had been urged to return – next to Patrice Baudin; Madame Serre next to Pierre Rouzeau; and Guillaume Ladoucette at the end of a bench next to the baker.

Several sat silently praying for a mini-tornado every year as members of the committee placed on the tables platters of blushing beef; pork infused with white wine, garlic and thyme; spit-roasted ducks wrapped in bacon; whole golden plump chickens and chunks of mutton coated in garlic, rosemary and ginger mustard. As the villagers picked up their knives and forks and started to eat, a rare moment of tranquillity fluttered through Amour-sur-Belle.

Guillaume Ladoucette, however, was far from at ease. As he sat with his bare feet cooling on the grass, he failed to enjoy the succulence of the pork. Nor did he take delight in the mustard crust on the mutton. He didn't even ask for someone to pass him the Cabécou when the cheeses were served. Instead, he just thought of the châtelaine and the terrible death that had befallen her and how he was to blame for not having found her in time.

It was after everyone had been served one of Stéphane Jolliss's *puits d'amour*, a choux pastry 'love well' engorged with rum-laced *crème pâtissière*, that the baker nudged Guillaume Ladoucette and said: 'There she is.'

The matchmaker turned round and saw to his astonishment Émilie Fraisse walking barefoot towards them in an antique emerald dress that not only appeared to have been shorn off at the knees, but was ripped in several places. Her hair, which was usually pinned up with something that sparkled, trickled over her shoulders festooned with leaves. And her knees were no longer the colour of a raspberry stain, but smeared with mud that had been fermenting for decades.

Silence fell. The villagers put down their spoons and listened as the châtelaine explained herself. When the mini-tornado struck, she had been in the woods looking for summer truffles. As the trees let out their dreadful moans falling to their deaths, and the birds were too terrified to call, she became disorientated and was unable to find her way back to the château. Fearful that she may go the way of Patrice Baudin, she sought refuge under the still warm body of a wild boar that had died from shock. Upon waking the following morning, she returned home and was just crossing the courtyard when part of the crenellations plunged to the floor in front of her. Terrified, she fled back to the woods where she spent a second night, hiding underneath the door of the old hunters' shack which had spiralled into the sky and dropped to the ground some distance away. She had only just summoned the courage to return to the château and, seeing how badly damaged the village was from her bedroom window, came at once to see whether anyone had survived.

But the villagers had stopped listening by then. Their curiosity sated, their minds had turned to the tantalizing *puits d'amour* in front of them made by the award-winning fingers of Stéphane Jollis. As soon as the châtelaine drew breath again, they picked up their spoons and lowered their heads. Guillaume Ladoucette then gave the baker an elbow in his considerable flank. Instantly recognizing its meaning, Stéphane Jollis shuffled up and Émilie Fraisse sat down between them. The matchmaker pushed his *puits d'amour* with its caramelized top in front of her and passed her his spoon. Émilie Fraisse then turned towards Guillaume Ladoucette with eyes the colour of fresh sage and whispered: 'Thank you for the letter.' But the matchmaker was unable to reply.

When everything had been eaten and Guillaume Ladoucette had recovered his power of speech, he offered to accompany Émilie Fraisse back to the château. As they left the field, the châtelaine noticed Fabrice Ribou walk past Sandrine Fournier who had tripped over one of the spits. His failure to help the assistant ambulant fishmonger confused Émilie Fraisse as the last time she had seen the pair together was when she had gone into the woods with her engraved musket and discovered them naked underneath the blanket in the old hunters' shack. The other villagers who also noticed the bar owner ignore Sandrine Fournier as she lay sprawled on the ground naturally assumed that he couldn't bear to touch her. In fact the pair had been running their hands all over each other since becoming lovers a year after he banned her from the bar.

It was an arrangement that served them both. Fabrice Ribou thought their widely known animosity would serve as a perfect cover for an affair during his second marriage, which bored him as much as his first. Whenever he dwelt on his father's death, and found himself filled with loathing for the mushroom poisoner again, he simply accepted it as after two miserable marriages he had come to view hatred as a natural ingredient in a relationship. The mushroom poisoner, who had never forgiven the bar owner for the slur on her character, the nickname it had provoked and the devastating effect the ban had had on her social life, lived in the hope that their energetic contortions underneath the stained blanket would one day induce in her lover a fatal heart attack.

Once at the château, Émilie Fraisse and Guillaume Ladoucette stood on the drawbridge looking in despair at the courtyard pitted with enormous crenellation stones. The matchmaker, sensing the depth to which the châtelaine's heart had spiralled at the sight of such devastation, immediately strode inside and announced that he would hoist them back up himself, and if the rope snapped he would simply try again. Worried about her heirloom vegetables, Émilie Fraisse then led him to the garden through the scattered bones of the chapel roof. Despite the volley of roof tiles that had landed amongst them, the ancient varieties were largely unscathed. Hoping to take her mind off her despair Émilie Fraisse picked up a couple of baskets that had been blown against the garden wall and handed one to Guillaume Ladoucette. As they picked some of the round black radish, Émilie Fraisse asked the matchmaker whether he remembered the summer when the château was between owners and a group of them slipped in, dressed up in the dented breastplates and ran round playing hide-and-seek amongst the antiques and junk-shop furniture. And

Guillaume Ladoucette replied with a smile that he did. As they helped themselves to the square podded peas, the matchmaker asked whether she remembered how their gang, the Wet Rats, so called because they lived near the Belle, attacked the Bog Weeds every Thursday afternoon with catapults. And the châtelaine replied with a smile that she did. And, as they filled their baskets with strawberry spinach, Émilie Fraisse asked him whether he remembered when they baked stolen apples in the ashes of a fire outside the den they made in the woods. And Guillaume Ladoucette replied with a smile that he did.

As they walked back to the château, Émilie Fraisse fell silent and when the matchmaker asked her what was wrong, she admitted that she was still too frightened to stay there. Guillaume Ladoucette then said that she was welcome as his guest while it was being made safe, and she dashed in to collect a couple of antique dresses which had been shorn off at the knees.

When they arrived at the matchmaker's home, he put the bag of heirloom vegetables on the kitchen table and carried her case up to one of the spare bedrooms. As she was washing her hands and knees in the bathroom, he went outside and picked a white dahlia from the edge of his potager which he put in a vase by her bed. When he came back down, Émilie Fraisse was looking at the handbell which Madame Ladoucette rang in the street during the war whenever De Gaulle had been on the radio from London in order to irritate her neighbours, who were Pétainists. She then turned her gaze to his father's shotgun mounted on the chimney-breast which had claimed three wild boars, and the clock on the mantelpiece below it which had driven a relative to suicide. 'The house is just as I remember it,' she said. The matchmaker then took out the old Vittel bottle filled with homemade *pineau* and a couple of glasses, and they spent the rest of the evening at the kitchen table recounting the years they had lost. When, in the early hours, they both started to feel hungry again, Guillaume Ladoucette served them both a bowl of cassoulet. And it was then that Émilie Fraisse found her little green button.

Both too weary to stay up any longer, Guillaume Ladoucette decided to risk the wrath of the council and ran Émilie Fraisse a bath, leaving out for her the most exquisite bar of soap from the bottom shelf. Once she had finished, and disappeared into her room in her white cotton dressing gown with the dark-blue flowers, the matchmaker ran another for himself and experienced the unparalleled joy that he had been denied for too long. Again he saw the wondrous sight of his knees rising like islands out of the water and his hairy toes lined up underneath the taps. And he stayed lapped by the sweet-smelling water until he found himself falling asleep, his moustache afloat.

Quietly shutting his door so as not to disturb his guest, he then got into bed, pulled the sheet over him and turned out the light. As the perpetual breeze fluttered in from the window, he relived the moment when he turned round at the fête and saw Émilie Fraisse in her torn emerald antique dress. Again, he saw her mudstained knees, her hair festooned with leaves and the scratches on her arms. Just as he was wondering what delectable delight he would make her for breakfast, the door opened. He then heard the sound of a pair of small bare feet crossing the wooden floor, and felt the châtelaine, who was unable to bear being apart from him any longer, slip in next to him, her quicksilver hair caressing his arm as it fell. Pulling Émilie Fraisse towards him, Guillaume Ladoucette told her everything he had written in the letter, and when he had finished his outpouring of love, he started again. And by the time he had got to the bit about always loving her, he heard the rhythmic rise and fall of her sleeping. He then turned on his back into his usual position, his arms down the sides of his body as if already dead in his coffin. As he wondered what he would do if he ever lost her again, a tear suddenly ran down the side of his face into his ear. Promising himself that he would never let her go, he turned on to his side and tucked into the warm contours of her body. Sheltered in the harbour of Émilie Fraisse, he fell asleep and was lost in the production of his monstrous snores. And it was only Émilie Fraisse, woken by the uproar, who heard the sound of a freshly laid egg rolling across the landing.

Acknowledgements

With grateful thanks to the people of the Périgord Vert, in particular my kind and generous hosts. Thanks also to my agent Gráinne Fox, all at Transworld, my sister and brother, and, of course, Digby the Brave.